a novel

karma

a novel

karma

Nancy Deville

Vitasta

Vitasta Publishing Pvt. Ltd.
New Delhi

Published by
Renu Kaul Verma for
Vitasta Publishing Pvt. Ltd.
2/15, Ansari Road, Daryaganj,
New Delhi-110 002

ISBN 978-93-80828-06-0

First Published in 2010 by Heavenly Clouds in the US

Cover Design: Nancy Deville
Layout by Vitasta Publishing Pvt. Ltd.
Printed by Vits Press, New Delhi

DEDICATION

In Memory of Thaddeus and Genevieve

PROLOGUE

Medicine is a system that processes human beings. Rich and poor, stoics, pragmatists, deniers, liars, and hypochondriacs—they all get processed. I thought about this some time after I was raped. Once I had the luxury to think beyond my immediate survival, I realized that what had happened to me was no different than what doctors like me do to patients in hospitals. I was being processed through a system.

It didn't matter that I was wealthy, educated, and American. I could have been one of the poor ignorant gypsies I'd seen at the bazaar in Istanbul. The process was rape/conditioning. Until I was abducted, I thought things like that only happened to poor Eastern women—not to women like me. But I was wrong, and my life changed the instant the rape began. I was reminded of the innocent people whose lives changed when I spoke the words "stage four cancer." What terrified me most was how ill prepared I was to deal with the cruel hijacking of my planned-out life. I suppose my terror was no different than the fear of those who are freshly diagnosed as terminally ill.

Fear is primitive. I learned that from my father, a corporate law litigator. His militaristic training that passed for parenting enabled me to get through the stress and fear of four years of medical school and one year of internship. He hammered into me how to keep a cool head during a crisis. *Do not panic. Breathe deeply. Be realistic*. It was unreal, actually, the way I remembered and was able to act on the lessons my father taught me. First of all, having been told my entire life to *accept, accept, accept*, I did not deny what was happening to me. How could I forget my father's credo? He would look at me eye to eye, and only when he saw the light of recognition flash in my eyes would he straighten his spine—rising to the full towering height that had intimidated legions of plaintiffs—and bellow, "Then deal with it."

When I think about it now, I'm sure that even Dad would have given me credit for "dealing with it." I could have easily lost it. I knew from medical training that the instant the *fear* signal reached my brainstem that neurons informed the amygdala lodged deeply within my brain's temporal lobe. This primitive ganglion of my limbic system alerted my adrenal medulla to shoot epinephrine into my bloodstream, tripping my blood pressure and heart rate into high gear. I experienced tachypsychia, a neurological phenomenon of time distortion, which slowed events and heightened my perception. My heart rate ripped to its tipping point. Once over 145 BPM I would begin to disassociate. To maintain control, I started survival breathing, what my father called "ream the other guy" breathing. Four counts in. Hold for four. Exhale four.

During the rape, I was hyper-focused on staying alive, on avoiding any movement that would cause the icy cold razor switchblade pressed against my neck to slice through my pulsing carotid artery. I analyzed every possibility to gain an advantage over my attacker, including fighting back as soon as the razor was safely away from my neck. It was a nice try, as Dad would have said, though it gained me nothing but three cracked ribs. Even seriously injured, I had reached in vain for the blade when it lay in the rapist's slack hand as he dozed, his body a dead weight on top of me, his long black hair flopping over my face as he snored, filling my nostrils with the sickening sweet smell of his oily scalp, and the rankly sweet odor of licorice on his breath.

Only those suffering from acute post-traumatic stress can understand how the mere scent of things so benign and seemingly pleasant as candy and flowers can produce hallucinatory torments so profound that reality and sanity spin out of control.

But I am getting ahead of myself. Like many stories, mine will end with conclusions, leaving some frayed ends that will likely fester into more heartbreak and even greater frustration. This again was really no different than what occurs in hospitals. Through various tests, doctors gather as much evidence as they can. They knit together as many bits and pieces of history as they can garner. They reach conclusions. A series of actions, they are the means to an end to heal the patient. Sometimes a patient has no other choice but to come to terms with an end result that is far from optimal. But I have seen with my own eyes the lengths that humans will go to accept. That's the purpose of writing my story down. Memoir or a confession, you must decide. Regardless, this recording of events is part of an effort to heal, despite a less than optimal end result. You see, I'm damaged and feel like an outcast. All I have to cling to now is the hope that Dad was right, that if I could just accept. . . then maybe I could move on with my life.

ONE

A sad-eyed hotel valet snapped his fingers and a TAKSi darted out from a predatory phalanx of cabs. With a slumping gait, the valet lugged my carry-on bag over to the cab and opened the door. I handed him a couple of American dollars and scooted over the lumpy seat, settling my purse on my lap. Inside was my wallet, mobile phone, *Fodor's Istanbul*, toiletries for the plane, my laptop, and a plastic freezer bag containing my father's ashes. Even as a doctor I was still a little surprised that the ashes of a human being were so heavy. It seemed significant to me. The weight.

It was a mere two weeks since his death. The funeral director had tried to sell the idea that a mausoleum internment would be "appropriate for a man of Mr. Fitzgerald's stature." My father had once mentioned that he wanted to be cremated, but wasn't sure where his ashes should go. "Meredith," he grumbled, as his mood was always on a slow boil, "I could lie forever with my grandifloras, floribundas, my polyanthas." But after his death when the house was on the market, I didn't feel right about kneeling in his garden mulching his ashes around the thorny bushes between real estate showings. Besides, I had my own plan.

The TAKSi thumped as the valet hoisted my bag into the trunk, then again when he slammed it closed, rattling the car. He rapped his knuckles smartly on the top of the cab. The driver cranked his neck to look at me, a leer spread over his face. He was child-size. As part of my training in infectious diseases, anthropometric history was of interest—studies that establish the historical record of the overall nutrition of a population by tracking average adult heights. Even though the man was underdeveloped, he had the ubiquitous five o'clock shadow, black caterpillar eyebrows, and Saddam Hussein moustache of the Middle Eastern male. "Where you go, lady?"

"Can you take me around Istanbul and wait for me? I want to go to the Egyptian Spice Bazaar first."

"No problem, lady. I can drive you anywhere, anytime. You can look at carpet too. No need to buy. Just looking." He trained the rearview mirror on me reflecting the hungry eyes of a man who spent his days grasping for intimacy with his fleeting fares. Trying to make an extra shekel, as my fiancé Paul would say.

"How much in American dollars?"

"Not too much. Very good price for you."

In the closed cab his body odor was inching into the back seat. "How much is not too much?"

"No meter for you. Just seventy-five American dollars, whole day."

"I need to be at the airport by four. So okay, I guess."

"*Very cheap price*," he pushed, having to get the last haggling word in.

"American?"

"Yes."

"Beautiful girl." When he didn't get a rise out of me, he said, "You go back to America?"

"No. India." *I'll see some of Istanbul, then to Varanasi, return to LA the following weekend, sleep sixteen hours, and back to the hospital to start my fellowship.*

"Why you go India?" he asked, butting into my thoughts.

"Just visiting."

"Why you not stay in Istanbul? I make lady very nice tour. Very cheap."

I pretended not to hear him over the cacophony of honking horns and the grind of hundreds of revving engines. My Indian mother had died of preeclampsia after childbirth. She'd been my age at her death, twenty-seven. Her parents had told my father that death was her karma for marrying against their wishes.

Dad had swallowed his hubris and traveled to India to scatter her ashes in the Ganges River . . . just in case.

"Why you not travel with husband?"

I smiled again at the driver's dog eyes in a way that was intended to shut him up. Kind of a pathetic, spinsterish smile of one who spent her *life* cooped up behind a blubbering TV set spooning Häagen-Dazs down her throat. He looked away, drumming his fingers on his steering wheel, then said, "No husband?"

I was not going to open the subject of my engagement up for conversation with the little man. "I'm a doctor," I replied, hoping to satisfy him. "I was attending a U.N. medical conference at the hotel. 'Preventing and Treating Infectious Diseases in Developing Countries'."

"Ahhh," he breathed, but this information only seemed to ignite a flame of curiosity in his probing eyes. "My wife, she is dead."

"Oh, I'm sorry."

"Evil eye."

"Excuse me?"

"My neighbor have evil eye. He angry with me. He kill my wife with very big fever."

I sat silently looking out through the window, feeling a creep of emotion for the man, for his loneliness, his superstitions, and his obsequiousness, as if it were a cluster disease that warranted pity. I opened my bag for the *Fodor's*. There was the sterling Tiffany pillbox Paul had given me containing ten-milligram Valium. Paul, a movie producer, traveled a lot and knew that benzodiazepines provided the best sleep during the disruption of jet lag by slowing down the nervous system. I punched speed dial on my phone to hear his voice, but saw there was no service. Regret began like a flu that signals its onslaught with a faint musky throb of lung tissue. Paul wanted to meet me after the conference so we could travel together to India. But no. I always had to show the independent spirit that had made my father so proud. If Paul were with me, the taxi ride would be fun. We'd suppress giggles and eye rolls. Paul would have already mapped out the new section of Istanbul, built on the Asian Continent where Istanbul's financial and business district and five star hotels flourished. When we crossed the Galata Bridge over the Golden Horn inlet of the Bosphorus to the old city on the European continent, he would ignore the driver to fiddle with the GPS on his iPhone to get his bearings. At the end of our tenure in the sad little man's cab, Paul would have tipped him heavily to cleanse us of any guilt associated with our elitism.

Indeed, we had crossed the Galata Bridge and were now in the old city of Istanbul; the black and gunmetal gray Mercedes and Jaguars disappeared, replaced by Kartol station wagons, tinny Fiat Sinhans, Opel Vectras and, surprisingly, American classics from the late fifties and early sixties, one after another. Chevys mostly. Besides the cars, there were elephantine Mercedes Benz buses filled with middle-aged German tourists peering with vague interest from their upper berths. The TAKSi slid along the ancient wall and huge towers as if spoiling for combat. Correspondingly the sky darkened, with rain only moments away. An indifferent wind, a prelude to rain, whistled against the windshield.

We passed a moss-covered fortress. "Prison," the driver said, when I had thought we had settled into a quiet ride. "Many, many American hippie. Life," he took his hands off the wheel and crossed his wrists in a pantomime of bondage. "Antiquity smuggling, possession of the Afghani." He toked vociferously on an imaginary joint. "I can sell lady doctor very excellent Hindu Kush Red. I swear on my mother is very, very good shit. Not to worry. You smoke here in my car and . . . ." He smacked his palms together as if brushing off dirt. "You take carpet. Very nice carpet, make your house very proud. You no need to buy. Just looking."

"No thanks. Really." I smiled at him, feeling again that sense of responsibility for being a privileged American while this man had to scrape for extra income, however nefariously.

"You visit Topkapi?" he asked, hoisting his skinny body a half a foot off the driver's seat so that he could sling his arm over the backrest, looking at me.

I had seen it with a few other residents the day before. My face must have said it all because the driver laughed, showing off blackened teeth and the inflamed gums of periodontal disease. "Ah, I know," he said patronizingly. "Liberated American woman no like *haram*." I looked away, creeped out that he'd invaded my thoughts. He took both hands off the wheel, making a circle with the fingers of one hand sticking the index finger of his other hand in and out in a sexual gesture. "No men!"

"Watch the traffic!"

The little man plopped back in front of his wheel. Rain fell. Big fat polluted drops over the cold, dank, wet tomb of antiquity. Minarets all over the city began transmitting the melancholy Arabic call to prayer over antiquated loudspeaker systems jarring in their lack of synchronization. When the TAKSi driver defiantly flicked his radio to belly dancing music, a chill crept under my skin. He continued multitasking: flicking his lighter and sucking at his cigarette till the tobacco lit, switching radio stations, jamming his foot on the brake just millimeters before slamming into the car ahead of him. My bag slid off my lap as he turned the wheel sharply, cutting off a dirty Rolls.

"No more *haram*." The driver belched smoke, not wanting to leave the subject alone. "*Haram* mean forbidden. Atatürk, he father of modern Turkey, he say no more sultan, no more *haram*. Nineteen twenty-two, sultan go away. No more eunuch." He fluffed them away with flicking fingers. "Eunuch mean, in Turkish, 'no beard'. Eunuch guard *haram*, like the peacock, only mean, like mad dog."

"Uh-huh," I said under my breath, wondering if there was a way that I could switch cabs at this point, but probably not.

The TAKSi nudged its way through the rubble-strewn street, pausing impatiently for a donkey, scattering chickens lured into traffic by mounds of garbage. The driver maneuvered the car through the bustling street, going from a dead stop to flooring the accelerator and miraculously slipping into spaces between cars, a terrifying fraction of space on either side. He hit the brakes to avoid a bus that careened into the next lane—such as it was—narrowly avoiding a collision with a truck hauling two milk cows in its bed—throwing me forward; fortunately I managed to brace myself before my nose met the heavy plastic liner on the back seat. *The Song of God Bhagavad Gita* flew out of my bag onto the floor. I had planned to read it on the plane to India. It seemed about time to learn something about my mother's faith. I opened the book. Inside I'd slipped a photo of my parents. Dad, young and blond, dressed in a suit, my mother at his side, wearing a sunset-orange sari with a pink blouse. Ray Bans hid her eyes. Her hair, like long strands of black silk, flickered around her smiling mouth, her lips painted cherry red like the bindi placed over her third eye.

I'd gotten over any girlish fantasies about my parents shortly after reaching the age of reason. At least for my father, it wasn't the kind of soul-mate love little girls romanticize. He'd simply been in lust over the intrigue and drama of a woman who had to break with thousands of years of tradition to marry him. He wasn't the type of man to stay faithful to one woman. His "little black book" had been more like the Los Angeles telephone directory. My mother's death was a bitter victory that had saved her from heartbreak. But still, his making the trip to India inspired in me a romantic notion that urged me back to that same holy river to unite them.

The TAKSi fishtailed to a stop. "Okay lady, Egyptian Bazaar. I wait for you."

I shuffled the book back in my bag and then glanced up at the sound of voices arguing so loudly they penetrated the window. It was a peasant couple with a little girl. The family was grimy, sun-baked, their features blurred by desperation. The woman, hunched and cringing, wore ballooning pantaloons of flowered cotton fabric, a dingy shawl, and a voluminous fringed scarf over her head. The man was lean and tall. Baggy pants flapped against his calves, in the wind. The girl seemed about six years old. She was blonde, a throwback from some ancient migration. Her cheeks were raw, her mouth blistered. Her hair was gummy and tangled, a few dreadlocks having volunteered. She was barefoot, her face streaked with grime. A sackcloth dress sagged over her fragile frame. She hid behind her mother's legs as the man's balled fist punched the air in front of their faces. This exhibition of hostility regularly occurred in the hospital parking lot, followed inevitably with an E.R. admission and a swarm of cops making an arrest.

But the TAKSi driver was unfazed. He reached over the seat for my bag.

"You leave here. No problem."

"Thanks. I'll keep it with me."

Avoiding the potholes, I tiptoed cautiously across the garbage-strewn cobblestones toward the bazaar. Young men hawked knocked-off Gucci purses, key chains and Playboy socks. I mounted a flight of broken concrete stairs following the garish music that squawked from overhead speakers. Heavy drops fell again, racing down the neck of my leather jacket to settle around the waistband of my jeans as clammy reminders that I could have whiled away the afternoon in the hotel tearoom chatting with the other docs.

The hall was gloomy and glitzy. Merchandise crushed down upon the shoppers: frivolous tourist junk, foods, gaudy jewelry, leather goods, carpets and more carpets, and every conceivable souvenir capitalizing on Turkey's history. Thunder reverberated through the maze-like structure off the tall ceilings and stone walls like phony sounds from an old black and white Sheik of Araby movie. Vendors flipped around long-handled squeegees, a kind of show, deftly directing pools of water on the muddy pavement away from their stalls and rushing to place rain buckets. All business as usual, this controlled pandemonium, along with the cacophony of innumerable radios.

One minute everyone is scurrying around making sure the rain didn't do any damage; the next it's all one big tea party, the little boys dashing to and fro wielding delivery trays of hourglass tea glasses and cubes of sugar to placate the soggy tourists.

I got out my mobile phone again, punching in Paul's number, but received only one of those frustrating robotic messages about entering my mail box number. I clicked off and pocketed the phone. A touch of cool flesh brushed against my palm. I jerked my hand away in an involuntary response and was taken aback to see the peasant woman who had been arguing outside. She offered me her little girl's hand. I dug out some coins from my jeans. I was only going to be in Turkey for the weekend and the other docs had advised me to avoid the hassle and stick with dollars. So all I could give the woman was a handful of pennies, quarters, nickels, and dimes. But she refused my money, a look of frustration twisting her drawn features, a hint of a curse on her quivering lips. She wasn't more than eighteen or twenty. Just a girl herself, with tufts of blonde hair escaping her scarf, and gray eyes clouded with emotion. She picked up her daughter and shook her, roughly, like she was offering me a sheaf of wheat at the market. The girl's head flopped on her neck as her mother spat at me in Turkish.

"Calm down," I said, using my gentle-but-firm doctor tone.

Just then a shopkeeper from a nearby stall caught my eye and gestured to me.

"Come, come, just sit here." He offered a chair. "I have rose oil, very nice from Isparta."

"Roses?" It seemed so convenient as I'd been thinking of some kind of ritual at the river, something to do with roses since the garden is where my father went to tamp down the intensity of his life. Ironically, he'd died there of a massive stroke.

"Yes, yes, roses," the man said, beaming.

I flashed a weak semblance of a smile at the peasant woman, feeling apologetically like the ugly, selfish American. But what could I do? If she didn't want money then I didn't know what else she wanted from me. I ducked away from my guilt and her accusing eyes and entered the man's shop, bracing for the overkill sell. The man had a delta of wrinkles on sun-hardened cheeks, his white whiskers defiantly growing in patches like brittle bushes which manage to emerge from blistered earth. He wore a black woolen cap. "This is *gulab*." The man with the goatee launched immediately into his pitch. "Rose water from hundred petal roses. Old-fashioned roses, gallica, Damascus, moss, centifolia." His heavy horned-rimmed glasses fell down his nose as he peered above them at me. *Progressive ptergygiums*, I diagnosed, examining the thickening of tissue, like blobs of yellowed wax, creeping from the sclera of both eyes onto his irises; if he didn't have the masses surgically removed, he'd be blind soon.

The man produced four chemist beakers filled with oil. One was the color of burned caramel. "Opium oil from poppy." The next, a curry color. "Isparta rose." The next, sunflower yellow. "Mixed roses. " The last, the color of lemonade. "Wild roses." With a syringe-like instrument he extracted drops from each beaker and massaged the oil into my hands. The attar of roses exploded pleasantly. The old man grinned, knowing he'd gotten his hook into me. "In Turkish, *Attar-t Cihangir*. Essence of Jahangir. *Attar* is Arabic. It means scent. Rosa damascena, the essential oil used to making all fine scents. Its scent is at surface. Just the slightest touch releases fragrance."

He scurried to gather up a bouquet of pink roses. "Isparta rose," he announced.

"I don't know," I mused out loud. "I'm going to the Ganges River with my father's ashes. I wanted to take something sentimental." I realized I'd said too much.

"In Asia, white is the color of mourning," he replied with feigned sympathy, proffering a white rose to finish me off.

"I can't take fresh roses with me all the way to India."

"Not roses; just petals, you see." He produced a clear plastic container, like a take-out box, and began plucking off white rose petals from a bouquet, filling the container. "I put underneath plastic bag. You go through security at airport then you fill with ice. Keep rose petals fresh."

I don't know why I stood there while he went on about roses and perfume, all the while stuffing the box with petals, because normally that kind of presumptuous behavior on the part of a salesperson would have launched me out of the door. But I kind of liked the idea. Who knew if I could find white rose petals in India? This way I'd have them with me. I envisioned myself floating on a boat, the Ganges River water the color of parrots, the white petals undulating, finessed by a tender current as my father's ashes filtered down to join with my mother's.

"I'll take them."

The man chortled, "Of course."

Outside, the rain showed no signs of letting up. Finished with the bazaar, I was happy to head to the airport to wait for my flight. An old man hobbled toward me, tugging up his coat. His lower spine had caved in toward his abdomen from the weight of the upper deformity. *Kyphosis*. Probably a congenital anomaly, or caused by tuberculosis, or maybe syphilis. It was kind of cool to see a case of it. He held out a knotty hand. "*Baksheesh*," he spat. I gave him the handful of American coins the peasant woman refused. He limped away from me.

I peered through the drape of water falling from the eaves. Several other beggars were making their way slowly toward me and so I chose to run, landing immediately into a pothole, my toes squishing in my hiking boots. Then to my utter amazement I noticed that the peasant woman, with Herculean strength, was trotting beside me, holding up her girl. I stopped, out of breath, blinking raindrops from my lashes, hiccupping a little incredulous laugh. "What in the world?"

The woman set the girl down. I bent to her, and took her little pointy chin in my hand, tilting her face upward. "Are you hurt?" She smiled halfheartedly, with her mouth shut, like kids do when their parents yell *smile* for photographs. There was nothing wrong with her that a good meal wouldn't cure. I'd take them over to a food vendor in the bazaar. But when I rose to standing, the girl's mother was gone.

The rain, which at first seemed to carry a hint of summer, now seemed more like the temperature of dead winter.

I urged the girl back to the bazaar, out of the downpour, watching her blonde head as it bobbed along in the rain, the way that little girls prance. She burped little squeals and grunts with each step, patrolling my face with traumatized curiosity. Once inside she attempted to bolt, but I followed her into a darkened nook where she crouched into a ball. I snatched up a handful of her dress, and yanked her out. The girl's eyes, caked with dried rheum, filled with tears. She opened her mouth and slipped her thumb in the empty space where her two front baby teeth had once been, sucking with grave intensity.

"Oh, I'm so glad to see you again," I called out, when the rose man walked by.

"This woman came up to me and left her little girl, just like that."

"Gypsies," he sniffed. "I will call the police. Don't worry. I bring you tea."

"Oh, thank you. Thank you so much," I said, watching him shuffle nonchalantly in the direction of his stall on loafers with crushed out backs, like slippers.

In just a minute or two, a woman appeared, heavily veiled in a black chador, with only a tiny triangular opening exposing her nose and downcast eyes. She modestly proffered a small gilded china saucer, which held two hourglass-shaped glasses of tea, each on a saucer with two rough cubes of white sugar and tiny longhandled spoons. The shrouded woman motioned to the shopkeeper's stall. The tea was from him.

My teeth were chattering. "Oh, thanks."

I stirred in the two sugar cubes. I'd have the tea, get the girl situated, then get to the airport where I would change into some dry clothes before the flight. I'd talk to Paul for an hour on the phone, and worry about my phone bill later. The woman handed a sugar cube to the girl, who lodged it where her baby teeth used to be. She held a glass of tea so the girl could slurp it through the cubes. It was a nice moment, the way that happens sometimes, with the three of us, complete strangers, sharing a window of time that was simply about hot tea and sugar, and nothing else.

"I don't want to be rude, but I have a flight to catch so I've got to get this girl to the police as soon as possible." The woman nodded, eyes downcast, then walked away.

Flaxen eyebrows. Lashes fluttering over downcast eyes. She was way too delicious for that old rose man. The taxi driver said that Turkey outlawed harems. I gulped the rest of the tea, not eager for any images of the repulsive ancient polygamist and his sexy young bride sticking in my head. My core warmed with the tea in my stomach, the heat permeating into my wet extremities.

It was the first time since I'd received the call at the hospital that I hadn't had my father in the back of my mind. It was good. I was turning a corner in my grief. I rummaged in my bag for a handful of hotel bedtime chocolates and poured them into the girl's cupped palms. She plopped onto the dirt floor of the bazaar and began to methodically unwrap the candy, gumming one as she unwrapped the next.

The shopkeeper was taking a long time and I checked my watch, feeling pressed to get going. "Come on." I reached my hand down to the girl and she clamored to her feet, clutching my hand with a chocolaty grip.

In that instant—too late for me to scream or form the words that could save myself—I knew that the tea I had just consumed contained choral hydrate, the drug used in a Mickey. Having an empty stomach, the well-absorbed sedative was taking hold of my consciousness and dragging me down into its dark web. The voices in the bazaar echoed large and small at the same time, as if packaged somewhere in my brain where I couldn't sort them out. My vision blurred as the bazaar music turned into a high pitched-whine. The girl's hand slipped out of mine. I staggered. A firm hand gripped my arm as I looked into the eyes of the black shrouded woman who had brought us the tea. Her eyes were *green*. I stumbled into a delicious free fall as a billow of black fabric enveloped me.

A honeyed voice filtered through the material, "Just let go, darlin'. I got you."

TWO

I worked feverishly at loosening the plywood boards that sealed the windows of the prison room to the outside world. After the rapist was finished with me, he had taken my clothes and locked me inside the small room. My adrenals were still pumping adrenaline and cortisol, triggering a flood of opiate-like neurotransmitters in my brain. The natural analgesics served to blunt the pain of my bleeding fingers, as I tore several fingernails to the quick. I stumbled back as the board peeled a few inches away from the windowsill. An incongruous ray of mote-swarming sunshine streamed in through a broken windowpane. Birds tittered and whistled, kids laughed and shrieked, singing songs that drifted up from a hollow courtyard below, sounds that flooded my entire being with the kind of lightheaded joy that can only be experienced when hope chases terror.

"Up here, help me!" I yelled. Somewhere close by was a heavily travelled highway and the kids couldn't hear my voice above the traffic. They ran off.

I stretched my fingers through the crack and brushed a film of spider webbing away from the window. I was in a room on the second floor. The garden was in new bloom, with clusters of grapes sprouting along vines which roped the building, little black beads dusted with white. In haphazard rows, a cutting garden developed where shoots had broken through the ground, their blossoms open in the afternoon sun. Papery fuchsia flowers exploded prolifically on woody bougainvillea vines, which had been cut back, leaving tracks of untarnished paint. The building I was in abutted several other ramshackle pre-nineteenth century structures, virtually identical, topped with clay roofs and mottled by weather and adorned with carpets and laundry hanging from windows. Minarets, telephone poles, and power lines crisscrossed the skyline.

I put my fingers into my mouth, sucking on my wounds. The taste of my blood renewed my fear. The rays of the sun that had so dazzled me with hope now shone on the blotches of dried blood on the plywood. The leaden realization that other women had been there before me fell over me like an executioner's hood. The dregs of my strength drained from me forcefully, like life's blood sucked into a Vacutainer. Next to the door stood a chrome table with a cheery yellow Formica top, and one chair, its yellow marbled vinyl torn, regurgitating tufts of cotton batting. I stumbled over to the chair and rested there. Borrowed light oozed in from the fissure at the window. The room had once been a luxurious bedroom, with green and silver flecked wallpaper peeling here and there like the drooping leaves of a neglected houseplant. The ceiling was made of ornately hand-carved wood. A frayed electrical cord swayed from a chipped, old-fashioned plaster ceiling medallion where a chandelier must have once hung. It seemed like a slum. The panic started to well up again. Who had seen me leave the hotel? The valet? I had not paid the TAKSi driver his seventy-five American dollars. He would go to the police with my bag and report my disappearance. The police would call the American Consulate. They would call Paul, as his number was on my bag. He would come to Istanbul and track me. Paul was enterprising, resourceful, and well-connected. He would find me.

"Paul!" I cried out in despair.

I'll be right back, I'd said, leaning into the open passenger window to blow him a kiss. I'd walked toward the thick glass doors of the Bradley International terminal at LAX, turning around just in time to detect a trace of anxiety on Paul's face as he jumped out of the car to yell over the pre-recorded white-zone announcement, *You be safe*!

His words had been a portent. *I'd been raped*!

Raped women in the E.R. were given a rape kit exam. Offer the patient levonorgestrel to prevent ovulation or fertilization. Order baseline tests for STDs. Advise a follow-up exam for HIV in three to six months. Collect physical evidence for a criminal investigation. Call a psychiatrist. I drew a hitching breath. The loneliness was alive as if it were something tangible with a slithering tongue and dank breath. I closed my eyes for a moment, psyching myself into being strong, reminding myself that I had to be strong—because there was no other choice. "I will find a way out," I said aloud.

Tasks had to be compartmentalized. Each situation had to be dealt with systematically. It was the only way to maintain psychological equilibrium and survive. I evaluated my injuries by palpitating my ribs, gasping out loud as the white pain shot through my core. I was moving air. That was good. It meant that the breaks in my ribs were clean and that the bones had not pierced my lung. I scooted to the edge of the chair to examine my genitals. My labia majora were swollen and tender. My labia minora were swollen and abraded. I slipped my index finger into my vagina, probing for any signs of traumatic genital fistula—a tear between my vagina and bladder or rectum. The tissue was inflamed but didn't appear to have sustained any serious damage. What was so strange was that the rapist had not sodomized me, which was typical of most rapes.

Just then the strains of an opera came from somewhere in the house. It was the Marriage of Figaro. Mozart. My father was an opera fan and had taken me with him to the opera on occasion when he didn't have a more interesting date. Opera was a thinking person's music. Now I knew that my rapist was a thinker. I didn't have time to dwell on it, as the heavy scrape of shoes on wooden treads outside the room became louder, and then the footsteps approached on planked flooring. "Hail Mary full of grace . . . " My palms were slick with oil and sweat, the attar of roses stimulated by panic. "The Lord is with thee . . . " What was he going to do to me? "Blessed art thou among women . . . " I felt faint with terror. "And blessed is the fruit of thy womb, Jesus. " I hadn't attended church since grade school when my father stopped taking me to catechism classes. The scowling nuns and their *fear of God* came to me, and my prayer caught in my sternum like a malignant tumor.

The deadbolt turned and the door opened. There he stood at the door, backlit so that he appeared like a huge black cut out. Adrenaline licked up my spine as I rose from the chair and backed to the wall. "Holy Mary Mother of God."

"Deva," the man said from the doorway. His voice was deep and hoarse.

"Who are you? What do you want?"

"Deva, *viens ici*."

I had studied Spanish and didn't understand what he was saying.

The man walked with determination across the expanse of the small room, his heels hammering the wood planks. He struck me across the face with a balled fist. My body thumped against the wall, unhinging the injuries that all the systems of my body had worked so hard to put into a healing sync. A throbbing hematoma gathered in the connective tissue under my cheekbone. I touched the new injury in disbelief. For a few moments there was silence except for my erratic breathing and the music. My heart palpitated wildly. I was aware of my blood pressure spiking and adrenaline flowing as his hand tangled in my hair, yanking my head back. Looking up, I saw the first stars of the night appear through the cracks of the window. Then I began to breathe.

The man dragged me across the floor and threw me down onto the mattress. I screamed, the pain torch-like in my ribs. I began to experience time distortion again, with time seeming to run slower so that I detected each detail with great clarity. I went limp to signal that he had won the fight. He reeled away, panting like a feral underworld animal, straightening his tie and pulling down on the edges of his jacket as much to smooth the fabric as to sooth and gather his composure.

When he bent to look at me, I stared directly into his eyes to personalize myself to him, in hopes that if he were to see me as a fellow human being he would not lash out again—or kill me. He was dressed like a businessman in a white shirt under a black sports jacket, and gray gabardine trousers. He looked about forty-five; he was clean-shaven, squared-jawed handsome in an aging playboy kind of way, with brown eyes fringed in black lashes, an equine nose of nobility. He reminded me of the French venture capitalists who sit in cafés in Beverly Hills, legs crossed like women, sipping espresso, and making deals to buy shopping centers. His long, straight black hair fell over his eyes, but even so, it was receding severely at the temples. He had had a blepharoplasty to minimize the bags under his eyes, and that said a lot about his psychology. He was vain.

"No screaming," he said with a thick French accent as he held up his switchblade again, "Or I cut off zee nose."

"I'm an American doctor." I forced the words into coherent shapes. "You have to let me go."

The man smirked.

"I'm with a U.N. delegation. They'll be missing me."

"I am also wis zee U.N. *délégation.*" He chuckled.

"Please don't hurt me again. I'll do whatever it is you want. I can get you any amount of money. Just let me go."

He planted his boney knee on my sternum above my cracked ribs. A fiery pain encompassed my rib cage. He fumbled in his coat pocket and expertly wrapped a rubber cord around my upper arm, as if he had done it a thousand times before.

"What are you doing?"

"I make you mine, stupid girl." He extracted a hypodermic from his coat pocket.

"You have the wrong person! My name is Meredith Fitzgerald. Doctor Meredith Fitzgerald," I said, my voice a hoarse whisper. "I'm an American. A medical doctor. This is all some kind of a mistake."

"You are Deva," he said matter-of-factly.

With the prick of the needle into my vein, I slumped onto the mattress gliding on shallow breath along a narrow corridor of ecstasy. The experience was solitary and I felt the aloneness of it as if standing apart, observing. There was no emotion, no awareness of my senses other than pleasure. It wasn't an earthly voyage, but a space within my mind that was vividly alive with thoughts, imaginations, visions and dreams flowing, intermingling.

The rush ended, leaving an immediate longing to experience it again. My eyes fluttered open. My nose ran and I felt drained with no awareness of how much time had elapsed. The reality of my situation carved its way into my consciousness. I felt myself being hurled into the darkness of overwhelming shame that sucked me down, obliterating the pleasurable sensations. I immediately understood the secret of the drug, a scrambled formula of desire and remorse. My innocence had ended. I now saw the rapist vaguely, as if through the amniotic fluid of my rebirth into hell. "What do you want?" My voice sounded strangely unfamiliar.

He ignored my question and went about sealing with duct tape the crack I'd made at the windows. The door slammed and the heavy bolt thundered. His footsteps faded down the stairs. Unable to move, I vomited onto the mattress. The odor mingled with the smell of the rapist's semen and the sweet scent of roses as the sound of opera started again.

THREE

Into the euphoric bubble of oblivion, the cloying scent of roses filled my nostrils with the shocking memory of the rape. I opened my eyes and recoiled at the sight of another face. *A eunuch*? A thirty-year old man with feminine characteristics, soft, beardless skin, blue eyes, thick, tousled blond hair, his full lips twitched in a smile. I'd seen men like this at the hospital. Castration was a perverted homosexual sub-cult, sometimes occurring as a result of "ball and cock torture," sexual play involving inflicting testicular pain. Fetishist practitioners— or "cutters"—non-medically trained perverts who indulged S&M fantasies for profit, also performed castrations.

This eunuch's head was disproportionately wide, a condition called brachycephaly. Most likely he had been left lying on his back for prolonged periods of time as an infant, causing his skull to flatten. Otherwise he had Mongolian facial characteristics with a protruding forehead and a nose that was narrow at the top, and broad at the nostrils. His eyes were hooded, yet not quite Asian. Crude tattoos in Russian cursive curlicued around his neck, disappearing into the front of his soiled white dress shirt. It was so odd that he wore a suit. He would have been less scary, more in character had he worn jeans and a tee-shirt like the goons in the movies. But he looked like a junior executive with a sociopathic glint in his eyes. Castrated men were said to possess "eunuch calm," but I remembered what the taxi driver said, *Eunuch guard haram, like peacock, only mean, like mad dog*. The deadness in the eunuch's eyes told me that he was like the T-Rex that possessed a human sized brain, but no cerebellum; like the T-Rex, living purely in the moment with no emotional response, even to his own pain.

"Something for blue-eyed bitch," he said atonally, with a syringe clamped between his teeth.

"I can pay you any amount of money . . . . " Before I could finish my plea he plunged the needle into my vein and I escaped into the dark joy of the rush. *The process of separating water from oil was discovered accidentally in Mogul India in the sixteenth century, at a feast for the Emperor Jahangir. Pools filled with rose water in his garden. The hot sun evaporates water, and oil comes to the surface. That is perfume*! I came out of the nod. The eunuch was gone but the loathsome smell of roses remained.

Each visit from the rapist was a recurring nightmare. But the heroin injections were even more worrying. Being highly soluble in lipids, heroin crossed the blood-brain barrier in seven seconds, a hundred times faster than morphine. Pharmacologically, the drug relieved my pain. Hypnotically, it lulled me into a fairy tale sleep. I could recover psychologically from the rapes, but I feared that the substance of my identity was dissipating with each heroin rush that was delivering me inexorably into heroin addiction. I prayed they would stop forcing the drug on me before that happened.

The blur of the drug made it impossible to tell how many days had gone by. I tried to tell time by the prayer calls, which invaded the prison room like clockwork. But eventually I lost track of the hours, and then the days. Ten days? I wasn't sure. I searched my memory for any detail of what had taken place, for clues that might be the germ of an escape plan. There had to be a way. I struggled off the mattress and went to the window. I'd seen the hacked up prostitutes being wheeled into the O.R. and was certain that the rapist would deliver on his promise to mutilate me. Nevertheless, I stripped the tape with trembling hands and tried again to peel back the plywood in hopes of attracting someone's attention in one of the nearby apartments.

Sparrows flapped into the sky, scared off by a stringy looking cat that cruised into the garden. Several blackbirds vaulted away, too, circling, waiting for the ruckus to end. My heart raced when a band of shepherds sauntered down the pathway, casually corralling their sheep with gentle switches of reeds. Their shoes were caked with mud, and over their shoulders a few of them carried newborn lambs. Mutts trotted alongside and helped with the herding. I had nothing to toss down to get their attention. I tore off a piece of dangling duct tape with my teeth. For the next half an hour I scratched HELP KIDNAPPED MEREDITH FITZGERALD into the tape with my fingernail. I shoved it through the cracked window and watched it fall to the earth. I said out loud,

"The door is locked, but I will find a way out. I will escape. I will be OK." I repeated my mantra, "I will find a way out."

They'd left me a small bottle of water on the table! I lunged for it, drinking it, gulping air, panting. A quarter of a liter—eight ounces. They were giving me enough for my body to flush enough toxins through urination so that I would not die. I needed much more water. A female body my size is made up of about fifty-five percent water. Dehydration becomes uncomfortable when the body's water volume falls only two percent. My water volume had declined more severely than that. The thirst was unbearable. I'd already stopped urinating.

The drug and dehydration robbed my appetite, too, though it didn't matter as I was not given any food. I had not eaten since the breakfast at the hotel. That innocent, innocent breakfast! I was wasting away despite the systems of my body that struggled to keep me alive. My thyroid slowed as my endocrine system raced to protect the infrastructure of my body. My immune system leached every last resource of my former robust body to ward off infections. But nothing could stop the cannibalization of my lean body mass that was taking place to keep me alive.

The rape, the unpredictability of the drugs, the thirst, starvation, and isolation had to be a method to break me. I tried to remain strong emotionally, and tried to encourage myself. I tried to adhere to the main objective of staying alive. I replaced the tape on the window, and then dealt with the darkness.

More time passed. I couldn't tell how many days. One day the rapist and the eunuch didn't come to my room. That night I lay awake all night, slapping at the repulsive tickle of the feathery cockroach legs scampering over my body. The effects of the last fix began to wear off. It must have been the middle of the night when I heard a voice singing *Con onor muore*. It was the aria in Madama Butterfly when Cio-Cio San reads the inscription on her father's knife that says, "Who cannot live with honor must die with honor." I tried to occupy myself by trying to figure out the singer playing the part of Madama Butterfly. But an hour went by and the same aria repeated over and over. An hour later, the repetitious music was driving me insane. I covered my ears and rocked on the mattress.

Incapacitating cramps seized the largest muscles of my body, the latissimus dorsi, trapezius, quadriceps and gluteus, and then slowly moved to the smaller muscles deep inside my tissues until I felt as if my bones were cramping. I couldn't stop yawning. My nose ran, my stomach knotted, and I sweated profusely. The nerve discharge of my sympathetic nervous system caused the contraction of the little muscles called the arrectores pilorum, elevating the hair follicles above my skin. *Gooseflesh.* My body, slick with perspiration, shivered uncontrollably. The itchy nose I'd experienced during heroin highs turned into whole body torment and I raked my face and arms with jagged fingernails. My intestines began the slow turn that starts when the narcotic constipation ends, intensifying into wrenching diarrhea. I scrambled off the mattress and felt around frantically in the dark for the bucket the eunuch had tossed into the corner. Then the stench hung inescapably in the air.

I couldn't afford to lose more fluids, and began to fear the very real possibility of death. But worse than the fear of death was what was happening to the essence of myself. The systematic injections that the rapist and eunuch had forced on me had instigated the viscous spiral of tolerance and physical dependence of heroin addiction. The physiological effect of withdrawal created a longing so extreme that I strained to listen for the Russian's heavy clomp on the stair treads, feeling a thrill of anticipation at any creak that might signal his approach. Once I began to desire the drug, I became fatalistically resigned. Dependency was like a fortress blocking my way back to my old self.

It happened so quickly.

FOUR

After the first hellish night of withdrawals, the sweet sound of a woman singing wove its way into my consciousness like an innocuous atmospheric disturbance. It took me some time to understand that I wasn't hallucinating, that the voice was American . . . and that it was right outside my prison door. The voice crooned a children's song. I rose from the despicable mattress, propelled through inertia by a storm of adrenaline and the innocent turbulence of hope. The fear of my abductors seemed like some kind of dirty trick on my mind that I no longer needed to heed. I limped to the door and banged on it. "In here, in here! Help me! Help me!" I shouted, surprised at the force of my voice. The singing saturated the door, having transformed from sound into matter. The voice of a little girl accompanied the woman's. "In here. Help me. Help!" I screamed, hammering harder.

The singing stopped. The deadbolt turned. The door opened. A hallway light shed a sickly yellow glow into the room. Just a few hours earlier, my pupils would have been pinned from the heroin. But now that the heroin was out of my system, and having been kept in the dark, my pupils were dilated and the light was painful. The relief was so profound, I crumpled onto the dirty floor, shading my eyes with shaking hands. "Thank God, you've come. You've found me!"

This woman would call the authorities. Officials from the American embassy would arrive with American military medical personnel. I'd receive medical attention, a hot bath, food, and water. I'd be transported by air ambulance to a hospital in the U.S. Paul would be at my side to hold my hand as I fell into a drug-induced coma where I'd remain for the first seven to ten days of my withdrawal. I would be brought out of the coma, heavily sedated until I made a full recovery.

My eyes adjusted and I recognized the little gypsy girl from the bazaar, hesitating at the woman's side. She'd been cleaned up, and her tattered sackcloth frock replaced with a blue flowered garden party dress with a smocked bodice, white socks trimmed in lace, and yellow leather dress shoes. The mats and dreadlocks in her hair had been carefully clipped away, and her hair was washed and plaited with little blue satin bows tying the ends. She slipped her thumb between rosy lips and sucked as her eyes took in the spectacle that I had become.

The woman sashayed over to the window where she stripped the tape away with bold strokes. Sunlight darted into the room in long sharp shards. When she turned, her eyes were green rays of another kind, a light that pierced into me with the painful truth. These were the eyes I had seen the instant before I lost consciousness at the Egyptian bazaar. This woman had been complicit in my abduction. I crawled toward the door, but she grasped me by the shoulders and pulled me back. I sprawled naked on the floor, trembling, sobs rising out of me like spasms.

The woman went about her business as if I didn't matter. She dragged the shit bucket into the hall. "Wait on me, hear? *Sen burada bekle*," she said to the girl who gripped the handrail of the stairs and stepped backwards down the staircase, her suspicious eyes never leaving me.

The woman shut the door. Without ventilation the room remained close, the smell of the bucket lingered in the air. She was about twenty and wore a red sheath dress. Seeing her glammed up as if she were going to a cocktail party added weight to my sensation of delirium. Since I'd been dating Paul I'd seen some of the most beautiful women in the world; actresses and models processed through hair and makeup and who had their own stylists to dress them. This woman, more stunning than anyone I'd seen at the studio, was naturally beautiful with lips and breasts that were full and real. She had a perfect, straight nose and firm, creampuff skin. Her lips bowed into a nubile pout. Her smile, when she'd flashed it encouragingly at the girl, was one of those larger-than-life toothy grins that leave men's hearts scattered by the wayside.

She squatted on her spike heels to stroke my forehead with a cool hand. "Yer burnin' up girl," she said, tarnishing the gestalt of her beauty with her painful Southern twang. "Gotta git you back in bed."

"Bed?" I whimpered feebly. She helped me limp back to the sweaty mattress, where I flopped down. She pulled a clean blanket from a bulky tapestry bag to cover me. This small gesture of kindness overwhelmed me and I began to sob.

"Hush," she purred. "Can't even cry tears now. Yer all dried up. I brung you some water." She helped me up so that I could gulp from a water bottle. "You best be careful," she said, pulling the bottle away. "Otherwise you just upchuck and it won't do no good."

Psychotic homeless men regularly sprawled around on the grass in front of the E.R. entrance to the hospital. Many of the interns, residents, and nurses avoided having to treat these men, finding something else more urgent to do. Now I was like those derelicts, and this strange woman with lotion soft hands and a décolletage bathed in cologne was helping me. "Why are you doing this?" I whispered.

"Got no choice in the matter."

"But of course we have a choice. *We're American.*"

She laughed merrily, though there was a somber timbre to her giggle. "And the rockets red blare," she sang wistfully as she pressed those cool fingertips to my feverish thorax, urging my body back down onto the mattress. "The bulbs bursting with air . . . . " She rummaged in her bag as she continued to hum the Star Spangled Banner.

"Who are you?" I asked, interrupting the inane humming.

"I'm called Nasreen."

"That's not your real name. That's not an American name. That rapist, the man who did this to me, he called me another name."

"That's Belhaj. He's the boss here."

The boss! What net had I fallen into? I had to find out. First I had to befriend this woman. "What's your real name?"

"Real name's Camille. But you best not go callin' me that."

I sat up, hugging my arms around my knees to try to quell the twitching of my limbs. "You've got to contact the police."

"Ain't gonna do that." She handed me the water bottle and I began to nurse it.

"I need medical attention. That rapist and that eunuch have hurt me!" She giggled. "Eunuch? Better not call him that to his face! Beat the piss outta me fer callin' him gong gong. That's China talk fer eunuch. Story goes Vadim lost the family jewels in Shanghai. Chugged a fifth of rice moonshine in some bar contest'n got down with some homos—"

Please!" I interrupted, not wanting to chitchat about that thug as if we were normal girlfriends who were gossiping. "You've got to help me!"

"That so? Who's gonna help *me* then?"

"What do you want? Money? I can get you money. How much do you want?"

"Ten million dollars!" she cried gleefully, then again looked somber.

I was getting nowhere with her and searched my mind for the vernacular of girlfriends, a way to connect us. "At the bazaar, I thought you were the shopkeeper's wife. The man who sold me roses," I said, failing miserably at sounding girl-friendly.

"Do I look like the old lady of some old fart shopkeeper?" she asked, affronted.

"Are you the rape . . . that man . . . Belhaj's wife?" The words stuck in my throat.

She snorted air indignantly through her nostrils, but I couldn't read her.

"What about the little girl? Her mother gave her to me to protect her and I—"

"Her mother was givin' us the girl," Camille interrupted. "Well, not *give*."

It wasn't true. Maybe the father wanted to sell his girl, but her mother clearly wanted me to help her. And now both the little girl and I had been kidnapped.

Camille sat on the vinyl-bottomed chair and hoisted her bag onto the table, the rush of air ruffling her hair like dandelion fluff. She produced a pink pastry box. "I could git in real bad trouble but I brung you some baklava." She cut the dessert into neat sections with a plastic knife. "The sugar'll do you good."

The muscle cramps and twitching, nausea, and headache hammered me worse than any flu imaginable. I flopped down and doubled up on the damp mattress. I needed a fix. *Fix*! My God, I was thinking like a junkie. *I was a junkie*!

"That's why they call it kickin' the habit," Camille said gesturing to my jerking legs with her plastic knife. "You best get through it now. Otherwise it's about the quickest way to hell."

"So you're saying they are not coming back with more drugs?" I chattered in a small, guilty voice.

"I could git in real bad trouble, but brung you some'a that too, if you want it."

"Yes, I want it."

Camille's green eyes examined me. "First you got to take a bite of this cake." She turned back to her carving of the baklava, her face emotionless as she lapped a stream of honey from her fingers. "Balls," she said under her breath, dabbing a drip of honey that had fallen onto the red crêpe fabric of her dress.

Under the blanket, I wrapped my arms around my bony ribs, recalling the chilled, solid feel of a corpse in the morgue.

"Shaky huh? Your belly hurtin' you too? Junk does that to you if you don't eat. Here." Camille proffered a glob of pastry. "Gotta eat no matter how puny you feel."

I snatched the baklava and ate it quickly, then another piece, and another, bolting the honey-sodden pastry like the starvation victims in the movies trying to satisfy an irrational craving for sugar created by the brain chemistry imbalance of heroin use.

"He's got you strung out. Up to two grams a day. Take my word for it, that's what old time junkies use. He's gonna fuck with you now. Give you just enough to make you his slave."

"He sent you here to do that?"

"Eighth of a gram is all I could score, but I brung it 'cause I knew he was withholdin' n' that you'd be in need. You ain't gonna get a high 'n yer *still* gonna be sick. So it's up to you. You could try and do without. Git over the next couple a weeks you'll be clean as a hound's tooth."

I tried to comprehend what she was saying but my need was too great. *I need it to think*! It was just a medicinal dose, after all, to take the edge off my pain. "I don't understand. You brought it for me, now you're telling me not to use it?"

"I'm havin' second thoughts, you know," she said, her voice prickly. "Now that we're talkin' nice 'n social, I'm sayin' to myself that yer too nice of a lady to turn into a dopehead."

But I couldn't think! Once I could think clearly, I could understand what she was talking about. I kept my pleading eyes locked on hers. Camille made a disapproving face, and from the tapestry bag produced a plastic bag that had the power to take away my suffering. She shook gray granules, like kitty litter, from a vial into a spoon. I watched her closely, as my reality again had become crystal clear and everything I looked at what appeared like images on a fabulous quality high definition monitor.

She had ordinary hands. Her fingers were short and the red polish on her flat uneven nails was chipped but appeared vividly red. She went on talking as she spilled a few drops of water into the cap from the bottled water and drew it into a hypodermic needle. She squirted the water onto the grains, and then she cooked it over a cigarette lighter, which was the addict's meager attempt at purifying the product. The heroin in her spoon bubbled, grey and tantalizing. She drew the liquid drug into the syringe.

"Is that needle clean?" I wiped my nose with the back of my wrist.

"Brand new, just fer you."

"What's inside the syringe?"

"Cotton. Filters out the bigger impurities what don't git burned off."

"What kind of impurities?"

"Stuff they hit it with, you know, coffee 'n powdered sugar'n all that shit. This ain't the U.S. of A where drugs are pure like the driven snow."

She was wrong. In the U.S. all kinds of adulterants were used, as dangerous as procaine, lidocaine, laundry detergent, and Ajax. Alkaloids too, like quinine and strychnine. We saw a lot of cases of poisoning come through the E.R.

Camille used a rubber cord as a tourniquet. She snapped at my median antecubital vein with the nail of her index finger to plump it up, but it rolled away. "Ain't gonna stand up." She plied the flaccid vein with her fingers.

"Let me do it." I snatched the syringe and clamped it between my teeth as I inspected my arms. "This vein is bad . . . phlebitis . . . inflammation of the lining of the vein." I moved haltingly, examining my other arm, talking to myself. "Hemotoma." I looked up at Camille.

She snorted a laugh through her pretty nostrils. "I knows what a blown vein is."

I went back to my search.

"You don't need to shoot. You can smoke it in a cigarette."

"I don't smoke."

"The coal burns off most of the smack anyways," she said, sighing. "You can pour it onto the baklava, but yer stomach acid'll destroy most of it before it can git into yer blood. You can snort it, or put it onto a piece of tin foil and heat it from underneath 'n inhale it with a straw. Either way it'll git into yer blood. They say the needle's masochistic, and that some folks just go fer that."

I gave up on finding a vein and did what the junkies in the E.R. talked about. I muscled it, plunging the syringe into my buttock and injecting. I lay rigidly on the mattress, waiting five minutes for the heroin to meander through my muscle into my bloodstream. Camille went on about kicking heroin and what I needed to do and not to do. When the drug finally reached the opiate receptors in my brain's pleasure system I melted loosely onto the mattress, consumed by the rush. But the high was over quickly. Reality snapped back into focus. Camille was right. It wasn't enough. It was different, too.

"He's been injecting me with unsterile needles," I said in a hyper tone, clinging to the infinitesimal high that instilled in me a false confidence. "I'm going to get septicemia. It's a serious infection. Or endocarditis. Look," I said, pulling the blanket aside. My skin was riddled with abrasions, black-and-blue spots and infected sores. My drugged sensibilities prevented me from being alarmed by what I saw. "I've already got some bruises," I said curtly. Suddenly I stopped talking, realizing what might have already happened to me, that I might have irreversible heart or liver damage.

"You sure got some moxie, girl."

I realized that on this smaller dose of the drug I could still function with very little loss of attention and motor activity. At the same time, a lesser dose had not rid me of the withdrawal symptoms. It had only taken the edge off enough to intensify the craving. "I need more!" I cried, slavish to my habit and crashing from the thready high.

Camille picked up the syringe. "I wanted to give myself a skin-pop too, but I'm givin' it all to you."

"What's a skin-pop?"

"Under the skin. Thought you was a doctor."

So she knew about me! I drew my hand over my upper lip, wiping away the beads of sweat that had collected there, wondering what to make of her privy status with the rapist.

"Don't need it anyways, I guess. Chippin's just playin' with fire."

"What's chipping?"

"Messin' around with smack."

I was learning the language of addiction. "Then it is heroin," I said somberly, mostly to myself, as I had entertained a stupid fantasy that it was all just a bad dream that I wasn't really an addict.

"Don't tell me you and yer doctor friends ain't never busted into the pharmacy fer a taste?" Camille smiled coquettishly.

"We don't use heroin in hospitals," I shot back, disgusted.

My friendly captor didn't seem to mind my irritability. She unwrapped another piece of baklava and offered it to me. "Here."

"Please, can't you bring me some clothes?"

"I brung you *all this*," she confided in a tone that implied the cake she was waving in the air, the thin blanket, and the bottle of water, were a grand affair. "Had that smack in my vajajay for three hours, so try 'n be a little more appreciative," she sulked.

"Thank you," I said, feeling the well of self-disgust that I had fallen so low, but also understanding that there was more to her than meets the eye. She was acting against the rapist's wishes. That meant she probably understood what I was going through. She had a heart someplace beneath the chintzy satin and lace push up bra. "Can you at least tell me how long have I been here?"

"Near goin' on three weeks. We're gittin' on to the end of June."

I shivered at the assault of a sultry summer breeze from the broken windowpane. "I was only supposed to be gone a week.

People will be looking for me. They will find me."

"That so? Well, I dunno know who *they* is, do you? *They* never did find me." Camille pulled a package of cigarettes from her bag and shook one out. She deliberately tamped down the tobacco, licked the paper with her wet, pink tongue, and struck a match, inhaling deeply.

There was small knock at the door. The voice of the gypsy girl called, "Nasreen."

"Hold on, little one," Camille's voice was pleasant, girlish.

"Please at least tell me what happened to my things. There was a bag of ashes in my tote bag. A plain plastic bag. It's my father's ashes."

The odor of burning tobacco veiled the smell from the bucket as she took two quick nervous puffs in succession, the cigarette's tip flashing orange as the coal grew long. She pursed her lips and blew ashes off her lap. "Best be goin' now." Her face was impassive, and delicate streams of smoke wound out of her nostrils as she spoke. She crumpled up the pink pastry box and tossed the cigarette on the floor, grinding it into the linoleum with a blue stiletto.

"Go? What do you mean? Please don't leave me here, Camille, *please*!"

Camille walked over to me and, crouching down, slapped me hard across the face. "I told you not to go callin' me that."

FIVE

The rusty clunk of the deadbolt slipped, and Vadim the eunuch kicked his way into the room. I battled through the squall of my delirium to understand why he had come, why he stood over me with malice on his face. The Russian hoisted me off the mattress by my arm. I hung my head, ashamed of my wretchedness. He shoved a dull yellow cotton robe at me, and it fluttered to the floor. I picked it up and put it on, cinching the sash. A modicum of dignity. He shoved me out of the room and I fell, scraping the papery skin of my knee. The hallway was unfurnished, just old plank flooring, and mottled wallpaper from a bygone era, a florid rose pattern. I stood up. There was a fulllength mirror on the wall, a deteriorating silver-glassed relic that reflected a blurry, mottled image. I was startled at the sight of a hollow-eyed hag in the mirror with greasy, lusterless hair, and protruding hipbones.

Without warning, the rapist, Belhaj, appeared at the foot of the stairs, dressed in a stylish European cut suit, white dress shirt, and tie. Vadim pushed me down the hall. Belhaj flung open the door of another bedroom. On the floor lay a young blonde, naked and unconscious.

"You doctor," Vadim said. "You fix girl."

I sunk to my knees on the mattress where the girl lay. I tried to shake off the heavy webs in my brain so that I could think. She was young, maybe seventeen. "I need more light," I ordered automatically, but no one paid any attention. In the relative darkness I assessed the girl, tilting her head back, putting my fingers on her carotid artery, leaning down, and hovering my ear over her mouth, watching her chest. "I can feel a pulse." But it was not the normal sinus rhythm I had hoped for. "Do you have Naloxone?" It made sense that if they were in the business of hooking women on heroin that they would have a supply of Naloxone to counteract a life-threatening depression of the central nervous and respiratory systems caused by opioid overdose.

"You figure out," Vadim said.

Belhaj stood behind him in the shadows, watching.

I pinched the girl's nose shut and gave her four quick breaths. Fluid had built up in the alveoli, the small sacs in my lungs. Giving mouth to mouth aggravated the edema and I coughed. But then I forced myself to stop the taunting thoughts of what could be happening to my health: *myocardial infarction, congestive heart failure, cardiomyopathy*. I focused on my patient. "Call an ambulance. If she stops breathing she's going to have cardiac arrest."

Belhaj's footsteps took him away, but I didn't get the impression he was rushing to call for help. There would be no efficient paramedics with their clean, equipped ambulances, disciplined nurses, or teams of medical intelligentsia to turf her case out to. I was there in the room with the girl, on my own. "Please let her live," I prayed. After several more breaths the girl began to breathe shallowly. "Call an ambulance!" I shouted. I gave her another four quick breaths, helping her. I checked her pulse. "Her heart's stopped!" I yelled. "Call an ambulance!"

But my words just echoed in the empty room and when I turned around, Vadim was gone. I paused just long enough to look at the girl, just a few seconds. I took in everything about her face, the upturned nose, splashed with girl freckles. Her lips a cupid bow, drained of color. Her lashes, thick and white, fanned over her pallid cheeks. I wanted her to know, wherever she had gone, that she wasn't alone. "I'm with you," I whispered. "I have you, girl, and I'm not going to let you go." I went to work, placing the flat of my fingers on her ribs and sliding my hand up to her sternum, palms down, one over the other. I began compressions, artificially flattening the girl's ventricles to stimulate a contraction in her heart. *One, two three.*

Camille appeared with a lamp and plugged it in.

"Call an ambulance!" *One, two, three.* "She's going to die." *One, two, three.* The girl's body felt gelatinous as if she were already dead, past rigor and disarticulating. But she was not dead. Her face twitched and her pallid lips suddenly flushed deep purple. I pinched her nose and gave her two more breaths, and resumed compressions. *One, two, three.* Sweat tickled down my face.

"Come on now," Camille said, her hand on my shoulder. "Ain't no use."

The girl was not ready to give up as easily. Her eyelids fluttered, and her hands jerked spasmodically. I resumed chest compressions, repeating under my breath, "I will not let you go. I will not let you go." I felt the girl's pulse again. It was slow but strong and growing stronger. But my elation was short-lived when the girl's entire body began to flail, arms and legs thrashing, her torso arching in hyperextension. Her head dropped back on her neck as her body jerked and heaved on the mattress. I fell over her in an attempt to hold her down, more out of respect than a belief that I could do her any good. There was nothing I could do for her, but make good on my promise. I would not let her go alone. She lay still, rigid in hyperextension, her lovely mouth fixed in a gruesome death grin. I held her in my arms willing her to know that I was with her even in death.

At the creak of a floorboard I looked up to see Belhaj standing in the doorway, the torn wallpaper behind him wagging on the walls like tongues carrying bad tidings. Camille ran from the room, her heels clicking and clacking down the hallway, her blue cocktail sheath flashing like a scared bird in flight.

"Ach, no luck?" Belhaj asked me.

"This was not a heroin overdose," I shot back. "Whatever you gave her was tainted with something she was allergic to, or worse, some kind of poison, maybe strychnine."

"*Impressionnant*," Belhaj said, turning to Vadim who had just rushed into the room. "You aired zee doctair. Make sure I get zee refund on zhat shit."

Vadim grunted in acknowledgement. I sat on the floor, watching the Russian hoist the body over his shoulder like a carcass, with the girl's arms flapping indecorously.

"Too bad," Belhaj mused, watching his goon carry the girl's body out. "I ave a client zhat would ave liked air very much."

They were going to sell her like meat! "Then I'm glad she died."

He laughed. "*Incroyable*," he said, with a hint of admiration as he grabbed my arm and half dragged me to a wobbly stand.

Though he seemed casual and relaxed while I worked on the girl, now he was in a hurry. He pushed me down the hall. We entered another sorry bedroom, but this one was set up as operating room with much of the room draped in clear plastic. The dead girl was laid out on a gurney.

"I want, *comment dit-on*, zee organs?" Belhaj picked up a box of surgical gloves and tossed it to me. "Art, liver, kidney."

I shook my head in disbelief. I had done a one year internship in surgery before switching to an internal medicine residency. But I was not competent to wing a fast organ harvest. Talking fast, I said, "The organs probably won't be viable. They weren't oxygenated when her heart stopped pumping. Her kidneys and liver are most likely damaged from the tainted heroin." I could see by his blank expression that he didn't care. "I'm not sterile," I insisted, knowing full well what a sensational understatement that was.

"Make it fast or you are next."

After three weeks of terror and torture, I didn't want to die. I made a split second decision to save myself by snapping a pair of surgical gloves onto my hands. There were 10-blades, and a Finnocetto rib spreading retractor laid out on a blue paper drape over a stainless steel tray. There was saline solution on ice to flush the organs and a half a dozen coolers filled with chipped ice. The instruments and supplies indicated that they had done this before. I picked up a blade.

Heart tissue is more muscular and therefore more sensitive to a lack of oxygenation than are the liver and kidneys. The heart would have to come out first. But because of how difficult it was to access the heart, if I went for that organ, the other organs would not be viable. "I can't get the heart," I said, "if you want the other organs."

"I do not want to air zhis bullshit."

There was no time to give him a tutorial on the deterioration of the cellular structures. I did what I had to do. "Vadim, have you watched this before?" I asked feeling more awkward about using his name than I did about the bizarre question I asked.

"Many times," he boasted.

"Then put on a pair of gloves *now*!"

We had but a few minutes to get the organs out, flushed and onto ice. Even though I doubted the viability of the organs, Belhaj would have an understanding about the time limitations of organ harvesting under these conditions, and he would likely hear from his buyer if the organs failed. I didn't want him to blame me for dawdling. Vadim was going to have to perform the thoracotomy and take the heart out because I didn't have the strength to crack her chest open. I would go after the liver and kidneys.

I cut a traditional Y incision into the cadaver, opening it up from just below the sternum to the pubic bone. Without the heart pumping there was no pulsating blood, but it was messy with a lot of blood leaking. I could feel Vadim's heat next to me. The compounded stink of male sweat, stale cigarette smoke, dental plague, and sour yogurt spilled on his crummy suit made me queasy. I considered plunging the scalpel into his thigh, through his trousers, to severe his femoral artery. But I would not be able to fight Belhaj even with Vadim bleeding out on the floor. Instead, I flapped open the girl's skin. Her breasts fell heavily to either side of the gurney. It was grisly.

"Vadim, pick up a scalpel and make an incision around the forth rib." He didn't understand. "Count down four ribs and cut through like you're cutting into a piece of meat." He followed my instructions. "Cut all the way down the rib," I instructed, half watching him as I made an incision through the omentum, the fatty layer of tissue that holds the internal organs and intestines into a neat package. Vadim had done a surprisingly precise job of his assignment.

"Now take the rib spreaders. Introduce the spreader into the incision you made between the ribs and crack the ribs open."

I cut through the muscular hepatic artery and vein that held the liver in place. Blood oozed into the cavity. I heard the crunch of the rib bones splintering as I went after the three main lobes of the liver and lifted the slippery organ out and set it into a bath of ice. I moved the slithering intestines away with my left hand, grabbing the left kidney with my right, slicing through the renal artery.

"There are three major arteries," I said to Vadim. "Really big veins. Find them and cut through them." I saw him sever the pulmonary artery, pulmonary vein and the veina cava and pull the heart out. At the same time, I pushed the intestines to the other side of the body, cut through the renal vein and took out the right kidney.

We had the organs out in less than four minutes.

"Open the saline bottles. We need to cool down the organs and get as much blood out of the arteries and cavities as possible. Like this, like rinsing out a chicken carcass." I took a bottle from him and rinsed the heart first, splashing it with the solution then squirting it inside to flush through the arteries as best as I could. He immediately picked up the liver and began flushing it with another opened bottle of chilled saline.

Within another minute and a half the organs were rinsed and dried with sterile paper towels. We nestled them in thick plastic so that they would not freeze in the cooler with chipped ice where they would be kept until transplantation into various patients. Vadim clicked the coolers shut. The plastic-sheeted floor was slick with blood and the room smelled like a butcher shop. I was soaking in blood and fluids. I wiped my forearm over my eyes, exhausted and feeling a churning dread in the pit of my stomach. The girl's body was mutilated. I carefully folded the flaps of skin back in place so that her breasts were repositioned. I was hyperventilating with bile rising in my throat at the sacrilege of what we had done to her. I swallowed hard, trying to steady myself.

Vadim's full lips held the suggestion of a smirk. In the lamplight, his face was a grid of defensive wounds. My eyes traveled investigatively to his crotch, which bulged, despite the fact that he was castrated. He saw me looking and cupped his penis with a bloodied-gloved hand, giving me a little bump and grind show. He must have read my revulsion because he immediately kicked me with a heavy boot. It was graceful and for a second I felt a sense of wonder that Vadim had been a ballet dancer, and my mind formulated all kinds of scenarios about him in just a second or two. As my mind spun, Belhaj intervened and easily shoved Vadim against the wall. "If I want my bitch kicked, I will tell you." Vadim seemed afraid of Belhaj even though he was broad shouldered and muscular.

I pulled a bedspread, a simple cotton weave of forest green and white, off the bed and drew it over the corpse. Vadim juggled the coolers out of the room. I heard him clomping down the stairs. Before I had time to further digest what we had done, Belhaj took me upstairs to another part of the house. The ambiance there was dramatically different. The floor was polished inlaid wood. Alabaster sconces mounted along the ceiling cast soft lamp light, illuminating several ancient stone reliefs. Turkey was rich in ancient treasure, according to the TAKSi driver's implications. I tried to get a better look at the stone pieces, and not paying attention, tripped over an Oriental runner. I knew enough about carpets from having helped my father decorate his mansion in the Santa Monica canyon. This and the other carpets in Belhaj's private suite were Turkish Oushaks. His were museum quality perfect, in the hundred thousand dollar range. It seemed that Belhaj was a man of discerning tastes, and such a man would require the finest in art, music, and women, which explained the gorgeous Camille.

Further down the hallway, we entered an old fashioned European styled bedroom. It was heavily draped in tapestries, a little on the gloomy side, furnished with massive, antique furniture of dark woods and exotics. Heavy, maroon velvet drapes were drawn, allowing light in only where the fabric didn't quite meet reflecting prisms through a crystal vase of fresh tulips. On a side table, masculine things were set out: a leather book, a comb, a silver tray of pocket change. What caught my eye were a pharmaceutical IM vial and a 3 cc syringe with a 22-gauge needle. I couldn't tell what the vial contained from that distance, but Belhaj was injecting something pharmaceutical.

He shut the door to the bedroom, the minute *thunk* of the latch reverberating in my brain as if it were a massive metal clank of a penitentiary door. I stifled a withdrawal yawn that I could not suppress, and wiped my running nose on my hand. Watching him as he crossed the room, I yawned again. I was in trouble now, in imperative need of another fix. He threw open the drapes with a flourish. The mid-morning, bright sunshine shone brightly through voile sheers. He went to a serving tray and poured a milky alcoholic beverage into an awaiting glass, splashing it with water. Pernod. He sipped noisily. Though he was good looking, he was what nurses called a *double glove* kind of guy, the type they would have refused to treat. There was something unsanitary about him. It was his psychic slime.

As if on cue, Belhaj smiled diabolically at me. "Deva, zee Bosphorus is splendid, no?"

I was dehydrated, malnourished, in heroin withdrawals, traumatized by the torture and isolation of the last few weeks, and in shock from our butchering of the girl'. Ironically though, working as a doctor had awoken a little of the old Meredith, so I said, "My name is Meredith. Doctor Meredith Fitzgerald."

He snuffled mucus as he sipped his drink thoughtfully and gazed out of the window. I took the opportunity to glean as much information as possible from the room. Exercise equipment: a full set of free weights, a Nordic track and a treadmill. There was an open armoire and, inside, suits and clothing colorcoordinated and stacked with anal precision.

"So what kind of doctair you are?" he asked.

"I'm just beginning a fellowship in infectious diseases."

He made an ah ha expression. "I see zhat you really are zee doctor. For me, it is *intéressant.* You see, I ave zee, *comment dit-on* . . . zee quacks all over zee world zhat give colored water I.V. drips to zee bitches to keep zhem quiet." Belhaj smiled as if I would think that was funny. "Girls are dispensable but I do care about customer *satisfaction*. Your services we can offer customers zee disease free goods. Beat out zee competition. And zhen zhair is zee Chinese. Zhey love zee organ trade." He finished telling me about my future career and then a quizzical lookcame over his face and he pointed to his nose. "So what is zheez red spot? I have tried everything."

"Acrogmegaly," I said without question. I hadn't noticed his condition before. But he was a little too masculine with frontal bossing—an unusually prominent forehead and heavy brow ridge. He also had oily, thick skin, thick lips. Soft tissue swelling of internal organs, including the vocal cords accounted for his deep, husky voice. Now I saw too that he was sweating and that his body odor was abnormally excessive. Even if he had seen a doctor for annual check ups it was an easy diagnosis to miss in its early stages because of its slow progression. Of course, he was a body builder. His shoulders and chest strained against the fabric of his jacket. He likely misused human growth hormone, which is associated with the onset of acromegaly. He was impotent from the disease, and that's why he didn't sodomize me. He couldn't keep an erection that long. The prescription IM vial probably contained depo-testosterone, which allowed him some sexual function. I was about to examine him more closely to try to determine how advanced his condition was, but he interrupted my train of thought.

"Infectious disease?" he asked.

I recognized the typical anxiety of those who do not immediately understand their diagnosis. "It's a pituitary disorder," I replied as crisply as I could under the circumstances. I chose my words carefully since I could not tell this psychopath that acromegaly could result in severe disfigurement, complicating conditions, and premature death. So I cut to the treatment instead. "You could take a synthetic form of the brain hormone somatostatin to stop the growth hormone production in your brain, or you could have surgery on your pituitary gland using a method called transsphenoidal surgery to remove the pituitary tumors, which will reduce growth hormone production—"

Like a striking snake, Belhaj wrenched a handful of my hair. I collapsed onto the floor, tears springing to my eyes. I heard the warbling of a tin canister being milked, felt a cold liquid spray, and smelled the chemical odor. He was spraying me with lighter fluid! The flammable hydrocarbon mixture was oozing in my hair and saturating the shabby, blood-soaked kimono. I shielded my eyes with my hands, choking and sputtering. He put his hand into his pocket and held up a gold cigarette lighter from which a distorted reflection of my terrified eye stared back at me. He flipped the lighter open with a tiny metal *clank*. His thumb hovered over the small black rubber roller that would trip the flame.

"Don't try to play me, bitch. I invented zee mind game." He

brought the lighter closer. His thumb rolled over the wheel and a tiny blue and orange flame approached my now volatile hair.

"It's just a little irritation," I said with as much authority as I could summon. "Probably from soap."

I was about to go on in a desperate attempt to mollify him, about the type of soap likely to produce such bumps, when Belhaj singled out a clump of my hair and, wrapping it around a finger, wrenched it from my scalp. It hurt, but I remained still, except for a slight flinch of my nostrils, blinking away stinging tears, watching him. He held the clump over the flame and it exploded, drifting, filling my senses with the burnt dead odor.

Prayer calls invaded the room. I remained crouched, paralyzed, barely drawing breaths, wondering what to do next, feeling like a chameleon when it changes to the color of the rock it clings to and becomes rigid and cold as its predator stalks by. The Arabic voices droned on, oblivious to my plight. I had been right in my fears. What they were doing to me was called seasoning. The breaking of my will. Belhaj was a trafficker of women and girls. He was grooming me and now I knew what he had planned. I recalled from those long ago psych classes that people who were aware of the process, who knew that their captors were trying to break them, were less likely to cave in. People like trained military personnel. Or people who were stable, who knew they had a loving support system, were less likely to conform to brainwashing. The exception was when the victim was subjected to isolation, rape, and drugs—like what was happening to me.

There was a draft and then I heard the familiar clomp and scrape of Vadim's boots on the stairs. "I put in trunk," he said in his taciturn way as he entered the room. "I take later to bye-bye land." He snorted graphically, like a pig, and winked roguishly at me. Of course there were Christians in this Islamic country and there would be at least a few pig farms. Pigs were indiscriminate scavengers and tonight ravenous swine would be digesting all evidence of the young blonde.

"What now?" Belhaj groused as the little gypsy girl skipped into the room, giggling, shrilling and hugging an old stuffed teddy bear. On her heels was Camille, with what I now saw as a familiar nervous furrow between her brows. "*Merde*," Belhaj muttered, his rage churning. Like the chaos theory characterized by the butterfly flapping its wings a hemisphere away, everyone in the room recognized it and tensed up, waiting for the storm.

"Zarina," Camille hissed. She hurriedly spoke to the girl in hushed Turkish. The little girl left the room, looking at me all the while with large reproachful eyes as if I were the cause of her exile, the interrupter of fun.

"Get air cleaned up," Belhaj snapped at Vadim.

Vadim stepped forward but I slipped by him and ran out of the room.

SIX

Warm June temperatures had driven Northern Europeans south to Istanbul in search of mussels and caviar and hummus to feed on. They spilled out of cafés, ignoring the polluted air, enjoying their holidays, sipping red wine, smoking, laughing and carefree, so close but yet impossible for me to reach out to.

Before we left the house, Belhaj had supplied me with enough heroin so that I would be presentable. In addition to the drugs, Camille gave me more water to drink and fed me a real meal. Deep fat fried cheese. Crêpes, called *börek. Cacik*, which was whole plain yogurt topped with chopped cucumber, and parsley swimming in olive oil. My stomach was full and my veins were flooded with heroin.

I nodded out in the backseat while Vadim drove. We were in a late model Mercedes. Vadim's slanted eyes stared meanly from within the depths of the rear view mirror. Zarina sat up front playing with a Barbie doll and eating an ice cream sandwich that Vadim had bought through the window from a vendor. Camille was next to me in the backseat. Both of us wore black polyester chadors that covered us completely but for a small grid to look out of. The face mesh of my chador reeked of rancid saliva and mucous. The worst part of it was that I was naked underneath.

Camille leaned through the opening in the seat to talk with the girl. "You best be mindin' that ice cream. I ain't gonna take that dress a yer's to the washeteria."

"Wash-teria," the girl chimed.

"That's right. Now take this here washrag, 'n wipe off yer hands."

I leaned against the window and looked up at the blue sky where a tenacious moon remained, flanked by fat white clouds. Sunlight filtered through the perpetual haze which hung over Istanbul. The car stopped in front of an ancient wooden door that led to a murky corridor.

Vadim pressed in the cigarette lighter on the dash. "O.K.," he said, his eyes on me in the rear view mirror. "Go now. Wash shit out of hair. Any funny business, you go prison, and this one . . . ." He leaned to the girl. I could see her face through the space in the front seats. One second she was smiling, the next her face contorted in a silent scream as her lungs spasmed. The moment of shock ended and she let out a high-frequency squeal that could have shattered glass. Camille pulled the girl into the backseat, cradling her. I stared numbly at the round, seething welt that rose between her thumb and index finger. Vadim had branded Zarina with the car's cigarette lighter.

Camille kicked Vadim in the back of the head as hard as a mule. "Ain't your mama ever taught you to pick on someone your own size?"

Vadim chuckled, tears pooling into the crow's feet around his eyes. "Is mosquito bite compared to what I do if you bad girl," he said to me, his voice eerily dispassionate.

Camille reached over me and opened my door, and then jabbed me in my bony hip with her stiletto. I scooted out and she followed, carrying the girl. I came to from my dream and walked with them into the darkness.

We entered a corridor between two medieval buildings. Zarina's wails bounced and echoed off the old walls. Camille led the way, and we hobbled down the cobblestone corridor. I looked back and saw the sun glint off Vadim's tinselly aviator sunglasses. He was watching us. The hallway was long and dark, reaching fifteen feet high. We crossed the threshold and stood for a few moments until our eyes adjusted to the murky light. The once-marbled veneered walls were chipped and worn in places all the way through to a layer of sandstone. The passage was wide enough for three adults to walk abreast. At the length of a football field another cavernous door stood ajar. A form peeked out, but all I could see in the dark was a little frame with a wild fuzz of hair, its bristles tipped with light from behind her. A woman's voice called out to us in Turkish.

I wore ill-fitting rubber shoes with T-straps, like Mary Janes. The friction of rubber against skin had produced plasma and blood-filled blisters on my heels as I struggled to keep up with Camille. We reached the cavernous door, and the tiny woman turned out to be a bath matron; naked but for red bikini panties and rubber flip-flops. The crone was shriveled and wrinkled, her empty breasts pointed toward the earth. Muddy irises swam in the waxy sclera of her eyes as she took us all in. Camille ducked inside the bathhouse, saying something urgently to the crone who turned toward her, as if to help. When I saw her naked back turned toward me something inside me clicked and I shifted into autopilot for survival. I grabbed handfuls of the chador fabric and sprinted.

The corridor between the buildings was dark and damp, as cold as a butcher's freezer, reeking of ancient mold, human and animal piss, fecal matter, blood, and rotting produce. Suddenly, I was in the blinding light of the full, warm sun. It was a neighborhood bazaar. Merchants with wooden huts, lean-tos, and carts under ratty umbrellas hawked produce, leather goods, polyester scarves, ground spices, grains, trinkets, cages of hens, prescription, and OTC drugs. Sheep's blood pooled between the muddy cobblestones. I slipped in a puddle of it, bumping into an elderly woman who wore a headscarf and was dressed in a heavy skirt despite the warm day. Multi-colored heirloom tomatoes tumbled from her basket and she scowled at me, annoyed, her facial skin a ruddy orange like a heavily tanned cowhide. She reached for the tomatoes with hands like root vegetables that had been left too long in the earth.

"Please," I said, urgently. "Help me!"

The woman ignored me, affronted, as she hastily gathered her purchases.

I helped her by picking up one of the fallen tomatoes and placing it with care into her basket. "I'm sorry. Forgive me."

She softened, smiling and nodding in appreciation, and a little ray of hope sparked in my chest. But then she turned away.

"Wait," I cried. "I'm American and I need your help."

But she had her own agenda and continued walking away.

"No, wait!" I tore at the grid covering my face, while she stood there, a cloud of suspicion brewing over her face. I managed to rip the netting free creating a window. The woman peeked inside, curious. Then she backed away, the storm turning into a hurricane of disapproval. "Natasha," she spat through broken, stained teeth. She grabbed the tomato I had touched and tossed it deliberately into a pile of donkey shit.

"What?" I was confused. Two gypsies sat among piles of acrylic dolls in garish Turkish costumes. "Please," I said, turning to them and begging. "Do you speak English?"

The old woman with the tomatoes called out to the other gypsy woman, "Natasha!" And the two gypsies spat in my direction.

55

I had to do something. Paul had lectured me on the chances of survival being higher if you ran toward someone wielding a gun rather than away. *Run toward danger*, he said. And so I did the only thing I could think of to help myself. I tore off the chador and stood before the groups of hookah smoking men, merchants, shoppers and gossipers naked, and screamed, "I'm American. Please help me!"

My act had the opposite effect than I had hoped. Instead of rushing to my aid, the crowd erupted in a frenzy of disbelief and judgment, hostile faces spitting, yelling, hooting, and screaming, "*Natasha*!" Everywhere I looked people were screaming, until I was *turning, turning, turning*, the world in a vertiginous whirl.

My head jerked back painfully on my neck. "You are nothing but whore to these people," Vadim crooned calmly into my ear.

I felt a searing jolt on my shoulder. And then another. The crowd was pelting me with rocks, bricks, and construction debris! Vadim covered my mouth with his hand so that I could not say another word and called out, like a demented preacher, "Stone her. Stone Natasha bitch." Several more people picked up stones and threw them, hitting my breasts and arms. Meanwhile, Vadim dragged me back inside the recesses of the dark corridor, probably to save himself from being accidentally hit by the projectiles. Thankfully the crowd didn't follow us.

When we were safe and the mob's voices dimmer, Vadim's hand slipped from my mouth and I used every bit of energy I had left to scream, "I'm an American doctor—"

"Shut up, cunt." Vadim said with his unnerving calm tone. He pushed me and before I could right myself, kicked me in the kidneys and I fell onto the slimy cobblestones, gasping in pain. He fell on top of me so that I choked for air, feeling a rise of blackness well up in my core, my consciousness spinning into a deep well.

But then his head was broadsided by the skinny bath matron's broom handle. Her pendulous breasts swung as she pulled me into the bathhouse where Camille hovered at the door. Vadim called out something in Russian.

Camille yelled back in English, "Loser."

Vadim looked worried, scared even.

The bath crone slammed the door, bolting and locking it, pocketing a huge key, the satisfaction sparking in her old eyes. She examined me, her eyes calculating. Her breathing was labored and her nostrils flared as she struggled to catch her breath from all the exertion. A hint of sympathy crept into her gaze, of camaraderie, as one woman to another, but the womanly empathy faded. I lay on her old carpet where she had tossed me, propped up on my elbows, my own breathing labored, trying to sort everything out. I wondered what Camille had meant by Vadim not being able to follow instructions. Would Camille tell Belhaj that Vadim had almost allowed me to escape? If he were afraid of being blamed for my escape attempt, he might not say anything to Belhaj.

The woman gave me a little kick with her flip-flopped foot as if to say get away from the door. I rose and followed her out of the foyer into a changing room. Decaying ottomans, musty divans, and cushions were strewn about the room. Chatting women shed their clothing into baskets, with the relaxed looks of those anticipating an afternoon of luxury. Several massive paintings depicting harem scenes in dark Renaissance style hung in heavy filigree frames, Victorian fashion, from cords anchored several feet above. The conversations of the women mingled and echoed throughout the bath. The heat felt heavy but not oppressive.

Camille sat on one of the ottomans with the little girl in

her arms, rocking her, singing under her breath. "Hmf! We got ourselves a naked doctor."

I grabbed an old towel and wrapped myself in it. The bath matron turned to sweep the floor with a bundle of crude rushes. A small radio whined statically, competing with another radio playing loudly in the room beyond. I headed immediately toward the door that led into the inner sanctuary of the bath. I would find another door out.

Camille grabbed me by the elbow. "Where do you think yer goin'? Ain't no back door here. No windows neither, but them." She nodded to stained glass windows thirty feet above us. Camille called out in Turkish to the bath matron who had gone behind an old oak desk to take money from other customers. The woman answered back and then disappeared. "She's gonna bring some more ice fer the girl," Camille said, "cold enough to freeze water."

Zarina's sobs were juxtaposed against laughter, murmured conversation and splashing that filtered out of the steamy bath like captured moments from long ago. The matron pushed past me to shove a pill between Zarina's wet lips. She held a glass for the girl to drink. I was worried. What if Vadim made good on his promise to hurt the girl because I ran away? Camille poured off melted water from an ice-filled shower cap and replaced it on the girl's hand. The pill was taking effect, and Zarina's eyes flagged. I knelt to examine the wound and Camille, though giving me a dirty look, laid the girl down on a divan.

Camille had taken off the chador. Underneath she wore another vintage dress of coral dotted Swiss fabric that had a form-fitting bodice, a gathered skirt with a ridiculous bow tied in back like a fifties party dress. But she was young and sexy and the dress suited her. As she undressed, she seemed to move for effect, as if she were stripping. Seeing her spectacularly naked, hairless and smooth as the little girl, I couldn't help thinking of all the male interns I knew who would have loved to run into Camille in a strange and lonely part of the world. I watched her as she began to probe into the depths of her mysterious tapestry bag, unearthing various jars of beauty preparations. She had a long, graceful, almost massive neck, like a Grecian statue. On one buttock a crude, angry-looking brand was seared into her flesh, incongruously the yin/yang symbol. Camille noticed me looking and laughed bitterly, smacking her butt saying, "Git along, little doggie."

No doubt Camille had a story and it wasn't pretty. The matron returned to tend to the girl and there was nothing I could do for her that she had not already done. Camille disappeared into the steam and the old woman nodded to me with her head that I should follow. I had to remain calm if I were to recognize any opportunities for escape. Now I knew that Belhaj had subcontractors, like this bath woman, there might be another opportunity. I sat down on a divan that was strewn with an old Kilim rug. The Turkish woman appeared again and pulled off my black rubber shoes, tossing them into a basket. It was nice when she turned her attentions to Zarina. I felt glad to see her speaking kindly to the girl, tickling her under the chin, to wake her up a little and the girl giggled sleepily.

"Barbie," Zarina said when she saw me. She held up the naked icon for me to admire.

I managed a smile. "Very pretty, like you."

She giggled again, though I wasn't sure if she understood me. "Zarinath dolly," she lisped.

The old woman left the girl lying on the divan and went about tidying up. She flicked imaginary lint from Camille's thrift shop dress with her claw-like hands, clucking with appreciation. When she finished hanging it on a hanger and making it all nice and pretty, she disappeared with the dress into the foyer. I followed and looked to see that there was another dark passageway. But she returned and even though I pulled my head back quickly, I knew that she had seen me. And so I went quickly into the bath. The room was large enough for a hundred women, and still grand after decades of the distress of soap, steam, and depilatories. Peals of laughter, murmured conversation, and splashing water floated on the moist air like captured moments from long ago. The bath was florid in a Byzantine fashion, with a massive dome over a courtyard-like center, surrounded by Carrera marble columns and hovering cherub statues. The inner sanctuary was laid with intricate colored mosaic. There were no tubs or pools. The water flowed from fountains and spigots where the bathers could gather it in buckets, first soaping their bodies, then rinsing. The floor had been engineered so that the water and soapsuds flowed into strategically positioned drains. The stone under my soles felt cool, slick, and in other places grainy and worn, the water pouring from spigots, hot.

Camille sat at the end of a marbled, tiled path. But I stopped fifteen feet short of her and sat with a group of bathers. "Do any of you speak English?" I asked in a hushed tone.

One woman, about thirty, with the wrinkled abdomen of numerous pregnancies, sat with splayed legs, vigorously and unabashedly soaping her vulva. She answered, "I speak a little."

Before I could draw a breath, the bath matron appeared through the steam and I was propelled to my feet by her mannish grip. I slipped perilously on the slippery stones, away from the group of women. The old woman spoke in a harsh voice to the bathers in Turkish and they responded by pouring soapy water over the bench that I had sat on, as if disinfecting it. The matron pushed me away as the woman who I had spoken with muttered with disdain, "Stay away, dirty whore."

I stumbled along the slippery way toward Camille. There was no other choice but to join her. I sat down next to her on a marble bench, covering an etched inscription. Camille, noticing me examining the inscription, translated, "'Completed in Eighteen-seventy-three, by Ludovico Moro de Guglielmi. Master mason, Venice, Italy. Dedicated to my beloved'." Before I could even think long enough to be impressed that this hillbilly with painful grammar could read Italian, she went on, "What a load of crap. Some slick Italian feller come up to Turkey to build baths 'n had hisself some fun with a poor harem girl. Just some ramblin' construction worker all wrapped up in a glittery package, that's all. Tack a hundred years on anythin' 'n you can romance it into whatever you want it to be." She shampooed her hair furiously.

"You read Italian," I said, thinking to try the girlfriend approach again to try and buddy up to her.

"Yes, ma'am."

"Russian and Turkish too?"

"Not read, but I can speak some. I speak a few languages real good, a few okay. I read some too, but only if they sound like they read. Can't read Arabic or nothin' like that. Can speak a bit of it though."

"How is it that you speak so many languages?"

"Well, la-de-da, doctor high 'n' mighty. Guess there's some things that just come natural. Belhaj has shown me a greater appreciation 'cause I knows languages he don't."

"You mean you act as an interpreter for the women he kidnaps? You're as much involved as he is. You could go to prison."

"You could go to prison," Camille said, imitating me uncannily before she went back to her shampoo.

The bath stood oppressively around me like a mausoleum. The other bathers yielded to the seduction of the warmth and humidity. The voices of the bathing women mingled contentedly in the balmy air. How casually were they enjoying their freedom. Never for an instant had it occurred to me that freedom was not an inherent right.

Bath attendants, wearing bikini panties like the matron's, roamed the bath, capturing lingering bathers and scrubbing them hastily in an attempt to keep customers moving along. In another few hours the thought of water on my skin would be unbearable. I made myself wash. "Can I have a toothbrush?"

Camille rose from her stool and sashayed out of the bath. I probed my ribs tentatively. They were healing. I examined the needle tracks on my arms, crimson, keloided holes, wondering how many years it would take for them to fade. Then I started to scrub, hard, using the loofah Camille had set down.

Camille returned and set a toothbrush and toothpaste on the bench next to me. "Mind what yer doin'! Yer gonna tear off chunks of skin." I scrubbed harder. "That smell ain't gonna come off with soap," she said as she snatched the loofah and tossed it into a soapy bucket of water.

Camille knew how I felt. She understood how desperately I needed to get the rapist's smell off of me. I couldn't tell how she figured into Belhaj's business. Maybe she was just playing with me by being kind. I was wary as she squirted shampoo onto my scalp and began to massage it in, twisting my long mass of black hair, squishing the shampoo out and flinging globs of soapsuds on to the marble floor.

"Keep yer eyes closed, this here's special shampoo to get rid of the critters."

Camille stopped lathering my hair and began bucketing hot water over my head. When she was finished she began to methodically comb the knots from my hair, laying clumps of tangles aside as she pulled them from the comb. When she was through with me, she opened a jar and spread gooey depilatory over her legs, arms, underarms, and crotch. An acidic smell hung stagnantly. Her face was blurred by steam.

Camille was unlike anyone I had ever associated with. Back in the states, women like her had been somewhat invisible. I would have registered her vaguely as a hooker, a low life, a junkie, an abuser of food stamps and other social services. But my imprisonment and torture changed my perception. In her quaint Madonna getups, her eyes smeared with iridescent blue shadow, I wondered who she really was, and how she came to be involved with these sociopaths. She was odd. But Paul used to say that sometimes the strangest people turned out to be the most normal. He was right. Really strange people were ordinary and really ordinary people *were* strange. Right then, the very strange Camille was my only possible ally. I'd been brought up by a man to think like a man and interact with others like men do. Men's conversations were hard and linear. You could bounce a dime off of a male exchange. Women's conversations were like quicksand. They often perplexed me with their many dimensions, double meanings, overt neediness, manipulative intensions, and neuroses. I didn't have many close girlfriends. Most of my friends were men. Now I was determined to figure Camille out and to get close to her.

"Where are you from?" I asked.

"Growed up on a farm in Mississippi. Had us hogs, dogs, cows, chickens, ducks, all kinds of farm animals."

Zarina appeared, slipping on the wet floor, falling into Camille's arms. She smiled at me tentatively as she rocked back and forth, lanky and swaybacked, her little pot belly moist and shining, her little hand bandaged crudely. "Zarina go pee pee," she announced, pressing the Barbie doll into her crotch. She was learning English quickly from Camille. The girl relieved herself over one of the drains, then began to play again, churning bubbles in a bucket. She pulled Barbie's head off the doll's body and tried to stuff it down a drain.

"Listen to me," I said to Camille in a low tone, "This is our opportunity. We can get help, we're Americans!"

Camille rubbed off a patch of the lemon concoction from her legs, testing, then turned a spigot and filled a bucket. "What's up with you, with this 'merican shit? Ain't no one gonna repatriate drug abusers in Turkey, 'merican 'r not."

"What about Zarina's mother? She must be crazed with grief by now."

"Face it, everbody ain't rich."

"Please, for God's sake, can't you tell me what's going on?"

"What's goin' on is that you fell for the oldest trick in the book. Didn't your mama ever tell you not to take candy from strangers?" Camille wrung water from a sponge in short quick bursts as if she were wringing the neck of some small helpless creature.

"I have money. If you help me, I promise I'll help you."

"You gotta understand he's got you now. You took them organs outta that dead girl."

My hand went involuntarily to my mouth.

"Learned a lesson from a Japanese girl once," Camille said

huffing a sigh as if she were obligated to reveal her survival secrets. "Called it *naki-neiri*. Means cryin' yerself to sleep." Camille mouth was set and her tone was practical. "That's what I do."

SEVEN

The Golden Horn inlet of the Bosphorus shared its waters with an odd assortment of floating craft from tiny sailboats to Nordic freighters to Turkish submarines, basking in the moonlight like dragons three-quarters submerged. The city lights reflected off the ancient buildings, casting a violet hue over the city. Even at midnight the city was awake. While a decades-old Chevy navigated the greater metropolis of Istanbul, I huddled in the backseat with Camille and Zarina. We had been forced to put on cumbersome blouses and skirts, kerchiefs over our hair. Even though it was night, Camille had donned a pair of sunglasses like a celebrity seeking to obscure her identity. I was feeling the hideous creep of heroin withdrawal again. Zarina, who couldn't take her eyes off the back of Vadim's head and sucked her thumb vigorously, sat absorbing our anxiety. Camille finally broke the silence by reaching over and pushing Zarina's bandaged hand down into her lap. "Gotta stop that, girl. Gonna end up like Bucky Beaver."

The new city of Istanbul offered the same snarl of traffic as the old, lanes and rules a mere formality. Traffic resembled a demolition derby, the air thick with diesel smoke. Stunning hand-loomed carpets hung, airing, from windows. Apartment dwellers used available space in enterprising ways to string clotheslines full of laundry, the freshly washed clothes lapping up pollution from the air. At a red light, an owl perched at the edge of a turret, fixing his gold eyes on me like a knowing evil eye. I looked out over the skyline of the blue-gray city. Over the water, dozens of night birds winged the lavender sky and in my agony I observed the beauty of Istanbul.

The driver, who sported the ubiquitous heavy moustache and three-day beard, had been chattering away about his classic American car. Vadim looked about ready to smack him as the man pulled the car up to a walled, eighteenth century mansion. A brass plaque read *Indian Consulate*. "Real visa," the driver assured Vadim. "No black market."

Vadim reached over the driver, opened his door and then booted the surprised man out of his own car onto the pavement. "Get visa." He tossed out four passports that landed on the pavement. I could see the familiar khaki green of the American passport, but couldn't tell what the others were.

I whispered to Camille. "Visas?"

She hissed back, "Belhaj's usual forger got hisself busted so we gotta go through official channels. Some dude we paid off."

"Why does he need visas?"

"We're movin' the operation. God, I do hate Mumbai in the summer time."

"Mumbai? We can't leave Turkey," I sputtered. "This is where they'll be looking for me." I saw Vadim's scarred face in the rear view mirror. I looked away, determined not to let him see my fear. We were parked next to a makeshift pen of sheep, marked with Day-Glo spray paint. The shepherds were dressed in suit coats and trousers, like college professors. They stood around trading news, blue clouds spouting from their lips, looking comfortable in the drizzle, having fixed lethally spiked collars onto their dogs' necks to ward off the razor sharp teeth of wolves hungry for a mutton dinner. I spent the next half hour trying to catch the attention of one of the shepherds, but the men refused to look our way.

The driver came back looking relieved, holding the stack of passports. He slid behind the wheel. Vadim grabbed the passports from him, and jerked his head. A minute later, the car careened through a ghetto of old crumbling walls, ancient buildings, decaying. Then we left the city and entered the countryside. The fifties Chevy, with its wide tailfins, rocketed like a futuristic vehicle against the rural backdrop. I wanted to get to the airport, around people. I would have a chance then. At the very least I could get a message to the driver, who didn't strike me as one of Belhaj's subcontractors. He looked too scared, as if he were not sure what he had gotten himself into. I was determined to make my escape at the airport, even though I could not stop yawning and sneezing and I was shaking so hard I could barely think straight.

"We gotta stop," Camille said, with a small amount of irritation in her voice.

Vadim glanced over his shoulder at me and frowned. He said something to the driver. A few minutes later the old Chevy pulled into a roadside café. Vadim and Camille paraded me past mustached, stubble-faced men to a W.C. in the back.

The W.C. was a reeking, putrid cell with a fecal smeared Eastern style toilet on the floor. As soon as Camille shut the door, I began to check the place out for an escape route, but the upper window, crusted over with grime, was too small to climb through.

"You gotta pull yerself together 'n act normal, 'cause the police are gonna be as thick as fleas on a coon at that airport," Camille said, juggling the heroin works from her tapestry bag, placing things, one by one, on a grimy, pathogenic sink.

"Good."

"Good, if you fancy gettin' gang banged till yer twat's hamburger meat." She bunched up my sleeve where keloid tracks glowed purple under the bare light bulb. "Turks won't give a hog tittie 'bout no sob story from you, 'merican 'r not."

"Those men out there. We could ask them for help."

"You ain't no high society doctor no more, girl. You fell a long ways down from there." Camille scooped a spoonful of heroin onto a bent spoon, drizzling on water from the filthy tap.

"Why are you involved with these people? Tell me. I deserve to know."

"You deserve." Camille cooked the spoon with a cigarette lighter. "I seen women like you all my life with built-in expectations." She drew the liquid heroin into a syringe. "See, I ain't got nothin' else 'n I'm grateful for this here situation. Belhaj's good to me. Better'n most."

"Don't be a fool. You're his flavor of the month. When he's tired of you he'll, he'll . . . . I don't know. What do they do with women? Kill them for their organs?"

Camille bit the syringe between her front teeth as she cinched my arm with a rubber tourniquet. "You got us all figured out."

I gazed past Camille at my reflection in the mirror as Camille mainlined me, then I free fell a million miles into outer space, caught by strong arms. Tears ran from my eyes, welling from the deepest pit of my tortured soul. Camille cooed into my hair, comforting me in my ugly bliss. "I know, girl. I knows all about it."

"Fuck me." Vadim's voice brought me out of my nod. I forced my head up by a sheer act of will to see the goon sitting ramrod straight in the front seat as the car slowed to a stop. The driver had stopped at a roadblock. Two uniformed jandarma with five o'clock shadows, serious expressions, and automatic rifles were marching over to the car. Vadim cast a glance at me in the backseat. His expression was neutral, too neutral for our present circumstance. His filthy nails dug into the soft leather upholstery as he twisted in his seat to reach over and slap me across the face. "I not afraid to die. I take you with me," he said. "Understand?" He slapped me again, harder.

Remembering Vadim's agility, I nodded.

A jandarma cranked his neck inside the driver's window, his eyes wandering greedily over Camille, pausing long enough to go through an entire sexual fantasy about her. "*Pasaportlarinizi gosterin*," he demanded finally.

Vadim handed the man the stack of passports. The policeman stood at the window so that his holster and pistol and the butt of his rifle were at my eye level. Say *something*, I screamed internally. *Scream now*! But my throat was closed, my terror complete. The atmosphere in the car was tense as the jandarma huddled, discussing us. The driver, cued to his own anxiety, turned on the radio to belly dancing babble.

"How you listen such shit?" Vadim asked, in a sincere tone as if he really wanted to understand.

"I can change. Mikhail Ja-hackson?"

"Mikhail, eh?" Vadim asked, with no affect.

The driver flicked off the radio but couldn't help knee jerk reacting to his nerves. "No problem. They talk about car," he said helpfully. Getting no rise out of Vadim, he gawked into the rearview mirror. "You American ladies?"

"None a yer beeswax," Camille shot back.

"What your name, little one?"

"Loretta Lynn," the beautiful Camille snarled.

Vadim pulled out a switchblade, slung his arm over the seat, flicking the glistening blade open and shut. The driver shut up, swallowing nervously and polishing a string of worry beads with his fingers. The jandarma motioned the driver on. He fumbled with the keys in the ignition.

"What we gotta do?" Camille asked tartly. "Light a fire under yer butt?"

The old engine ground to life, the car's tires burned rubber onto the road, and the big rocket ship bulleted off. I turned to watch the jandarma fading into the night. Why had I not acted when I had the chance? Why was my throat closed when all I had to do was scream?

The rain had stopped and the landscape appeared awash with mud. A movement outside the cab caught my attention and I looked, expecting a jandarma vehicle to be in hot pursuit after the old Chevy. But it was a pack of greyhounds. They raced the car, their petite tongues flagging the wind. Backdropped by the lush countryside and the crisp cloudless sky, they ran, wild and free. The car pulled ahead and then it was only harsh-faced men in shirtsleeves sitting in doorways enjoying the short respite from the rain. Foraging sheep and goats roamed the edges of the highway looking for sprouting greens, and chickens pecked for their last morsel before heading off to roost for the night. A few women picked their way through the muck, eyes cast to the ground, their hair hidden beneath scarves. They labored under various loads, firewood, blanket-wrapped bundles, stacks of long flat breads, and cages filled with chickens. When the car hit a dead zone away from cars and people, Camille rolled down her window and hurled her tapestry bag out.

Soon after we arrived at a private terminal at the Atatürk Airport. I was disappointed that we were not going to go through the commercial airport, as there would have been many more opportunities to grab attention. As it was, there were more jandarma roaming, strutting their male superiority. Turkish men kissed each other boisterously while their women stood around looking coy. Otherwise there were mostly foreign travelers bustling about with the spoiled glee of those who could afford to fly by private jet. A herd of obese Russians dressed in garish sportswear and pounds of gold jewelry overtook the sidewalk, nearly jostling us into the shrubbery, accosting us with their underarm odor, heavy perfume, and garlicy stomach gas. "Help," I said under my breath like a ventriloquist, with Vadim's hand heavily on my shoulder. "If anyone speaks English, I'm an American doctor. I've been kidnapped." Vadim couldn't hear me but neither could the Russians with their honking and bleating conversations, all talking at once.

Camille had gotten out of the backseat had scooted into the front across the long leather platform seat, and it seemed like she was flirting with the driver, giggling and stroking his arm. I caught sight of him licking his lips. When Vadim let go of me for a moment I leaned inside the car, snatched a wad of Camille's skirt and yanked her out so that she nearly tumbled onto the concrete sidewalk. "What are you doing with that man?"

Camille righted herself and brushed off her skirt as if my indignation was something tangible, like lint that she could dust off. "Son of a bitch, I was just fixin' to give him a little gratuity for all he done for us."

"Gratuity? Is that what you call it?" Vadim was counting money to the driver. "Vadim's paying him so you don't have to give him a piece of yourself, too."

She looked at me curiously as if this was a new concept and it gave me a sick feeling in my stomach, knowing that if I continued on the way I was that I might someday feel that way about myself, too. Vadim was pulling suitcases out of the trunk. I leaned into the car and whispered, "Help me."

"That *rus serseri* will kill me," the man whispered back, his eyes darting furtively, pushing open the heavy door and climbing out, as if he needed to get away from me.

Belhaj arrived in a TAKSi. He looked unruffled, composed, dressed in another designer suit and tie. His driver unloaded several suitcases and miscellaneous bags.

The owner of the Chevy sat on his haunches within the safety of a group of TAKSi drivers. He sipped Turkish coffee from a demitasse cup while a six year old boy waited at his side holding a tray. I looked at him, meeting his eyes, begging him, but he looked into the safety of his coffee cup. He muttered as we passed by, "Allah go with you."

Except for a perfunctory check of our passports and visas, the security for private jet travelers was virtually nil. I did what any heroin addict would do crossing one of the world's most drug-hostile borders. I filed silently through the airport with my head down and my eyes fixed.

Fifteen minutes later, I held the driver's blessing in my heart as the Gulfstream took off from the tarmac. Istanbul's mystical ancient turrets and domed mosques shrank until they were mere child's toys and then disappeared like a dream beneath the clouds.

EIGHT

As a cauterizing sun rose, the jet came in for a landing over Mumbai. The flight had been uneventful, as Belhaj, Vadim, and Camille smoked while Zarina slept through an Oxycotin haze, as Belhaj had forced Camille to give her a pill to keep her quiet. By the time we landed I was sick again as the therapeutic effects of the heroin Camille had given me in the grungy pit stop had waned. I hadn't slept all night but remained vigilant, rallying my courage and was prepared to throw myself on the mercy of the Indian authorities.

But we didn't land at the airport. The jet set down on a packed dirt landing strip far outside the city. A motley crew of men in mismatched Indian garb rushed to meet the plane, securing it, opening the passenger door, attaching portable stairs. Belhaj descended first, followed by Vadim. I was last, after Camille, who carried the sleeping girl. Leaving the climate-controlled atmosphere of the plane where I had shivered for ten hours, the wet heat hit me forcefully in the face. I stood on the hardened earth, shoulders slumped under the weight of the burning sun, wondering if it could get any worse.

A petite Indian man in his mid-forties ran toward us. He was dark skinned with a dandruffy comb-over. His beaked nose bristled with nostril hairs, narrow brown eyes blinking from beneath an overhanging brow. He laughed readily, showing a deep gap between his two front teeth and a lower mouthful of crooked teeth. He pressed his palms together in namaste, a prayerful gesture.

I knew from yoga classes that Indian hand positions were called mudras, and that the anjali or namaste mudra meant, "I bow to the divine in you." Not knowing anything much else about the Indian culture, I saw the man doing the namaste mudra and I felt a thrill thinking that he must be a holy person, there to deliver us from this untenable bondage.

"*Namaskar*. Velcome to India, Bel-ji," the tiny man said to Belhaj, ignoring Vadim and us.

"*Bonjour, Monsieur* Pawar," Belhaj replied.

"I am trusting that your journey was a pleasant one," Mr. Pawar added. His head wove back and forth, in the way that Indians indicate the positive. "You are coming this vay."

He showed us through streamers of rising heat from the earth across the road opposite to where the plane had landed. "My sincerest apologies for the impending long journey into Mumbai, Bel-ji."

"Fucking *sécurité* bullshit," Belhaj groused. "*Merde*."

"I am understanding, Bel-ji. Since nine-eleven ve are having all planes land at our secret landing strip to avoid exposing ourselves to the possibility of the eventuality of dangerous security procedures."

Belhaj looked tired and pissed off despite the man's attempts to mollify him.

"I am having a line on the American university textbooks you requested," Mr. Pawar said in a placating tone. "First rate, old man." His head wove again. "Hooray for Bollywood and all that pish-posh nonsense," he added, chortling sophomorically.

I wondered what he meant by university textbooks, but nevertheless my fantasy of his holiness faded. Vadim went with another Indian man in another SUV with the luggage. Mr. Pawar showed us to an SUV. The vehicle's black paint was waxed and polished and for all intents and purposes this Mr. Pawar person seemed well off.

Mr. Pawar drove while Belhaj sat in the passenger seat. Camille, Zarina and I shared the back seat, hanging on as we bounced along on rutted, potholed dirt roads. Bucolic countryside sprawled out to the blue horizon. The car passed by hundreds of hectares of rice paddies where laborers toiled waist deep in the water, bent and sunburned. Bullocks, the color of ivory, with slender ankles, their ribs, coccygeal vertebrae protruding, roamed unmolested, sleepily chewing water lilies and lotuses in gently flowing streams rich with vegetation and tall grasses revitalized by a recent rain. Women scooped up pots of water from these streams and carted them off on their heads, hips swaying, heads as still as statues. Water buffalos pulled carts, and plows, and tractors filled with people. Further on, one less fortunate water buffalo lay dead in a ditch; several looming vultures gorged industriously, stopping their meat shredding only momentarily to watch the car go by. Women winnowed rice, tossing rice grains on woven trays, and sat at the roadside picking nits from one another's scalps. Men in white walked by the side of the road carrying large black umbrellas to and from village after village of mud shanties with bleached grass roofs and stone temples.

With Belhaj, the Indian man, and Camille all smoking cigarettes they were forced to open the windows. Camille had changed on the airplane into a tailored, white cotton Indian blouse with slim tangerine colored capris, and a silk scarf that covered her hair and wrapped around her neck. She wore the oversized sunglasses again, too. She looked hot, all bundled up.

An hour later the car motored into Mumbai, the old world

meeting the new in a frenetic, hallucinatory tailspin. Riotous sounds of sitar music, chanting, honking horns, yelling, bartering, singing, crying babies and wailing beggars jarred, yet oddly, soothed the senses. Into the car charged the assaulting odors of smoldering cow dung, diesel exhaust, burning tires, smoking incense, marigold pollen, curry, cumin, hashish. It was hard to believe that so many people could coexist: Women in saris and other Indian dress, mini skirts, blue jeans, Gucci, Chanel, adorned with henna skin ornamentation, bindis, silver, precious stones, glass bangles, and gold. Men charged through the streets in business suits, while others, swathed in ancient Indian dress, tramped along with rickshaws. Merchants hawked tin, recycled car parts, hemp ropes, and maritime chains. Street sleepers peeked out from hovels attached to high-rise buildings and temples like barnacles. Imported luxury cars, pedicabs drivers, rickshaw pullers, rattletrap Indian Ambassadors, trailer-tractors, trucks, bullock carts, motorcycles, and bare feet vied for passage, breaking all rules in frenzied anarchy. Sadus, Sikhs, tourists, holy cows, mongrel packs, begging urchins with babies on their hips, lepers, foreign hippies, businesspeople, pickpockets, the spiritual and the depraved went about their business in a cataclysm of organized disorder. I could not help but notice that everyone, including a lama in red robes, *was talking on mobile phones*. If I could only get my hands on a phone!

We left the metropolis high-rise and business center and drove into a seedier part of the city. The car paused for a circus troop that led a road-worn bear across the highway, pulling him by a chain attached to a ring in its nose. "My bear!" Zarina cried.

"Sugar, that rag baby only had one eye and its tongue was fallin' off." "My bear!" she insisted.

"We'll git you a much prettier one. I promise."

We were all distracted when the vehicle swerved to avoid a collision with one of the circus elephants. Watching the mayhem was a fifty-something Caucasian hippie wearing a sweat-soaked black tee-shirt with worn jeans.

He shaded his eyes with his hand, observing us, a mala—something like a Buddhist rosary made of rudraksha seeds—dangled from his wrist. He had a suntanned, clean-shaven face, his eyes hidden behind sunglasses, and his shoulder-length, wavy blond hair pulled into a loose ponytail. We drove off, leaving him in our dust.

A few minutes later, our impervious late model vehicle skirted an open fire in the middle of the road, scattering chickens and goats on our journey into Falkland Road, the bowels of Hades. There human suffering was laid out like so much depraved confectionary delight. Hundreds of girls and young women in garishly decorative saris were incarcerated, exotic creatures in row after row of cages; on display for horny men to ogle and select for purchase. Above the cages rose apartment structures—wooden brothel rooms stacked like boxes, painted prettily in shocking hues, layered with generations of crud, and flapping with vibrant laundry moldering in the wet heat.

Ditches the length of the road ran stagnant with contaminated water, littered with debris and frothy with chemical pollution that glistened in iridescent hues of neon green and blue. Into these oozing sewers, men peed, naked children frolicked, and women spat red juice. Emaciated mothers squatted on stoops, hollow eyed, with baby bumps between their thighs, smoking bidis while skinny infants enswathed in the drapes of their tattered saris hung on their breasts. The women's eyes, heavily lined in kohl, stared bleakly at the futures ahead of them. One mother accommodated her infant by holding her over the fecal ditch. Elimination communication was the mode mothers used in all societies before the developed world created the diaper, as babies will let their mothers know when they need to eliminate. It was the first time I had actually seen the practice in use and I turned to watch. Another mother held her limp baby in her arms. *Infantile hypotonia*, I diagnosed, better known as floppy infant syndrome. The mother was trying to get the baby to breastfeed but hypotonic infants do not have the mouth musculature to maintain a beneficial breastfeeding latch and suck-swallow pattern. The baby would be dead soon.

"Suck and fuck," one girl wearing greasy hot pants called through the open window, pulling down her top to show Belhaj breasts stretched marked and riddled with cigarette burns. She backed away when her eyes flashed recognition. *They knew him here in this hell zone*. The weather was seething, but I felt a chill.

The vehicle stopped at a huge wrought iron gate. Three women forms huddled there swathed in identical ashen colored cotton saris, the fabric hardly more substantial than cheesecloth. They wore saris draped over their heads, hiding their faces while they cooked chapattis over a portable kerosene stove. The gate was unlocked by two men and the SUV entered the compound, driving down a simple driveway just wide enough for the vehicle to navigate. On the driver's side was a wall made of stone and sloppily covered with plaster. On the passenger side, where I was sitting, was a twenty-five foot stone wall. Both walls were edged with bales of concertina wire.

The SUV came to a stop in front of a fortress door made of wood and metal slats, which lent an impenetrable air to the compound. The door opened and there stood a small man, about thirty, with a modest, dark skinned face and a frame of delicate bones. The bushy black hair that tumbled out of his white turban was dusty as if he had been caught in a storm. He wore a simple dhoti, the traditional male garment in India—unbleached unbound cotton cloth, wrapped around the waist and knotted. His short-sleeved shirt of pale gray seemed freshly laundered and pressed. But at closer inspection the fabric was old, the collar deeply soiled, as if no amount of washing would clean it. At his throat, where a button was missing, was a small safety pin. The man appeared to be nothing more than a humble servant, and indeed, when Mr. Pawar slid out of the car, he stood back as if not to contaminate the great master with his unworthiness. Once inside, the compound appeared more like an Indian version of a bed and breakfast. Immediately inside stood a lavish house—by decaying shabby chic standards. It had worn and stained marble inlaid steps leading to arched, open-air entrances also constructed of ages-old marble and decorated in the same inlaid style. Inside the house lazed inviting yet grimy velvet divans in deep maroon and royal blue. Sheer silk fabrics, somewhat tattered but threaded in gold and silver, hung as room dividers and drapes, flowing lazily in the humid breeze. That was all I could see of the house from that vantage point. Facing away from the house, along the side where the driveway and fortress wall stood were four bungalows, painted in pastel shades of yellow, blue, pink, and green. At the far end of the bungalows was a two-story stucco structure, like an apartment building, also with open windows. The interior of the compound flourished as an exotic jungle garden lush with flowers, coconut palms, banana trees and other tropical foliage. Facing the garden to the right of the flora stood another unassailable wall, also edged in concertina wire. The compound filled maybe half of a hectare—about one and a quarter acres.

You'd think it was paradise. The jungle garden teemed with fauna. Monkeys screeched and chattered, birds cooed, hooted, and flapped, fruit rats ran up trunks disappearing into fronds. A peacock stirred, spreading its fan and strutting. A microcephalic Siamese cat peeked from beneath a hedge of Calla lilies. Several kittens frolicked maniacally behind her. Zarina squealed and skipped after them.

The man who let us inside the compound was a gardener. After he locked the door behind us, he went about raking the earth around the bamboo, palms, pandanus, the umbrella trees with their pleasant nutty aroma, the Indian pines, and the banyans, huge shade trees that protect from the sun and, not least, add privacy. Like many poor Indians there was something ascetic about the gardener, the dignity with which he went about his business. He did not deign to look at us or at any of the three servant men who had appeared and were balancing luggage on their heads.

A woman's voice called out from an open door just above us in the palatial house. "Yoo-hoo!" A toilet flushed, with running water.

Camille ribbed me. "Act natural, hear?"

A three hundred pound sari-swathed figure filled the archway, puffing a cigarette clamped in nicotine stained fingers. At the sight of her, Zarina darted behind Camille. "Bel-ji, splendid to be seeing you," she gushed, her face aglow and eyes gleaming with delight as she descended the marble steps.

"*Namaskar*, Shabana," Belhaj said, folding his hands in namaste, which seemed a little mincing and dainty for a hardened rapist.

"*Namaskar*, dearest Bel-ji." She leaned, grunting, and Belhaj kissed both of her cheeks. A solid gold skeleton key fell from within her massive bosom, dangling on a gold chain. She snatched it and stuffed it out of sight into the depths of cleavage packed into a gigantic, hot pink top. Her continence clouded like the sticky sky above, and she pouted. "It is appearing that you vill be greeted by the monsoon. The veather of Mumbai is being the veather of the Arabian Sea."

We all looked up at the threatening clouds. Above Shabana Pawar, palm branches swayed under the lithe weight of a baby Ginger monkey with bright orange fur. He swung down as if performing for us, followed by several others, screeching and swinging away on the branches. His face was defined by brown fur, his eyes like little round black marbles. Orange ears, trimmed in brown fluff, stuck out at right angles. A tuft of orange fur stood on the top of his head as if slicked up with styling gel. He swung down close to us and I saw that he had a wire wrapped around his neck. Someone must have tethered him and now he was free, but growing into the wire that would soon asphyxiate him.

"So this is being the American doctor?" Mrs. Pawar said, uninterested in the monkey, and tossing the loose end of her lime green, gold-trimmed sari over her shoulder. She smiled engagingly at me. I managed a weak smile. "It is my pleasure to be making your acquaintance." She pressed her palms together in namaste.

"Mrs. Pawar allow me to introduce you to Doctair Deva," Belhaj said.

My brow knit in dismay at the introduction but Camille pinched the flesh above my hip, hard. "It'sway importantway orfay ouyay otay ayplay alongway." It took me a second to register that she was speaking pig latin. She was telling me to play along—and it went right over Belhaj and the madame's heads. I returned Mrs. Pawar's namaste.

"Oh, my dear, but you are exhausted. Nap time! Nap time!"

Belhaj smacked his lips, a hint of disgust wanting to settle on his features, but nevertheless he continued charmingly with the social civility that was clearly a sham. It was the first time I had seen him smiling, ostensibly or at least feigning happiness. He had nice teeth, straight and bleached white that he undoubtedly flashed at girls before kidnapping them.

"I have been preparing your apartment with starched linens, fruits and French vine, and, of course your Pernod, Bel-ji," Mrs. Pawar said coquettishly, batting her puffy eyelids at him. "The doctor and Nasreen can be staying at the far end. Keeping the girl vith them for the time being," she said in her bubbly tone, but at the same time staring somewhat salaciously at Zarina. "The doctor must be recovering from her fevers." Her tone was comforting and oozing with concern and I felt a warm rush of tears, as no one had spoken kindly to me in weeks. At the same time, I stared at her, trying to sort out the cryptic message from within her fractured syntax. And then she added, "The doctor must be recovering quickly and then ve vill get to vork on our new project. Oh, my it is exciting after all these years to breathe fresh air into our endeavors!"

I felt a tug on my sleeve. I followed Camille and Belhaj, who strolled arm and arm with the obese Indian woman along a path that led to an open bungalow door. She nattered on about her garden as if there were nothing out of the ordinary about our situation. "Oh my," she said at last. "The time has arriving to my bidding you adieu," she offered politely, leaning to allow Belhaj to kiss her cheeks again. "Rest and rejuvenate, my dearest Bel-ji."

"*Oui*," Belhaj said, noncommittally. "Bonjour, *cheri*."

"Oh! The French language," she emoted. "So evocative. How I have been missing you, Bel-ji." She brayed a laugh from within lungs tanned by years of cigarette smoking. She tossed the trailing end of her sari over her shoulder, her wrist-load of gold bracelets making a shimmering tingle as they fell down her arm, and then she lumbered back in the direction of her house. "Ekanta! Vhere is that stupid girl?" she said loudly. "Oh, these disobedient ingrates, abandoning me every time a few rain drops are falling."

We all went inside the room that we were assigned to, leaving Mrs. Pawar to sort out her problems with her servants. Unlike the well-appointed bungalows we had passed with silk curtains fluttering in their open windows, our room was dingy and a mere three by three meters, about ten by ten feet. There were no windows facing the garden. Only a portal, high up on the side of the room that faced the driveway and fortress wall. It was braced with metal bars, fashioned like eyelet openings of a decorative screen. I was disappointed to see that even if I could get the grate off, the opening would be too small for even Zarina to squeeze through. Then of course we would have to scale the twenty-five foot walls and somehow avoid certain impalement on the barbs of concertina wire.

The coolies put everything down, bobbling their heads and doing namaste as they backed away. The room was furnished with two low-to-the-ground Indian beds, shrouded in mosquito nets, with tightly woven rope platforms in lieu of mattresses. Above the two beds an oscillating fan rippled the fine netting. There was also a simple wooden table and chairs, painted sky blue. I was glad to see Zarina clamoring under a gauzy drape, milking her thumb drowsily.

"I gotta pee immediately, if not sooner," Camille declared,

going into the adjoining W.C. and shutting the door.

Belhaj sized me up. I kept my eyes steady on him, my rapist, not letting him see how scared I was. Behind him, a gecko, a pretty bright green, clung to the cruddy pink stucco wall and I, in turn, clung emotionally to that creature, suddenly and painfully reminded of a vacation I had taken to Tahiti where Paul was filming and where we'd named our room geckos Bertha and Melvin. Right then it seemed so impossible that I had ever been carefree.

"*Tres joli* zee blue eyes," Belhaj said, my reality jarring me away from the bittersweet memory. But there was something else in his eyes? *Sadness*? *Longing*? I couldn't tell.

"They'll look for me," I said, forcing words out that I knew could mean serious consequences. But I felt reckless in my terror. "They know I'm missing by now."

Belhaj reached around my waist and ran his wrist down the slope of my hip, clutching my buttock with a firm grip. "*Oui*. Missing in action."

Then he did something worse than the rapes. His eyes locked on mine, his face came closer and closer until his thick lips were brushing mine. He forcefully, but tenderly, kissed me like a lover, with an urgency that was genuine, though my lips remained wooden. The entire kiss lasted no more than four or five seconds. He pulled away, but remained close, his lips parted so that I could smell his labored licorice breath fouled by a night of smoking and air travel. And then he turned away and walked out of the room.

When I heard the slip of the padlock, Camille was just coming out of the W.C. "News at eleven. Beelzebub cut hisself a big one in there."

I pressed by her and went into the room, nothing more than a concrete closet that housed a hole with two sodden wooden planks to step on. There was a faucet and a tin can. Above this makeshift toilet was a showerhead. She was right. Being inside the room was like being inside a diaper pail. The walls were diarrhea green and soiled with decades of fecal matter, mucous, and other dried fluids. The smell Camille referred to stung my eyes and caught in my throat. I rinsed my mouth at the sink with careless disregard for the contaminated water, fearing amoebic dysentery less than I detested having his taste on my lips. I stared at myself in the small mirror above the sink. I was looking better since I'd been let out of that room and been given food and water. I touched my face, my mouth, not wanting to think of what was in his mind, of why he kissed me.

Afterwards I scraped a chair over to the window and climbed onto it to look outside. I could see the gate and a bit of the street! Three wild mutts ran through the alleyway in an excited chase, nipping at each other's tails and yapping. They had to have gotten in through the wrought iron gate that led to the street. I wondered if Zarina would be able to squeeze through the iron bars if we could get her through the fortress door. Then I noticed a long-necked buzzard sitting atop a turret, devouring a rabbit, its carrion beak dripping with blood, his beady eyes fixed on me like another evil eye. I was just about to come down from the chair when the three beggar women walked by the gate. One of them squatted down, leaning against the wrought iron bars. The others followed suit, and then the three of them were simply sitting there. They didn't appear to be talking, but just sitting there like a vigil.

Camille flicked a wall switch. "Gotta keep the fan on. Little fuckers'll eat us alive."

I came down from the chair and, pushing away the mosquito

netting, sat on one of the beds. "Those cages," I said, reeling from the sight. "Did you see those girls? Some of them looked prepubescent. Get up on that chair. You can see them."

"Indians believe that havin' sex with a virgin'll cure 'em AIDS 'n other sex diseases," Camille said idly as she unzipped one of her suitcases. "Not just Indians, Arabs too, 'n all manner of chinks, you know, yer Cambodians, yer Vietnamese, yer—"

"My God, we have to get Zarina out of here!" I interrupted. "Did you hear what that woman said, about keeping her with us 'for the time being'?"

"I'm keepin' her fer good. Belhaj says I could."

"It's not like finding a puppy. You can't just *keep* her."

"Possession is nine tenths. 'Sides, what parents would sell their own flesh and blood?"

I walked over to where Camille stood. I snatched her cigarette from her mouth and threw it on the floor. "For God's sake, what kind of aberration are you?"

Camille lifted her skirt to reveal the brand on her buttock. "This is who I am! Just another girl that lost her way n' ended up like branded cattle."

"Like *Zarina*, you mean?"

Camille dropped her skirt, licked her finger and drew an imaginary vertical hash mark in front of my face. "Score one fer the lady doctor." She turned her back on me and reached through the mosquito netting. "Wake up, girl. Yer gonna have yerself a nice cool shower, okay?"

"Okay," Zarina agreed wearily, as if all the energy of her youth had been sucked away by the vampirism of the long flight and car trip. She clamored out from underneath the netting and followed Camille into the W.C.

Before I knew it, I'd fallen asleep only to be awakened by the door opening. The breeze created by the fan riffled the mosquito netting where I lay in the scorching heat. I opened my eyes to see Vadim chasing Camille into the room, the door slamming against the wall.

"What you sneak, bitch? I know you get shit from gardener." He shoved her.

"You can't push me around. I'm gonna tell Belhaj on you."

His face blanched, and he scowled at me. Since we'd gotten to India he'd changed from his cheap suit and dress shirt into loose cotton pants, a white sleeveless tee-shirt and a navy blue gabardine suit vest. Despite his lack of testosterone his bare arms were muscular, and heavily marred with primitive tats. He shifted his caustic gaze from me and sniffed, his eyes darting around the room, a grimace gripping his thug face. "Ach. Is stink like red day of female dog."

"That right? Sure it don't reek like rottin' nuts?" Camille grabbed her crotch.

He shoved Camille again. I beat the mosquito netting away and rolled off the bed, rising on wobbly legs. "Leave her alone."

He laughed. His blunt fingers rammed into the tender fascia beneath my clavicle. I fell hard onto my butt, my head slamming against the wall. But then the sound of opera blasted from the two storied apartment cattycorner to our room. We all looked up, like the weaker listening to the roar of the dominant beast. Vadim snorted an indignant blast of air through his nostrils, then turned and stormed out of the room.

"Igpay uckingfay erkjay!" Camille yelled as he locked us inside. She helped me stand. I steadied my fall with my hand, gingerly pouring myself onto the rope mattress. I felt chilled, feverish, though it was not the fever of illness. She sat down next to me and swung her legs onto the bed, getting settled in.

"Are you okay?" I asked.

"Fine."

"Why are you here? I mean, why aren't you staying with Belhaj? I'm sure he's got a very nice apartment."

She shrugged. "I dunno. Guess it's like that Chinese proverb, 'Fuckin' not fartin'."

She didn't look like she wanted to discuss it any further, so I let it drop. "So who is Vadim?" I asked, massaging the bruises that were rising on my chest.

"Belhaj's whippin' boy."

"He's afraid of Belhaj."

"Belhaj likes 'em physically tough but mentally challenged."

"Why?"

"'Member I told you how Vadim got neutered in China? That was Belhaj's doin'. Punks like Vadim 'r more obedient when they's cut. Vadim's not long fer this employment though. Done fucked up one too many times."

Part of what she said rang true, but I suspected that Belhaj's deep animosity for testosteronized, potent men had more to do with what he did to Vadim. It was chilling to know the extent he would go to mollifying his own twisted ego. Right now, I was more curious about what they intended to do with me. "Will they bring me more heroin?"

"No," she said without hesitation. "Circumstances have changed. They ain't gonna fuck with you no more. Now they want you clean 'n sober for good."

My heart sank.

"Here's somethin' to take the edge of the creepy crawlies." Camille pulled a brown ampoule from her cleavage.

"Morphine?" I asked incredulously.

"Pharmaceutical grade. Ain't got no needle so yer gonna have to snort it."

"Where did you get it?"

"That mali. You know, that gardener. Give him some rupees to git it fer me."

I was dumbfounded by her generosity, the way she seemed to always be looking out for me. "Thank you," I stammered. "Where did he get it?"

She shrugged. "Drug store."

"Without a prescription?"

"They ain't got no FDA here, meddlin' in people's business. Only don't go tryin' to score from him. You'll just scare him off."

"How did you get out of here?"

"Mrs. Pawar come by 'n let me out while you was sleepin'. Wanted someone to practice playin' bridge with her. She got her ladies comin' over."

I laughed a small bitter laugh at the idea of Camille playing bridge. "Who is she?"

"Says she's a Maharani, but that don't mean shit no more. Plus that would make her old man a Maharaja 'n there's just no way in hell that little cretin coulda been a king. Nah, she's a gharwali. That means she's like a mother to her girls. In real speak, she's a madam." Camille expertly snapped off the top of the ampoule. "Tilt yer head back. That'a girl." She poured drops into my nostrils. I sniffed. "She ain't like the other gharwalis 'round here, though. Done give up pimpin' out Indian and Nepalese girls now that she cooked up this new business with Western girls." She poured a couple more drops into my nostrils and I sniffed greedily. "It's clean. In one day, out the next. Don't have the constant brothel bullshit to stress her out," Camille added, dropping the final dregs into my nostrils.

Within a few minutes the warm rush built in my brain until I was *tumbling, tumbling, tumbling* down onto the comfortable place next to Camille's soft thigh. I stayed like that for awhile, enjoying the respite from the stress. Since my experiences in that horrible prison room in Istanbul, I could not stop the horrible voices that plagued my waking hours. I knew it was the psychological trauma, but it didn't make it feel any better. The voices just went on and on no matter how hard I tried to shut them up. They were like nipping dogs herding me deeper and deeper into insanity. The relief of the morphine allowed me to relax under the cool breeze of the fan. Camille looked particularly beautiful, like a saint with an undulating halo around her blonde hair. "You're my best friend," I said, surprised that I said it, but more surprised by the reality.

"That's the dope talkin'."

"It's true. I don't even know you, but you're the best friend I've ever had."

"I'm grateful for the compliment." Camille gazed down at me, her flitting eyeballs studying my face as if deciphering truths from its lines and contours. I could see that my declaration struck deep within her, penetrating a walled off area of her heart. She rose from the bed. "Gonna take me a shower, too."

Maybe it was the jet lag wrecking havoc with my circadian rhythm, but the morphine acted paradoxically as a stimulant and I suddenly felt agitated. I got out of bed and climbed back on the chair at the window, the screen casting patterns on me. I just wanted to see the sky and the stars, to cast my gaze upon something of the universe that wasn't evil. A man stood at the gate, the Western man I had seen earlier that day when Mr. Pawar's SUV stopped for the circus. He was talking with the three beggar women, gesticulating with his hands. I could hear frantic words, but I couldn't hear what language he was speaking. He walked out of sight but the women huddled together and remained at the gate. A half hour passed, while I watched the street and the stars.

As I stood on the chair looking out at the sky, the voices in my head began the loop of taunts. These voices kept repeating my guilt over what we'd done in Istanbul to the dead girl. I knew it wasn't realistic, yet I felt beleaguered by my weaknesses and inability to protect the little girl, to defend myself and Camille, and to find an escape. My abject failure as a human being weighed down upon my shoulders.

Camille came back into the room, wrapped in a frayed towel, her head full of wet blonde hair that bunched in waves and curls around her shoulders. She pulled on a simple white linen caftan and tossed the soggy towel onto her bed.

I made the sign of the cross, something I had not done since I was a child. "Bless me father, for I have sinned," I whispered.

Camille snorted a hint of contempt as she plopped down onto the rope bed and began tugging a comb through her tangled hair.

"I have sinned, a mortal sin," I said grimly. "I'm wounded, don't you see? Mortally wounded." I hung my head. "The Catholic Church teaches that when you die, everyone will know everything you ever did. What will people think of me?"

"You ain't the onliest person in the world with skeletons."

"That's an absurd and cruel thing to say. Stop tormenting me for God's sake, and be my friend. I can't go on with this loneliness."

Her face softened and she looked contrite. "Belhaj done give me yer stuff when he put you in that room," she said lightly in a singsong tone. She rummaged in one of her bags and handed me my wristwatch.

I stepped down from the chair, steadying myself on my wobbly addict's legs. "It's a Piaget. Why didn't he sell it?"

"Ain't no common thief," she said airily. "You know, bigger fish to fry 'n all a that."

"My fiancé gave this watch to me. Paul. He's looking for me," I insisted.

"Nobody doubts he's *lookin'*," she said with hint of impatience that meant I better get used to the fact that *looking* didn't mean *finding*.

"My engagement ring?"

She shrugged. *So that he could sell. Or maybe he kept souvenirs.* Then Camille handed me the little pillbox that Paul had filled with Valium. I immediately calculated what one hundred milligrams of Valium would do for my withdrawals. I opened the box but it was empty. At the bottom of the little box I noticed a scrap of paper, folded tightly. I picked it out with my fingernail and opened the note. It was Paul's handwriting. *Meredith, Please take care of yourself and come back soon. Thinking of you. Love, Paul.* It was so bizarre to see the note, to hold it in my hands, this link to Paul, my soul mate. It gave me a thrill to read the note but then, like the rush of heroin, I crashed. What was Paul's reality right now? Wrapping his film while he waited for a call on his mobile saying I had been found? The thought of him blowing me off, and going on to live his life was worse than any of the torments my captors had put me through.

"What's that?" Camille asked.

"A note from Paul," I admitted, then regretted letting her into my personal life. But it was too late.

She snatched the note and read it. "That yer fiancé?"

"What difference does it make?"

"Makes a difference if you let 'em steal yer dreams."

"Are you just trying to mind fuck me now? Because these people—*you*—stole my dreams."

Camille wasn't offended though. "When I first saw you, I knowed he was after the girl 'n I didn't think he'd keep you. Not that yer not pretty 'r nothin'. Yer real pretty. Even in yer jeans 'n leather jacket I could see you weren't some stupid student tourist like the rest of 'em. You acted like a lady. Then we come to find out that yer a doctor. When I give you that morphine earlier and you says we was friends? I knowed what you was up to. No lady doctor's gonna wanna be friends with a ignorant cracker like me."

I was half listening, fixated on Paul's handwriting, thinking, *No, he's not just sitting around waiting. He's looking for me.*

"I had me one real good friend," Camille said dreamily. "We was in Tokyo together, at a club. We was supposed to work the customers fer drinks 'n such . .

. . " Camille's words fell off. She went back to her bag and then handed me my book, *The Song of God Bhagavad Gita.* "This yer's too?"

The book was still permeated with incense from the bookstore. The photo of my parents was missing. Before I could feel a pang of regret, she tossed me the plastic bag of ashes. "This too."

"My father's ashes," I said, barely catching the bag. "You brought them from Turkey." I stared at the weight in my hands. Dad was not the type to go for a Ming vase. And some corny nautical theme would have had him haunting me from the other side.

A cardboard box would have been good enough for him.

But since I was traveling, I had the mortuary pour his ashes into the plastic bag and secure it with heavy-duty rubber bands. And the bag had made it to India. I couldn't believe it. "That was so generous of you. I don't know what to say. I'm overwhelmed with gratitude. How can I thank you?"

"Must'a loved yer Daddy to lug them remains around in yer pocketbook at all times. Kinda creepy though."

"I was going to take them Varanasi."

"What call you got taken a dead person's remains to Very-Nasty?"

"The Ganges River. I was going to scatter his ashes with white rose petals."

"I git it. Like some people dump their loved one's ashes into the ocean?"

"It's a holy river, whatever holy means." I turned over the bag in my hand marveling at the dusty gray matter that was once the man who ruled my life. "Our relationship was complicated," I said, thinking that I should stop talking, but needing human connection. "It was all about what I could accomplish. I'm here because of some stupid romantic fantasy of pleasing him."

"You had yerself a noble purpose. That's what you need to hold onto. 'Cause you got yer work cut out fer yerself if you wanna get clean."

"I'll never be clean." I gazed up at the portal in the stucco wall where I could see a tiny cutout of stars. "It's not like all the songs and fairy tales we grew up with, is it? In that room, in the darkness I realized it's hate, not love, that breaks your heart."

"Yer still the same person inside," she said as if she had pondered this herself.

"Like you said, I've fallen too far to ever go back to where I was."

"All yer booklearnin' and them accomplishments ain't nothin' compared to what you got ahead a yerself. After you git through that, you can decide whether 'r not yer still ashamed to stand before other sinners."

"I will not rest until I am either dead or out of here. And I am not leaving without you and Zarina."

"When Satan wraps hisself 'round you, try 'n remember those intentions," she said in her matter-of-fact way. She was finished with me, I could see in the way she turned away, humming tunelessly as she finished combing out her wet hair.

Contrary to Mrs. Pawar's complaining about all of her servants jumping ship during the monsoon, at least one girl was left. And later that evening, a servant girl brought dinner: Potato filled samosas, the lentil dish dahl, and the Indian flat bread, chapatti. The barefoot girl wore a white cotton midriff blouse with capped sleeves and a short gathered skirt of a flower print. She moved with an ethereal gracefulness. No older than thirteen, her clear brown eyes were the deep wells that had inspired the poetry of Indian ancients. A long black braid like a thick, shiny rope fell over one shoulder. Her fatal flaw, and in this case her redeeming feature, was the congenital deformity cheiloschisis, commonly known as a harelip. The formation of the upper lip occurs during the first six to eight weeks of pregnancy and though genetic, can also be the result of environmental influences, like pesticides, poor maternal diet, drugs, nicotine, nitrates, and solvents. Poor countries had high incidences of cheiloschisis. Her sloppy sibilance also indicated palatoschisis, or a cleft palate. She set the tray down, and left, locking the door.

I forced myself to eat, knowing I would not have an appetite soon. Camille woke Zarina up and helped her eat. I couldn't tell if giving me some of my things meant that she was warming up to me, or if it was just pity. I would go through withdrawals. Then I would think of how to solidify my friendship with Camille, how to get her to work with me.

NINE

That first night in Mumbai at the Pawar's brothel compound, not much more than twenty-four hours after being let out of the prison room in Istanbul, I laid under the mosquito net while Camille and Zarina slept, thinking. My brain was on fire; I thought of the trauma I had been through, this strange new venue, the fact that I had no other choice but to kick heroin cold turkey. Camille was right about Satan. I'd witnessed too many junkies going through withdrawals not to be terrified. I would go through cold turkey in this concrete room under a bare light bulb, a sweating, convulsing feast for the clouds of mosquitoes that blew through the portal. The yawns welled up, the jitters crept into my sympathetic nervous system, the cold sweat formed like gel on the surface of my skin, and my muscles bunched into painful cramps. If I were to make it through this, I had to think it through scientifically. I needed that anchor.

I thought of my father. *You want to win*? was one of his mantras. It didn't matter if I answered yes or no or kept silent. He would go on reading his paper, buttering his toast, or pounding on his laptop, and speak the next three words I heard too many times to count: *Do your homework*. In this case, what was I to do? When Dad talked about winning, he began with spelling bees and worked up to SATS, applications to medical schools, facing off with senior residents. What would he tell me now? I reviewed the simple things I could do, like taking a shower and washing and braiding my hair. I started hydrating, as I laid there with my head propped on the wall, drawing deeply from one of the bottles of water Camille had brought back after her bridge game with the madam. While I was still able to rationalize, I got out of bed and paced the small space, reviewing what I knew scientifically about heroin in an attempt to steel myself for what lay in store for me.

Heroin would not be addicting if the human being had not been designed with a reward system doling out pleasure for actions that perpetuated survival and procreation. Humans suffered hunger pangs, the dryness of thirst, the throb of a full bladder, the churning of the colon, and the lust for sexual satisfaction. These sensations and urges compelled humans to eat, drink, sleep, urinate, defecate, and have sex; each action reinforced with a zing of pleasure. The pleasure reward for our actions sprang out of the brain's treasure trove of chemical messengers. Without the dopamine reward, humans would have felt too depressed to go through with the actions that led to survival and procreation. Pleasure was the big motivator.

Then came the Neolithic Age when the wild poppy seed was discovered. By ingesting the poppy seed with its active opiate ingredient, humans got the same flood of pleasure of the action-inspired dopamine reward. This easy access to reward without action was the route to addiction. About ten thousand years later, medical doctors began using opiates as analgesics. In the late nineteen hundreds, scientists, looking for a way to create an analgesic without the addictive aspect, synthesized morphine into diacetylmorphine, AKA heroin. Many times more potent than morphine, it went directly to the brain, producing the infamous heroin rush. It was one of the most addictive drugs ever created.

I pushed aside Camille's mosquito net and sat on the edge of her bed watching her sleep, a plan formulating in my mind.

The brain and spinal cord produces chemical messengers called endorphins that are natural analgesics. Natural opiates explain why people who have been seriously injured do not immediately feel excruciating pain so that they are often able to help themselves survive, such as running out of a burning building. Natural opiates also explain the high that joggers experience. The body suffers cellular and structural injuries during a run, and reacts by flooding opiate receptors with endorphins in response to these injuries. As it turned out, plant opiates are close enough in chemical structure to our natural endorphins to mimic and even do a better job at killing pain.

The yin/yang brand on Camille's butt summed up my situation. The human body is in a constant state of yin and yang rebalancing called homeostasis. In normal life we are in a constant state of tissue destruction and would be in agony if it weren't for the up-regulation of endorphins. But when heroin artificially fills up the opiate receptor sites, the body down-regulates the production of our natural opiates. If an addict attempts to quit using going cold turkey, and suddenly there's no more heroin onboard, it takes the body a couple of weeks to up-regulate the production of the opiate chemicals. There was no way to speed up the process. I would suffer agony as my body gradually up-regulated the pain-killing neurotransmitters in the effort to reestablish homeostatic levels of neurotransmitters. But I also knew how to reduce my suffering.

"Wake up." I shook Camille's shoulder. I was careful not to say her American name out loud, but I would not call her Nasreen.

"What's goin' on? Bless yer heart. Yer sick, ain't you?" Her words were muzzy and slightly slurred as she wiped a goo of drool from her full lips. "What can I do fer you?"

"You can ask that gardener to go back to the pharmacy."

Camille rolled over toward me, rose on one elbow flinging aside a frayed block printed Indian bedspread. She cleared her throat and, looking exasperated, said firmly, "I ain't got the cash flow to feed yer habit."

"You misunderstand," I said. "Do you have something to write on?"

"Over there, in my bag's a People magazine."

I flipped on the small lamp between our beds, retrieved the magazine and a pen. I jotted down *2 milligram flunitrazepam* and showed it to her.

Camille squinted at my scrawl.

"Get thirty of them if you can. It's generic for Rohyponol."

"What call you got fer roofies?"

"It's not just a date rape drug. Flunitrazepam is a nitrobenzodiazepine, a sedative-hypnotic drug that depresses the nervous system."

"I knowed some folks that mixed roofies with booze so's not to crash too bad from cocaine, but they ain't ended up so good."

True, I'd seen the body bags on the way to the morgue. But I'd also treated heroin addicts in the E.R. who used flunitrazepam to ease withdrawals. "I want to be unconscious when I go cold turkey."

She flopped back onto her back. "Guess all them years a hittin' the books pays off at a time like this. Sure, I can ask him tomorrow mornin'."

It was late and Camille fell back to sleep, her lovely lips parted, her eyelids twitching in a dream. I curled on the rope bed beneath the revolving fans where the mosquitoes couldn't fly. Like Camille, I was scratching bites and in my feverish state I was getting more and more paranoid about the disease-carrying vector. In my studies in infectious diseases I had reviewed the dreadful illnesses spread by the mosquito: yellow fever, malaria, dengue fever, West Nile virus, a myriad of types of encephalitis, and the filariasis worm, a parasite that causes elephantiasis. It was only the female that was hematophagous—a blood sucker—while the male flitted around in the Pawar's garden feeding on nectar. The female arthropod determinedly traveled up to ten kilometers—six point two miles—to hunt blood, following her keen detection of carbon dioxide from breath and sweat, which was another reason to stay under the breezy fan. She would light on her victim, inject saliva into the skin causing vascular constriction, blood clotting, platelet aggregation, inflammation, immunity, and angiogenesis, the promotion of new blood vessel growth. Her host thus prepared, the female sucked out the blood she needed to develop her eggs.

Time and time again over the night I jerked awake, only to lie back, relieved that I was shrouded under the net. As the sun began the slow burn into day, the mosquitoes disappeared and the rain began hammering on the roof. Water blew into the portal, soaking the mosquito netting. It was the monsoon Mrs. Pawar had predicted. The obstinate gooseflesh rose over my arms and legs. I yawned, sneezed and coughed, as the flu-like symptoms of withdrawal chased me. I kept moving my arms and legs, urged on by electrical charges throughout my nervous system. I couldn't wait any longer. I woke Camille. "Please," I begged.

She slipped into a pair of loose salwar trousers and a kameez—a svelte tunic—with a long scarf, called a chunni, which hung around her throat and trailed behind. The salwar kameez outfit was bright red and orange with gold threads and multi-colored embroidery around the neckline, and, down the front tab, a dozen tiny mother of pearl buttons. She gathered her hair into a ponytail with a scrunchie. "Gotta take care of the girl's needs. Then I'll see what I can do 'bout talkin' to that mali."

Zarina was crying and carrying on like a normal kid, but it grated on my nerves. I was glad when Camille's pounding on the door finally got someone's attention. It was the same servant girl. She had the key to our door, and it struck me as so odd that this deformed fawn would be our jailor. I just wanted Camille to come back with the flunitrazepam. It seemed like they were gone for hours but it must have just been thirty minutes or so. When they returned it was apparent that Camille had been industrious as she carried with her a plastic bucket, more bottled water, blankets and towels, and a washbasin.

"Did you talk to the mali?"

"He's here fixin' things from the rain. But I gotta be careful 'bout approachin' him."

I fell onto the bed and curled into a ball.

Zarina sat on her bed and ate from a tin of rice and yogurt on her lap. "I'm hot," she complained.

Camille peeled a banana and presented it to her by way of consolation.

"I don't want it," Zarina said defiantly.

"I'm gonna sing you a nice song then." Camille began to sing. Zarina caught onto the refrain quickly.

"You no thing, Deva?" Zarina asked, smiling her toothless smile and slithering her pink tongue over her gums.

"My name is Meredith," I said irritably. "Not Deva."

"She's just pullin' yer leg, sugar. Her name's Deva."

"Whereth Barbie?" Camille rummaged through one of her bags. Miraculously, Barbie had made the trip. Camille handed Zarina the doll. "Barbieth hot, too," Zarina announced. "Thath why she ain't got no clothes." Zarina held out the doll for my inspection.

"She doesn't have any clothes," I corrected. I was impressed with Zarina's quick grasp of English, but annoyed that she was learning how to talk like a redneck.

An hour later my mental reserves were ground down. I could not stand the physical pain. "Please," I begged, twisting on the hard rope mattress. "Please help me."

Camille knelt at my side to wipe vomit from the floor where a swarm of flies buzzed. "Gotta be quicker with that bucket, girl. I'm fixin' to go out again in a few minutes. When I come back I'll have some chai for you. Yer goin' to drink it. You got to drink fluids, it'll flush it out quicker, you hear me?"

She pounded on the door again and waited until the servant girl came with her giant key. Zarina sat on the other bed, playing with an imaginary friend, babbling in a mixture of Turkish and English. Where was that damned gecko? He was always in a different spot, but I had never actually seen him move. Then I spotted him, clinging to the ceiling. My dristi. My link to Paul. I focused on him, taking deep, long breaths.

Camille returned some time later with the chai and held me while I tried to drink the scalding liquid. Unlike the Turks who drank black tea with rough cubes of sugar, the Indians drank Darjeeling chai garam, a rich brew of black tea, hot whole milk, and sugar. I drank, craving sugar. "What about the mali?" I asked between gulps.

"I gave him all the rupees I had left, 'n that note from you to show the pharmacist."

"When will he be back?"

"Soon," she promised. "Soon, girl."

"Get me more sugar," I demanded. "Sugar cubes, I don't care what."

"I can't go out again right now. Don't want to piss off Mrs. Pawar whiles she's in the middle of her bridge game with her girlfriends."

"Girlfriends? God! Has the world gone *insane*?"

The weather was hot, but I shivered. Camille covered me with several blankets. A few minutes later I tore them off, sweating. Camille urged me to drink more of the *chai* that had grown cold. "It'll help them stomach cramps." I knew I needed to drink the tea she brought me, but with my body's down-regulation of opiate chemicals even peristalsis was starting to be painful, just as lying in bed, which stimulated the nerve endings under my skin, was painful.

The rain lulled. With the door locked, the room was a suffocating tomb. I forced myself off the bed and clamored onto the chair to try to get some fresher air. Below our room a half dozen women, their diaphanous saris in hot colors, flowed like tropical birds as they flitted down the driveway energized by the female agitation of having spent the afternoon gossiping. They wafted tiny purple bundles, and tucked fat brown paper envelopes into their sari tops.

I sunk down off the chair and got back onto the bed. "It looks like Mrs. Pawar's bridge game has broken up. Is she paying them off or something? I thought she was the big cheese around here."

"Told you. She don't like to git her hands dirty no more with all the abortions 'n what not. Still's got them hands in the pie, though. She's got herself a fleet of peeps to do her dirty work. But what them women git is nothin' compared to the cash she rakes in from shippin' Nepal girls to various parts unknown."

"Her, um, peeps were holding little purple bags."

"Lavender sachets," Camille said. "Party favors fer under their pillows."

"The world *has* gone insane."

By that evening I had lost all perspective. I sobbed and felt as if the world had turned into black sorrow, and that I had fallen into a deep pit. I became more irrational. There was nothing else but my need, an out-of-control desire for deliverance. "*Please help me*," I cried. I flailed on the rope bed and screamed, "Please help me!"

"You have got to *shush* now, girl." Camille pressed a towel over my mouth.

"She's sick!" Zarina said.

"Get back in bed and shush up yerself."

I heard my groans bouncing off the smeared walls but I couldn't stop myself.

"You got to lower yer voice, girl. The Pawar's got a houseguest."

"Houseguest?" I said, remembering the lavender sachets the evil brothel keepers had taken away from their civilized bridge game.

"Mrs. Pawar's brother's is stayin' here. You gotta be cool."

But I could not help the involuntary moan that flooded out of my lips.

Please, I am attempting to sleep here, came a man's voice through the walls.

"Now shush. Shhh."

But I cried out involuntarily.

If you vould kindly quiet yourself, madam!

"Where is that mali?" I cried. "Did you talk to him?"

"*Shhh*!"

Zarina crawled out of her bed onto mine, looking worried.

"Did you? Did you talk with him? Did you ask him?"

"Yeah, I done asked him."

"You're lying," I cried, turning to sob into my pillow.

"Whath lying?" Zarina asked.

"Not now, sugar."

"Liar!" I screamed, writhing on the rope bed like a snake, wriggling, urging off the desiccated sheath of scales.

Camille looked up at the window portal. "Where's that fuckin' monsoon when you need it?" she mumbled. She tore a towel into strips and crammed a gag into my mouth. I was too weak to resist. I trained my eyes on her, hoping she would watch to make sure I didn't aspirate vomit. For the second time in recent history I feared the possibility of death.

TEN

My soul left my body and hovered over my sick bed, waiting for the tempest to pass. I suffered as the sun rose and set and rose and set, but I was not aware of anything but my need. Camille didn't leave me. The monsoon pounded and raged and flooded the room so that Camille and Zarina sloshed about. When I retched, Camille was there to tear away the gag from my face and hold the red plastic bucket. Still, the room got messy, with the puke and the flooded toilet.

My first coherent moment came when I registered the scratching of a broom on the floor and opened my eyes to see Camille sweeping water and bodily excretions out of the door. Later I saw her hauling in buckets, and the caustic stink of ammonia permeated the room as she splashed the disinfectant around the floor. When the room had drained and she had tidied up, she ran a clean wet towel over my arms where I had raked long red marks into my skin. Camille still wore the same salwar kameez as she had when my withdrawals started. Now it was stained and there were dark rings under her arms.

She picked up my hand to inspect it. "Lordie girl, yer in need of a mani pedi."

She made me laugh.

During my convalescence, Zarina became my nurse, holding the glass of chai carefully in both hands. "Drink thith," she said imitating Camille and holding the glass to my lips. When the glass was empty she set it back down on the table and then lay down next to me. "Feelin' better?"

"Yes," I whispered, hoarsely.

"Becauth I worry 'bout you." She reached up and placed her cool, baby hand on my forehead.

Camille brought me food and for the next few days I ate, drank water, and slept. I wondered vaguely where Belhaj was and why he was leaving me alone and was being so benevolent. I was too weak to think much more about it. It was the heat that woke me finally, that and the creaking of the monsoon-rusted door hinges. Zarina stood in the doorway, holding a scraggly brown kitten. The kitten's amber eyes caught the light.

"You vill have to be giving the kitten to me." There stood the huge madam, Mrs. Pawar. "Its mother vill be sick with vorry."

"No," Zarina pouted. "*My kitty.*"

"Zarina, sugar, give the kitten back," Camille urged sweetly.

"No," she whined, clutching the kitten so hard it mewed.

"Give the kitten back, Zarina," Camille said firmly, then softened. "Someday you're gonna have your own kitten."

"Promith?"

"Yeah, sugar, I promise."

"*Liar! Liar! Liar! Liar!*" Zarina repeated, becoming the demon child. "I want *my bear*!" During the long, shrill shriek, I remembered the bear with the red tongue that she had dangled from one paw the day she ran into Belhaj's boudoir, the day he threatened to set my hair on fire.

"What is all this commotion, Nasreen?" Mrs. Pawar asked, looking piqued, her fleshly nostrils twitching ominously at the sharp stink of newly sanitized illness in the claustrophobic room.

"Oh, nothing," Camille answered breezily, fear radiating from her bright eyes. "We lost her bear."

"Goodness gracious," Mrs. Pawar replied, turning to Zarina with a look of mock astonishment. "Vas it such a furry creature?"

Zarina nodded, as if Mrs. Pawar had finally gotten it.

"Vell, then. I am knowing of just the shop to replacing said bear." She smiled, showing decaying teeth, long familiar with various indulgences. She eyed me on the rope bed. "I am seeing the doctor is recovering vell from her bout vith jungle fever."

"She wants drugs!" Zarina cried.

Camille drew Zarina close to her with a maternal not-another-word kind of hug. "The girl's just pooped out from the heat."

Mrs. Pawar was clearly comfortable with the charade, her head bobbling affably. "Ah. I haven't been myself either, lately. I do not know vhat it is. The veather changing every day. One day it's varm, the next day cool."

"Cool like hellfire," mused Camille.

Mrs. Pawar held out a pudgy hand. "Come child. Ve shall have the best bear in all of Mumbai."

With sinking dread, I watched Mrs. Pawar take the precious girl's hand and lead her from the room. My muscles had atrophied and I was too weak to protest. It was too late. Zarina was gone with Mrs. Pawar.

ELEVEN

Camille pulled off my sweat soaked kameez top as if she were undressing Zarina. "I'm gonna give you a shower now," she said, her facial expression showing me nothing.

"Is Zarina okay?"

"How the fuck should I know? You seen yerself she left with Mrs. Ton-a'-Blubber."

I was too drained to think more about it. I barely had the energy to take a shower. I held onto Camille to stand under the stream of water. After I got out, she combed out my hair and dressed me in a fresh salwar kameez of baby blue cotton with silver embroidery, and a pair of leather flip-flops. She strapped my watch on my wrist. She took me by the hand and led me out of the room into the garden. The rain had ceased long enough for the river of water to drain off and the garden was quickly reviving with the resilience typical of a jungle. It was glorious to be out of the foul room where I had lived through my nightmare. There were two rope beds in the garden in lieu of chaise lounges, and we both sprawled on them.

To say that Mumbai was hot and humid was to conjure up images of Georgetown, New York, Boston, or even New Orleans in the summer. But Mumbai was not merely hot and humid. The city had arisen out of the briny swamps surrounding seven sea-level islands that had for centuries been flooded by the Arabian Sea during high tide and the monsoon. It took over one hundred years to join the soggy islands into one body of land that was originally Bombay, then changed in 1995 to Mumbai, named after Mumbadevi, the stone goddess of the deep-sea fishermen. It is said that she fled with the fishermen, but I am certain she left because Mumbai is just too damned fetid.

Despite the wet heat, I hoped to recover from sunlight deprivation in the hot sun that filtered through the dense foliage. I napped there on the rope bed underneath the dappled shade of a sprawling kumquat tree, with the intention of gathering my strength so that I could think of a way to break out of the compound. I didn't realize I had fallen asleep until I awoke to a splash. I blinked through the daze of my sleep at the mali who was netting smelly, dead koi from the garden pond.

"Poached fish," Camille said, when she saw I was awake. She wore a bikini top and drawstring cotton pants and sat cross-legged on a bed across from mine. "That's how hot it is."

I rose, heavy-headed, onto my elbows, reveling in somber happiness that I was sober and that the fevers of withdrawals had broken. I was on the mend. The mali seemed to avoid my gaze, though I watched him penetratingly, wondering why he had not brought me the drugs and what he had done with Camille's money. Despite the heat, the garden was restful. A peacock spread its fan and strutted around boldly, indifferent to our captivity. The sleek Siamese cat peeked from beneath a hedge of Calla lilies strategically planted under a shady eve, their fresh white enclosing sheaths and fiery orange spikes of flowers, erect and regal. The gardener worked, raking the packed earth around the bamboo, palms and pandanus, the shrubby Indian pine trees. There were no weeds under the banyans, which, on that first day we had arrived, Mrs. Pawar had proudly referred to as her mulberries.

As if worrying about Zarina and the quandary of getting us

all out of there were not enough to weigh anyone down, I had another nagging anxiety. I could not stop thinking about what I would do if I did make it out alive, and if I could return to my old life in California. Of course there was no old life to return to since I was now changed forever and could no longer just pick up and resume my same career in medicine. I tried to imagine myself returning to the teaching hospital to begin my residency. The medical community did not take drug addicts lightly. Would I be allowed back to finish my training and practice medicine?

Camille sat on a bench in front of a banyan tree and a rubber tree plant, its shiny variegated leaves creating a lush backdrop. The mother cat jumped onto her lap and settled in. Camille began industriously fashioning a dovetailed joint, crumbling a block of tarry hashish into morsels and mixing them with shredded tobacco. She squinted at me through the piercing rays of sun that had reached its zenith and now shot through the foliage like heat-seeking laser beams. "Wanna smoke some hash?"

"I've never even tried marijuana," I stammered, astounded at Camille's cavalier mentality about sobriety.

"Ain't you the virgin." Camille finished constructing her masterpiece and licked the cigarette paper with a flickering pink tongue. She lit the joint with a sulfuric match and toked on it so explosively that a cloud of smoke the size of a bed pillow hung without moving in the soggy air.

Sobriety had brought with it a bizarre kind of clarity about the world around me. I watched a Monarch butterfly, its wings flapping thunderously in the cavern of my mind.

Camille nudged the cat off her lap. It hit the ground, and immediately began the arduous task of licking off her attentions. "Why don't you try a hit? Relieves the heat."

"It just seems like you would be a little bit more considerate under the circumstances."

"I got my own set of circumstances, you know."

"I don't want to be around drugs after what I've been through."

Camille looked at me through slit eyelids. "I need some relief after all's I been through. No offense." Her eyelids draped shut, her expression serene as a small smile played on her lips. Camille picked up the rest of the black blob and rolled it between her fingers. She sniffed it as one would savor a cork from a bottle of fine wine.

I could not help but think of the pleasure of mainlining, the euphoric rush that engulfed my whole body after the prick of the needle, blocking the pain of awareness. The medical community defined dependence differently than addiction because addiction was considered physical dependence. My own physical need was gone now, but my emotional and psychological cravings were not.

After Camille finished her joint, she lit a cigarette and puffed on it. She piled her long blonde hair on the top of her head and leaned back against the banyan tree and began to hum to herself, the smoke sputtering out of her nostrils. Her hand fell lazily onto a cluster of small tubular flowers called paintbrush. Their colors, red, orange, and pink seemed too cheerful for me at the moment.

"Where did you get hashish?"

"Where did you get hashish?" she said, mimicking me. She must have noticed my intense stare because she finally said, "Some old hippie I met at the market."

"Come again?"

"When you was sleepin', Mrs. Pawar sent me 'n Vadim to the market to buy her some of them marigolds fer her Ganesh." Then my face must have shown utter mystification, because she added, "The elephant god what brings good fortune. Mrs. Pawar's in a dead heat to keep him happy."

"I don't understand. You left the compound?" I stammered again, not giving one moment's thought about some heathen god's desires. She gave me one of her famous looks as if I were daft.

"Then why wouldn't you escape? Go to the police?"

"First of all, I was with Vadim. He turned his back fer two seconds 'n I just had a brief opportunity to speak to the 'merican gentleman. Second, I take it you never heard'a baksheesh?"

"For God's sake," I hissed, nonplussed and stammering like a fool. "I can pay anyone more baksheesh than they'll ever need."

She continued smoking her cigarette, her emerald eyes blazing at me. "Yer an educated person, but in this here situation you don't know jack."

"There has to be someone who would help us."

She shrugged, smoking absentmindedly. Her voice was thick as she observed, "All the saints come marchin' in ain't gonna git you outta here."

Once again I'd hit an impenetrable roadblock with Camille, and pursuing it seemed fruitless for now. "Well, you shouldn't talk to people like that. You're in enough trouble as it is." Inane as it seemed I was starting to worry about her, about her judgment, her brainwashed state, her vulnerability under all those layers of makeup and what seemed to be her feigned street smarts.

Camille bent to peek in a compact, clamping an eyelash curler to the lashes of one eye. She looked up with her cranked-open eye. "Don't go worryin' yer purty little head," she said vaguely.

I still didn't understand Camille's purpose in Belhaj's organization. Maybe he wanted her to keep tabs on me, to report back to him if I had any escape plans, how broken and malleable I was, or wasn't. She could come and go as she pleased, or at least she could come and go at someone else's bidding; more freedom than was likely to ever be allotted to me. As I watched her primping her melting makeup in the compact mirror, I felt awash in tenderness for her. I didn't know anyone from my past life who would have nursed the junkie version of myself. It would have been nothing but referrals to rehab clinics and well wishes dashed out by email. Camille was impenetrable and probably living somewhat of a double life, which made her volatile and dangerous, yet she really was the best friend I had ever had.

The mali dragged two buckets containing garden material and smelly fish by us. "What happened to my flunitrazepam?" I whispered to Camille.

"Indians ain't got no sense of urgency."

"Oh." It occurred to me that if the mali did end up getting me the drug eventually, we could use it on our captors. I would not share this idea with Camille just yet. She wasn't ready to hear any more about escape plans. It was highly likely that the mali had an urgent need for the rupees Camille had given him, and so he conveniently forgot all about getting the flunitrazepam. And so my hopes of using it on our captors were more or less squelched right then and there.

I picked up a white rose, dropped by the mali. I thought about the rose peddler in Istanbul. I probably could have found white rose petals in India. I could have called a florist and had them delivered from Holland. I stopped myself from thinking. I was there, and no amount of revisionist history could undo the facts.

Mrs. Pawar's roses were not doing well in the rain and humidity. The buds, drooping and withering, were suffering from bud blast. The stem of the bud was broken and blighted with botrytis, the gray mold that thrives on damp roses. Still, the flower was beautiful to me and I sniffed it. The fragrance of the flower shattered the peacefulness of the setting, the attar of roses exploding into an image of the room where Belhaj raped me. I felt as if I were tumbling into darkness, the rapid thudding of my heart reverberating in my head with flashbacks of the rape. The glint of the razor switchblade, the prison room, the rancid mattress, the act of rape, the smell of his breath, his sweat, his semen and the fragrance of roses. I watched in disbelief as the rose buds opened, like stop-motion photography.

My own shriek shocked me out of the hallucination.

Camille was clearly inured to the tormented screams of those suffering from posttraumatic stress. She was as calm as a seasoned E.R. doc looking down at me lying on the ground. "Heard about a dude that flipped out on LSD here in Mumbai," she said informatively as if I were in any condition to absorb this bit of lore. "Hog-tied him to a pole, carted him right to the hospital 'n give him shock treatments."

I lay there, staring up at the foliage of the trees to the bright sky and the pulsating sun that sought to dehydrate the life out of us while I pulled myself together mentally. "That's a silly apocryphal tale," I croaked, my voice dry and brittle. "Who told you that, anyway?"

"It were that old hippie."

"Maybe it did happen a long time ago when all the hippies were here," I said, scraping my elbows on the wet earth as I clamored to rise, astonished to realize that I felt jealous of the mysterious man. I sat back on the edge of the bed next to Camille, collecting myself. "Thank you for helping me through withdrawals."

"No problem."

I picked up the offending rosebud, and placed it on her lap. "This flower is like you. It's beautiful now, but it'll be the most beautiful when it blooms." A tiny sob hitched up my throat as the emotion of gratitude welled up. This contradictory creature had helped condemn me to hell but she had also thrown me a lifeline. Camille smiled the smile of a woman who had received few compliments in her young life. Her eyes drew me in. I felt the urge to kiss her on the lips to feel a moment of closeness with another human being.

But then a voice interrupted. "Yoo-hoo!" It was Mrs. Pawar.

Camille pinched my shoulder forcefully, her face strained. "Best not be talkin' trash to Mrs. Pawar if you knows what's good fer you."

"I'm smarter than that," I said, annoyed that she continued to treat me like a naïf. "And I will find a way out of here."

Camille burped a cynical laugh. "That right? Little ol' you, weak as a kitten?" She let go of me as Mrs. Pawar's massive body stood before us fortuitously blocking the scalding sun. Zarina was not with her.

"Ah, I see you are recovering, Doctor. You are looking quite vell. Quite vell, indeed."

"Thank you," I replied hesitantly, knowing better than to ask about Zarina.

"As for me," she said in her lyrical Indian accent, "I continue to be suffering the curse of constipation. It is beginning years ago with a bout of toxoplasmosis. If it is not the diabetes, the insomnia, the psoriasis, the shingles, the asthma. Vhat I vouldn't be giving for a bowel movement today."

It never ceased to amaze me what people disclosed not only to perfect strangers, but to doctors, whether they knew them or not. However, I didn't hesitate, as the way to win a hypochondriac's trust is to play along. "Are you having any cramping?" I asked, furrowing my brow in mock concern as if I were discussing a serious illness.

"Yes, yes. Oh, the gas, the gas, the terrible gas." She massaged her massive gut like a genie rubbing a lamp. "There I am sitting, several hours a day on my vestern toilet in my battle with my bowels," she testified hyperbolically. "And in the process I am consuming a half a dozen pots of chai, two packages of Four Square cigarettes to no avail, no avail at all." She twisted a rolled up, dog-eared copy of the British gossip rag, *Hello*. Commode reading, I assumed.

I reached for Mrs. Pawar's wrist and took her pulse. This act generated a spark of light in her eyes. "You shouldn't exert yourself so much."

Mrs. Pawar responded to my sympathy, sinking onto the other roped bed that shrieked quietly as the tightly woven ropes stretched under her girth. "How vise you are to be diagnosing my exhaustion. Vith so many demands, vhat is a voman to do?"

"Someone with acute hypoglycemia should not be under such stress," I said kindly.

"That is vhat I am always saying!" she exclaimed, and then asked with baited breath, "Acute hypoglycemia?"

"We'll evaluate you," I said with the kind of officiousness she would appreciate. "You should be snacking more frequently. And we should test you for hypothyroidism." It occurred to me that I could crank up thyroid hormone replacement to precipitate a thyroid storm: *tachycardia, disorientation, heart failure*. I reached over and patted her arm, keeping my facial expression neutral. "I'll prescribe something for your constipation."

Mrs. Pawar was flustered, but pleased, her cheeks rosy with burst spider veins and dotted with perspiration. "As simple as that!" The gleam in her eyes reflected her happy brain that was being bathed in serotonin as she conjured up comforting fantasies of being tended by her own personal physician. She turned her attention to Camille, generous now in her state of bliss. "The poor child is not vell either," she breathed melodramatically. "Oh, dear. She must be having the jungle fever the doctor is recovering from. Vhat she is needing are bananas being mashed into blanched oats." Mrs. Pawar snapped her fingers at the servant girl who trotted over and bowed to listen to Mrs. Pawar's bidding.

"Like she can't tell the difference between cold turkey 'n Delhi belly," Camille muttered.

I shook my head at Camille to get her to shut up. At least we knew the girl was safe, and it sounded as if she was being tended to properly.

Mrs. Pawar turned back to us, smiling with her horse teeth. "As simple as that!" She rose as she flung the end of her sari, called a pallu, over her shoulder and waddled off, buttocks jiggling under her flowing silk.

I called after her, "I'll write out a prescription for the pharmacist."

She looked over her shoulder and smiled again. But before I could dwell any further on Mrs. Pawar, I felt a hand on my arm and turned to see an Indian man in his mid-forties, wearing Indian pajama pants, a long white Indian shirt with a slit neck called a kurta, and an embroidered vest that accentuated his potbelly. He was shorter than me, and so I looked down on him.

"Hello! You must be Doctor Deva. I am Mister Chandraram." Instead of doing namaste, he shook my hand with a wet little mitt.

"It's a pleasure to meet you," I said warily, but politely, as my father taught me to keep my enemies close and I didn't know who this Chandraram was or how he fit into the picture.

"My sister has told me all about you. Ah ha, I see the quizzical look on your face. Mrs. Pawar is my sister who has graciously allowed me to stay with her and her dear husband while my palace is being fumigated."

His palace. He was apparently in need of impressing people with his status, and so I gasped and smiled, feigning agog. I looked around and Camille was gone, but the man was not finished with me. He cleared his throat and looked at me conspiratorially. "After the kerfuffle in your apartment, my sister informed me of your . . . *recovery.*" He guffawed, his soft jowls bouncing. I smiled weakly at his characterization of my writhing agony as a *kerfuffle*. And furthermore, if he was Mrs. Pawar's brother he had to have been around the compound and must have seen the cellblock of a room that he referred to as an *apartment*?

"I trust you are feeling much better?"

"Yes, thank you," I said, my fake smile frozen.

"Vonderful. Ve Hindus do not believe in original sin as do you Christians, rather ve hold the concept of uncleanliness. That vhich is *impure* must be cleansed." He made a scrubbing motion with his hands. "Vashed away, so to speak."

So okay; behind the scenes they were openly admitting that I went through heroin withdrawals, but in public we were referring to it as "jungle-fever-kerfuffle." His smiling face was blank. He had the effeminate air confirmed bachelors tended to possess;

fussy about their home, their meals, their habits. It was hard to place Mrs. Pawar and her brother in the same family. Here was a seemingly educated, gentile man, so different than his sister who ran a sex slave operation. I wondered about him and how much he knew about this sordid business.

"Perhaps we could have dinner some night?" Mr. Chandraram suggested, his lips twitching timidly.

"Yes," I stammered. "Of course."

Was this Mr. Chandraram my ticket out? How could this bashful gentleman have anything to do with this heinous business? I smiled, locking eyes with him so that his head bobbed slightly, shyly casting his glance away from me. "Off I go, as my palace is aired and I am homesick."

"It's nice to be home," I said agreeably, though the whole conversation was beyond absurd.

"Good day, madam," he said, bowing his head.

"Good day," I replied, though I had never said good day in my entire life. I watched him stroll down the garden path and when he reached the fortress door, the mali was there to let him out.

TWELVE

That evening, Vadim barged into our room. "You come," he said to me. "Fat bitch want you."

I was just finishing a meal of naan (Indian bread) and dahl with spinach and country rice. I swallowed the last piece of bread that had suddenly dried out so that it traveled abrasively down my esophagus. It was a shock to see the thug Vadim again. I had put him out of my mind, hoping he'd been sent off someplace else. But there he stood, standing over me impatiently and I rose quickly to avoid angering him. I had no choice but to follow.

We found Mrs. Pawar dining in the garden, balling up food with her fingers and popping the large balls of curry into her cavernous mouth. Barefoot servant girls tended her, fanning hungry mosquitoes away. Vadim left me and I stood for a long time waiting, watching Mrs. Pawar, eyeing her pink mobile phone that lay on the table next to her plate. She must have known I was standing there, but she ignored me. Finally she spoke. "Deva is a Hindi name. It is meaning goddess. She is being the Hindi moon goddess. I am seeing that you are fair complected, as am I. You are being of Indian descent though, are you not?"

"My mother was Indian."

"How lovely, dear. Are you meaning to say that she no longer vith us?" She chewed her rice.

I decided to feel her out. "My father brought my mother's ashes here, to the Ganges River in Varanasi."

"Ah!" she gushed orgasmicaly, spitting little bits of rice. "The

Supreme God, that is Brahman. Over time three sub-Gods are emerging. Brahma the creator. Vishnu the preserver. Shiva the destroyer, who is representing all three. That is vhy ve are calling him ruler of Varanasi, the holy city, Kasi."

"Kasi?"

"Lord Kasi Viswanatha was one of Lord Shiva's many forms. That is why Kasi is the home of one of the revered twelve Jyotirlingas of our Lord, a shrine vhere Lord Shiva is being vorshipped in the form of a Jyotirlinga . . . a lingam of light," she added irritably. "Do not be looking so dull of the face as you are being an educated woman, with an Indian heritage who should be lecturing *me* on these subjects."

"Yes, of course, you're right," I replied brightly, understanding then that Hinduism's many layers could not be peeled back in any cognitive fashion by one such Mrs. Pawar.

"Vell," she consoled herself piously, "it is only those who reach the highest level of spiritual enlightenment who can see these lingas, so brightly shining as columns of fire piercing into the earth." In the background, the young servant girl who had been our jailer spread her legs to urinate into the flowerbed. Her act interrupted Mrs. Pawar's tangent. "Ah *babu*!" she called sputteringly out to the mali, but then she saw the feisty little Mr. Pawar marching in our direction and addressed him instead. "Do not let that girl to be making vater on my pansies, Vachspati."

Mr. Pawar was close enough to slap the girl across the back of her head, hard enough to make her stagger. The mali saw it but continued raking, not looking up.

"Ah, but I am going on and on," said Mrs. Pawar to me, as the girl struggled to rise. "And here are you, still appearing veary from your recovery. Not to vorry, India is a metaphor for renewal. You will soon be understanding that India is a symbol of endurance. Then you vill be feeling much better."

The purposeful Mr. Pawar delivered a first aid kit to us, a large white metal box with a red cross on it. Mrs. Pawar hoisted her massive body from her chair with an equally massive grunt and motioned that I should pick up the kit, which I did. "Shall ve be getting started, dear? Then you can be resting."

I didn't have a clue what she was talking about, but thought better of saying so and followed her instead down the garden path, past our room, to another door. This door was opened through much straining, grunting, and heavy breathing, with the assistance of several ancient old skeleton keys. Once we passed through that door, we were in a dark foyer with a dirt floor. Ahead of us a gigantic wooden door had been left ajar. It led to the street where the cages of women and girls were visible, and just beyond the cages sprawled the dusty street where men gawked at the merchandise and prostitutes ostentatiously plyed their business. The night air was thick with smoking kerosene, incense, perfume, human sweat, boiling vats of oil, flowers, all folded into a miry concoction with the moisture that clung to the air molecules. It felt claustrophobic and hard to breathe.

I scanned the street and located an alleyway that might be a good escape route. No doubt Mr. Pawar was a nimble rabbit, but he had not accompanied us and Mrs. Pawar could not catch a turtle. All these thoughts went through my mind in seconds but then Vadim startled me, stepping through the door. To our right a stairwell dug into the earth, the steps thick wooden blocks moldy and rotting from generations of monsoons and humidity. He forced me down the grimy steps into what seemed to me the festering bowels of the earth. I vowed next time not to think but to act, however impetuously. There had to be people out there who would be willing, out of goodness or greed, to bet on the American woman. These thoughts weighed heavily on me in my regret for the lost opportunity, the cacophony of Bollywood music, street hawking, crying, banshee screams, crowing and braying suddenly fading as we descended into darkness. Struggling with the heavy first aid kit I followed as best as I could, all the while fearing that they intended to incarcerate me down there. It was a hallway, tunneled into the earth with tarred railroad tie beams as shoring. Our sandals stuck to the sticky ties, flapping against leather soles. Bare light bulbs, strung on frayed electric cords in a random pattern, lit our way.

Mrs. Pawar removed a belt from around her huge waist, jangling her ring of rusty skeleton keys. She grunted again at the effort of opening an imposing lock, the ancient kind I had seen only in museums. Hinges squealed and my heart raced, wondering if this would be the last of my relative freedom. All three of us gasped, hands masking our noses, when Mrs. Pawar pushed open the door. Inside, crying out meekly, a dozen girls huddled: sweet young girls who could be cheerleaders, coeds, the girl who handed you your latté at the local coffee hangout; except these girls had been mauled, raped, and beaten, and were wearing nothing more than the panties and bras they had been abducted in.

"University textbooks," I said, barely audible, remembering the day we landed and Mr. Pawar telling Belhaj, *I am having a line on the American university textbooks you requested.* I stood there, dumbfounded. Camille had told me that these people were dealing in Western women, but somehow I had not put it together. Vadim shoved me into the room. The dirt floor was strewn with filthy straw. Flies buzzed frenetically over an overflowing latrine bucket. I understood. I was supposed to give medical care to the girls they had abducted, raped, and beaten into submission. I straightened my spine, hoping that Mrs. Pawar would be responsive if I behaved normally, as I would have in my former life: The American doctor, in charge. "Someone needs to clean that bucket out," I said with authority. "I need ice, boiling water and clean bandages. And some light."

Vadim only slammed the door shut, locking me inside. Mrs. Pawar's bulging eye appeared watching at a peephole, then disappeared. In the miserly dimwatted light the girls, clinging to one another, sobbing, now turned hopeful faces to me as if blooms to the sun. "I'm Doctor Meredith Fitzgerald," I said. "Does anyone speak English?"

"We all speak English," a blonde girl said with a British accent, her words spastic with fear. "What the bloody fuck is happening to us?"

I touched her arm, to let her know I heard the question, but I ignored it for now. "Whose injuries are the most serious?"

The shuddering girls parted and there in the filthy straw lay a young girl. The girls mewed and all murmured over each other.

"I can't look."

"It's so awful."

"I'm going to puke if I look at her."

I am a doctor. We examine with curiosity that which others look away from. But it was clear why these young women were unable to stand the sight. The injured girl was breathing shallowly. Caustic dermal burns on her face were gray as if made of putty, infested with squirming maggots. Her nose was melted into a mere nub. Frothy discharge, now dried foam, was caked around her eyes and ears.

The British girl's voice came from behind me. "They poured acid into her ears and eyes. They did it in front of us to shut us up. To scare us." She started to cry, loud sobs, heaving into her cupped palms.

I noticed a jar in the corner and went over and kicked it with my sandal, but did not touch it. In the U.S. the use of hydrochloric acid was strictly controlled. In India it was no doubt readily available in concentrations not found on the American market. The label on the jar read *Hydrogen Chloride 40%, Water 60%*. Hydrochloric acid is an alkali agent that penetrates the tissue causing it to liquefy and die, known as liquefaction necrosis. The ocular burns the girl had sustained had certainly resulted in opacification of her corneas and complete loss of vision. Her eardrums had probably melted, allowing the acid to flow and damage her auditory nerves, cochleas and Eustachian tubes. Inhalation of the acid would cause inflammation and destruction of the nasal passages, dental erosion, loss of voice, pneumonia, headaches and heart valve damage. That she was in shock told me she had ingested the acid during the attack, which rendered holes in her intestinal tract and resulted in inflammation of the kidneys. Even in the best hospital in the U.S. she would only be given life support and pain management.

"Tell us! What's going on? Why are we here?" the British girl cried out, nearly hysterical. She was pretty in a baby-faced kind of way, a girl-woman with biglashed blue eyes and a voluptuous body. Her hands clutched at my arm.

"I don't know what's going on," I lied, looking away from her as I could not look into those baby eyes. "I was kidnapped too," I admitted. "Right now, let's get you all well."

It would do no good to tell these girls the ugly truth. If I patched them up, then we might be able to work together. No doubt some of the girls needed surgery, but that was not in the realm of possibility. I braced myself to treat their superficial wounds and began by opening the first aid kit. It held the basics, a stethoscope, aspirin, tweezers, scissors, needles and thread, alcohol, adhesive bandages, ointments, hydrogen peroxide, instant cold compresses, exam gloves, sterile gauze. There on top were heroin works: syringes, cotton balls, a spoon, a rubber tourniquet . . . and a sandwich size plastic bag of heroin. I felt sick. These people were masters at the business of seasoning. They knew that I would be tempted to use the heroin myself. And they knew that I would be tempted to use it on the sickest and those in the most pain. But I couldn't do that. I would be going against everything I believed in. We didn't use heroin in medicine. I was not going to be complicit in hooking these victims on heroin. I was not going to help my tormentors. I felt close to tears myself but I had to stay calm. I started to breathe. Four counts in. Hold for four. Four counts out. After a few breaths I turned around to face the girls. "Who is she? Does anyone know?"

"I do," said another girl, her eyes swimming with tears. She had her arms crossed over her abdomen. I could not help but notice that she too had a sensual, curvy body. "We are Dutch, from Ouderkerk aan de Amstel, outside of Amsterdam. We came to Mumbai for summer vacation to work as extras in Bollywood films. My friend, Christyn is her name, thought it would be fun." As with her friend who lay dying, this girl had long thick hair, the color of champagne. "These men . . . Christyn fought them and they did this to her. She is going to die, isn't she?"

"Yes." With trembling hands, I picked up the heroin works and in that moment my life, and the person I thought I was, was further altered. I prepared a deathly dose, cooking it in a spoon.

"Is it heroin?" the girl asked me when she saw what I was doing.

"What is your name?"

"Maria-Maarens Van Vleck."

"I can ease your friend's pain, Maria-Maarens. If you want me to."

"Yes, please. It is good of you to do that."

The other girls nodded. They were sick with the grief and torment of watching someone die so gruesomely. They watched, silently as I tied a tourniquet around Christyn's arm and injected the heroin. Maria-Maarens held her hand and sang under her breath in Dutch. A children's song.

I took out the stethoscope and listened to Christyn's heart until it stopped beating. It was only a few minutes. I slung the stethoscope over my neck. "Now who has the worst injuries?"

An American girl, about seventeen, answered, "Olivia is really hurt." She pushed her friend, a doe eyed, African American girl, to the front. I blinked for a moment, as both these girls were gorgeous, too, and as with the others—*and Camille and me*—they were curvy. The two American girls' breasts looked augmented with implants—the current rite of passage among teenaged and college girls in the U.S. The others, the Italians, the French, all of them were well endowed. And they were all beautiful. Camille had said that Mrs. Pawar had given up on Nepalese girls and was concentrating on Western women. *Customer satisfaction*, was what Belhaj said they were interested in. T&A—tits and ass—is what they called it in the film industry. A sure sell every time, Paul had told me. These traffickers were cherry picking for certain sensual qualities to please a discriminating, well-paying clientele.

"Tell me what happened to you, Olivia?"

"We were in Goa on vacation with our parents, at the beach," she said in a girlish voice. "I was all, 'I have to pee, I have to pee', but I didn't want to go in the water. So my mom told me to go over to a restaurant and ask if we could, you know, use the bathroom. And they were saying, 'The bathroom is outside in the back'. Three Indian guys were hanging around trying to flirt with us, as if they wanted to hook up, or something. I was all, 'Fuck off'. Then they grabbed us and put something over our faces so we couldn't breathe. We woke up in a disgusting, gross room." She paused, tears tracking down her cheeks. "They raped us. Three men. We tried to fight but they beat us up. They made us take pills. We were here when we woke up. Some little Indian man came down here with a Russian dude and the Indian man, you know, fucking raped us again in front of everyone." She stopped talking and started to wail as though she were a seven year old. "*I want my mommy.*"

"I know, Olivia. I understand. But you have to calm down because I don't know how much time I have to help you. I need you to show me where it hurts."

She stifled her sobs and pointed. "My shoulder. I can't lift my arm."

Her shoulder was swollen and bruised. In a hospital we would send her for an x-ray, but all I could do was base my diagnoses on an educated guess that her shoulder was dislocated. Putting the humeral head, or the top rounded portion of the upper arm bone, back into the glenoid labrum cavity, or joint socket, was done under anesthesia. But I was not going to give this girl heroin. Maybe I was wrong, but I said, "Hold onto your friend. It's going to hurt, but it'll be over fast. It's okay to scream." The girls surrounded and held onto her as I pulled on her arm, hard. She screamed. We all waited for the pain to subside and when she smiled through her tears the girls hugged her and comforted her.

"It's okay, Olivia," her friend said. "The doctor's going to, you know, get us out of here and call our parents."

I turned to my work, concentrating as I squeezed an instant compress to burst the inner pouch. I pressed the cold compress onto Olivia's shoulder.

"Who's next?"

"My eye-a," a raven-haired Italian girl said, pointing to one eye.

Her raccoon eyes indicated bilateral periorbital hematomas. The eye is surrounded by fatty tissue that allows room for blood to accumulate after trauma. But something told me that this was not a simple black eye. "Can you see out of your eye?"

"One eye, yes. This eye-a no."

I covered the good eye and held up my finger and crossed it back and forth in front of her other eye. "Can you see my finger?"

"No. I cannot."

I began bandaging her eye, silently.

"What is it? What is wrong-a with my eye-a?"

"It could be the swelling around the eye," I lied. When retina detachment occurs, the most common complaint is double vision. The fact that she was blind in her eye meant that her condition had deteriorated. It was possible that her retinal tear could be successfully repaired with laser surgery or cryotherapy to seal the retina back onto the wall of her eye. But only an ophthalmic surgeon could perform such procedures, and it would have to be done soon.

Her companion, an eighteen-year old strawberry blonde Italian girl had a tooth knocked loose. I gave her a wad of bandage to bite down on. Next was a cheerleader type with brunette hair tied into a ponytail at the top of her head. She was German. Her earlobe was ripped where an earring had been forcibly torn off. I sutured it with a needle and thread. The first aid kit contained antibiotic powder. I stared at the box. It was made in India. My mind raced. Of course, India had a booming pharmaceutical manufacturing business. I kept thinking of what Camille said about India not having the same regulations about drugs as the U.S. The fact that prescription drugs were readily accessible here had to work to my advantage somehow.

Olivia's friend was persistent. "You're going to call the American Embassy? And get us out of here, right?"

"I'm going to try," I said, keeping my face neutral, knowing it was impossible. But I needed to keep her occupied. A girl from Germany had rug burns on her hipbones. Two French girls had cigarette burns on their legs. There were many other burns and abrasions. "I'm going to sterilize your hands." I poured alcohol over Olivia's friend's hands. "You can be my physician's assistant. Apply this antibacterial salve to the burns and any other abrasions. There are bandages to dress the wounds."

I looked over the girls, who sat in the dirty straw looking up at me. "Were you all raped?" They nodded. "Did they sodomize you?" My question turned on the tears again. "Okay, I'm going to pass out this antibacterial ointment. I want you to put it on yourselves. Hopefully you can see a doctor in a clinic soon." *God, why was I giving them false hope?*" I motioned to Olivia's friend, "Take this tube and divide it up between all of you. Give everyone two aspirin. Chew them, okay?" I said to the girls, and they nodded again.

"My name is Lauren," Olivia's friend said, her expression composed and suddenly looking years older. "Lauren McCarthy."

"Okay," I said, feeling numb, not really hearing her.

"No," she grabbed my arm. "I need you to remember my name. You're a doctor. My father's a doctor. He like, told me that medical school is all about memorizing. You have to memorize our names. All of our names."

"Yes, you're right." My father had emphasized memorization saying it was essential for success. From a very early age, he'd taught me methods of mental organization, visual memory, and association. I would need those techniques now. I looked around at the young women, some of them just girls, scared out of their minds, in emotional agony, knowing that if I didn't do something that they were on their way to unimaginable fates. "Tell me your names." And one by one, they recited their names and I memorized all fourteen. *Lauren McCarthy . . . Olivia Coolidge . . . Tessa Rizzo . . . Imelda Conti . . . Karen Yamagata . . . Rita Kagoshima . . . Claudia Yager . . . Amelia Getman . . . Joanie Patterson . . . Danielle Fournier . . . Gabrielle Rosseau . . . Sharon Martins . . . Maria-Maarens Van Vleck.*

"Don't forget my friend," Maria-Maarens said. "Christyn Landseer."

"I will never forget Christyn."

An hour later they had fallen asleep in each other's arms, seeking comfort and giving solace. I sat with my head between my knees, thoroughly spent. Mrs. Pawar and Belhaj were going to use me to help them do their evil work. Belhaj and Vadim were psychopaths, but in a way, Mrs. Pawar was even more complicated. Though I had only briefly studied the *Diagnostic and Statistical Manual of Mental Disorders* during my internship rotation, I was sure her diagnosis was a combination of sociopath and narcissistic personality disorders. I'd only had a handful of encounters with her but it was evident that she was mentally ill. If I were correct in my diagnosis, Mrs. Pawar saw the world through the lens of her infatuation with herself and her egotistical obsession. She would be ruthless in her pursuit of her self-gratification, dominance over others, and greedy ambition. She was certainly devoid of empathy and unable to acknowledge the feelings and needs of others, which made her capable of capturing, torturing, and selling women and girls into sexual slavery. Her grandiosity and need for recognition, her belief in whatever good qualities she had spun about herself, her belief in her unique status as a special individual, her entitlement would make her very dangerous indeed. If contradicted, she could fight back with brilliant verbal obfuscation. If crossed or thwarted in a particular quest, Mrs. Pawar's wrath would know no bounds. It was perilous to disagree or contradict a narcissist, and imperative for me to appear awed by her achievements, talents, and beauty. I also knew that I should never make any comment that might insinuate doubt about her inflated self-image and omnipotence. I made mental notes to always rapturously agree with her, and to patiently and accommodatingly fawn over her with medical care, as narcissists gravitate to individuals who can offer them something unique, though the infatuation period is brief. I would find my way in to these evil hearts, one revelation at a time.

As the door creaked open, the girls stirred but didn't awaken. Vadim kicked my thigh. I got up and followed him out.

THIRTEEN

Since our arrival at the Pawar brothel compound in Mumbai, Camille had been preoccupied with taking care of me. My absence had given her the opportunity to unpack. When Vadim shoved me inside our small room, I was immediately assaulted by Camille's wardrobe that had migrated from her luggage into a strange menagerie. Feathers, fake fur, leather, cocktail dresses, red fezzes, and feather boas gave off a musty, dead-animal-old-perfume-body-odor smell that competed with the inescapable stench-from-Hades emanating from the W.C. The floor was dangerously littered with stilettos. Camille, topless and wearing just the fetching salwar baggy pants of a teal green and silver, sprawled like an odalisque on one of the rope beds. The temperature was scalding and beads of perspiration rolled indolently between her breasts. She pulled aside the mosquito netting and hesitated just long enough to hear the scrape of the lock that signaled we were alone.

"From the looks of you, I take it you didn't fall fer their tricks," she said, her eyes at half mast and falling back onto a pillow.

"Fuck them." I said, rising. My throat felt raw from breathing the ammonia by-product of feces and urine in the dungeon, and my head pounded. "And thanks for the warning."

She shrugged.

"It's not just us now," I said. "There are other girls down there, in a . . . *dungeon*. I've never seen anything like it, except in the movies. We have to get them out!"

Camille was singing under her breath, ignoring me.

"Did you hear me?"

She looked up, blinking her profuse lashes, and smiling wanly. "Oh, I knows *alllll* about that hole."

"You?"

"Meeee?" she replied, opening her eyes in mock surprise. "Whaddya'll think? I done got here by signin' up fer Sex Slave 101?"

"But I thought . . . . Never mind what I thought. We have to help those girls."

"You helped them, I expect. That's what yer here for. That's why yer not rat food in some Turkish alleyway."

"What do you mean?"

"Yer *old*, girl. No disrespect meant by that. It's just that the only reason you made it this far is 'cause that taxi driver in Istanbul told Belhaj you was a doctor."

"The taxi driver who picked me up at the hotel, who took me to the Egyptian Bazaar?"

Camille shrugged again. "Don't know where he picked you up. All I know is that we was after the girl, but you had to be the hero."

The revelation that that little lecher taxi driver had primed Belhaj to abduct me was a psychological blow too unwieldy to process. And here I had thought all along that he would be the first to recognize that something was wrong, and that he would go to the police with my suitcase. For all I knew, the man took my bag back to his wife who pawed through it, greedily clutching my American jeans and other treasures. Without a heads up from the driver, it may have taken Paul a few days to come to grips that I was missing. He would have had to convince the American Consulate that I was not just a wayward girlfriend blowing him off by going on a jaunt in the Middle East. He would have had to convince Interpol. At that point the trail would have gone stone cold. The rose man could have suffered a heart attack or gone on summer vacation to the Dalmatian Coast. Any eventuality could have taken place to completely erase any clue that led to me.

"I will find a way out," I said under my breath, determined to fight the sensation of doom.

I left Camille lounging and went back into the W.C. where I showered, trying to clear my head of what she had just told me, trying to forget that I had just murdered a girl down in the dungeon, and that I had lied to the prisoners down there telling them that everything would be okay, that I would help them.

Just as I turned off the water, Camille appeared through the vapors as an apparition. She'd pulled on a blouse, and was holding up a towel. When I stepped out of the shower, she wrapped me in it, wiping me off. "Gotta get dressed," Camille said. "Somethin' fittin'."

When I went back into the room, the same servant girl stood at the door who'd gotten smacked for urinating in Mrs. Pawar's flowerbed. She spoke with Camille in Marathi, which I now knew was the official language of the state of Maharashtra, where Mumbai was located. The whites of the girl's eyes shone in the darkness of the garden as she peered inside curiously, patrolling the room, and me. I didn't have a good feeling about her being there.

"He wants you," Camille said, flapping a silky red caftan at me, something with glitz on it that I would never have dreamt of wearing in my former life.

"What does he want?" I asked warily.

Camille didn't seem to be in any mood to coddle me. She stormed around in the small space, her face set, her lungs pumping so that her breath came in little snorts of air. "Looks as if you's the flavor of the month now," she said angrily, waving the red silk.

"I don't understand."

"You was right. I was doin' him, you know, keepin' him happy, just so's he wouldn't trade me elsewhere. I been his girl fer six years, n' he even let me keep Zarina so I could feel more like a family. You come along 'n yer gonna spoil all that fer me."

"I thought you said you were his translator."

"He ain't gonna want me no more now that he's got you."

"He doesn't *have* me. He'll never *have* me."

"He's got you!" she shouted. "I don't know what it's gonna take fer you to git that."

"I'm sorry. I never intended to—"

"Fuck off."

"I won't go then."

"You'll go unless you wanna end up traded down and down till yer livin' in some cardboard hut with a shit-hole out back. Then, you won't be so purty no more 'n he'll get over you." Her full lips drew into a tight line, and I saw in graphic detail the terribleness of her situation and how, if she stayed in this life, her looks would wither along with her soul. "Just go and do what you gotta do," she said cryptically, "to stay alive."

"What?" I asked, needing her to say it, as though she were a judge handing down my execution orders.

"He's a man. He has needs."

My intestines began to agitate like the loads of laundry the servant girl did in her ancient wringer washer in the garden. "I thought I was his doctor," I said, realizing how naive I had been to even think of a second that he wouldn't want to continue raping me.

"He fancies clean, beautiful women," Camille said. "That's

why he keeps certain girls for hisself."

I was broken now and Belhaj could do with me as he pleased, safe in the knowledge that I would not give him a sexually transmittable disease. And now I knew that Camille had been with Belhaj all these years, ever since she had first been abducted. Was that my fate too? It was all too terrible to digest. The girl knocked again on the door-jam, little raps, reminding me of the Indian woodpecker that tapped for insects in Mrs. Pawar's jungle garden. Her urgency made me believe that my dallying would cost her.

"I can't do it."

"Ain't got no choice."

I stared at her, wondering about that, as she had said it so many times. *No choice.* When did no choice become my life? I put on the red caftan.

"Just pertend yer a princess 'n he's yer prince," Camille said woodenly. She gave me a little shove toward the door.

Outside our door, the mali tended a fire to incinerate garden trimmings he'd dead-headed after the latest deluge. Orange flames licked and crackled in a rusty and dented tin barrel. The heat was intense as he piled in more wizened foliage, stoking his inferno. The sky sprawled pitch black and milky with galaxies. The noise from the street seemed far away. I listened to the crackling of the flames, the night bird's songs, and occasional furtive rustle of some nocturnal creature hypnotized by the heat and weaving sparks. *So there was still glory in the universe*, I thought resentfully. I looked up into the man's eyes. Within them I read the truth of my situation. I was a sex slave, and there was nothing I could do about it. The mali nodded to me as if to say that I should go with the girl who had paused as though a timid jungle creature at my elbow, her eyes full of the mystery of the ages.

I followed her up an open stairwell, reaching a small foyer with an old wooden door hinged together with primitive hardware and copper decorative pieces. The girl folded her long hands in namaste, searching my face as if to ask why I was going to be with Belhaj who she knew to be a hater of women. I patted her shoulder and managed a smile to try to assure her that she was not responsible for condemning me to this encounter. She left me there. I knocked.

"*Entrez,*" he shouted.

Belhaj sat morosely on his bed. He perked up when he saw me and for the first time in my life, I regretted the assets that supposedly made me attractive. Though I felt ugly and dirty inside, my long loose hair rippled in the hot night breeze from the window. His eyes traveled from my hair, to my face, to my breasts swathed lightly in Camille's thin red, sequined silk caftan. Behind him candles flickered; demonic tongues. The fragrance of incense assaulted my nostrils with a pleasing scent that taunted me.

He left me standing there and went to pour a drink. When his back was turned I inspected his quarters, noting some of the same array of vanity products, the same OCD order to his clothing. His suite was elegantly furnished in Raj style antiques, reflecting the British reign of the Indian subcontinent that, if my history was correct, was mid-nineteenth to mid-twentieth century. Silk draperies, a sterling tea set, burning candles in candelabras. It was lived in, as if he had called this apartment home for a long time, years even. He walked over to me, sipping his Pernod. He was past his prime, and no amount of primping could alter that. A dangle of loose flesh under his chin was the tell-tale sign that age was, indeed, relentless. He salvaged what he could by diligent grooming, keeping nose, ear, eyebrow hairs clipped, nail ridges buffed. He probably employed Botox and derma fillers. Only a daily exercise regime could guarantee his shirt falling flat across his abdomen, and yes, he also had exercise equipment there in India–an elliptical trainer, free weights, and a few yoga DVD's scattered on the floor.

He put his drink down, sat down on his bed, and motioned me to come to him. "*Je me ronge de l' énergie*," he said. "How you say, zee energy is drain from my body," he translated irritably. "Why are you not speaking French if you ave the education?"

"You're right. I should learn."

He pulled me to him and wrapped his arms around my thighs so my crotch was at his face level. "I will teach you." He let go of me. "I don't zhink so. I am too tired. Zher is no life left in me.'

"Is there anything I can do?" I asked, incredulous that he was being so candid, but also understanding that I had to respond, to behave as if I cared.

He shrugged. "I am getting old. Maybe . . . something about zeez damned spots," he pointed to his nose. "Zee way you say in Istanbul."

I kept quiet then. I was definitely not going to go there ever again.

"Zhese girls. It is too much work for me now."

"I did what I could. I need more medical supplies."

"Whatever you want, I will give you."

I felt a lump in my throat. I wanted to help them, but I didn't mean to imply that I would willingly comply with their trafficking scheme. But that's how he took it.

"I need zee help with my medicine." He rose from the bed and went into his bathroom, where I could hear him rustling around and a drawer opening and closing. He returned and handed me the I.M. vial of depo-testosterone, and a syringe.

I tore the syringe out of the sterile plastic casing. "What is your dosage?"

"You are zee doctor."

"What have you been using that gives you . . . results."

"Two of zeez numbers." He pointed to the lines on the syringe.

"Two cc's?"

"Oui. Zhree is O.K. too."

Two to three hundred milligrams of depo-testosterone. It was a lot for a man his size and age. It was one of the reasons he was so aggressive, and also accounted for his receding hairline. I could tell him to take finasteride to block dihydrotestosterone, but I was not going to be the one to mention to this vain peacock that he was losing his hair because he had too much DHT onboard. Fuck him. I snapped the air bubble out of the syringe with my middle fingernail. "Okay," I said, signaling that he should drop his pants. And then I gave my rapist an injection to assist him in violating me.

When I was finished and the syringe was disposed of I was about to ask him if the girls could be released from the dungeon and instead be kept in one of the empty bungalows next to our room. But he picked up my hand. I had forgotten about the Piaget on my wrist and cringed, wishing I had thought to take it off.

"A woman as you should ave beautiful possessions." He touched my face. "A man as me should ave beautiful possessions." It made me ill to think that this was a date for him.

And then he raped me.

FOURTEEN

The servant girl was not summoned to escort me back to the room, but Belhaj had no fear that I would flee when he pushed me out of his door. There were no escape routes from the compound, but for those adept at scaling twenty-five foot walls edged with bales of concertina wire. I was exhausted anyway, and all I wanted was to take a shower and try to forget the last two hours that I had spent as the mistress of my rapist. I could not wait to soap my entire body, rinse, and soap it again and again, even though I knew I could not wash his smell away. I would shower anyway, then hide in the neverland of sleep. In the morning I would think about the girls.

The first thing I saw when I walked back into our room was a white parcel the size of a pound of butter, along with heroin paraphernalia laid out on our little table. Something told me that my evening had just begun.

From within the net draped bed, Camille said anxiously, "Been waitin' on you. How'd it go? 'Cause I fergot to tell you about his problem. Gotta suck his joy stick hard 'n stroke it at the same time . . . ." She must have seen the anger on my face because she stopped talking and pushed aside the mosquito netting and plopped her bare feet onto the concrete floor. "Don't strain your milk, girl. That shit ain't fer you."

"What's it doing here?"

"Them girls been carryin' on somethin' fierce down there. They's all purty and got good prospects so Belhaj don't want no more bruises. We gotta do somethin' to settle 'em down."

"I would never, ever, do something like that. And I don't understand why you would either if it's true that you came through that pit."

"I told you why."

"Please, help me understand why you are so fucking compliant."

"Hmmm, well let me see. Oh, that's right. I got myself a slew of options. After I get myself mutilated, maybe an ear 'r two lopped off, you 'n me 'r gonna escape with our knights 'n shinin' armor back to the U.S. of A. You'll rehabilitate my backwoods talk 'n trashy-sorry ways so I can go to brain surgery school." She had walked over to me and was drumming her fingers on the block of heroin as if to punch holes in it.

"I accept you as you are."

"If you did, you'd have to accept the fact that yer in bed with a connivin' whore that does whatever I gotta do to stay alive 'n protect myself." Her words were somewhat garbled, because as she talked she absentmindedly stroked her fingertips over her gums to rub in any residual heroin that might have been deposited onto her fingers. I understood then that no amount of trauma could erase the frugal sensibilities of a junkie's heart.

"So you're the biggest slut in the universe," I half shouted. "I have every intention of getting out of here and taking you and Zarina with me, even if I have to drag you."

She laughed. "Dude, picture me 'n you back 'n the States. 'Everbody, this here's my friend. Me 'n her turned tricks together 'n India.'"

I slapped her hard across the face. It shut her up, but the second I did it, I knew that I could not take it back. I picked up the heroin and rushed out of the room.

In the relative silence of the garden there was only the crackling of the flames in the mali's tin barrel. I stood there hypnotized by the inferno. The heroin was enough to keep a habit for a long time . . . or kill myself. "I will find a way out," I said aloud. "I will find a way out." I tossed the block into the fire and stood back watching a gaseous mushroom cloud billow, dissipating very slowly into the wet, black sky. The fire exploded and blazed. I breathed in the burning narcotic and felt a warm rush flow dangerously through me and experienced the sensation of my brain deliriously softening. A breeze began to blow, sucking the cloud of heroin upward and I staggered backwards, suddenly aware of the narcotic's stealthy effect on me. I walked around the garden, taking in deep breaths of the muggy night air to clear my head. All I wanted to do now was go back and apologize to Camille. I had to get her on my side if I had any hope of getting to those girls before another one died.

When I went back to the room, Camille was lying on her bed with her back to the door. "Are you asleep?" I whispered. A small movement of her body indicated that she was still awake. "I'm sorry."

She didn't reply and after a while I thought she might have fallen asleep. I stood by her bed watching her, thinking about what it must be like to be her. She accepted whatever situation she found herself in, and then made the best of it. I found myself admiring her, wishing that I could be more like her. I wanted to lie down next to her and put my arm around her to feel her body rising and falling with each life-giving breath, to feel the closeness of her. But before I could lift my knee to scoot onto the bed, the door smashed open and Belhaj marched inside. His face was trancelike, his lips drawn into a scowl, his eyes dark, pupils dilated. He shoved me aside and I fell as he tore at the mosquito netting, breathing noisily like a mad bull. Camille awakened groggy and confused. He dragged her out of bed by her long blonde hair.

"Ow. Shit." She hit the floor. He dragged her out of the room, her feet floundering, bicycling for purchase.

"Stop!" I shouted. I followed them to the door but it closed, and locked so that I could only hear the muffled sounds of Camille begging. I banged against the door, yelling, "Please don't hurt her. Hurt me! *Hurt me, for God's sake*!"

Camille's cries were further away, and I knew that Belhaj had no intention of switching gears. It was one of those moments in life when you feel like jelly and your body can't do anything but fall onto the floor like a helpless blob, and that is what I did, bursting into tears. I had not cried in way too long and now I needed the outlet. I needed just to sit there and sob helplessly to purge my system of all the angst, anxiety about Zarina, the horror of seeing the raped and beaten girls in the dungeon, of what I did to the acid burned girl, or being raped again myself, and now my fear for Camille. It was all too much to bear, yet there was nothing else I could do but weep.

After a while I calmed down. Bollywood music, distant screams, grunts, moans and other animalistic noises came from the street. I put off taking the shower and instead waited for Camille. I stood on the chair to look out of the window. A feral cat sat on top of the barbed wired wall with a lifeless bird under its paw. The cat, momentarily distracted from its prey, watched me back. He was black with a white chest and it reminded me of my father's body laid out with a black suit and white shirt and tie before the cremation. Although my father did not attend mass, nor was he big on the Catholic Church in his later years, the funeral director had folded his hands over rosary beads and a missal. Then I pictured the memorial ceremony I had planned with the white rose petals flowing with gentle determination in a course charted by the currents of the Ganges. My thoughts shifted to survival. If I could get the cat over to the window I could attach a note around its neck. The cat began to eat its dinner, the bird's body snapping between its jaws. "Meow," I called in a high alluring voice. "Meow, meow, meow." The cat ignored me.

The lock turning startled me. Camille was tossed inside the room and I scrambled off the chair to help her up from the gritty concrete floor. One of her eyes was swollen, the lid a purple slit. She fingered her nose, mashed against the side of her face.

"Can you fix my nose? I think it's broke."

"Oh my God, what did he do to you?" I lifted her chin to see her face.

Camille curled her tongue, licking at the stream of blood. "Already told you. You gotta suck and stroke. Otherwise the onliest way he can git it up is by maulin' 'n rapin'. And there's also that little matter of burnin' up his brick."

"I'm sorry. I didn't realize he would take it out on you."

"Yer really a piece a work."

"I know. I'm sorry. Do you have a needle and thread?"

She went to her suitcase and rummaged, then handed me a hotel sewing kit.

"What about the Valium that was in the pill box Paul gave me? Do you have any left?"

She dug in her bag and handed me a tissue. "Can you get ice?"

"Just git on with it."

"All right then. Lie down," I said. In a medical setting she would be referred to an ENT. It wasn't optimal to attempt to set a nose while it was swollen. But Camille wasn't going to have the luxury of seeing a specialist. My hands trembled as I shook out the small blue tablets into my palm.

"I'm ready," Camille said, but then added, "This is gonna hurt, ain't it?"

"Here," I said, unfurling the tissue. "Take four of these and chew them." I handed Camille the pills and she obeyed, chewing.

I examined her face. "The eye that's swollen shut will go down in a day or two." Camille had a wound along her collarbone. "What did he hit you with?"

"Threw me against the dresser drawers."

"Lucky you missed your larynx. You're going to need a few stitches or it'll heal badly." She was an unnerving sight with her nose flattened. "You can cry, just let it out."

"Nah, I ain't gonna cry for his benefit. Just makes 'em wanna hurt you more. Can you fix my nose 'r not?"

"I'm not sure I can set your nose until the swelling goes down."

"How long will that take?"

"At least a couple of days."

"Best do it now before he get a notion to separate us, 'n he might, just to make sure I stay ugly fer good."

"Take some deep breaths," I told her as I put my hand on Camille's chest. "I want you to breathe with me, together now, come on." I took a breath and felt Camille's chest rise. "Another." We breathed together for five minutes. I felt Camille's lungs expand and the tops of her breasts swell under my palm. I closed my eyes and breathed out, letting her catch the rhythm of my breath. I needed a few minutes to gather my courage, too. It was a small thing, setting a nose, stitching a wound. But I was nervous, imagining how a poorly set nose would mar such beauty. Camille's nose was ballooning and I would be lucky to get it in place. But Camille was right, I had to do it now. I readied myself. Camille seemed calmer. "One more huge breath." Camille inhaled and as she exhaled I pulled her nose swiftly up. The cartilage crunching was audible. Camille cried out and reached for her nose, but I intercepted her hands and held them. "Don't touch. Just lie still."

"Stung real good." I thought she might cry, but she remained steely and composed. "Sorry about what I said, you know, earlier. I know the difference between hookin' 'n rape."

"I'm sorry too, for what I said. Truly sorry."

"Sticks 'n stones'll break my bones but names'll never hurt me."

"But I did hurt you! Please accept my apology. You're a better person than any of the brain surgeons I've ever met."

She hiccupped a sigh but still didn't cry. I remembered the bathhouse when she told me that she cried herself to sleep, but I'd never actually seen her shed a tear.

"I'm going to stitch you up. It's not going to hurt that much, okay?" I selected a sharp from the sewing kit, but it took me a few minutes to guide a strand of white sewing thread through the needle's eye.

Camille shut her good eye. The lashes of her bruised eye clumped together. Her face was smeared with blood and mucous. I only had a rag from the W.C. to clean her up. As I wiped, a galaxy of freckles appeared across Camille's cheeks and nose, collected in childhood but faded with time, visible again now that blood had drained from her face. I dabbed around the wound. "OK, here we go. Just a pinprick." I guided the needle through the tear in her skin along her clavicle. Camille flinched. "Why don't you tell me about your home. It'll take your mind off what I'm doing."

Camille started talking, as if reciting as I pulled the thread through. "Mama and Daddy was the nicest folks you ever wanna meet. Bet they wonder what happened to their purty little girl." She laughed bitterly.

"Here's another stick," I warned.

Camille's good eye looked down, straining to see the needle, but she remained still, almost stiff. Two stitches were finished, then the third stitch was in place. I knew that Camille was talking but I felt immersed in the procedure as I pulled a fourth stitch through neatly, and shifted on my knees. I stuck Camille again and again. I put in fourteen more stitches. "I'm almost finished. You're doing great." I tied a knot. A long white thread hung down across Camille's neck. "If the wound heals well you might only have a hair-line scar." I leaned close to Camille and found the thread with my tongue, then severed it between my front teeth. I pulled back, the thread hanging from my lips, then spit it onto the floor, wondering if I could get that mali to bring us some alcohol.

Camille was wistful now. "Saved up my own money workin' three jobs to buy me a ticket on the Internet." Then her attitude changed and she got off the bed and started mugging a catwalk. "Got me a ticket all the way to Tokyo, Jae-pan." She struck a model's pose. "Whaddya think?"

"Don't."

"Ta da! Lookie at what Eunice and Jimbo's little girl made a herself." She laughed a fake laugh and then said incredulously, "I got here *babysittin*!"

I sat there, stone-faced.

From Belhaj's quarters came the sound of opera. "I swear that man can't hear hisself think," said Camille. She stomped her foot on the wooden door. "Turn that noise off, will you?" she yelled. This brazenness struck me as funny and I laughed. Camille giggled. I laughed harder. Camille grabbed her stomach, laughing. Then we started stress laughing, uncontrollably, falling into each other's arms. I could see that Camille was struggling not to cry now. I lay down next to her and took her in my arms. Her skin felt clammy, little beads of perspiration dribbling down from her forehead. Camille's eye had puffed out further; the skin looked smooth and shiny blue, like a baby bird's eye. Her nose had burgeoned and was pulsing with blood. The wound across her clavicle was Frankenstein-like against her white skin. But she was drowsy from the Valium and looked like she might sleep.

I got up, feeling antsy. I climbed onto the chair to look out. On the windowsill beyond lay two tiny bird feet and a few feathers, where the cat had finished its dinner. The street was mostly abandoned and some of the lights were off, but this was Mumbai, a city that did not ever fully go to sleep. I climbed down and sat on the chair, conscious of the tightness across my shoulders. I picked up the paperback *Gita*. The first page read, *On earth there is no purifier as great as this knowledge* . . . . I closed my eyes and started thinking about Paul, how hard we worked but then how carefree we really were. All the trips we took together. Telluride to ski. Calistoga to the mud baths. Hawaii for surfing lessons. New York for the theater. I wanted to stay at the W but he liked the Plaza even though he admitted the inherited-wealth-of-the-upper-crust décor was a little too precious. I visualized the foyer of the Plaza hotel so clearly it was as if it were my reality. It was incredible that people were actually there right now without a care in the world.

They were passing by the mammoth flower arrangements without thinking of girls in cages who were being raped tonight. I put myself there, at the Plaza, walking over the miles of gleaming marble that paved the way to an open tea room where white tablecloths, crystal stemware, and polished silver-adorned tables. I sat down among the rich European tapestries, overflowing cornucopias, carts of pastries, berries out of season, beveled mirrors in Baroque frames, bronze statuary, priceless antiques, and crystal chandeliers. I would order tea and have a scone . . . .

"Stop it, Deva!" Camille grabbed me by the shoulders and pulled me away from the wall. "Yer gonna break yer head open if you keep on bangin' on it like that."

I snapped out of my trance. "Don't call me that. If you can't call me by my real name, don't call me anything."

"Thank you for fixin' my nose. But you best not get too many ideas. This is the way it is."

FIFTEEN

Along with my own troubled thoughts the rhythmic white noise from the oscillating fan masked the tormented screams from beyond the compound. With the help of the fan, I managed a sound night's sleep and felt a welcomed surge of vitality the following morning when I rose from the rope bed. Meditating on my mantra, I sipped a cup of the sweet chai the servant girl brought us. Finished with the tea and the contemplation, I gave myself three more days to rescue Zarina from the clutches of the deranged madam, and to spring the kidnapped girls from the hellhole. I may have gone on indefinitely, but was interrupted from further heroic fantasies by Camille, who paced the cramped room as she puffed on one cigarette after another, muttering under her breath, "Fuck, fuck, fuck."

The smoke blasted out of her nostrils like smoke signals.

Her spoken anxiety echoed my own sense of doom, not only about Zarina but for the young women awaiting their fate unawares. My own isolation in the darkness, the terror and uncertainty fresh in my mind and worrying myself into heart palpitations, I couldn't stop obsessing about the girls.

Adding to my anxiety, the door was locked again and so I could not get the medical supplies Belhaj promised he'd let me have for the girls. "You have more freedom than I do. You have to figure out a way to get out so you can take care of the girls down in that pit," I demanded after we passed two days in confinement. "They need fresh water, food, aspirin. That bucket needs to be cleaned out."

"Can't promise somethin' like that." She pouted.

"They'll die down there."

"No," she said definitively. "They ain't gonna let them die. They just wants to break 'em, that's all. It don't seem like it but there's ventilation 'n the rain cools things off a bit." As the day passed in the stuffy room, I feared Mrs. Pawar and Belhaj were going to keep us imprisoned indefinitely as punishment for my escapade with the brick of heroin. Then the key turned in the lock on our door and there stood the servant girl, with her head down and I knew what she wanted. Camille sneered as I followed the girl out of the room.

Every night from then on Belhaj raped me. When I was with him, I was afraid to bring up the subject of the girls again because after the heroin business there was no more talk. He just raped me and pushed me back out of his room.

During the day, the hours dragged by endlessly. I had nothing to do but shower endlessly under the cold water spray or read my copy of the *Bhagavad Gita*. I got it in my mind to attempt to clean the W.C. with the scrub brush and the left over ammonia that Camille had used to sanitize the floor during my withdrawal. My obsession with hygiene got on Camille's nerves.

On the fourth day when I rose from the bed and picked up the brush and the bottle of ammonia, she just looked at me, nodding her head. "Them fumes could bring tears to a glass eye."

She sat at the table going about her ritual. I watched her as she fiddled in her bag. Her pillowy lips formed a little O of concentration as she peeled back a bit of newspaper from a tiny package. Inside was the tarry lump that looked like mummified shit, thus the moniker. Running low on cigarettes, she resorted to spearing a bit of hashish with a safety pin, then lighting it with a match. She held the burning hash close to her puckered lips and sucked the yellow smoke into her lungs. After escaping into a tetrahydrocannabinol stupor, Camille squirted toothpaste into her mouth and sprawled onto the rope bed chewing it like cud as she browsed the month old *People* magazine I had used to splat mosquitoes against the wall.

"Doesn't swallowing that make you nauseous?" I asked, annoyed.

"My mouth is dry enough to spin cotton, 'n it's minty."

Although Camille didn't seem as bothered by the heat or the boredom, I didn't enjoy lounging as it was completely foreign to me, and I also found that idleness only allowed more time for disturbing thoughts to invade my mind. It was as if time had stopped and the longer we remained at the Pawar's the more stagnant my soul. I was transported by my inability to deal with my trauma and the inertia of India, into a place where time no longer mattered. Camille's resentment made matters even worse. I'd patched her up to the best of my abilities in our crude situation and I kept my eye on her wounds. But aside from the occasional comment she would have nothing more to do with me. As the ironies of all ironies, she held a grudge against me for Belhaj's fondness for raping me.

Five days into our incarceration, we heard Belhaj's voice penetrating the thick stucco wall of our cell. He was outside our room, speaking loudly, the way people do on mobile phones.

"What is he saying?" I asked, as Camille spoke French.

"He's got a buyer."

"He's going to sell the women together?"

"Could be an auctioneer or a private sale, can't tell." She

listened and then when his voice grew dimmer she said more somberly, "Shippin' them off today."

"Where?"

"Don't know. Saudi, maybe. Tokyo. I ain't sure 'cause they goes to a middle man first."

It seemed the worst day of my life. Losing the girls was a shock because, idealistic as it sounded, I really thought we could do something.

That night, after raping me, Belhaj wanted me to stay. He seemed to crave pillow talk, like I was his real lover. He lay naked in bed, one arm cradling his head, the other holding a smoldering cigarette. I kept quiet and let him talk. "Oh là, là, my *goolies* are going smaller," he said, flipping his grape-sized testicles. "What I make for this?"

I had to think fast. Sociopaths were only drawn to people who could offer them something, and, as the alternative was untenable, I wanted to keep B. lhaj believing that I had something he wanted. He was in denial about the acrogmegaly causing his impotence, and I was not going to bring it up ever again, even if he asked me about it. He'd been self-medicating with the testosterone injections, and his hair loss was not his only problem. An artificial bump in testosterone shuts off production of natural testosterone, leaving the testicles to lie dormant, and his had subsequently atrophied. If he had had been treated by a doctor, he would have been put on cycled gonadotropin to encourage his own testosterone production. I was in a bind, because first there was nothing he could do to reverse the damage he'd already done, and second, if I told this psychopath he had shrunk his testicles out of stupidity, he might put my eye out with his cigarette. All I could do was what women do when they want to take men's minds off a topic.

After an hour of fellatio I could see that he felt more like a man, preening and stretching on the bed. "I detest zis India. Zee heat, zee mosquitoes, so much filth. Zee poor people. *Déplorable.*"

It seemed I had something in common with my rapist, though outside of the heat, mosquitoes, and germs, I thought that I would have fallen in love with India given a chance to experience it beyond the walls of the brothel compound. I almost kept quiet, but then asked impetuously, "Where will you go next?"

He studied me, as if he knew I was sleuthing, and I cringed internally, reliving the day he told me not to play him; but I kept my eyes locked on his, batting my eyes slowly and smiling innocently. "Not Istanbul. We are finished there."

I held my breath.

"*Help me, help me. I am zee American doctor,*" he mimicked in a high, piercing voice. Vadim *had* told him! Belhaj didn't smile and I held my face impassively, waiting. My terror was complete. In just one instant I imagined all the ways in which he would torture me, and then kill me. But he just laughed as if he found the whole escapade of my attempted escape in Istanbul amusing. "Perhaps we go back to São Paulo. *La Brazilian femme*, uuhh." He grunted a sexually explicit noise of delight.

"Brazil is hot, and has poverty, and mosquitoes," I said flatly, taking insolence to a dangerous level.

"In winter, zee weather is good. Okay. You win." He reached over and stroked my cheek with the back of his index finger. "You are not breaking so easy." I didn't reply, but let him talk, hoping he would say something I wanted to hear. "Nasreen is beautiful woman, but you are more my type," he said, drawing me near and kissing me on the lips. "I get rid of her. She is, how you Americans say, zee drama queen."

"I would like it if she stayed," I blurted, then immediately tried to look blasé. "She keeps me company."

He reached over to his nightstand and downed the rest of a glass of his Pernod. Then he lit a cigarette, belching smoke forcefully out of his nostrils. "As you wish. But nothing is forever."

"It would be nice to have Zarina back with us, too," I added breathlessly, hoping I hadn't gone too far.

He shrugged, puffing. "You women with your children."

Just then we both heard Mrs. Pawar in her garden, singing along to a Bollywood tune in a painfully flamboyant operatic voice.

"I think we go soon. *Oui, Brazi*l."

He jerked his head and I rose from the bed and dressed quickly. Belhaj had picked up a TV remote and was channel surfing through American cable channels. Without saying goodnight, I left his room.

The servant girl was waiting for me at the bottom of the steps. "Thank you," I said, as she unlocked our door. The girl waited for me to enter. I heard the padlock slip, then saw that Camille was still awake, sitting in the dark, just the glow of her cigarette lighting a small space around her face as she dragged on it. The acrid smoke was thick in the room and so I knew she had been up fretting for hours. Camille continued puffing on her bidi, not saying a word, just sitting there in a cloud of spiraling smoke.

I brushed my teeth with her precious toothpaste and showered. When I came back into the room I flipped on the light switch and a single light bulb hanging from a cord on the ceiling blasted the room with light.

Camille crushed out the primitive cigarette into a tin ashtray and folded her arms over her chest. "Thought you were gonna be my role model, but I guess not."

"I don't know what you want from me. You're the one who told me I had to go along." I struggled with the knowledge that Belhaj wanted to sell her off, and then take me to Brazil. I wanted to tell her, but I was too exhausted. I needed to rest, and then we would talk. "I should take out your stitches before they leave indelible scars."

"If I want yer opinion, I'll ask you to fill out the necessary form," she said peevishly, picking up her magazine and strumming furiously through it.

"I know you're pissed off at me, but don't take it out on yourself. You're the one who said you didn't want to be uglier than a bucket full of armpits. So where are your nail clippers?"

She acquiesced, swinging her long legs off the bed and stomping over to her bag like a disgruntled adolescent, where she rummaged for her nail clippers and then flung them at me petulantly. She flopped back down on the bed, her arms crossed over her chest.

"I would not let anyone come between you and me, ever," I said as I snipped out the stitches.

"Yer just sayin' that."

"No, I'm not. I will never leave you. I told you that."

Her scar was going to be ugly, but I consoled myself that I would someday introduce Camille to a world-class plastic surgeon I knew in Beverly Hills. I felt my jaw harden with determination. I lay down next to her and soon she drifted off to sleep. I was too wired to relax. It reminded me of the feeling I had during my internship, when I was beyond exhausted yet too worked up to get to sleep, thinking about my patients and all the doctors and other medical staff I had dealings with on the previous shift. I watched the fan revolve, thinking about the hospital and how the other residents were going forward with their careers. Here I was on the subcontinent of India in the most unbelievable situation.

"Why don't you git yerself some rest?" Camille asked sleepily.

"I can't sleep, and when I do I have nightmares."

She turned and wrapped her arms around me. "I'm gonna keep them nightmares away."

I settled into Camille's arms, allowing myself the closeness of another human being. And then I slept.

The next day, the servant girl brought the girl back to our room. Zarina was determined to show off the teddy bear the madam had bought for her. "He's mine, 'n you can't touch him!"

"Hush yer trap, girl. Deva can play with that bear if she wants to."

"It's okay, Zarina. I can admire him from afar. Besides he looks so comfy with you."

"Cause I'm purty, 'n I'm nice."

"It ain't polite to tell folks yer cuter than all get out, smarty pants."

We were both anxious to find out what happened during Zarina's tenure with the madam. Camille was savvy enough to couch it in terms that would not scare the little girl. "Tell us all about them games you played with Mrs. Pawar," she asked casually.

"No games."

"What did you do then, all them days?"

"Nothing." She played with her teddy for a few minutes then said, "We went visitin' her brothers."

"Really? How many brothers does she have?"

Zarina held up one hand. *Five.*

"Where did they live?"

"Great big houses. Big purty houses."

"That's nice, Zarina."

She nodded but added solemnly, "They's all *sick*!"

Camille and I exchanged stressed-out glances.

Zarina's face was flushed, her hair damp. "I want thith off." She tried to pull her blouse over her head.

"What do you say?"

"Pleath, Mama," she said, probing the depths of her nose with her finger.

I did a double take. When did Zarina start calling Camille Mama? The girl needed a mother, but I felt unsure. Shouldn't we try to return her to her birth mother when we got out of here? I felt a catch in my throat.

Camille undressed Zarina. The girl stood naked except for the multi-colored bead necklaces and the bangle bracelets. "I want a thower," she demanded. Shards of light reflected on the walls from her iridescent glass bracelets as she stood with her hands on her hips, like a little dictator, then whined, "Pleath." Serrated tips of her permanent teeth probed their way tenaciously through her gums and she ran her tongue over them as if to scratch an itch.

Camille led her to the W.C., and turned on the spray so that it came out in a gentle stream.

I wondered if Zarina had originally been procured for some wealthy freak who was smitten with AIDS or some other terminal sexually transmitted disease. Camille had used her wiles on Belhaj who had agreed to allow her to keep Zarina. But now all bets were off as Mrs. Pawar was hearing the jingle of the cash register every time she looked at the little girl.

While Zarina was in the shower, Camille came back

"Mrs. Pawar's shopping Zarina's virginity out to the highest bidder," I said.

"No, she ain't. She's shoppin' her out to all five of 'em."

"What?"

"The highest bidder will rape her and she'll scream. He'll see blood on the sheets and feel all warm 'n fuzzy about gettin' his cure. Then you, the famous doctor, will sew her up inside, so's the second one'll also get a screamin' 'n bleedin' show for his money. When she's done the five a them, Mrs. Pawar will shop her to other rich men with sex diseases. When Zarina's dog meat, they'll have you hack her up fer her organs. Kid organs fetch a purty penny."

I was speechless.

"I don't have to tell you what they'll do to you if you don't cooperate." Darkness fell over her features.

The lock on the door rattled and then the door swung open on its noisy hinges. Mrs. Pawar's humble servant girl spoke in Marathi to Camille. "Mrs. Pawar wants you," Camille said.

She went to get the girl out of the shower. I would talk with Camille as soon as I got back to the room. I needed to approach the subject carefully, so she didn't completely freak out. Still, she needed to know that Zarina was not the only one in immediate peril. With both of their lives in danger, Camille would have the motivation to overcome her fears and to cast her considerable ingenuity and resources in with mine to help formulate an escape plan.

Before I left the room I took a Valium out of the tissue and put it in the pocket of my salwar kameez pajama like trousers. Then the girl ushered me down the garden path where Mrs. Pawar sat at breakfast in a patio area in front of her house, her enormous buttocks blimping over the sides of the chair. I stood there at attention, worried about what she wanted from me. I waited for such a long time, shifting from foot to foot, that I began wondering if she registered my presence when she finally wiped her swollen lips with a tattered linen napkin, and spoke.

"And so Doctor Deva, I vill be having the prescription for the pharmacist you so promised me for my constipation." She handed me a pad of recycled paper and a pencil.

As we were calling this scribbling on an ordinary piece of paper a "prescription," I decided to order Bisacodyl, a toxic laxative that's used to empty the bowels before procedures. Bisacodyl irritates sensory nerve endings and mucosa in the gut to stimulate peristalsis. It carries a high risk of causing atonic colon, which means that the colon loses normal reflex activity and from that point on the only way to avoid a chronically impacted colon would be to use an irritant laxative on an ongoing basis. Even with these risks, I wanted to make sure that she got the relief she so desired. I would worry about any side effect later. Best get her habituated to any and all drugs so that I could have a chance of controlling her.

"Vhat is this?" she asked suspiciously, as she reviewed the so-called prescription and absently fingered a plate of jalebi, deep fried batter in pretzel shapes soaked in syrup that were the consistency and color of earwax. She eyed me suspiciously as she forced an entire jalebi into her mouth.

"It's a commonly prescribed medication for people with your condition," I said, feigning concern as I surreptitiously inspected her breakfast of Indian desserts. Stale leftovers were occasionally brought to our room, dubious relief from the eyeball melting curries we usually got. The fried crap would kill her eventually, but not soon enough to save us. She broke off a piece of stuffed paratha, a flat bread fried in ghee, and shoved that into her mouth too as her bloodshot eyes roamed my face.

"It's an effective, yet gentle cathartic," I lied, worrying now about the possibility of projectile diarrhea in the middle of the night.

She munched a bite of a fried dough-round, called puri, and while chewing she spooned into a block of halvah, a pistachio confection. She shoveled a blob into her mouth and washed it all down with a cup of sweet lassi, the yogurt drink.

"You might also add prunes to your breakfast."

Her lips pursed like the prunes I'd suggested as she inhaled liquidly. Her face blanched. Drool dribbled out of her mouth down her chin as she clutched her throat, where a massive mouthful of her sweet breakfast treats had apparently lodged into her trachea and was obstructing her breathing. She lumbered off her chair and began to stumble about, her arms flailing the air like prizefighter jabs, which I did not want to encounter. If I allowed her to asphyxiate, hypoxia—inadequate oxygenation of the brain—would only take about five minutes. Cerebral hypoxia would leave her in a vegetative state. Given her obesity and numerous medical conditions, it might also lead to cardiac arrest. But I could not take the chance of being blamed for not trying to save her.

"Mrs. Pawar, calm down, I'm going to clear your airway," I said loudly, with the dead calm necessary in hysterical situations.

But she was too panicked to hear me, and continued to flounder. By now a group of servants had collected, and Mr. Pawar had run down the marble steps from the house.

"She's choking," I explained. "I need her to remain still so that I can help her".

Mr. Pawar latched onto one of her forearms like a monkey hanging for dear life onto the jungle branches that swayed in the monsoon. He managed to talk her down from her panic. I don't know what he said but her body stopped moving around, while her eyes darted to and fro, reflecting mortal skepticism.

The back slap is the protocol of choice among knowledgeable practitioners as the Heimlich maneuver can cause serious abdominal injuries and broken ribs. The percussion of the back slap creates pressure behind the blockage, causing enough vibration to assist the patient in dislodging the obstruction. But several pounding smacks with a clenched fist did nothing. I mounted her from behind but she was too huge and I could not get my arms around her ribcage. I circled to the front of her and shouted, "Bend forward at your waist, just a little, Mrs. Pawar."

She obeyed, fear bulging her eyes. I clenched my left hand into a fist and placed it in the center of her chest, and with my right hand jammed, hard. I repeated the thrusts several times and finally a blob of dough propelled from her mouth, splatting on my foot like a giant glob of warm mucous. She melted at her waist, gasping. Mr. Pawar knelt to catch her tears tenderly in his palms, kissing her fat cheeks, and then leading her back to rest upon her chair at the breakfast table. They spoke in Marathi and though I couldn't understand the words, his tenderness was apparent.

Finally, she said, "I have recovered, Vachspati."

He smiled, relief plumping his taut features and tears springing to *his* eyes.

"Now I shall finish my breakfast."

He snapped his fingers. "Hot *chai*!" And the servants ran off.

"You are busy, Vachspati. Go. Go."

"I cannot be leaving you in such a state as this, Shabana."

"I am in the care of Doctor Deva. Ve shant be vorrying.

He hesitated.

"Get to your vork, and leave me," she commanded darkly.

His face blanched, but he obeyed, rising from a supplicant kneeling position at her side and departing, humiliation twisting his features as he walked down the garden path in the direction of the foyer door that led to the dungeon. I hoped he wouldn't take his mortification out on the captive girls.

"If you are such a distinguished doctor, then you must be curing my insomnia as vell," Mrs. Pawar said to me, reaching for a fresh cup of tea delivered by one of her girls.

Her lack of gratitude was one for the books, as they say, but I kept quiet, realizing that her entitlement was part and parcel of her sociopath/narcissistic personality disorder. My lips curled into a fake smile and I wiped a slick of moisture off my upper lip before replying. I thought of all the ways I would like to permanently cure her insomnia. But if I just wanted her to sleep and not to die I could knock her out easily. Suggesting flunitrazepam was out of the question as she undoubtedly had used it on girls she abducted. It made me wonder why she hadn't tried it herself, but then I guessed that with her limited medical knowledge she most likely didn't realize that the "date-rape" drug was actually a legitimate medication intended for therapeutic purposes, namely to treat recalcitrant insomnia. I had to think of something else that wouldn't scare her, a potent, highly addictive drug that I could experiment with on her to get her habituated.

"Yes, of course," I said, taking back the scrap and writing on it *100 mg phenobarbital, #150.* Since she was the weight of three normal women I suggested she try three before bedtime. "You don't want to take the laxative at night if you're taking sleeping pills," I said, trying to convey urgency in my voice so that it would penetrate the pleasure she was experiencing in munching on another piece of puri. I could see she wasn't registering and so I added, "Unless you're planning on wearing a diaper to bed?"

She swallowed. "A *vhat*?"

"Take the laxative in the morning when you wake up."

"I see."

"Buy a blood pressure cuff too," I said to the servant girl, casting a quick glance at her, conspiratorially mumbling, "Large circumference," hoping she understood. "And we'll get a glucose meter too. We need to monitor your *acute hypoglycemia* closely." Mrs. Pawar's eyes lit like dancing flames at the mention of one of her pet infirmities.

Mrs. Pawar spoke briefly and harshly to the girl in Marathi, and when she was finished hammering her orders into the "girl's feeble head," the servant folded her hands in namaste and flitted happily away from the huge madam, down the garden path. "Ve vill see," Mrs. Pawar said to me, her eyes now like the storm clouds that threatened us once again. "Ve vill see." She scraped her chair back from the table and rose. "My sciatica," she groaned, wincing. "The assault of your fists has set off an attack. Oh dear, I must be getting comfortable in my parlor."

I trailed her up the marble steps, through an archway, past a stone elephant god garlanded with marigolds, into an open-air parlor decorated in a Victorian Raj style. The royal blue and maroon velvet sofas, settees and divans were beyond shabby, the velvet pile having worn out and showing patches of bald cotton fabric. The veneered side tables, coffee tables, chests of drawers were peeling and moldy. The Oriental rugs were threadbare, the fringe grimy and tangled. The potted houseplants were riddled with mites and mealybugs like little white tufts of cotton. It reminded me of the moldering old-money décor of some East coast blueblood's homes, a bygone moribund style that some people just could not let go of.

Behind the parlor grouping of sofas and settees stood a grand desk upon which sat a laptop, a printer and fax, and a huge black telephone from another century. My laptop was long gone, but I knew Paul's email address. If I could just get in here some night when the Pawars were sleeping. The security within the compound was lax given the high walls. During the monsoon storms all the servants disappeared, either because they were dismissed or because they took it upon themselves to take their own leave to attend to their families. *Some night*, I thought, *I will sneak into this room*.

While Mrs. Pawar got situated on a sofa, one of her servants brought in an oxidized sterling tray set with more tea and cakes, and another removed her rubber Bata sandals and propped her scaly, toadstool feet onto a needlepoint footstool, I scanned a salon grouping of framed photographs. The first one was of two children, ostensibly Mrs. Pawar and her brother standing in front of a school. She wore a pleated blue and black plaid shirt and white blouse, white knee socks against brown knee caps. He wore gray flannel shorts and a white, short-sleeved dress shirt. He stood with his arm draped over one of her skinny shoulders, his fingers creeping like tentacles across one cheek. He was taller than she then, though he had been chubby as a boy. She had had extremely exaggerated features, oversized eyes, giant fleshy nose, piano key teeth, overly plump lips, a cleft chin, which gave her a gawky and strange appearance, like an alien being.

My eyes traveled to other photos and I saw that Mrs. Pawar's exaggerated features had purposefully mellowed with puberty and adulthood resulting in the ingredients for striking beauty. From within various shots, Mrs. Pawar blinked seductively, age twenty or so, weighing in at one hundred fifteen pounds, a tall, willowy girl with breasts like melons, eyes like the turbulent Arabian Sea, hair falling like the black veil of night over one shoulder. She wore form-fitting saris that wound around her frame with the same ultra eroticism of the famed Kama Sutra sculptures. She was adorned with exquisite jewelry: an intricate necklace of emeralds and gold, diamond chandelier earrings, and the small fortune in gold bangles she still had on her wrists. She held a hint of a smirk on her vermillion lips and a smoldering Gauloise between her crimson-lacquered fingertips as she sat among groups of attentive, ogling men at tables set with white linen, overflowing glass ashtrays, French wine bottles and stemmed glasses of red wine. Waiters in long white aprons wrapped around their hips filled glasses, served plates of steak and *pomme frites*, and stood at attention in the background.

Then I noticed that Belhaj was the man who claimed the honored seat next to her in every photograph. He was in his twenties, sexy, with thick black hair tumbling over his forehead, the cleanly square jaw, the handsome flashing, white-toothed smile. In one shot Belhaj leaned toward her laughing, the dashing ruffian with the shock of black hair tumbling jauntily over one eye. She laughed too, a single tear having escaped prettily from the clutches of her false eyelashes. I searched the photos quickly but could not recognize Mr. Pawar or her brother, Chandraram. No, it had just been her, forging out into the Western world alone.

I turned slowly to look at her, fussing over her tea tray, her girl lighting a fresh cigarette for her as she slurped a cup of sweetened tea, the cup clattering into the saucer. Though morbid obesity obscures defining characteristics, turning people into anonymous moon-pies with Mr. Potato features, there was no doubt in my mind that the breathtaking woman in the photos was the vulgar monstrosity sprawled precariously before me on a groaning dilapidated sofa. Mrs. Pawar had been a dazzling beauty. Then it dawned on me. Mrs. Pawar didn't start out in the business as a madam. First she had been a high priced Parisian call girl. Then something had happened that had caused this tragic metamorphosis.

"I shall be having a complete physical examination," Mrs. Pawar exclaimed, oblivious to my investigation of the photographs. "Please be providing a detailed inventory of the medical supplies you vill be needing to conduct such an assessment of my health."

I stared at her for a moment, and then my eyes shifted to the tea tray that held the nauseous chai brew of which I could never drink another cup and it would be one cup too many. I remained immobilized, staring glumly at the tea tray. All I could think of was how very much I would love to have a cappuccino with frothy milk and two lumps of sugar. At that moment, the reality that I could *not* have my silly cappuccino was emblematic of my plight. And I think it was then that the determination solidified inside me. I squelched the burning desire for Italian coffee and replied, "Of course."

The servant handed me a notepad upon which I began to jot down a lengthy list. Then I could hardly contain my glee, realizing that Mrs. Pawar was playing right into my hands. There she sat, smoking like the condemned, while I itemized my inventory. I finished writing down everything I thought necessary for my exam, including Vacutainers, with which I would draw copious amounts of blood, have it analyzed and then scare the living shit out of her with blood sugar numbers that were guaranteed to be off the charts. Next I'd order insulin. I could find my way out of the compound with enough insulin filled syringes in my possession as an overdose of the hormone reduces blood glucose to a level that starves the brain of necessary sugar, resulting in hypoglycemic coma, and death. I handed her the list.

"I am assuming you vill be including the female examination?"

"Yes."

"I can confide in you prior to the probe, that I am suffering from the plague of leakage."

"Urinary incontinence?" Flames raced up her cheeks providing my answer. I sunk to the settee in front of her and rested my hand on hers. "When you sneeze?"

"Yes, but sometimes the leakage is happening vhen I merely set eyes upon the loo."

"How many pregnancies have you had?"

Her head wove almost imperceptibly, like the gamblers' tell. A single tear slid from the same eye as the one in the photograph. She sucked in her lips to quell her emotions. She'd been pregnant, but had had abortions.

"No babies?"

"None."

But a lot of sex, and now I was beginning to think that she had been raped and brutalized too. There had to be a reason she self-destructed. I would wait to inquire any further. First I had to gain her trust. "Urinary incontinence is a treatable medical condition. I can teach you some exercises to strengthen your pubcoccygeal muscle. We can start right now."

But without the usual social niceties she was finished with me, waving me away with her fingers. "I vill be notifying you vhen your services are required."

Then I saw him, right outside the arched doorway. The baby

monkey, dangling by one long, stringy arm, his little black fingers clutching a mere tendril of foliage, so slight was his weight. I left her quickly, walking down the marble steps, passing by her breakfast table where I took a banana from a bunch. The banana was red, called Chandra Bale, and the fruit was ripe and sweet. I took the Valium out of my pocket and mashed it into a tiny bit of the fruit. It would be a huge dose for the tiny creature, but I wanted him to be fully anesthetized. I left the treat, cradled into the nook of a banana leaf, and waited. It didn't take long for the little monkey to find it, as he'd followed me, curiously swinging along. I sat down on the path, my back leaning against the bungalow wall and waited as he ate, smacking his lips, grinning at me, and showing his gums. Within a few minutes, he swung down from his high perch, weaving a little and then fell. I tried to catch him but missed. Still the dense foliage buffered his fall. When I picked him up, I felt that his body, not more than a kilo, was nearly skeletalized. He was deeply asleep, his little eyelids flickering over quivering eyeballs. Yes, I had been correct. The wire around his neck was strangling him and preventing him from eating. It was only that the sucrose in the banana had drained into his esophagus carrying the sedative into his system.

"I see you have catching the monkey."

I turned, startled. It was the mali. I was surprised that he spoke English and that he would deign to speak to me. And he seemed tentative to do so, as he looked apprehensively around him, on guard.

"Do you have wire cutters?" I made *snip snip* motions with my fingers.

He pulled out a pair of clippers from his belt.

"No, too big, you'll hurt him."

He found another pair among his garden tools, small as a pair of scissors, and the man held the monkey while I carefully cut the wire from around his neck. It had embedded in the monkey's flesh and when I unwound the wire away I had to pull a patch of orange fur attached to raw, infected flesh. I wished I had some antibiotic powder, but it would have to come from the first aid kit Mrs. Pawar hoarded for the girls. "I need medicine," I said to the gardener.

He wove his head. "I am having for you."

"Okay then, get it." He left me and I wrapped the baby Ginger monkey in my chunni scarf, and rocked him, comforting him, and myself. I stroked his palm and his cool baby fingers curled reflexively over my forefinger. He was so cute and precious and I teared up at his plight, and hoped that he would trust me when he awoke and that I would have a friend in the garden, a creature whom I could tend to and who would be there for me. I bent to kiss his little head.

"Vhat do you have there?" Pawar stood over me. He didn't wait for me to answer but pulled my hands away from the sleeping body. "Ach!" he spat and snatched the monkey roughly from me.

"No, please!" I cried, alarmed, as the baby's head lolled back on his neck.

But before I could reach out and grab him back, Mr. Pawar hurled the little monkey above his head and smashed the creature with all his strength onto the concrete walkway. Above us a deafening cacophony of simian screams and hysterical chatter burst forth from the dense jungle of the garden. I screamed too, a horrible involuntary sound that I never thought I was capable of. I picked the monkey up, with shaking hands feeling for his pulse, but there was none. The monkey's neck was broken and his skull fractured.

His sleeping black eyes had popped open and were now staring blankly as blood gushed from his cracked skull. Before I could react, the mali's hand was firmly planted on my wrist, restraining me. I looked up into his brown eyes, soft and compassionate, filling with tears. In his other hand, which he hid from Mr. Pawar, he held a tin of ointment. I gulped hatred down into my gut as the evil man's lip curled in satisfaction as he casually strolled away, humming a Bollywood tune. The mali nodded to me and I gently handed him the monkey.

Later that night I smelled the scent of burning embers. Our door had been left unlocked and we'd left it open to try and get some ventilation in the room. In the garden the *mali* was burning more clippings in his drum. He picked up a small bundle. It was the monkey corpse, wrapped in banana leaves. The man gently tossed the bundle into the blazing inferno. The hatred I felt for the Pawars was ameliorated by the fact that I now knew now that the gardener was an ally.

I stared at the revolving fan, thinking of Paul, wondering where he was, what he was thinking this very minute, would he forget me, would we ever be able to have normal sex if we were reunited? What would ever be normal for me again?

The room was dark, but when the door opened, I recognized the little body of the heinous Mr. Pawar standing there, the glint of the whites of his eyes making him scary looking, as if he needed any help. "You are coming with me."

He took me back to the dungeon. Twelve new captives huddled down there, aged sixteen to twenty, I guessed as I surveyed them. Their injuries were the same. The tears, the pleading, the terror, a replay. Again, they were shapely and beautiful.

“Who has the worst injury?” I asked, knowing now what to expect.

The girls parted, and I saw the girl curled in the corner, catatonic, babbling incoherently, spittle caked on her chin. Her eye sockets were empty and bloody, black hollows like some B-movie special effect. Another girl hovered, speaking softly to her. The two girls were willowy Japanese girls, but both had had breast implants.

An alluring Czech girl with a broad forehead and eyes spaced apart spoke with the charming staccato accent of a Slav. “After they rape us she fight and fight. We are all fighting, but she is not to give up. They gave her such a pill. They force her to swallow. We think it is LSD because she start to trip. Then they came in and they held her down and put such a thing in her eyes. Something bad we think.”

It was there, in the straw. I squatted to examine a small glass pot, then picked it up with the tips of my fingers and sniffed it. My eyes smarted and watered, my olfactory membranes seared by the scent. *Chili paste.*

“She, like, clawed her eyes out *with her fingernails*,” an American girl whimpered, her declaration ending in staccato forte. She was a little flower, with big breasts, wide shoulders and slim hips.

I’d only witnessed one surgical enucleation, or surgical removal of the eye. Even with a patient with a malignant tumor being operated on in a hospital O.R. it had been disturbing.

“When she came down from the LSD she was screaming bloody murder,” the American girl said. “We were . . . . ‘You can’t see because you, like, *tore your eyes out*.’ Then she, went like, she just fucking *flipped out like that*.”

Told what had happened to her, the girl had suffered a psychotic break. The other girls were just watching me. They weren't all American and EU, I noted. There were the two Japanese. But again, they were exceptional beauties. Then I understood. The old scheme was to turn quantity: Nepalese girls from the north, Tamil girls from Sri Lanka, Indian village girls. But Mrs. Pawar had grown tired of the humdrum and bothersome annoyances of dealing with human flesh that menstruated, conceived, and deteriorated before her very eyes. She had never stopped dreaming of her golden years in Paris as a high priced call girl. She wanted to resurrect that cache, that feeling of being above the fray. So she rewrote her business model. Now she dealt not just in Western girls with their expensive orthodontics, but any high society girl with stellar genetics would do, perhaps a boob job thrown in for good measure. She'd even branched out to well-bred Japanese girls with boarding school educations for those desiring more stylized goods.

"I'll bandage her eyes, then I'll see what I can do for the rest of you," I said, feeling the squirm of nausea hatching in my throat. This time I didn't make any promises to the young women about escape. I withheld any words of encouragement or hope, and that made me sick, too. It was just another layer of indoctrination convincing me how broken I was. How despairing I felt. The most I could do was hang my hope on Camille coming around, and on the gardener. He had to help us.

SIXTEEN

The next morning I was let out of the dungeon room and ushered into Mr. and Mrs. Pawar's house, up the grimy marble steps and through the open archway, through the parlor, though an enormous wooden door and into a bath that was more like a spa. There, in the style of the Taj Mahal, stood a decorative inlaid marble bathtub, the size of a Jacuzzi for six. Immediately behind the bath, an equally ornate yet ancient marble staircase led to the second floor of the house.

Mrs. Pawar held an audience with me while bathing. Even though she was submerged, she was swathed in a canary yellow sari that floated around her, as it was not socially acceptable in India to go around naked—even when washing, swimming, or having sex. Mrs. Pawar, as large as a sumo wrestler, soaked in a mountain of suds. Her immense breasts sprawled beneath the wet silk fabric, across her protuberant stomach. Nestled in her spongy cleavage was the gold chain that bore the solid gold skeleton key.

"Your ministrations have performed miracles, Doctor. Miracles! Naturally being a physician you are understanding the toxic nature of constipation. Poisons festering in the colon! Cancerous toxins! Not that death is an event ve Hindus are fearing as you in the Vest."

Cued to her need for attention, I picked up an enormous sea sponge and went to work, lathering her back, probing deeply into her fat rolls and fascia to massage her trapezius, and deltoids. She groaned in pleasure. "We shall all be departing this incarnation someday, though I am not being prepared to depart prematurely."

This was the sociopath's way of thanking me, I suppose. "We're going to keep you healthy, Mrs. Pawar."

"Yes, Doctor, ve shall do vhat we can, shan't we? Nevertheless, my husband and I have been pledging a mutual vow. Whomever is surviving shall be escorting the dear departed to the Ganga. You see, Mother Ganga is coming from the head of Lord Shiva." She reached over her head to point to an area where her rhomboids ran just below the base of her neck, and so I scrubbed and massaged them. "Ve Hindus are believing if your ashes are scattering in the Ganga then Shiva vill be blowing on your soul and after that you vill be spared the endless process of reincarnation." I found this bit of trivia interesting and perked up a bit. "Thus the fires in Varanasi have never gone out! For many thousands of years! Hour after hour, day after day, the bodies are burning!" A startled look came over Mrs. Pawar's face and she panicked. "Quickly! Quickly now! I must use the loo. Oooh!" Six servant women's faces bobbed over the edge of the banister to see what the urgency was all about. "Oooh! Oooh!"

The women rushed three by three down the stairs to her aid. They got soaked themselves as they sloshed into the tub to hoist the monstrous madam to her feet. Mrs. Pawar strained and groaned, exerted in her effort to raise her beefy leg over the edge of the tub, all the while sputtering, "Loose motions, loose motions, Doctor!" And then, dripping blobs of suds and pools of water over the marble inlaid floor, she was escorted, doddering, to the nearby W.C. She slammed the door. "Oh, your ministrations, doctor. Your ministrations!" her voice echoed. Relieved through an obscene explosion of flatulence and rectal sputtering, Mrs. Pawar continued her monologue, calling out through the thick wooden door, "The *Gita* teaches that enlightenment is the goal of every individual. Elderly and ailing journey to Varanasi to die. Alas, many pilgrims vait and vait! But they are not necessarily disheartened by their circumstances. Because you see, purification is coming from bathing in the Ganga! From bathing!"

I squeegeeed suds off my arms with my hands as the servant girls helped Mrs. Pawar from the W.C. up the staircase. I followed. It was the Pawar's master boudoir, decorated in red satin, more worn out velvet and tattered gold embroidery. Like a beached whale, Mrs. Pawar flopped onto her ornately embroidered bed, her blubbery stomach rising and falling as she gasped to catch her breath after the climb up the steps.

One of the girls lit a cigarette and handed it to the madam. Mrs. Pawar took a billowy puff, her stack of gold bangles ringing as they cascaded down to her wrist. "You are the vorker of miracles, doctor. I have never slept better in my life. Oh, your ministrations!" She rocked on the bed, coughing up sputum from her lungs.

I noticed the bottle of Phenobarbital on her nightstand. "If you want to sleep a little deeper you can try doubling the dose," I suggested. I didn't doubt that I could easily habituate her to the drug.

One of the servant girls called out from below in Marathi, but Mrs. Pawar called back in English. "Oh, do be sending him up." She smiled at me with those horse teeth. "I am being deliriously hot but relief is coming forthwith!"

Up the stairs trudged a man carrying large tray over his shoulders in the concept of a "cigarette girl" but this tray held a mound of ice and several chrome spouted glass bottles containing liquid: bright yellow, crimson, and confederate blue.

"Vhat color are you vishing today, madam?" the man huffed, exerted from the climb and breathing heavily.

"Red," Mrs. Pawar replied delightedly. "My favorite."

I suspected that the pigment was something potently toxic, not even Red Dye #40, but most likely cadmium. I smiled at her encouragingly as the man began expertly shaving off shards of ice with a curved knife. He scooped a globe of shards into a paper cup creating something like a snow cone. He lavishly poured the allegedly poisonous red syrup over the ice from a crusty glass bottle.

While she was distracted I looked around. Off the bedroom was another smaller room that I could see through an open door. It was decorated in a masculine style, with a brown bedspread on a twin sized bed, and a simple chest of drawers. It was Mr. Pawar's room. He'd either been exiled or had fled to the safety of an empty bed where he could sprawl without being endangered by one of her limbs falling on him in the middle of the night like a bridge collapsing.

Then I saw the Pawar's wedding portrait sitting on her nightstand in a tarnished silver frame. She was in her mid-twenties, overweight by then, dressed in an extravagantly gilded sari, bejeweled and staring unsmiling at the camera. Mr. Pawar stood next to her, several inches shorter looking pimply and adolescent with a full head of unruly hair and an eager grin plastered on his face. So okay, this was step one toward her current state of being.

Mrs. Pawar accepted the cone and waved the man away dismissively so that the cigarette smoke spiraled around her.

I wasn't surprised to see an extra-extra-large blood pressure cuff on the nightstand too. The servant girl was no fool and knew that Mrs. Pawar would melt down into a vindictive rage had the girl brought back a cuff that mocked the madam for being so fat. I picked the cuff up and wrapped it around Mrs. Pawar's upper arm, pressing the diaphragm to her brachial artery while my other hand squeezed the ball. She puffed enthusiastically on her cigarette as the *scritch, scritch, scritch* of the rubber ball resounded in the stone room. I released the ball and waited as it whined down.

"One hundred sixty eight over one twenty," I said as I removed the stethoscope from my ears. "A little exercise will bring it down. We'll take a walk in the garden."

"Have you not heard the most glorious news, my dear?" She dug those teeth into the melting ice. "Scrumptious!"

"Heard what?"

"Vhy, there is no time for indulging in constitutionals," she sprayed shards of red ice out of her mouth as she talked. "Ve have much preparation to be attending to. Tonight you shall be the bride," she made air quotes with her little fingers, "of my dearest brother. Oh, it vill be topnotch amusement!"

The stethoscope slipped from my fingers, rattling onto the marble tiles. "Mrs. Pawar, Mr. Chandraram is a very charming... and deserving man, but I can't leave you. I need to be here, as your personal physician, at all times."

"Mercy! My brother saw you sunbathing in the gardens and has developing a taste for you."

"We need to test your glucose levels," I admonished her, kicking myself for not having pressed this more, and worried now that I would not get the opportunity to start her on insulin. "Someone with acute hypoglycemia should not neglect blood sugar testing."

"Tut tut," Mrs. Pawar said. "If my brother requests it, then so be it. But not such long faces. I have always vanting a daughter and it will be grand funs."

“What about your physical? You can’t be neglecting your health. If you don’t have your health, you don’t have anything!”

“Yes, you are being correct.” She slurped the last bit of melted red liquid from the paper cup then shoved the soggy cup into my hand. “However, it vill take some time for such a long list of supplies to be compiled. Perhaps next veek, or next month even.”

There had to be a way to talk her out of her plan. Maybe if I reminded her that Belhaj needed to be consulted? “But what about Belhaj?”

“Vhat about Belhaj?” she asked me, her eyes squinting as she peered in my direction. “Belhaj does *my* bidding, dear girl, and you best be not forgetting it.”

This bit of information surprised me. I was convinced from looking at the photographs that Mrs. Pawar had something going with Belhaj way back when. I guess I assumed that he was her pimp. But maybe I had it all wrong. Maybe she was in control from the beginning and he just latched onto a good thing. If that were true, then I was beginning to understand the chain of command. Belhaj worked for Mrs. Pawar and Vadim worked for Belhaj. I glanced at the monastic room that adjoined her queenly boudoir. It was likely that Mr. Pawar worked for Mrs. Pawar as well, as the spouses of sociopaths often subjugated themselves to their abuser.

“Ve vill begin your transformations after lunch,” Mrs. Pawar said, yawning. “I must be napping presently.”

I left her to sleep off the half-life of the barbiturate and ran down the path to the bungalow I shared with Camille and Zarina. I was sweating in the humidity when I banged the door open. Camille was calmly plaiting Zarina’s hair and one side was already braided into a pigtail.

“You have to save me,” I said without preamble. Camille

continued to flip one section of hair over the next, braiding away, ignoring me. I grabbed her arm. "*Please*, I'm serious. Mrs. Pawar's planning some sort of mock wedding between me and her brother."

"She likes them Indian weddin's."

"Don't sound so casual. I was supposed to be a doctor, nothing more."

"Yeah, 'n where's that written?"

"This is rape, do you hear me?"

She tied off the second pigtail with a pink satin ribbon. "Go outside 'n play with them kittens, Zarina."

"I wanna hear 'bout the weddin'," she whined.

"It ain't that kind a weddin' little one. Now go on."

Zarina planted her thumb in her mouth and spoke over it, garbled, "Yer no fun!" she shouted at me.

"Git!" Camille furrowed her pretty brows, and the girl made a face before reluctantly running from the room. Within seconds she was squealing, chasing the kittens. Camille turned to me, her hand on her hips. "I'm gonna tell it to you plain. We's poontang. Comprende? Mrs. Pawar wants her a weddin' and yer gonna give her a performance. That's the way it is. Don't know how many times I gotta explain to you."

"You said I was too old. That they would rather kill me than have sex with me."

"The male of the species 'r not ponies I would bet on when it comes to their dicks."

"What if I don't cooperate?"

"Then you'll be a shit-pot worse off, that's what, 'n nobody can predict what'll happen. At least this here's fairly predictable." Thus Camille's reason for clinging to this despicable lifestyle. "Besides," she said, thinking. "This ain't such a bad thing. I mean, you don't want *me* to get traded off do you?"

"What do you mean?" I asked guiltily. I still had not told her what Belhaj had said to me about getting rid of her. And I didn't have the stomach to kick the stool out from under her right then.

"What I mean is, play it right and you can be Chandraram's, you know, his—"

"Mistress?"

"Sure, yeah. Then Belhaj 'n me can get back together. We can start all over."

Zarina came back into the room and climbed under the mosquito netting on my bed, curling into a ball and sucking her thumb. Camille paced the room, smoking a bidi, her face tense in obsessive thought as if she were willing her fantasy to come true. I understood. She was scared enough to sacrifice me to Chandraram because having me around meant that she would likely be sold off. She had figured it out, as it appeared to be the logical next step in a situation like this.

Her smoke was gagging me. I knew about bidis from an anti-smoking campaign the hospital had launched. They are hand rolled cigarettes made of tobacco wrapped in the leaf of the plant *Diospyros melanoxylon*. They're tied on both ends with string and drenched in a toxic brew of flavorings. Camille preferred cloves.

The bidi contains more than three times the amount of nicotine and carbon monoxide and five times the amount of tar as a manufactured cigarette. Passive smoke causes acute lower respiratory tract illness, asthma, chronic respiratory symptoms and middle ear infections in children. I reached under the net to draw the cotton spread over Zarina.

Camille stamped the cigarette out, a happy involuntary smile stretching over her face. In her mind it was all settled and she began rummaging through her wardrobe, selecting and rejecting, humming the tuneless tune as her mind spun fantasies of her reunion with Belhaj.

I turned away, not wanting to see any more of that. After having spent the night in the dungeon giving medical care to the captive women, my head felt full of soggy wool. My eyes burned and my stomach gurgled sourly. The drama with Mrs. Pawar had left me further drained. I had to lie down. But there was nothing more I could think or worry through, and rest was imperative now, to unwind, to gather strength. I closed my eyes and breathed deeply. In my exhaustion sleep sucked at the edges of my consciousness. Fear, anxiety, and pain softened around the edges and melted into blackness.

Reality returned like a lightning bolt, accompanied by a throbbing headache and disorientating brain fog. Vadim stood at the door, banging it back and forth with a smirk on his ugly face.

Camille followed us down the garden path to the Pawar's house where hysterical Bollywood music was blasting. When Mrs. Pawar set eyes on Camille, her eyes lit up as if she had just had an idea. She fingered a tendril of Camille's blonde hair. "Oh, how my dearest brother vould enjoy hair sun-kissed by the gods. That is it, then! Nasreen, you are to go to the market and fetch hair-coloring products. Doctor Deva vill be a blonde bride for my dearest brother!"

"What?" I asked, feeling as if I had not heard her correctly.

"The chemist vill put it on my account," Mrs. Pawar said,

thinking of practical matters and ignoring me. "Be running along now." She waved Camille off in her inimitably dismissive manner.

Camille wrapped her chunni around her head, carefully tucking in every wisp of blonde hair, drew it across her lower face and pulled out a pair of sunglasses from her pants pocket, donning them so that her appearance was completely obscured. "Be right back," she said and turned to go. Vadim accompanied her.

While the two were gone, Mrs. Pawar set about preparing me to "marry" her brother. A team of servant girls seemed to find the process as fun and titillating as Mrs. Pawar who stood by cheering us on, offering suggestions like a nervous, happy mother of the bride. "She can be bathing in this," Mrs. Pawar said, proffering a gray cotton sari to hide my nakedness.

The servants dressed me in the common sari. They directed me into the tub where they gossiped in their language as they unselfconsciously reached under my sari to scrub my armpits and crotch. By the time they had finished my shampoo, bath, manicure, and pedicure, Camille, accompanied by the lurching Vadim, returned with a kit to bleach my hair. Her salwar kameez was wet with perspiration and her face was flushed. The goon looked bored.

"Blonde ambition!" Mrs. Pawar gurgled, hacking up phlegm from her emphysemic lungs at the excitement of seeing the bottles of hydrogen peroxide. To punctuate her exhilaration she clutched her chest with both hands in what seemed a mock parody of a torch singer, and belted a stanza with all her heart along with the film tune that was playing.

Camille and two other young girls snapped on rubber gloves and set about dabbing Vaseline along my hairline. Working quickly they sectioned my hair and painted it with bleach, using sponges. Once the hair shafts were covered in bleach, they spread it over my roots and scalp. It burned into my scalp and now I began to worry about hair follicle damage. Meanwhile, another young woman squeezed half a dozen lemons, the tang of the rind springing into the air so that we all salivated.

"Hang yer head here," Camille said. "Keep yer eyes shut. We's gonna neutralize that bleach." The women poured the lemon juice over my head and they all pitched in, massaging it into the hair shafts, then rinsing my head. Camille shampooed and conditioned my hair, humming tunelessly under her breath, with the same anticipatory smile playing on her lips, the gleam in her eyes telling me she'd convinced herself that her rapist lover would want her back.

Mrs. Pawar was beside herself at the sight of my new blonde hair. But I refused to look in a hand held mirror she held up. I pushed it away. Several hair and make up artists descended, then and appeared to be discussing what to do with my appearance, making up their minds, nodding and chattering away in Marathi. While my hair was being blow dried, makeup was applied.

"*Mehndi*," Mrs. Pawar ordered. Two women plopped down at her command and began to trace intricate patterns in henna on my hands, utlitmately dipping each fingertip into the solution, dying my fingertips. The process took about an hour. Meanwhile, my hair was heavily oiled and swept tightly back in a chignon. One of the girls applied a line of vermillion dye along my part line. "A sindoor," Mrs. Pawar explained. "It is being the Hindu vife's expression of undying love for her husband, and desire for his longevity."

"Uh-huh," I said, noncommittally, noticing that there was

no sindoor in the part of her thinning hair.

When I was fully made up, black kohl traced around my blue eyes, my lips ruby red, a red bindi on my forehead over my third eye, the servants dressed me in a sari.

"The sari, very mysterious to American women, is being an intricate affair," Mrs. Pawar gleefully elucidated. "The sari is being from four to nine meters in length. It is being draped over the female body in numerous ways. Typically it is going around the vaist. First, you are seeing, it is vorn over a petticoat called a pavada." The servant girls helped me step into the half-slip. Mrs. Pawar tossed a stack of European made bras on a chair for me to find my size. I went through them. Expensive silk and lace, sophisticated in design for maximum uplift. Sexy. I put one on. It was a relief to have some support after all these weeks of going braless.

"The blouse is being called a choli." The choli they put on me was a tight, cropped top, with short sleeves and a scoop neck. The fabric of my wedding sari was red silk, embellished with real gold embroidery so thick that the loose end, called a pallu, flopped heavily over my shoulder.

Mrs. Pawar directed me to sit on a stool. "These are being called Queen of the Night," she explained, holding a string of small white flowers. "They are very fragrant." She wafted the flowers under my nose.

My head jerked away involuntarily at the sickly sweet scent of the flowers. Mrs. Pawar, Camille, Zarina, the makeup artists, and all the servant girls seemed to shrink in size, disappearing into the shadows. The red bindi over Mrs. Parwar's third eye blinked at me. The jungle garden zoomed in large, the leaves huge and strobing. The fragrance of the flowers had turned into the reek of my rapist. My breaths came in short gasps as visions of the night Belhaj first raped me exploded in my mind's eye. Mrs. Pawar's voice echoed, her strident words probing into my subconscious, but it was as if I were out of my body watching someone else struggle to hear her, to understand. When she touched my head to tie the flowers into my hair I let out a shriek, jumping and stumbling off the stool, lying in a puddle of silk sari as if I had fallen into a pool of fire. As quickly as the hallucinatory flashbacks began, everything returned to normal and I held my stomach as though just ending a gut-wrenching roller coaster ride. I tried to force a smile that must have looked like a grimace. "Sorry," I mumbled feebly.

Mrs. Pawar's mouth smiled back, dismay was fixed on her face along with a hint of doubt. Two servant girls pulled me up and settled me again on the stool where Mrs. Pawar proceeded to tie the flowers around my chignon. The sweet smell hovered around my face and I shut my eyes, taking deep breaths.

"I want one too," Zarina said, pointing to the flowers, hopping excitedly.

Two of the offending blooms had fallen onto the ground. Mrs. Pawar grunted as she bent to retrieve them; then, removing a hairpin from her own hair, fastened the flowers into Zarina's blonde hair.

"Am I beautiful?" she asked Mrs. Pawar.

"Very," the madam replied noncommittally.

Zarina clung to Mrs. Pawar's gigantic, sari-draped leg. That Zarina was fond of Mrs. Pawar worried me. Children were not like animals; they could be deceived by people. Animals had the best instincts. They starved themselves to death and ate their young to spare them from captivity.

"Vadim, you may go," Mrs. Pawar said, and the horrible man lumbered away, probably to get high.

When the door to his bungalow slammed, Mrs. Pawar clapped her hands, triceps flapping, and two of her harried looking servant girls scurried into the tub, scrupulously mopping it clean as fast as they could with her standing over them frowning and muttering under her breath about what stupid idiots they were. The girls who Mrs. Pawar treated with such disdain respectfully helped her climb into the tub, one holding onto her with all her might, putting her own safety in jeopardy, the other gently lifting the woman's enormous leg. Once both legs were inside the tub, Camille climbed in to help Mrs. Pawar establish her equilibrium and gather her wits about her. She allowed herself a moment to snort heavy breaths through her nostrils. She dramatically yanked the golden chain, drawing the magnificent solid gold key from within her impressive bosom. The servants shoved a large embroidered pillow beneath her. Once again the fragile girls endangered themselves by the sheer proximity of much weight sinking toward the pillow as Mrs. Pawar's knees slowly descended.

Peeking over the ledge, I could see a cleverly hidden keyhole beneath a secret sliding plate of marble, and beneath that, another panel that opened into a safe. "Open it," Mrs. Pawar commanded, once she had inserted and turned the key in the lock. The girls struggled to lift the heavy iron lid, and from within the hiding place they extracted a jewelry chest and lugged it out, straining and panting.

Once out of the tub, and having reestablished her equilibrium once again, Mrs. Pawar threw open the chest, which contained a sultan's treasury of emerald, diamond, ruby, and sapphire-encrusted jewelry. Camille's features twisted in envy as the madam dangled a gold earring to my earlobe, then selected another, musing to herself and fussing over the selection of jewelry I would wear to complete my nuptial ensemble. Frowning with belabored breath as she toiled over the task of deciding, she finally held a pair of diamond encrusted drops to my earlobes and motioned for me to put them on. Then she placed the magnificent multi-tiered emerald necklace around my neck that she had worn in one of the photographs. The piece was heavy, resting on my clavicle, and cold against my skin.

Just when I thought she was pleased, she announced, "The bride must be having a nose jewel!"

I shrank from her. Cartilage piercing can become easily infected causing the cartilage to collapse. "Wouldn't just a clip-on do?" I asked, my voice trembling.

I could see from the way she was puttering about that she wasn't listening, nor did she notice that my neck had become taut and my eyes fearfully darting to take in her every move. "This is being a very ancient tradition," she insisted, gathering the supplies she needed to make this permanent alteration to my body. I was relieved at least to see that she intended to use a needle, since a gun could harbor *Staphyloccocus Aureus* microorganisms, and because of the close proximity to the brain Aureus was potentially fatal. "Sixteenth century Moghul emperors are bringing us this tradition," she emoted, thrilled by her new idea. "Shall we be using a phul?" she pondered, proffering an emerald stud on her fingertips. "Or a nath?" She selected a gold ring and dangled it in front of my impassive face. "Ve are piercing the left nostril," she went on to explain, "It is according to Ayurvedic medicine to be helping vith the female reproductive organs. The piercing is making childbirth easier."

At this insinuating comment, I felt a sharp stab in my heart. What was she planning for her brother and me?

"The piercing is also making less *rajah krichhra.*" Her voice had trailed off to a hush and she flashed an embarrassed look at the servants and then sputtered into my ear, "The pain of passing one's monthly impurity." I'd stopped menstruating since being held captive. But I was not surprised, given the malnourishment, the drug addiction, and the stress. All the time I had been raped by Belhaj I had hoped fervently that I was not ovulating despite the amenorrhea, but now I began to visualize my future as the harem wife of that unctuous little Chandraram, a passel of his little brats running under my feet.

Without so much as a surgical glove or cleansing the area with alcohol, Mrs. Pawar probed into my left nostril and darted her needle through my nostril cartilage. I cried out, but she was oblivious. One of the servant girls flapped a rough tissue in my direction. I pressed the wad to my nose while Mrs. Pawar busily searched for the stud. She found the emerald and turned to me, her eyes squinting in concentration as she once again grappled with my nostril and forced the shaft of the stud through the newly created hole. I yelped. The makeup artist stepped in, daubing at my tearing eyes and applying more pancake makeup around my assaulted nostril, ostensibly to cover up the glowing redness of the fresh wound.

Bejeweled to Mrs. Pawar's satisfaction, the madam came behind me, draping the pallu over my hair. She stood back to survey her work. "Splendid, just splendid. Oh, my brother vill be delighted."

Just then a servant girl appeared carrying a large platter piled high with a peppery ground lamb dish with boiled eggs, accompanied by Jasmine rice. "For this occasion of celebratory festivities, I have been making my very special recipe, kafta, handed down through generations," Mrs. Pawar gushed.

Clearly, cooking was one of this sociopath/narcissist's supposed talents. Although I had no appetite, I could not refuse; in fact, I realized, it was imperative for me to demonstrate my admiration and awe over her cooking. The four of us sat on stools in the garden while the girl scooped portions of the lamb into bowls. Mrs. Pawar dug in with her right hand, deftly shaping the lamb and rice mixture into neat balls and popping them into her mouth. "Eat, eat," she said, with a mouthful of rice. "It is being a celebration!"

I was feeling sick to my stomach about what she had done to my hair and nostril, not to mention the idea of soon being raped by her nauseating brother. Sometimes, my father used to say, we have to be our own adults. And so I treated myself like a child because I knew I needed strength to navigate the evening. Who knew what this encounter might bring? Methodically I forced myself to chew and swallow. "Mmmm," I crooned, looking at the beaming Mrs. Pawar. "This is delicious. I have to have the recipe." Camille looked at me sideways as if I'd 'lost it' for sure this time.

"I am being known all over Mumbai for my acclaimed skills in the culinary artistries," Mrs. Pawar shared conspiratorially, motioning her servant to deliver another helping.

"It's really to die for," I agreed apathetically, the grease starting to bog me down. But she giggled, eating like a wrestler, while I too kept chewing until I felt a little queasy.

We all paused when Belhaj walked into the house. I was surprised to see him saunter in without so much as announcing himself. Mrs. Pawar didn't seem ruffled, but rather gushed effusively at his arrival. "My dearest Bel-ji. Come, come and being partaking of our vedding feast."

Belhaj sat down on one of the velvet stools, his face set in a frown. Since arriving in Mumbai, Belhaj had switched to lightweight summer suits, remaining impeccably dressed at all times, though something of a caricature in his sky blue linen suits and tangerine ties. Perspiring, obviously uncomfortable, he looked me over, his eyes filled with a rapist's longing; then turned to Mrs. Pawar. "What is this *mariage*?"

"*Oui*, my dearest Bel-ji. Ve shall be alone tonight," Mrs. Pawar cooed. "Dr. Deva vill be the entertainment for my brother, whom ve are most devoted to." She dolloped out a huge portion and handed Belhaj a plate. "I am cooking another such gourmet feast for just the two of us. Ve vill dine in the garden, shall we? Go ahead, eat, eat."

His plate remained untouched as he glowered at me, the fury building in his core, and then I did feel ill. Was Mrs. Pawar oblivious that her flirting was repugnant to Belhaj and that he was jealous of me? All the rapes I had endured, playacting to get on his good side, but now as I tried to catch his eye to let him know I was being forced to betray him, you could see his eyes had glazed over. All the while, Mrs. Pawar continued her filibuster, "Belji, you are appearing to be veary of late. I fear that you have been vorking the vorkaholic schedule of the Vest. Here in India, ve are having a much slower and, might I be adding, a much to be healthier vay of living. You are knowing this, Bel-ji!" she scolded. And so it went on. Mrs. Pawar offering up sympathy for Belhaj who was out scouring the Bollywood casting calls and discos for voluptuous foreign college girls to abduct and sell into sexual slavery. "Eat, eat, eat," she encouraged.

"*Merci*, Shabana," Belhaj said, rising.

Then, as if things weren't bad enough, Camille was also there at his side, smiling her most drop-dead smile at him, taking his plate as she brushed obviously against him.

"You are correct, *cheri*," Belhaj said to Mrs. Pawar. "*Je suis fatigue*."

"Oh, the French language," Mrs. Pawar swooned. "Until tonight, my dearest Bel-ji."

It made me wonder if she had noticed how many evenings Belhaj had called for me, and had she arranged this sham wedding just to get rid of me so that she could have some alone time with Belhaj. I didn't have much time to think about it.

"Come, come," Mrs. Pawar demanded. "Freshening her makeup!"

Her servants, despite their lack of training in clinical psychology, instinctively understood that excessive pomp and fawning was the only way to keep the psychotic Mrs. Pawar sated. The makeup artist snapped to work, dabbing on another layer of rouge and lipstick with exaggerated flurry and excited commotion.

A few minutes later I was escorted out of her house by the entourage, down the crumbling marble steps, to the fortress door guarded by the mali. At Belhaj's second story apartment, I saw him standing at the open window looking down at me being pushed along like a bobble carried by the current of excited women. The jealous rage on his face transmitted over the distance and I wanted to crumple onto the dirt path and scream. All my plans of gaining these people's trust so that I could devise an escape plan seemed to be crumbling, and I had no choice but to placate Mrs. Pawar's idiotic wish to have a fake wedding with her brother. I was facing an uncertain fate at the hands of Mr. Chandraram, and I still needed to ingratiate myself again to Camille whom I needed to help me with my escape plan. If all of that were not bad enough, my rapist was no doubt spinning a dark fantasy about my betrayal and likely fantasizing about what brutality to put me through when I returned.

The driver had backed Mr. Pawar's SUV into the narrow drive. A rough prod on my arm forced me into the coolness of the car. The door slammed and then the metallic slip of the door locks filled me with panic as I had *fallen, fallen, fallen* into what seemed like a jungle of red roses. The fragrances of dozens of roses filled my lungs with asphyxiating sweetness and the flashbacks began again, firing horrific images of the rape, the prison room where I had been kept in dark isolation and forced into heroin addiction. *Flash, flash, flash*, like demonic explosions in my head. I shredded the flowers, beating them away as if they were coiled snakes ready to strike. Then my face was struck hard, first one cheek and then the next. I registered Vadim's thug face, close to mine, his brutish eyes ordering me to get a grip.

I nodded. "I'm okay," I gasped. "Okay, okay."

"You drive now," he said to the driver.

As the car left the squalor of Falkland Road, a gang of prisoners chained around their waists and tethered with heavy leg irons shuffled out of the way. They were dead men walking, with long scraggly white hair and beards. I understood why they shuffled, why they hung their heads. In two very different, but equally hopeless life circumstances, I looked at them and they looked at the SUV's tinted windows, with its prisoner huddled in another kind of despair. It was not just the chain gang, but the teeming humanity deluging all of Mumbai that filled me with a horrible dread. I found it difficult to comprehend the meaning of it all. Did the gods look on, selecting judiciously, or at random, lives to be radically altered, forever ruined like mine, or fantastically transformed by, say, winning millions of dollars in the lottery? Then I noticed the European hippie man again watching the spectacle of the prisoners too, a look of sadness over his features. Who was he? I had no time to ponder as the SUV traveled out of the brothel district into a posh part of the city.

The car slowed at an intersection. At the window popped a brown face with my rapist's eyes. I screamed.

"It vas but a monkey at the vindow, begging," the driver said. He wore a brimmed driver's cap and all I could see was the top of the cap over the headrest.

"I thought I saw his eyes," I sputtered, feeling delirious.

"Yes. The monkey's eyes."

The driver accelerated and drove on.

I started survival breathing. Four counts in. Hold for four. Four counts out. The driver's head was ramrod straight, his silence was deafening as he pulled the car up to a wrought iron gate, flanked by thick and very tall walls made of plain stucco. Two white-coated servants wearing red caps with gold tassels opened the gates and the driver pulled the car inside. The dull exterior belied the majestic palace hidden inside. It was not the decayed and dingy former grandeur of Mrs. Pawar's brothel compound. Before me sprawled a majestic white marble Mughal palace. The car pulled around a circular driveway up to white marble steps that led to the grand door of the palace. Two more elaborately white-uniformed male servants flanked the door, awaiting my arrival. When the SUV came to a stop, they marched down ceremoniously in lock step to open my door.

And then I found my voice. "My family has money," I whispered to the driver. "They will pay whatever you ask if you take me to the American Consulate."

He swiveled in his seat. My God, it was Mr. Pawar. His beady eyes bore holes through me as he spewed venomously, "You had better be shutting your gob." His look was so evil and penetrating that it took my breath away. He reached over the seat and fingered my chin, "I vill be pouring acid into your eardrums and eyeballs and splashing it onto your face."

I gasped and my hand rose to my cheek involuntarily.

"Do not tamper with my disposition as it is highly volatile. You are to be pleasing to our Mr. Chandraram as he is being the bestower of our bounty." He slipped his cold fingers into the neckline of my choli and pulled me over to him. Our faces were so close that the enlarged pores on his nose appeared magnified with the black hairs growing out of the follicles. In the lamplight, his lips were maroon, like leeches, moving in a downward arch, a permanent scowl of a deeply unhappy man. "Are ve having an understanding on the matter of this subject?"

I nodded, yes. I understood, finally. Mr. Chandraram was the boss. His sister worked for him, Mr. Pawar did her bidding, Belhaj was an abductor of gori—foreign women—and Vadim was the gora goonda lackey for all of them, the foreigner goon who did their bidding. The last piece of the puzzle had snapped into place.

The car door opened, and a white-gloved hand was extended for me. I stepped out of the car at the very moment that millions of bats suddenly emerged from some nearby hidden chamber to feed on night insects. Vaulting into the sky, circling in a vortex to gain lift, they were gone as quickly as they came. A clutch of fear grabbed at my heart. I was escorted up the carved and inlaid white marble step and into the palace foyer that was refrigerated to morgue temperature. Huge potted palms and erotic Hindu statuary were the ornamentation around a pool of water, in which highly manicured lily pads floated, their blossoms like decorations on a cake.

A regal male servant arrogantly showed me his tight swaying buttocks as he preceded me into an inner chamber of the palace. There an ethereal blue light filtered through paper fine alabaster shutters, casting elegant shadows over the room. Like the exterior of the palace, the chamber was constructed of white marble. It was decorated in Raj style, but clearly much more expensive and maintained than his sister's house, all of the furnishings being museum quality. Elaborately painted urns were potted with manicured palms and exotic tropical foliage that was unfamiliar to me, though beautiful. The marble walls were swathed in heavy tapestries, and plush velvet divans and puffy chaise lounges stood about invitingly. Mr. Chandraram had attended Oxford, I noted, His framed diploma hung among gilt framed photographs of him playing polo, and trophies—ostensibly won at such matches—boasting his athletic skills. There were taxidermy trophies, too, trumpeting his prowess at big game hunting: elephant feet, entire bodies of lions, tigers, alligators . . . . I'd transferred out of art history to avoid sullying my grade point average, but it seemed to me that many of the paintings installed on the walls were Impressionists and Picassos, and that they were real. This was a frightening revelation, since that kind of money meant Chandraram's trafficking of women and girls was indeed a lucrative criminal endeavor, that the situation I was in with him was dire . . . and that I had to please him at all costs.

And then Mr. Chandraram lumbered into the room, his pudgy cheeks flushed and perspiring. He palmed his soggy hands on his silk trousers and patted down his bright blue raw silk Nehru jacket as a pleased, yet timid look gripped his features. "Good evening, Doctor Deva."

Paresthesia: The abnormal sensation of the skin. Numbness, tingling, pricking, burning and creeping that has no objective cause. Yet the cause was standing right in front of me. "Good evening," I managed.

"I trust you had a pleasant journey?" he asked, his beady eyes revealing a nauseating anticipation.

"Yes, the roses were lovely," I lied, forcing a grimace that he might interpret as a smile. "I see you are a romantic," I added quickly, though my brittle tone betrayed me. He grinned broadly nevertheless, showing off his unfortunate British orthodontics, proud of himself in his self-absorbed hubris. Would he even care if I told him that the fragrance of roses triggered post-traumatic stress flashbacks of violent rape?

"Let me look at you." He stood there appraising me with a smarmy smile on his chubby face. I wondered what Chandraram's psychological diagnosis would be. The abnormal appetite that drove him to hurt women had to have had its genesis somewhere in his childhood. In addition, what normal man would want something as ridiculous as a pretend wedding? "Vhat a long day you have had with all this elaborate preparation," he went on in his oily way. "Vhat vould you like to drink? California Chardonnay? French Champagne?"

"Bottled water," I stuttered, my mouth still bone dry from reliving the rape just minutes before.

"Splendid." Chandraram appeared crestfallen that I refused his offer of alcohol, as if I were ruining his big plans for the evening. On a wooden table inlaid with semi-precious stones waited a magnificent array of Indian dishes for our pleasure. "Shall we dine then?" he gestured floridly like a game show host showing off potential prizes.

"I'm not really hungry," I said truthfully with Mrs. Pawar's homemade kafta fermenting its way through my digestive tract.

"As you vish," he replied, flustered.

"Maybe later?" I said to be polite.

"Perhaps."

He fetched me a bejeweled, solid gold goblet of water, then unceremoniously uncorked a bottle of Dom Pérignon, making a mess with the cork ejecting like a missile and wine bubbling over his hand. He picked up a Hermès scarf that was lying about and wiped off his hands, and then tossed it onto a sterling tray. Goblet in hand, he plopped onto a jewel-encrusted throne, trimmed in carved ivory. He waved for me to sit and when I was situated at his feet on a small crimson velvet stool, he sipped his champagne, examining me with his wet eyes. Now that I knew that he was the boss of the operation, I didn't doubt that Chandraram was a rapist with the worst of them, yet he was treating me deferentially, like a date he wanted to impress.

I couldn't figure it. Surely Chandraram had his pick of Bollywood actresses and high-class call girls. Still he looked awkward and was perspiring profusely. I could only conclude that something about me punched his buttons on a deep subconscious level. I didn't know anything about him, except that he had been chunky growing up. The trading of women had made him rich and powerful, but he still harbored the chubby boy inside of him who schoolgirls had giggled at. I decided then to go along with him, to make him feel like a *man*, to see how far I could play him. Besides, I still had Mr. Pawar's ghastly threats ringing in my ears. And I would never erase the sight of the Dutch girl, Christyn's melted face from my mind, and the nameless Japanese girl with the empty, ravaged eye sockets. I forced myself into the greatest acting role of my life and smiled to put Mr. Chandraram at ease. It worked, as he immediately sighed and appeared more relaxed and confident.

"So tell me, Doctor, vhat have you learned about India that pleases you?"

"I have been reading the *Bhagavad Gita*."

"Ah, yes, India's favorite Bible." He sighed, bored, but then brightened. "I, myself, am extremely enamored of the writings of the *Kama Sutra*," he said, changing the subject eagerly as if he had planned on talking about the book and now stumbled impatiently into it. He leaned over his belly, unselfconsciously letting out a toot of gas to reach for an oversized coffee table book that lay on an intricately white ivory table with the kind of colored inlaid marble pieces that I'd seen in photographs of the Taj Mahal. He opened the book and showed it to me upside down so that I could not actually register much more than the fact that it contained four-color prints of erotic Indian paintings separated from the vellum pages of text by sheets of creamy tissue paper.

He wore a big gold and ruby ring and a golden threaded bracelet around one wrist. Strumming affectionately through the book, he crooned, "*The Kama Sutra of Vatsyayana* was translated from Sanskrit. Listen to this sensual bit of prose." He cleared his throat, *hck, hck, hck*. And with a twinge of stage fright, read, "'Blows vith the fist should be given on the back of the voman vhile she is sitting on the lap of the man, and she should give blows in return . . . '" His words hitched in his phlegmy throat and then he stopped in mid-sentence and the book clattered from his lap. He rose, slithering to my side. Kneeling, he removed my veil, studying me as I sat as still as a statue. He quoted the *Kama Sutra* from memory, "'Abusing the man as if she vere angry, and making the cooing and the veeping sounds.'"

"I don't see anything sensual about that," I said in a plain voice, shattering the moment, immediately regretting my outburst and asking myself why I couldn't be more acquiescent even in the face of such imminent danger.

"Excuse me?" he asked, taken aback by my boldness, his face suddenly falling as if the nerves, sinew and tissue were directly connected with his lack of selfesteem.

Still my tongue refused to obey this lunacy and seemed to have a mind of its own, answering, "I don't see anything—"

"I'm afraid I heard you correctly the first time, madam."

He looked hurt. Maybe he did have a heart. I decided to take a chance and throw myself on his mercy, "Mr. Chandraram, you seem like a decent man. I see kindness in your eyes and your face."

He smiled tentatively at the compliment.

"You must understand that I just want to go back to my life." I wiped away a tear that had slid with ease from my nasolacrimal duct that was already irritated by the rose pollen. The terror welled, like a rolling wave from deep within me pushing up from the depths from my gut to my chest into my throat so that I felt I could not draw a breath.

"You just said that you are a student of the *Gita*."

"I'm reading it. I wouldn't call myself a student," I forced the words, my eyes fixed on him, watching him for any clue of decency or mercy.

"Let me help you then." He sat back on his heels, still closer to me than was comfortable. "My sister is enormously impressed vith your body of medical knowledge."

"Thank you."

"You have taken the position of her personal physician."

"Yes."

"And you've treated our girls."

I nodded hesitantly at the possessive "our," thinking of the young girls I had patched up so that they could sell them to the highest bidder, and of Christyn, whom I had murdered.

"There vill be others, many more for you to care for. This is your dharma." I stared at him.

"Your sacred duty."

"My duty is to return home to my family and friends, to finish my fellowship and to pursue my career."

"And who vill take care of the poor girls?" he asked, feigning the sulk of a petulant schoolboy, which did not do him justice and made me wonder if my attempt at manipulation was equally as transparent. Also, he'd backed me into a corner because the only obvious answer to his question was for me to suggest that they stop abducting, beating, drug addicting, and trafficking women in the first place. But I decided to stay quiet and to allow him to spin his crap. I thought of Paul's admonition again, to run toward danger. As a confirmed bookworm and wallflower, and as awkward and unstudied as I was in the art of flirting, I had no other weapon but my alleged beauty and undeveloped charms. I smiled at him again as if I were captivated as he went on, a little gleam of anticipation sparking in his creepy rodent eyes.

"Nirvana is the attainment of enlightenment and freeing of the spiritual self from attachment to vorldly things, ending the cycle of birth and rebirth," he lectured as I adopted a spellbound expression. "Of course you are attached to vorldly desires you just described. But the *Gita* teaches us that true enlightenment comes vhen ve transcend our identification with our false self, vhich is the ego. Ve learn that acceptance is the vay to nirvana. To pursue enlightenment you must seek attachment to the immortal self."

"The God Krishna doesn't preach that we have to give up the physical world to seek attachment to the immortal self."

"I see that you have a better understanding of the *Gita* than you originally let on. You are right that the Krishna does not admonish us to neglect the physical world. He tells us to live in accordance vith truth. Ve must mindfully embrace our temporal dharma—our duty. In so doing ve vill enjoy our lives and even achieve enlightenment."

He was talking shit and I blurted, "Mr. Chandraram, no God, Jesus Christ, Krishna, Allah, or Buddha would condone hurting women."

"The Buddha vas not a god," he said impassively, examining his fingernails that were polished with clear nail lacquer, as one nostril twitched.

I would have to work hard to soften him up again. "In the *Gita*, Krishna preaches that without action there would be no order in the cosmos, no truth."

"Indeed," he agreed, sniffing as he scrutinized my face for any tell tale sign that I was playing him. "Vhat you are experiencing now is called mumukshutva. It is the passionate desire to achieve liberation from suffering. But you see, the root of all suffering is the anguish of the mind that is stirred up by selfish desire. Selfish desire like you have to abandon your dharma and return to your vorldly pursuits. Krishna teaches of the three yogic paths of devotional service, and that is vhat I'm trying to explain to you."

I'd wondered about the mention of yoga in the *Gita* and muttered, "Yoga?"

"Not yoga like your American health club vork outs with

your blasphemous oms and shanti shanties," he spat with disdain. He reached for his goblet of champagne and drained it, burping unceremoniously. "Krishna vas talking about three yogic paths of devotional service: Bahakti Yoga is the loving devotion to God as a route to salvation. Kharma Yoga refers to doing your righteous dharma duty vithout concern for the results or gain. Rather by dedicating your profession to God, you can realize the Truth. Jnana Yoga is transcending knowledge by meditation." He closed his eyes and quoted from the sacred scriptures, "'Those who see vith eyes of knowledge the difference between the body and the knower of the body, and can also understand the process of liberation from bondage in material nature, attain to the supreme goal.'"

Mr. Chandraram was like the American felons my father had told me about, who mixed up praising Jesus with references to fucking. He was just another sociopath, but this one had power over me. Whatever I said next would be critical. "Mr. Chandraram," I asked softly, "What about your dharma?"

"My dharma right now is to please you." His hand cupped my breast and I felt the heat of his moist palm penetrating all the way to my heart; an evil wetness. I don't know what I expected. That he would prostrate himself before me and beg forgiveness of Brahmin, Krishna, and Vishnu for his crimes against women? If that is what I expected, I guess I was beyond naive. Mr. Chandraram wanted me, and to thwart him would mean facing Mr. Pawar and his jar of acid. On the other hand, since it was probably no longer possible to be Belhaj's "mistress" and gain his trust, going along with Mr. Chandraram could mean that he would begin to trust me and perhaps even give me enough freedom so that I could make my escape. It was revolting, but I did what I had to do. I opened my lips to invite him and I saw that this small movement excited him. I took his hand and placed it between my legs. "Show me what you like about the *Kama Sutra,*" I said, forcing disobedient eyes to meet his hungry gaze.

Mr. Chandraram led me to his bedroom. It was another Raj room, with a colossal carved mahogany poster bed, draped with a canopy of white linen, thickly embroidered in white floral patterns and monograms. The timid Mr. Chandraram unbuttoned my choli and unhooked my bra and pulled them off. He sputtered, "Undress me."

I reached up to unbutton his shirt, and just then he pinched one of my nipples, cranking it, hard. I shrieked. He balled his fist and backhanded me. My body flew across the bed, the back of my head smashing against the headboard. He leapt onto the bed and crawled across it, straddling my legs.

"Vhen I stimulate you according to the *Kama Sutra* you are to show pleasure on your face and vith erotic voices escaping your lips. Do you understand?"

I nodded.

"Good girl."

He pulled off his shirt, and came at me showing his sadistic side, his proclivity for slapping and pinching, conduct he insisted was espoused in the *Kama Sutra.* We may have been in his bedroom for an hour while he enjoyed his acrobatic cruelty when Mr. Chandraram suddenly froze and squinted at the pillow where crushed Queen of the Night blooms were strewn and my blonde hair, which had come unfurled from its updo, spilled. His face registered a flash of recognition, and he virtually flew off me as if my body were on fire.

"By golly," he sputtered. "I dare say I was fooled. You are nothing but a bloody trollop."

I pulled the lace-trimmed sheet over me. "Mr. Chandraram?" I asked, confused.

So distraught was he that he appeared to be speechless and could do nothing but point a trembling finger. I turned my head slowly looking to where his trembling finger was pointing. Crabbing its way across the white linen pillow toward my incredulous eye was a black *pediculus humanus captis*.

The louse, a tiny wingless parasitic insect, feeds on blood sucked from the human scalp. Unlike other hematophagic ectoparasites like mosquitoes and fleas, lice are wingless and handicapped by short stumpy legs that don't allow jumping; thus they are compelled to live their entire lives on their host. Head lice were an all too common problem in schools even in affluent communities in the United States. How the louse got on Mr. Chandraram's pillow, I could not say. Even if I had had head lice prior to the bleaching of my hair only a few hours earlier, a living organism could not have survived the hydrogen peroxide bath. The louse could have come from the hairstylist's comb, or it could have traveled onto Mr. Chandraram's own head from any number of sources.

He wasn't interested in alternative theories, as he was backing away from me as if I were demonically possessed. Slowly, his face surging with emotion, he picked up the receiver of a vintage European phone. His eyes never left me as spoke into the receiver.

SEVENTEEN

It was just moments before a burly, dark-skinned servant burst into the room, a sight that, in my fear-induced perception, appeared in slow motion yet was all too real. He approached, brandishing a long bamboo switch, his paunch jiggling fascinatingly beneath his ill-fitting polyester uniform. The switch rose above my head and then time snapped into place and the whipping began. The man drove me, thrashing and lashing, so that I darted out of the grand bedroom. The servants, mercifully, were asleep and the palace stood empty and still, sparing me any further shame as the wrathful servant drove me, naked, through the earache-cold hallways, through the grand palace's foyer, out the magnificent grand palace door, down the grand marble steps where I dove to relative safety into the waiting SUV. I huddled in the vehicle for a few minutes, squirming around on the now sticky, semen-smeared leather seat, trembling, when a young woman arrived dressed in bell bottomed jeans, rubber flip flops, and a tee-shirt with Brittany Spears face stretched over her double D's. She carried the bridal sari draped over her arm. As the SUV navigated Mumbai, the woman impassively dressed me in the complicated sari, saying nothing more but, "Lift your arm," "Turn to the right" and so on. I was relieved not to have to travel through the city naked, but it was a small consolation, as I knew that I was in trouble.

We pulled up to the compound. As Mrs. Pawar had regularly complained, the guards and servants had disappeared for the night as the smell of the monsoon was in the air. A few rumbles coming from Shiva's heavens announced my arrival, though inside the compound it was still and even the jungle garden was asleep.

I stood once again in Mrs. Pawar's boudoir and looked above the furious madam out the open window to the sky. Mr. Pawar was notably missing and I wondered where he was, as his presence would have terrified me much more than the blubbering woman who stood over me. I'd never seen her made up before but apparently the makeup artists who had worked on me had glammed her up for her dinner with Belhaj. Now her lipstick was smeared onto her planked teeth, and kohl ran her bleary eyes. The cloud cover had lifted over a small window for me to gaze upon the sky scattered with stars and laced with galaxies. I fixated on the universe above us, contemplating my smallness and this relatively miniscule drama that played out, wondering what it all meant. All the while Mrs. Pawar paced back and forth in front of me, pausing to pluck jewelry from my ear lobes and from around my neck, depositing the pieces into her treasure chest. She finished stripping me of the jewels, and slammed her treasure chest shut with a definitive clack that rang in my ears.

"Mrs. Pawar, I really don't understand—"

"Dear girl. Insulting my brother, of my own flesh and bloods."

"I would never insult Mr. Chandraram."

"All evidence being to the contrary, my dear girl, as the verification of your insulting vas crawling on his bed linens!"

Bereft of servants Mrs. Pawar heaved the chest back into the tub where she leaned to lock the secret door, grunting and perspiring. When she was finished, she stuffed her gold key into her bosom and yelled in a loud uncouth screech, "Vadim!"

It was all a blur and before I knew what was happening to

me, Vadim was dragging me through the garden passing by an elaborate, yet untouched dinner party.

We were headed toward the door to the foyer that led to the dungeon. I fought, but Vadim wrestled me effortlessly toward the door where Mrs. Pawar already stood, opening the locks with her many keys. But we didn't go to the right and down the stairs to the pit, as I had feared. Instead, Mrs. Pawar fumbled with her keys and then yanked opened the door to the street with a flourish that reflected an equally ominous outcome. The next thing I knew, Vadim tossed me into one of the cages Mrs. Pawar had allowed to stand idle these months since she had given up tending to the enslaved, ovulating Nepalese children. I sprawled on the cage floor, catching my breath, then rushed the gate, but it closed, *clanging.*

I had expected Mrs. Pawar to scold me dementedly like a loving but frustrated mother. But what she had in mind was much more hideous than anything I could have imagined. She stood panting in front of my cage, out of breath from the hasty walk and the effort of opening all the complicated antiquated locks. She jangled her ring, searching for the right key and then locked a huge padlock of the cage, huffing boisterously through her fleshly nostrils as she cranked the key so hard her bangles pealed into the night. She waved Vadim away dismissively and he retreated back into the compound but not before flashing me a twisted, satisfied smile.

"Mrs. Pawar, you are a very sick woman." I hoped that this approach might actually get to her, for her eyes gleamed like kerosene lanterns at my words, and so I went on insistently. "As your personal physician I can see that your exhaustion has led to an acute episode of hypoglycemia."

"My blood sugar has been erratic, even with your ministrations, doctor!" she spat leaving the spittle of anger on her lips.

"That's why we need to test your blood sugar, and we must start you on insulin immediately. You wouldn't want to fall into a coma some night when there was no one around to help you."

"You said yourself I should be snacking more regularly."

Behind Mrs. Pawar were the three beggar women who sat at the gate of the compound day in and day out. They walked back and forth now, their heads down. Again they were completely covered by their saris so I couldn't see their faces. But their heads turned to me from time to time, and they were clearly watching what was going on.

"You're ill, Mrs. Pawar. *Seriously ill.* I'll make sure you get the attentive medical care you deserve. We haven't even discussed your perimenopausal symptoms or your hypothyroidism. "

"Vhat you are saying is veighing heavily upon my burdened heart," she mused softly as her inner voices churned chaotically.

"Mrs. Pawar, who will tend your plantar warts, your adult acne, your eczema, your sinus headaches, your shingles, your dry eyes, your hemorrhoids, your bunions, your dandruff, your restless leg syndrome, your vertigo, and tinnitus?" I asked, arbitrarily rattling off ailments.

She appeared to be thinking hard to figure out the answer. "No one," she said sadly, wiping away a fat tear that had run down one cheek and pooled around her diamond nose phul. "You are speaking the truth as I have been cursed with so very many medical conditions to be needing the tender ministrations of a personal physician."

"You know deep in your heart that I will devote myself to you and I will make sure that you have many nurses tending to your every need, and other doctors as well!"

Mrs. Pawar's eyes glowed at the imagery that danced in her head of legions of doctors and nurses at her beck and call.

"A complicated, and I might add *fascinating* case like yours is bound to attract teams of specialists from all over the world," I said passionately, hoping to fan the flames of her grandiloquent self-image.

I thought I had convinced her but then she harrumphed dramatically. "You Vesterners are overly concerned with the physical manifestations of the being. Vesterners believe if the body is being defiled then the person is defiled. You are believing that a person is a body vith a soul. But you see ve Hindus are believing that ve are a soul vhich carries a body."

I had to reestablish a rapport with her. I could not let her leave me there. "Yes, you are right, Mrs. Pawar. We Americans are way too concerned with the physical manifestations of the flesh. And you are so right to place your primary emphasis on spiritual pursuits. The flesh is weak," I said nonsensically, remembering a fragment of some Bible phrase, which was the best I could do right then.

"Indeed, my dear, indeed."

I was completely winging it, like a sideshow psychic frantically sleuthing out clues from Mrs. Pawar's reactions. "But you were once concerned too with the flesh, weren't you?" She eyed me, waiting to see what I was getting at, and so I plunged on. "You wanted to have a baby, didn't you Mrs. Pawar?"

More tears sprang to her eyes. "And vhy, after all these years should ve be bringing up this subject now?"

Oh my God, *I had her*. "Because you want to talk with someone, and I'm your physician. You trust me." I made eye contact with her finally and reached through the bars to touch her arm. Slowly she raised her hand until she was squeezing my hand tightly. I watched her carefully, scrutinizing her body language for anything, however minute, that would lead me to into the depths of her troubled heart. "All those years ago, all those men. At first it was a power trip."

"*Oui,*" she said, giving herself up to me. "*J'ai passé une soirée merveilleuse.*"

I guessed at her meaning. "But then the fun ended."

"You are correct, Doctor, I vanted that one last baby. So very, very much."

"After so many . . . " I watched her eyes pool and then I was certain where to go. "After so many, many abortions."

"Just one," she whispered.

"And it was so violent."

She let out a belching sob, nodding, weeping soundlessly.

"It hurt, didn't it?"

"Ten men. I vas being torn up inside. I vas screaming. I vas crying for help."

"But there was no one to help you."

"Not a single soul in the vorld."

"And then your baby . . . "

"Still born. A beautiful baby boy. So very small he could have been fitting

into the palm of my hand. He looked just like him."

"You were very much in love, weren't you?"

"Bel-ji, my love," she said sadly. "But he was not a Brahmin." Then her voice held a hint of contempt as if after all these years she had finally bought into the argument.

I went out on a limb, my heart beating, *thud, thud, thud* so that I could hardly breathe. "Your brother did this to you."

She belched another sob, then continued to weep until her pallu was sodden. Finally she sniffed, wiping her wrists over her eye, one and then the other. "Our parents have been losing their royal purse, you see, after the revolution," she said huskily.

Clearly, the family clung to those times, which explained the Raj furnishings in their homes. "And so you went to Paris and made your own fortune from your astonishing beauty."

She smiled, the memories dancing in her eyes, but then her smile turned weary. "It vas my duty to support my family."

"Your sacred dharma," I said, feeling ill.

"Yes, my dear. And vhen I lost sight of my dharma, my brother's duty vas to remind me."

I stared into her eyes. From the little training I had about the psyche I knew that post-traumatic stress victims believe that they deserved their trauma. I had to lob my next comment directly into her broken heart. "Mrs. Pawar, it's not your fault that your baby died."

Her shoulders slumped perceptibly. "Thank you, my dear. After all these years, it is a balm to my troubled spirit to hear those vords being spoken aloud to me, as my pain has filled oceans. Not my fault. Perhaps it vas not the reason I also lost my Bel-ji?" she asked hopefully, then cast her gaze upon the ground as if searching for the answer there. She struggled again against the tears and when she was composed said, "I vanted to kill myself. But my brother came to my rescue. 'Shabana,' he is telling me, 'Karma must be vorked out. The suicide ghosts of those who have tried to escape to roam the earth until they vork out their karma. There is no other vay'. And so I remained, the living dead for many years. In the meantime, resulting from my success in Paris, my brother began to be recognizing the potential in the sale of vomen and girls. So profitable is the business and so plentiful the merchandise. Belhaj vas recruited into our business and he came first to India, and then he has been dispatched all over the vorld, as he is enterprising and clever. At first ve thought that my brother vould allow us to eventually be marrying." She smiled wistfully. "Did not the Prince carry on those many years until the Queen is acquiescing to Camilla? But alas, it vas not meant for being. My brother is arranging my marriage so that I vould be having a suitable partner of the Brahmin persuasion, a Maharaja no less, and I had been knowing Vachspati since childhood. But I have never found happiness vith him as my heart has never ceased in its yearning for my beloved. Now my marriage has becoming nothing more than the arrangement that it vas. And so I have been determined to go against my brother's vishes and reunite with my true love. But you are seeing, no matter vhat I do I cannot vin him back. Even tonight I have preparing a lovers' dinner, but he did not come."

"Where did he go?"

She sighed. "In Paris he used to say, 'Cheri, do not drink the vine or your tears vill be showing on your faces'. He vas a teetotaler you see, in the beginning. But soon his tears began to show on his faces as vell." She sighed again and went on with the bitter melancholy of a woman who lived in the past. "And there have been many vomen over the years who he has turned to in an attempt to stanch the flowing of his tears. There vas Nasreen, and more recently he has turned his attentions on you, my esteemed doctor, as I am being infirm but I am not being blind. Still, the vomen are not enough, you see. It is not that you are not being beautiful. You are being very striking and your intelligence is an intoxicant to us all. But mere sexual congress is not being enough of an analgesic to quell the pain of a rendered heart. He is out finding solace in the drink," she ended flatly.

Now that I had her talking I thought I might as well milk as much information from her as I could. Besides, as bizarre as it sounds, I felt sorry for her. I almost wanted her story to end happily. "Maybe he just went out for a few hours and he'll be back and you can still have your dinner."

"No, there is no hope of that. Vhen he becomes enraged vith emotions, he is being gone all night until the vee hours of the morning. He vould rather attain obliteration of his consciousness than to spend one solitary evening vith me as I am no longer being beautiful."

I couldn't say something like, "You're beautiful inside." It would only inflame her. Mrs. Pawar's primitive defenses kept her in a state of dissociation, identifying with her aggressors—her brother and Belhaj. I thought to try to lure her in with my sympathy. And it wasn't all an act. I felt true pity for her at that moment. "The loyalty of a friend is sometimes greater than the love of a man." She smiled. The tension between us had dissipated. Her face was serene, and the relief I felt was palatable. "And now, Mrs. Pawar, you can let me go, as you know that I will never leave you."

I immediately regretted this fatal mistake as sociopath/narcissists have a short attention span even when there is something in it for them. My words were like a dousing of cold water on her face, as she morphed immediately into the unhinged dissolute madam, dropping my hand. "Tut tut, my dear. I cannot be letting you go. Go vhere, I might be asking? To the American authorities? Do you not see how cleverly ve have hidden ourselves from the vorld here on Falkland Road? Indeed, many years and much vork and effort have transpired to build our small but thriving family business—"

"And your brother takes all of the profits into the coffers of his palace while you are here struggling along."

She looked mystified. "But my dear, he is being the head of the family."

I had to convince her of the value of my friendship. "I would never betray you, Mrs. Pawar. Doctor-patient confidentiality is *my* dharma." I had to shore up her paranoia and make her believe that she was *safe*. I held her gaze and spoke quietly, "Besides, you have nothing to fear. Your hypoglycemic events have triggered numerous dissociative fugue states. You can't remember any thing you've done. Nor can you ever be held responsible."

But Mrs. Pawar did not bite, rather she became unglued, speaking in rapid fire. "Mercy, my dear, you do go on, and rather impertinently I must say. And I have been being indiscreet despite our alleged doctor-patient pact of secrecy. But I am having no choices. My brother was villing to be paying me an allowance of one hundred and twenty thousand rupees for the pleasures of your company. These men vill be paying sixty each. But ve shall be doing vhat ve can to be making up our losses, shan't ve?" A crowd of untouchables had gathered around my cage, staring slack jawed, their black eyes unblinking. Their unworthy bodies were unsavory to Mrs. Pawar, a Brahmin, and her eyes darted about like the mongooses in her parlor looking for an escape route. "As you are saying in America, you can be calculating the arithmetic yourself!"

"Please Mrs. Pawar. Please consider the consequences of neglecting your medical care."

"No!" she shouted. "*You* consider, dear girl. For you shall be thanking me for this experience. The knowledge of the *real self*, that is vhat vill ultimately be saving *your soul*." She peered up at the rumbling sky. Raindrops were beginning to fall. "Now getting to vork before the monsoon is driving away all of our customers." She laboriously turned her ponderous body like an unwieldy craft in swampy waters and departed.

"You sick freak!" I yelled spontaneously. It was satisfying but nothing more. And as the crowd of men pushed and shoved against the cage, bartering amongst themselves for the cash to pay for a turn with me. Now I understood why Mrs. Pawar had asked her brother to have my gilded sari put back on. She wanted the bling to draw more customers.

She was gone and she was not coming back. She would go to bed with her earplugs and eye mask and the prescription I gave her and sleep like a baby while I was gang raped by hoards of these displaced village men eager for the opportunity to forget their woes for just a few minutes of illicit pleasure. The panic welled up inside me but before I could think any further about it, through the chaos I heard chanting, and I saw two Indian women in threadbare cotton saris, chanting, "Brides are not for the burning!" They streamed passed with a banner that read, *Brides Are Not For The Burning* in English and two other languages, presumably Hindi and Marathi.

"Here!" I yelled. "Over here! Please, help me!"

The women dropped their banner in the dirt and dragged it as they shoved through the crowd. "Ah *babu*, move aside. Taking your depraved intentions elsewhere." The women gasped at the sight of me, with my long blonde hair, and my silken finery.

"My goodness, what trouble you appear to be in," marveled one woman as if she could not believe her eyes.

"Stop pushing, you dogs. Go home to your wives and children," said the other, shoving back at a skinny young man.

One ratty older man took particular offense. "If we are the dogs, you are being the bitches." He spit in the first woman's face.

This act of depravity incited the crowd and they began to shout and shove, the frenzy building. The man and two of his friends pushed the women who fell to the ground. The men punched the women's shoulders and backs with their fists, and kicked them ruthlessly in the ribs with heavy sandals made of old tire treads. The women crumpled under the attack, yelling and crying out. Men from all corners of the busy street ran toward the mêlée and stood dumbfounded, watching the beating as entertainment, giggling timidly, then laughing and finally shouting in hilarity, enjoying the show, and barking encouragement to the attackers.

"Stop it! Stop it!" I yelled but the men had lost their lust for me in the heat of the attack. I did the only thing I could think of and started to unbutton my choli, exposing the tops of my breasts. "Come and see what I have for you," I yelled. No one looked my way. I yelled louder, "See the naked American woman!" Still, I had no takers. My father taught me how to wolf whistle, and so I inserted two fingers into my mouth and blew hard, producing a shrill signal. A man turned his jaundiced eyes on me and grinned, showing teeth broken and jagged, and thickly stained with red betel nut juice. I displayed a little more of my breasts, egging him on. He nudged a friend and they both turned toward me. Others noticed too, and slowly peeled off from the mob. They stood around my cage, quietly watching me strip, their mouths hanging open. Soon a hush had fallen over the crowd and, like one being, they turned their collective desire in my direction. Behind the team of horny, dumbfounded men I could see the two women stumbling, rising, their saris soiled and bloodied. I couldn't see anything else because Vadim stepped into my view. Then my attention was on him, unlocking the cage.

"Good you give show. Get customers ready. We go." I cringed from him, but he pulled me out of the cage roughly, and I fell into the muddy dust. He pushed me inside the door into the dingy foyer that led down to the dungeon. I feared that was where he was taking me, but instead he pushed me into a room off the darkened foyer. It was painted dark turquoise, and smeared with the smoke of cooking fires from some bygone era. There were three rope beds. Drapes of tattered indigo cotton were pulled across wires for privacy, ostensibly for three women to entertain men at the same time. Before I could contemplate the sordid circumstances, my wrists were handcuffed above my head, tethered to the bed frame. No sooner did the old iron cuffs go around my wrists than they began to chafe and bleed. The glorious wedding sari was bunched underneath me, stained with dust, and greasy with sweat and hair oil. My armpits were drenched, my blonde hair streamed around me unfamiliarly.

Vadim flopped down on top of me, and began to grind his pelvis into my crotch, his labored breath stinking of hashish, vodka, and cigarettes. "My family is wealthy. They can make you rich." His face was close, his animal eyes fixed on mine as he huffed his sour stench into my face. "You could get away from here. Set up your own business."

"I think no. I live. You die."

"I can guarantee you two million dollars," I replied, exasperated.

He chuckled, clearly not believing me. My father's estate was worth much more, but it would be impossible for this depraved

Russian to grasp the unimaginable wealth of a Southern Californian corporate litigator. How could I convince him that I would give him my entire inheritance for my freedom?

"Belhaj had you castrated."

He laughed. "So what."

"I will give you all the money you need to go anywhere in the world. You can get away from him."

He fingered a tendril of my blonde hair. "Where you get such money. From ATM?"

Okay, he was curious. I had to keep him interested. "I'll have it wired to you through Western Union."

"American police to deliver? No. I queer with no balls, but I not stupid."

Before I could say anything else, he pushed off of me and slid the flimsy drape aside. I heard the door slam and his voice outside in the hallway. "Highest bidder is go first with virgin bride."

I was numb to the shouting of the men queued up outside the room giving their week's earnings to Vadim for a premature ejaculation with the blue-eyed, blonde virgin. "Oh my God, I am heartily sorry for having offended thee," I prayed, having nothing else to offer up to God but some long ago memorized prayer. "And I detest all my sins because of thy just punishment."

I prayed for what seemed like a long time as the heavens released lightening bolts and the rain pounded and hammered against the wooden walls. Time stopped during my prayer and I felt my soul slide out of my body and hover above me. There was some physical pain to it, as if the exit required an incision. Once my soul found a perch above the bed, I saw myself as mere flesh and blood. I stayed like that for a while, feeling neither pain nor pleasure. Then suddenly my soul smashed back into my body and a chaotic spiral of activity ensued as the door opened. I blinked.

My first customer was the Caucasian man I had seen the day we first arrived in Mumbai. I would never forget him, with his shoulder-length blond hair parted in the middle and sixties style headband. I had seen him talking with the mali at the gate, and then earlier this evening when I saw the chain-gang of prisoners. I had thought I had read empathy on his face. But now I knew that he was just the same as the rest of the evil men. His muscles bulged as he forced the door shut, forcing back the nearly hysterical crowd of men in line to rape me. "Get back, *babu.* I am first in line." Then he spoke again in Marathi, this time sounding fierce. He finally managed to get the door shut and bolted and he came over to the bed, standing over me. I wanted to beg for my life but the words stuck in my throat. He bent to me and, sliding tools from pocket of his jeans, went to work on one handcuff with a rusty screwdriver and a safety pin.

"Lucky for you I was once of the criminal element," he said with a German accent. "If you want to call the pick pocketing and petty thievery of a starving boy a life of crime."

My God, he was letting me go. "Where is Vadim? The Russian?"

"He left your fate in the hands of Ghanshyam. He works for the Pawars, but he is my friend."

"What about the Pawars?"

"My friends and I have been fighting that filthy element for years."

"Your friends?"

"The two women you saved from being beaten to death with your strip tease performance. They have good intentions. Ending suttee—that is bride burning. They have many crusades, ending dowries and abortion of female fetuses. She and her sister have worn me out."

"Will your friend, Ghanshyam, allow me to go free? Doesn't he fear the Pawars?"

"*Jawohl*, he fears them greatly, so he cannot let you go free, even though he knows that I am up to something in here."

"But there is no other way out than through that door."

He grunted slightly, smiling devilishly as he worked on the cuffs, reaching to pat a sling bag that hung from his shoulder. He continued working, concentrating as he spoke. "The Hindu society was divided into one thousand Jatis, or castes as they are called in English. Originally it was a theoretical system founded to actually help society function better. The Brahmins were the priests and intelligentsia, the Kshatriyas were the military and ruling order, the Vaishyas were the merchants and cultivators, the Sudras were the artisans and workers." One cuff opened and I pulled my hand free. "The Dalits are the untouchables who clean up human waste and work with dead bodies who are thought to have no varna. It's a Sanskrit word meaning that they don't belong; they are cast outside of the club so to speak." The second cuff opened more easily and I was free. I rose from the bed, rubbing my chaffed wrists.

"*Namaskar*. I'm Kilmar. It's a pleasure to meet you." He did namaste.

"Meredith Fitzgerald." I returned the mudra, but I was distrustful of this man. Was he really who he said he was? I asked hastily, "What does the caste system have to do with me getting out of here?"

"Animal entrails are unclean to Indians. But I have no problem being friends with a Dalit butcher. And we will find these entrails useful tonight. Follow behind me and look frightening."

"I'm not sure I could look any more frightening," I said, touching a long lock of my absurdly platinum hair.

Kilmar opened his bag and scooped out a mess of bloody entrails, rubbing it into his crotch. "Please, may I?" he said, offering me some of the bloody tissue. I cupped my hands and he smeared them with gore. "Just a little on your sari, if you please."

I smeared the mess on my sari, and some on my face.

Kilmar staggered from the room, holding a glob of animal entrails between his legs. A pall fell over the crowd and the men moved away from him. To my astonishment there stood the mali, and then I understood, this was Kilmar's friend, Ghanshyam, who Vadim had left in charge. I caught his look of apprehension that quickly turned to fear when he saw what was happening, that I was escaping. He pressed his back to the wall, trepidation turning to terror for his own safety. Kilmar rattled something off in Marathi with a panicked tone of voice and held up a handful of shredded bloody tissue. The men shrank away as he lurched, smearing them with bloody gristle. He yelled and the crowd broke out in terrified yowls and dispersed, screaming like girls, pushing each other ruthlessly, and shoving to get away, knocking over the weaker, then trampling over them. Among the departing was Ghanshyam, who ran willy-nilly out onto the street.

Kilmar panted from the exertion of his performance, and probably too from fear, as we both knew we were treading into dangerous ground defying the Pawars and Mr. Chandraram.

"What did you say?"

"I told them that your cunt ate my manhood," he said. "There is nothing left. You have evil powers, and so forth and so on."

Like a feral ferret Mr. Pawar rounded the corner, soaking wet from the rain, and hollering, "Vhat madness is this?"

The scuffle was short as Mr. Pawar was as small as a girl and was quickly handcuffed to the bed, struggling. "Shut up, *ghochu*," Kilmar spat, as he tore a strip from the indigo drape.

"You are being the fool, my friend—"

Before Mr. Pawar could finish his sentence, Kilmar crammed the soiled drapery fabric into Pawar's mouth as a gag. Mr. Pawar continued to make muffled noises. Kilmar, exasperated, slammed his head against the bed frame and the little man's eyeballs rolled back into his head.

"*Auf los*!" Kilmar said, urgently, waxing into German out of sheer nerves. "Out, out, out. Go, go, go."

"No. No. I have a friend . . . and her little girl."

"We go get them."

Mr. Pawar must have gone out onto the street to check on me in my cage. He'd left that door ajar and we could now see out to the street. The door to the compound was also unlocked. It was raining hard as I led Kilmar down the garden path to our room. But the door to our room had been locked. I thought Mrs. Pawar might be asleep. She said Belhaj was out getting drunk. I didn't know where Vadim was, though. In reality, any one of them could walk down the garden path any minute, or lock the outside door and we would be trapped. Maybe that was this man's plan? Was he trying to trick me? Maybe he was just going to steal us for another sex slave operation. That was why he had gotten to be friends with Ghanshyam. I watched Kilmar working on the lock with his meager tools, muscles flexing in his forearms. "*Shiesse*," he muttered, raindrops dripping off the end of his nose, every time the cylinder slipped. Finally, he managed to open it and he pushed into the room.

Camille and Zarina were sound asleep on the bed. "Jesus

Christ on a popsicle stick," she muttered thickly when her eyes opened, heavy with sleep. I continued shaking her until she finally jerked her legs off the side of the bed and hunched there with her head hung so that her hair fell like golden waterfalls over her round, white shoulders. "My head's full a cotton. That mali finally brung yer roofies. I just took a quarter 'n I was out." She peered up and noticed Kilmar. "Won't even bother to ask what the fuck your doin' here." Her nose scrunched as she looked at his crotch. "Got me another gong gong on my hands?"

"I've been looking for you at the market," Kilmar said quietly. Then it made sense. Kilmar was the hippie Camille had met at the market when Vadim took her there to buy flowers for Mrs. Pawar's Ganesh. But I still didn't trust him.

"Mrs. Pawar said that Belhaj went out for the night, drinking," I said.

"Yeah. He done come in here all lickered up. But he didn't stay. Guess I'm not that purty no more."

I couldn't believe that she was echoing Mrs. Pawar's words. But it only made me more determined. I could not let her get that damaged. "What about Vadim?"

"Took my stash! That's why I took the roofie. I need sedation you know."

My voice vibrated with pent up nerves as I said urgently, "Okay Belhaj is gone, Mrs. Pawar is asleep. Maybe Vadim got stoned and went to sleep too. We have to take the chance. We're getting out of here."

Camille batted at the mosquito netting fidgeting back onto the bed. Her voice was heavy with anticipatory sleep and she said over a yawn, "How many times do I gotta tell you that there ain't enough baksheesh 'n hell to buy our ways out a here, Deva."

I snatched Camille by the shoulders and lurched her out of bed, shaking her so that her blonde tresses undulated like flames licking. "Listen to me, my name is Meredith, and your name is Camille. We're getting out of here tonight." Even as I said it, it sounded insane but I was running on adrenaline and focused.

"Ixnay onaway atthay illiantbray anplay," she mumbled.

I slapped her hard across the face. It woke her up and this time I didn't regret it. "You know what they are going to do to Zarina. Belhaj told me he's going to sell *you. I get rid of her*. Those were his words."

Her face blanched, and she stammered, "Yer, yer, yer right. I can't let them do that to Zarina. Maybe we should kill 'em. Teach 'em a lesson they won't never forget."

Okay, so she was in. But I was perplexed about Kilmar. I didn't know what to do about him. I said the only thing I could think of. "Kilmar, please wait in the garden. I need you to watch to make sure that Belhaj doesn't come back. We'll be back in five minutes."

"You are making a big mistake. You must come with me now."

I debated. Maybe we should run right then? But I didn't trust him—or anyone. Who knew if the people at the American consulate were honest? It seemed to me that the entire world was corrupt and evil. We needed money if we were going to stay safe, and I knew where to get it. It had to be three in the morning. If Mrs. Pawar downed several Phenobarbitals as I thought she might have, she would be in a tranquilized stupor. At least that was what I was betting on.

The Pawars didn't lock themselves in at night as their house was well within the compound and so it was a mere matter of mounting the marble steps, walking through the open air archway, strolling inside. I had thought I would send Paul an email if I ever got into the palor unsupervised, but now creeping up the marble staircase to the bedroom, with Camille shushing me all the way, it was the last thing on my mind.

As I hoped, Mrs. Pawar was indeed in a drugged state of unconsciousness. She wore a lacy white nightie, with eye mask and earplugs, and sprawled on the bed on her back, snoring like a water buffalo, long and deep. Camille waited by the steps as I tiptoed across the floor, tracking rainwater. I crouched by Mrs. Pawar's bedside and took a deep, cleansing breath to steady my hands. When I felt composed, I ever so carefully slipped my hennaed fingers onto the radial artery on her wrist. Her heart rate was sixty-eight BPM. It had been over one hundred a few days earlier in the garden when I had instinctively decided to capitalize on her hypochondria. Phenobarbital, a barbiturate, depresses the central nervous system. She was reaching peak serum concentration. Her respiratory system was depressed, with respirations shallow and far apart.

Mindful of every movement, I carefully picked up the gold chain around her neck and pulled it through the folds of fat. *Slip, slip, slip*. My breathing was measured and I didn't take my eyes off her face. I located the chain's clasp feeling a thrill at the feel of the round little knob. Mrs. Pawar stirred and grunted. I didn't move, but continued my breathing. She snorted, then settled into a contented snore and I unfastened the clasp, freeing the key.

I scuttled away from the bed and whispered to Camille, "I'm going to watch her. You saw where the jewels were hidden. Go downstairs into her tub and get the chest."

"Are you certifiably bojangled?"

"We need money."

"I got more nerve than what I need money for."

"You must have your own independence, and money will buy you that."

"What if someone comes?"

"The servants are all gone home because of the monsoon. The only person left is Vadim. You said he was stoned, so he's asleep by now. Go."

She looked skeptical, but obeyed. I watched from my perch at the balustrade and soon Camille rounded the marble newel of the staircase. She looked up and I waved from my perch encouragingly. She returned a tepid, girlish wave then climbed into the tub. Carefully she slipped the key into the lock and turned it, opening the trapdoor, and hoisting the treasure chest out.

I was as surprised as she was when Vadim jumped from the shadows, straddling her, holding a knife to her throat. "Why you sneak in middle of night, if not to die, bitch?"

"Shut yer pie hole 'n git off'a me while yer at it, you backwoods douchebag," her voice carried upstairs and I glanced at Mrs. Pawar who stirred, smacking her lips. But the rain was pounding now, creating a subterfuge of noise.

Vadim motioned with his knife that she should get up. I watched him as he opened the chest and saw the back of his head flinch back in startled awe of the jewels within the chest. My plan, such as it was, had gone awry. My thoughts flew in a thousand directions, the muddled mush of panic. Instinct took over my desire to save Camille, Zarina, and myself. The only way I could think of sparing us was to blame Vadim. Blame him for letting me out of the cage. Blame him for stealing Mrs. Pawar's jewels. I darted the few yards back to Mrs. Pawar, plucked an earplug out and cupped my hand around her ear. "Vadim has your key, Mrs. Pawar. He's in your tub, *stealing your jewels*!"

The madam's eyes shot open. She clutched her breast and then surprised me, when I thought I could not ever be surprised again. She bolted out of her bed like a hippopotamus in flight. With such girth propelling her, her arms flailed as she plunged toward the marble balustrade, slipping on the slick of rainwater. Unable to stop the momentum, she flipped over the balustrade, screaming as she plummeted. It took me no longer than three seconds to reach the balustrade. Vadim's disbelief held him back one second too long. Mrs. Pawar splatted on top of him. Her head hit the edge of the tub, exploding like one of the ripe guavas she so loved to gorge on in her garden. I stood for a moment, looking incredulously down at what I had done.

By the time I reached them, Mrs. Pawar was dead. Even if she hadn't hit her head, it was likely that the fall fractured her upper spine, tearing open her aorta and with no blood flow to the heart she would have suffered immediate heart failure. I stared at the woman who had revealed her shattered heart to me less than an hour ago. I had not meant to kill her, but there she was, dead and gone, never to hurt me or another woman or girl again.

Vadim struggled to breathe with a crushed chest. Camille emerged from the shadows and ran to my side, clutching my arm. "That's what you git fer bein' a yaller dog, you motherfucker."

The T-Rex managed a blood-gurgling grin. "I love my mother," he sputtered. "She good woman."

Yeah, I thought, *a good mother who left her baby in his crib until his head flattened*. Every one of these people had a story, but I couldn't think of it now. Vadim's eyes followed as I hastily collected the scattered jewels and extracted the chest from beneath

Mrs. Pawar's arm.

Camille grabbed my elbow. "Don't say nothin' to Kilmar about Mrs. Pawar 'n Vadim meetin' their maker. We gotta play this close to the vest, if you knows what I'm gittin' at."

"Agreed. And don't tell him what's in this chest." I extracted the emerald necklace and a handful of astonishing bobbles from the treasure chest and stuffed it all into my choli. I closed the lid, flipping its thumb turn. I looked one last time at Shabana Pawar, wanting to reach out and touch her as my heart felt squeezed in the vice of her last confession. Instead I picked up my end of the chest and nodded to Camille.

Neither of us spoke a word as we struggled to carry our bounty down the garden path where Kilmar waited. I was out of my mind trying to figure out what to do next. Camille was breathing hard, scared out of her wits as we went into our room. All I wanted was my father's ashes, the *Gita*, and the wristwatch Paul had given me. Camille grabbed a chunni that she wrapped around her head, tucking in her hair. Although it was still night, she donned a pair of sunglasses. On second thought I said, "Give me the flunitrazepam." She gave me the blister packs and I stuffed them into my choli.

I reached inside the mosquito net and shook Zarina gently. "Wake up, sweetie."

She was out of it, like kids get, sleeping through tragedies and all manner of psychological train wrecks. She squirmed and grumbled, sucking her thumb, and clutching her bear as Camille pulled her out of the mosquito netting. "Upsadaisy," Camille crooned. "We're gonna skeedaddle."

I couldn't carry the jewelry chest alone. "I take this for you," Kilmar offered.

We reached the dark foyer that led downstairs to the dungeon and to the street. "Let's go," Kilmar said, flinging open the door to the foyer.

"There are other women here. I am not leaving without them."

"It's fuckin' pourin' down bullfrogs," Camille shouted. Indeed, as if a spigot had been turned on full, the monsoon was pouring torrentially out of the sky, falling like sheets onto the dirty street, creating pools in the stinking black sludge that had festered from the last rains. The rain had driven most of the red light district's residents to find shelter.

Kilmar looked at someone over my shoulder. "What are you doing here? You must leave immediately. You are in danger, *yaar*."

The mali, the man Kilmar called Ghanshyam, stood before me. "Madam," he said, his head bowed.

"We need your help. The keys to the underground room. It's okay," I reassured him. "I will help you get far away from here."

"I vill be returning to my village in the south?"

"Yes, with plenty of money."

Just when we didn't need another interruption, the three beggar women approached. We didn't have time to deal with them but I felt sorry for them in the rain, and so I motioned them inside, and they accepted, stepping over the threshold and sinking into lumps of gray sari inside the dark foyer.

A pedicab pulled up and Camille climbed in with Zarina settling onto the seat under the shelter of the bonnet.

Kilmar and I followed Ghanshyam. "Get Mr. Pawar," I said. We stopped in the brothel room where Kilmar undid the cuffs that held Pawar to the bed. Mr. Pawar grunted and snorted as Ghanshyam grabbed the chains of the cuffs from Kilmar and roughly dragged Pawar down the stairs to the pit, the soles of his sandals slipping and sticking on the tarred railroad ties.

The young women in the dungeon, having heard us unlocking the padlock, were waiting at the door. They burst from the room screaming as if a detonated grenade had just been lobbed inside. Kilmar picked up the catatonic girl and carried her out. Ghanshyam shoved Mr. Pawar inside and when he slammed the door and I bolted it, it gave me a rush of relief to see Mr. Pawar's eye peering through the peephole, knowing that he could not escape that room.

Camille ran down the stairs and kicked the dungeon door. "Shoo. Git back where you belong!" She whirled on me. "We're getting' attention outside. We gotta split."

I knew the goondas were all protective of the operations in the red light district, and we had to get going fast. An assortment of pedicabs, rickshaws, and three-wheeled tut-tut cars had pulled up outside the brothel compound and the girls scrambled in. In the mere fifteen minutes that had transpired since Kilmar had let me out of the handcuffs the water had risen nearly a foot and we were sloshing up to our shins. Customers were fleeing the red light ghetto, a throng of men wielding identical, huge, black umbrellas pressed by us.

Camille sat back fetchingly in her pink and gold salwar kameez, smiling nervously like a belle on her way to the ball. "Look incognito," she called out giddily over the rain. Then a dark film of foreboding fell over her features and she pulled her chunni around her head, wrapping it over her mouth so that her identity was obscured behind her rain spotted sunglasses. "Best not to be overly confident."

"Take us to the American Consulate," I called over the clamor of the rain and the chaotic shouting of the other drivers. I climbed into the pedicab. "Make sure the drivers watch every single girl go *inside* the guard gate. Do you understand?" The man's head wove in the affirmative and he yelled over the rain to the other drivers who took off, bicycling hard, an unlikely parade of pedicabs and rickshaws. Their way was lit by streamers of lights sagging heavily off tangled power lines flanking the potted, crumbling asphalt Falkland Road. I watched them pulling away, feeling a well of relief.

But before our driver could gain traction peddling, a strong grip seized my arm and dragged me from the pedicab into the water and I heard the shrill sound of Zarina screaming. Two goondas stood over me menacingly. Ghanshyam yelled over the clamor of the rain, "The American police are to be coming very soon. Mrs. Pawar is vanting to clean out fast all the girls." One of the goondas spat a glob of red sputum into the rapids that the rain had created and they retreated into one of the dark alleys.

Ghanshyam took my hand to help me back into our pedicab. Before I could step aside of the flow of flotsam that carried with it a frantic half-drowned rat, the creature latched onto me and scrambled up my leg. He was the size of a small cat, nasty looking with black beady eyes and brownish-gray, mite ravaged fur. The rat wanted to use me as a life raft. He sunk his razor rat incisors into my forearm and then scrabbled with his hind legs for leverage, leaving long red scratches on my arm. "Get it off me," I yelled, my mind reviewing just some of the zoonotic diseases an Indian slum rat could transmit into my bloodstream: *rabies, typhus, rickettsialpox, leptospirosis, salmonella, lymphocytic choiromeningitis,* not to mention *yersinia*, better known as the plague. The rat was equally freaked by his own risk factor of drowning or being beaten to death by Ghanshyam who had grabbed a length of rubber hosing floating by and was slamming the animal with it. The rat retaliated by plunging his teeth deeper into my flesh. I fell back over the threshold that led to the darkened foyer. Ghanshyam hopped inside, swinging the tubing like a cricket bat. The rat's jaw disengaged as his body flew against the mud wall. I clutched my bleeding arm and looked straight into the headlights of a vehicle.

"It's Belhaj!" I heard Camille's scream from outside.

Ghanshyam cranked his head out of the foyer door and yelled in Marathi to the pedicab driver. Ghanshyam ducked back inside, slamming the door, closing us into the darkness. "They have escaped," he said, panting. "The driver, he has taken them away. They are gone. Gone. Gone. Gone." His tape was stuck in a loop of terror. "Ve are hiding here. Our owner vill not find us until the American police are coming."

I could see the fear in his eyes and smell it on him. He didn't believe for a minute that we were safe until the police came. That could take hours, even days. "He'll kill us," I said, my throat constricted by esophageal blood flow. I had but a few minutes while Belhaj's driver entered the gate, opened the fortress door and escorted the drunken man through the garden up to his apartment. "Help me open this door." It took both of us to open the inside door against the rushing water. Rain blew across the Pawar's jungle garden and into the dank foyer, and the stairwell that led to Belhaj's apartment.

"Stay here!" I ran, my heart in my throat, up the stairs to Belhaj's apartment.

His room was shuttered and draped, the air heavy with moisture. I found his bottle of Pernod and clutched it to my breast. I was shaken, hugging the bottle, my hands trembling so badly I could barely function. There was enough Pernod for the hair of the dog that Belhaj would need for the hangover that was hitting him like a sledgehammer right about now. I grappled into my choli for the flunitrazepam and frantically pressed a tablet out of the carded blister pack, crushing it against the bureau with the bottle then swiping the dust and bits into the palm of my hand, funneling as much of it as I could into the neck of the bottle. I screwed the cap back on and shook the bottle hard, praying the flunitrazepam would dissolve. I repeated the process with a half-full water bottle that sat there, crushing two tablets and funneling the drug into the water, shaking the bottle.

I went into the closet. My soggy sari itched against my skin and the flame of heat rash creeping over my skin. I waited there, behind my rapist's suits, hugging my rat-bitten arm. Hydrophobia is a viral zoonotic neuroinvasive disease that causes encephalitis, and is almost always fatal. The rabies virus travels to the brain via peripheral nerves, incubating for a few months. The initial symptoms are malaise, headache, and fever, followed by acute pain, violent behavior, depression, and the inability to swallow water, culminating in mania, lethargy, coma, and death. I had to get to a clinic within a few days. But now I had more immediate concerns.

It was no more than three minutes when the door battered open. I had a clear view of Belhaj staggering inside. I smelled his rank Pernod breath and the acrid stench of alcohol being secreted from his pores. He reeled over to his bureau, sloshing the rest of the bottle of Pernod into the water bottle, then swigging from the bottle, once, twice, three times, killing the drink, then belching. He stripped off his wet clothing and dropped everything on the floor. It was quick. His hangover was converted into another drugged sensation. I was at his side when he fell. He was suddenly lucid for one long moment as he saw me standing at the end of his bed, dressed in the tattered red and gold sari. The sari was draped over my head, but he recognized me and knew that I had drugged him. I could see it in his eyes. His fear. It was gratifying, but I had no idea what was to come. I stood there staring at him until his face became a blur. I started as the door banged open.

There stood Ghanshyam brandishing a trenching hoe from his garden tools. He panted, panic radiating from his eyes. "Our owner is not to be hurting you."

"Our owner can't hurt anyone now. He's drugged." I stared at him flopped on the bed. "Let's go."

"But ve cannot be leaving in the immediate future, madam. The rain, it is becoming dangerous vaters, you see there are being like the rapids of a river."

"It's okay, we'll go slow and we'll make it."

"No madam, this is being the zopadpatti."

"The what?"

"Zopadpatti. It is being the slum. Every year during the monsoon peoples are being svept into opening drain holes never to be seen again. My cousin, he is being gone. One minute I am seeing him and the next minute he is no more. Ve must wait."

"How long?"

"One hour. It could be as long two hours being to vaiting. Maybe it is three hours. Four hours, it could be if the rain is continuing—"

"Okay. Okay. Then please, stand guard at least."

He wove his head around in agreement and left me.

I went immediately into Belhaj's bathroom and soaped the rat bite with a bar of LUX, rinsed it with a bottle of water, and dried it with one of Belhaj's clean towels. My bladder throbbed. There were bottles of water on the sink top, which I drank, one after another, sitting on the toilet, drinking and peeing. I washed my hands, staring in the mirror at the oddity with bleached hair, splendid but greasy sari, smeared makeup, and the emerald nose phul that Mrs. Pawar, in her demented fury, had neglected to retrieve. An electric razor dangled from a hook. Without thinking I picked it up and flipped it on. I ran the razor over my head, again and again, the long golden strands falling, leaving just a red blotch at my partline where Mrs. Pawar had dusted the sindoor.

I pulled my pallu over my shaven head, and in his room I sat on a chair, listening to the rain pound. It must have been four in the morning then, and it was still dark outside with a heavy marine layer socking in the city, sodden with precipitation. When would the police come? Camille would tell them about me, and so would the young women who had been held captive. I was the doctor who treated their wounds. Everyone would know what had happened to me. They might even blame me, for being complicit.

I remembered Dad's training, and visualized an image of him to get myself together psychologically. My father said that life threw unpredictable curveballs, but smart people made confrontations work in their favor. I thought about what Paul said after some fiasco on the set or with the studio. It was useless to worry about things you couldn't change. He was like my father in that way. He focused on problem solving, not blaming or fretting. Right then I realized that while I thought of my father frequently, I had pushed Paul out of my mind. But for flitting memories, Paul no longer factored into my life. Maybe it was the constant drama and the hypervigilance necessary for survival that had stopped me from thinking too much about the things that I had done. But now that freedom was so close, I realized how damaged I felt, how deeply changed and altered I was. I could never, ever go back to being the old Meredith Fitzgerald. I knew then that I could never marry Paul. I was no longer the woman Paul had fallen in love with, and that was perhaps the greatest pain of all. And I loved him too much to saddle him with this radically altered woman who *I* didn't even know.

I couldn't think about it or I would go crazy. I got up and started rummaging around in Belhaj's things. In a wooden chest carved with figures of elephants and snakes, was a stack of cash: rupees, euros, and dollars. I stuffed it all into my choli. There were also dozens of passports from Swiss girls, American girls, French girls, Italian girls, Swedish girls, and on and on. There were the passports of the girls I had treated down in the pit. This is what Belhaj meant the day he raped me, when he said that he was from a U.N. delegation. He kidnapped women from all over the world. There were so many passports, I couldn't find mine. I tossed all the passports onto his bureau.

My engagement ring. It rested on the top of monogrammed handkerchiefs. I stared at it a long time, then I slipped it on.

Then they came. Tattered saris swished damply around their ankles as they climbed the steps on bare feet. The door opened and there they stood, eerily shrouded in the gauzy saris so I could not see their faces. One of them spoke, saying simply, "Bel-ji have sexy fun. Fuck and suck." These shrouded women had seemed a thousand years old, but this was just a *girl's* voice. "Fuck and suck," she repeated, and lifted her pallu.

As a doctor, I've seen a lot of horrible things. But nothing so ghastly as the girl's face. Maybe I should have tried to reason with the women. But to tell the truth, I was in sync with them. The next few minutes were remarkable on many levels. It was my first experience with freedom, it was my first undertaking as the new Meredith Fitzgerald . . . and it was my first premeditated crime. I needed to hurt Belhaj, to hold him accountable, not just for what he did to these three women, and to Camille, Zarina, and me. I wanted to hold him accountable for all the wrongs traffickers had wrought against women and girls. I wanted to hurt him for abandoning Mrs. Pawar. For not protecting her from that evil brother. For Belhaj's role in destroying her psyche. The women began undressing him. He was naked, sprawled on the bed, semi-conscious. "Wait," I said, and they turned to me, still shrouded, just heads covered in gray pallus, watching.

I found two vials of depo-testosterone in the bathroom and returned to the room, drawing the hormone into a syringe. Once, twice, three times, I filled the syringe and plunged it into his buttock. I must have given him 800 milligrams. It was a supraphysiologic dose—much more potent than what would occur naturally in a man's body. But that much testosterone would insure he got an erection.

I lay down next to him and shook him. He awoke and grinned lopsidedly, trying to lift a hand, but he was too sedated. I rose, and he stirred again when the three bodies lay down next to him. I stood at the foot of the bed so that he could see my face again, and stood there long enough to see one of the women's hands working, and that the depo-testosterone had kicked in, then I turned away, leaving the women to their grim task. They were giving this sexual deviant an erotic experience he would never forget.

An hour or so passed. The women emerged from Belaj's room adjusting their saris, swishing the air on the stairwell where I'd been waiting. One carried a pillowcase. Several strands of blonde hair escaped the bag. They were going to sell my hair. “Okay,” I said. And then they floated away like phantoms down the stairwell to the garden.

Maybe I had been reckless not to run for my own life. But I couldn't have left Camille, Zarina and the women in the dungeon. By the time help arrived, they could have been killed. Now Camille and Zarina were on their way to a new life with riches to keep them safe. My watch said six forty-five. The rain was abating. The rising sun was starting to bleed through thinner layers of cloud cover. It was time for us to go.

EIGHTEEN

There was shouting and chaos outside the compound. I clutched Ghanshyam's arm. "You said it wasn't possible to leave in the rain."

"Valking no. But the police are having four vheel driving vehicles."

Mrs. Pawar's servant girls had hung the cotton sari under an awning in the garden to dry after they'd given me the wedding bath. "Tell them to change me," I said to Ghanshyam. And so the beggar women helped me quickly change saris, cleverly, so that I was never undressed, adhering to the modest Indian tradition. I covered my head with the drab pallu, obscuring my identity like the three beggar women. "Don't betray me, Ghanshyam."

The Indians were suddenly there, swarming the compound. An American accompanied them. He was mid-sixties, clean-shaven, in shirtsleeves, tie loosened. He had the pasty, flabby appearance of those who eat American food. There was another Caucasian man in his late thirties, rugged, dressed in jeans and teeshirt, with the unavailable aura that many women found irresistible—but that I had always thought was a turn-off since it reminded me of my father. There was also an Indian inspector, crisp in the melting sun. He sported an impressive handlebar moustache, a creased khaki uniform and an immaculately neat black turban. He stood in the middle of the garden, his legs locked in a V, smacking a lathi sharply against a muscular thigh. The Indian police truncheon was a brutal looking weapon, with a heavy blunt at the end, and the inspector wielded it like a nervous tic. It was strange, that he, like Chadraram, had a manicure with clear lacquer gloss on his nails.

"You work here?" the man in the jeans asked Ghanshyam.

Ghanshyam's head wove in the affirmative.

"I'm Agent Ralph Berkshire," the man said with a British accent. "Interpol.

This is Steve McCarthy from the American Consulate. Inspector Rajkumar Singh."

Ghanshyam did namaste. I tucked in my hands and feet beneath my gray cotton sari and remained mute, standing huddled beneath the dense canopy of foliage with the three beggar women. The inspector spoke to Ghanshyam in Marathi and I heard my name. Ghanshyam shook his head, a subtle variation on the Indian head wobble.

"What did you say? Speak English," asked the American diplomat, annoyed.

The Indian detective looked perplexed that these gora were horning into his investigation.

"He asked him if he had knowledge of the American woman, Dr. Meredith Fitzgerald," the Interpol agent, Berkshire, translated.

It was exhilarating to hear my name spoken by a total stranger. It meant they had been looking for me, that someone out there had cared. My eyes teared up and I felt dizzy, as if the contents of my head had been vacuumed out into the hot, wet air and I was in danger of floating away, up into the clouds where I would disappear. Standing in front of the Indian police, the American diplomat, the detective from Interpol, I realized that my thinking about the exact sequence of my escape had begun to change after the accidental deaths of Shabana Pawar and Vadim. I guess I had not really thought it through but was just going with the flow, seeing how things would play out. Now I realized that I had never really visualized myself going to the American consulate. I had not imagined dashing through the guard gates into the welcoming arms of some Liz Claiborn-clad receptionist. No, I had not envisioned that at all. But now that I stood there in front of these men, I realized why. I didn't relish the idea of being debriefed about my experiences, a procedure that would undoubtedly be fraught with humiliation, debasement, and utter disgrace. All I could think of were the hookers I'd treated at the hospital and the disdainful stigma that dogged them despite the coercion and kidnapping that had initially recruited them into the life. My situation was worse than just prostitution. What would these men think of me if they knew all the things I had done?

"Well?" asked the American diplomat. "Do you know where she is?"

"She vas being here, but she has been going avay," Ghanshyam blurted, his voice palsied with guilt.

"Is there anyone here who might know her whereabouts?" Berkshire asked.

Ghanshyam head bobbled more enthusiastically. "Please, you are coming after me."

I trailed the men as they followed Ghanshyam into the dark earthen foyer, down the stairs made of railroad ties, and into the shorn out tunnel to the dungeon door. I thought it wouldn't appear odd if I tagged along, as Indians are rabidly curious and, in fact, the other three women eventually followed. And so there we all stood, huddled together.

"This is the prison," Ghanshyam said to the agent.

"The women who came to the American Consulate said they

were kept underground," Berkshire said.

"What is this, like a bomb shelter or something?" McCarthy asked, looking pallid.

Before Ghanshyam could produce the key, there was more frantic yelling as the police battered down the door. The stench was like a wave that pushed us back, and we all gasped and gagged. One young Indian policeman vomited, then made an awning with the flat of his hand to hide his eyes, as if ashamed. The agent, Berkshire, clapped him on the back reassuringly. By then most everyone was inside where Mr. Pawar lay snorting through his nostrils like a camel, crumpled on the shit-soiled straw. Berkshire lifted him by his cuffs. Pawar whimpered through his saliva-soaked gag.

"Vachspati Pawar!" the inspector exclaimed, with a look I couldn't read. Fear? Complicity? Though if he knew him, he must have known that this was his brothel. I started thinking about Camille then, what she said about baksheesh and that this inspector wasn't to be trusted.

"Where is she?" Berkshire asked roughly. "What have you done to the American woman, Doctor Fitzgerald?" The agent impatiently tossed Mr. Pawar to the ground. "Take him to the station. We'll get it out of him."

"There are other peoples," Ghanshyam said.

"Show us," said Mr. McCarthy.

The group of us reached Mrs. Pawar and Vadim. They were unmistakably dead. Their faces sagged and had taken on a gray-white pallor. Vadim's eyes were open, the eyeballs clouded with film, dull and flat, the pupils dilated. Both bodies were waxy looking, their extremities purplish. Their bladders and sphincters had relaxed. Urine and feces had leaked into Mrs. Pawar's magnificent bathtub. Flies buzzed around, lighting in clumps on Mrs. Pawar's decomposing brain matter.

"How in the hell?" Berkshire looked upward at the marble balustrade that flanked Mrs. Pawar's boudoir. The rest of the men stood around mutely staring at the sight of the huge woman with the splattered head, and the male crushed beneath her.

"Shabana Pawar," the inspector sniffed. "I am not to believing to see her like this."

His tone told me I could definitely not show my face, no matter what. Sooner or later the detectives would discover the hidden safe in Shabana Pawar's bathtub, and learn from Mr. Pawar about the missing treasure chest. This inspector with his incendiary sneer might find it suspicious that the missing American woman was sneaking around, hiding a stash of cash and jewels stolen from his dead benefactor. He could accuse me of murder and then Chandraram would use his influence to have me condemned.

"Vhat is the name of the goonda?" the inspector asked, but Ghanshyam only shrugged his shoulders. Vadim was dead and not a soul in the world would mourn him. His body would be burned and disposed of with less decorum than garden compost. He was an evil person, but his nothingness was unsettling.

McCarthy's face was gray and he stifled a gag. Yet he could not help himself and leaned in a little closer, rubbernecking, with the pulsing eyes of a voyeur. "How are we going to get them out of here? Are they in rigor?"

I could have told him. Rigor mortis, or cadaveric spasm, is the stiffening of the muscles that occurs as a result of dissipating adenosine triphosphate, an organic compound that transports chemical energy within the cells. Rigor typically starts two to six hours after death, beginning in the eyeballs and then moving to the neck, jaw, face, down the arms, into the chest, abdomen, and legs, and subsides between twelve and forty-eight hours. The air was moist and the temperature was hot, which encourages faster onset of rigor. Vadim was athletic and trim and so he would have gone into rigor faster, and from the stiffness, his body appeared to be in full rigor. Mrs. Pawar was obese and probably would not go into rigor. But they would still have the task of moving her off of Vadim and out of the compound. They would have to do it fast. In the heat and humidity, fungi and bacteria were decomposing the bodies in an accelerated fashion. Moving that much rotted flesh would be a challenge. But then again the Indians were masterful at turning challenges into art forms, and no doubt a team of them would arrive shortly to cleverly devise a jerryrigged pulley system.

"My detectives vill take care of it," Inspector Singh said, echoing my thoughts, his voice reflecting a tinge of disdain for the Westerners who sweated—what was in his world of compulsory creative artifice—the small stuff.

"Who else is here?" Berkshire asked Ghanshyam. "Is there anyone else?"

Ghanshyam bobbled his head.

"Take us to them."

I followed, my heart beating rapidly, clutching the humble sari around me and making sure that my face and head remained covered. We all went down the garden path and up the stairs to Belhaj's private apartment. The men exploded into Belhaj's room, but were stopped by the sight of him naked and spread-eagle on the bed, his flaccid penis lying on his hairy thigh, his shriveled testicles glowing purple. The Indian men appeared stumped by the sight, embarrassed, drifting into loose gaggles where they stood with their rifle muzzles impotently pointed downward, disappointed expressions gripping their faces.

The agent felt Belhaj's carotid artery and then nodded to the American diplomat. "Got him," he said.

Got him? What did he mean by that? Did they know of Belhaj before now? I was curious, but not curious enough to let my identity be known. Meanwhile, there was a lot more chaos and police vans arriving, people coming in and out.

Belhaj was hoisted onto a stretcher and taken out of the room by a group of policemen. But before the agent and the inspector left the room, using a penknife, Berkshire picked up the cardboard section that I had torn off the blister pack. I had not realized that I had dropped it. "What's this? Flunitrazepam." He put the blister pack into a plastic bag. "It's why he's sedated," he said, mostly to himself.

I ducked out then, realizing that I was not cut out for a life of crime, making such a stupid mistake as to have dropped the prescription blister pack section with my fingerprints all over it. I went down the stairs and found my Indian women waiting patiently in the jungle garden and I stood near them as if I were just another beggar.

"Who are these women?" McCarthy asked Ghanshyam, taking him by the arm and leading him off to speak privately.

"They are randis," Ghanshyam said. "They are sold to Mrs. Pawar." That was all I could hear but I could tell that Ghanshyam was telling McCarthy about the women and what they had done to Belhaj because McCarthy's facial expression registered disbelief and disgust. He called out, "Berkshire, get over here and hear this. Tell him, tell him what you said about the prostitutes."

Ghanshyam filled Agent Berkshire in. The Interpol agent was clearly the more worldly of the two, as his face showed no disgust or disbelief. On the contrary, he looked positively ecstatic, a smile stretching across his craggy face, and he laughed the cynical laugh of a man who had seen enough evil that he probably did not have a problem with vigilantism. He turned and eerily looked in my direction as if he knew it was me. My heart pounded and my respirations increased but I had no reason to be afraid. I was invisible to him in my gray shroud.

When all was in order at the compound, Ghanshyam, the women, and I were ushered into a police van. On the street hung the goondas who had threatened us earlier. Heavily made up women and girls and a contortionist, some with tribal tattoos, others with white powder heavily applied to their faces, stared with open mouths.

"Where are we going?" I asked Ghanshyam.

"Not to be vorrying, madam. They are only going to ask us over and over the same questions out of formality, then they are going to be letting us go."

The Mumbai Police Headquarters was a sprawling two-storied building befitting a metropolis of more than thirteen million people. The structure was of a British style in brown and white, like a luxury hotel, landscaped with towering palms. The vast foyer of the headquarters was air-conditioned, light and breezy with all the glass windows. We were left to wait, guarded by a policeman. There were wooden benches, but the women sunk onto their haunches, and I followed suit, not wanting to stand out. My thighs began to ache in just a few minutes. I felt out of place in the headquarters with its modern efficiency, policemen standing stiffly at attention, and other officials marching purposefully to their various tasks while officers filled out forms pursuant to the raid on the compound. The over-the-top rubberstamping, initialing, and filing of multiple triplicate forms went on for over an hour as the bureaucratic underpinnings of the British Raj intensified the already excruciatingly slow Indian-time mentality.

This was a different India than I'd experienced at the Pawar's brothel, and even at Mr. Chandraram's Raj style palace. It was clear that India had two distinct, polar opposite cultures. One was the professional and wealthy society that built the high-rises, shopping centers, and theaters. This India of the twenty-first century generated the technology tycoons, the starlets, the trust fund kids with their Rolexes and Gucci bags, an economic sector that supported a burgeoning middle class, many of whom were the usurpers of outsourced American jobs. For the most part, this culture had gone Western.

But alongside the unimaginable prosperity of the rich, and the booming economic growth of the middle class, lived Indians in despicable poverty, heroically hanging onto their cherished, spectacular 9,000-year old culture. Some lived uneventful, though struggling, lives. There were the truly holy devotees; others had devolved into strange and sundry cults. But the worst off were the slaves and those damned to remain in the Dark Ages. Pondering these contradictions only brought to light my own feelings of being out of place. It was uncomfortable, to say the least, to be a criminal sitting in a police headquarters with the stolen cash and jewels and the residue of Mr. Chandraram's semen caked on my pavada petticoat that could be used as evidence to accuse me of prostitution. Even though the air was cold, my armpits were drenched and I shivered under my sari, my thighs screaming in pain but I dared not move or show myself as any different than the three other women who squatted in ease, waiting.

Under my breath I recited the names of the girls I had memorized, the girls who I had failed to save, who had been sold by Belhaj into a lifetime of sexual slavery and certain early death. Their passports had been among those collected by the Indian inspector, Berkshire, and McCarthy. At least someone would be looking for them now. But as Camille had made it so clear to me, *looking didn't mean finding.*

Ghanshyam said they would question us and then let us go. Go! Go where? I could not grasp the normality of it all, with the surging crowds of foreign tourists, guest workers, and Indians coming in and out of the station to report crimes. I had not imagined the jitters that overtook me as I once again was about to be among those blessed with the same prerogatives as these people who were going about the business of life. What would I do when I left this station? The privilege of freedom was about to cast me off into the unknown subcontinent alone.

Mr. McCarthy interrupted my tempestuous thoughts. "Please follow me," he said to the five of us. We rose and followed McCarthy through a maze of gleaming corridors.

I stopped short when we climbed a few steps and pushed through swinging doors. There stood Paul with his arms crossed over his chest, talking with the Interpol agent. *My Paul!* I was paralyzed at the sight of him. Never in my wildest imaginations did I think Paul would be in India. Would Paul hate me if he knew the things I had done? I had seen husbands turn away from their wives and girlfriends after they were raped. There was nothing I could do to erase what had happened to me and the things that I had done. *If he only knew. If he only knew. If he only knew.* My inclination was to bolt away from the police station so that I didn't have to see Paul's face, hear his voice, feel his pain. But a young guard stood behind me ushering me along with the group.

We were led through another labyrinth of hallways and corridors. I couldn't take my eyes off the back of Paul's head. He was real. I could reach out and touch him. Paul and Agent Berkshire stopped to look through a grate to an interrogation room. "Okay, Paul. You all set?" the agent asked.

"Yeah. Let's do this."

The hum of the air conditioning ceased when we stepped into a room that was as hot as a kiln, stifling, airless, and claustrophobic. Belhaj had already been there for several hours. Inspector Singh was there too, looking sweaty and weary as if he'd been put through his own psychological wringer. Belhaj had been revived and sat at a rickety table, with his shoulders hunched, clearly still foggy headed from the flunitrazepam I'd given him seven or so hours earlier. The half-life of a drug is the period of time it takes for the plasma concentration to be reduced by one half. The half-life of flunitrazepam is eighteen to twenty-six hours. Belhaj had a way to go before he would feel awake, much less clearheaded. He looked greasy, and his diseased nose was inflamed. His arms hung limply at his sides like a boxer between pummeling rounds.

Berkshire launched into his interrogation without preamble, slamming a hand on the table next to Belhaj. "You fancy yourself a ladies' man, Noël?"

Noël? I found myself smirking. No wonder he went by his last name. The agent smacked him on the back of the head but Belhaj still didn't reply. "Because these three ladies said you had sex with them last night. *At the same time.*"

Belhaj smiled. He leaned back on his chair, crossing his arms over his chest, looking smug as if he thought they had nothing on him—that the agent was just reaching. His grin faded when Paul set down his bottle of Pernod on the table. It was in a plastic bag, marked as evidence.

"Funny, is it?" Paul asked. "We've got something to tell you that'll wipe that smirk off your face."

"You had better be listening to Mr. Veller," said Inspector Singh, his voice holding a hint of insecurity.

The British Interpol agent went on, "Someone slipped you a Mickey in your Pernod, old man." He thought for a second. "Scratch that. A Mickey's what you give your victims, isn't it? Chloral hydrate. What you got was no Mickey."

"No, no it wasn't," Paul said. "You know what flunitrazepam is?" Paul asked Belhaj. "Maybe you know the brand name Rohypnol? The date rape drug? *Of course* you do. You're in the business of rape, aren't you?" Paul waved the plastic bag that contained the empty blister pack section in front of Belhaj's face. "Recognize this?" Paul's voice was calm, but murderous rage was in his eyes. It was something I'd never seen. In fact, I had never seen Paul truly angry. He was always so composed. "Better pay attention, Christmas boy, because you got some gifts you might want to know about."

Belhaj looked nervous now, sweating profusely, dark moons under his arms and drops of perspiration falling down his cheeks like the drops that were falling outside. The monsoon. We all paused, looking up at the windows as rain pelted them again.

Berkshire nodded to my beggar women, his face softening, encouraging. "*Kalji karu nakoo*," he said. "Don't worry."

The first woman carried the bag of my hair under her sari, which gave her a distended belly, adding to the gruesome gestalt. She slowly removed her veil and even I was shocked to see her appearance again. The beautiful, thick and shiny black curtain of hair that typically graced the head of Indian women was no more. She had but a few motley patches of fuzz on her scalp. Her skin was covered in a hot rash. Her eyes were milky, her lips blighted with syphilitic chancres. She smiled a twisted, painful smile and stared directly at Belhaj. "Sexy fun Bel-ji?" she asked. "Fucky sucky?"

Paul had a book with him with pages bookmarked. It was a medical dictionary, tattered and dog-eared. Once Ghanshyam had told them about the women, he must have gone out and found it from a used bookstore. "Advanced syphilis," Paul read. "An infectious chronic venereal disease characterized by lesions involving organs and tissues ultimately resulting in loss of coordination, muscle control, paralysis, numbness, blindness *and insanity.*" He looked up and smiled grimly, his lips drawn into a thin line.

Agent Berkshire had his mouth to Belhaj's ear. "This precious young girl was sold into the Pawar's brothel at age twelve. She's only eighteen now. *Eighteen years old!*"

Belhaj had no time to react before the next woman unveiled. Her face was riddled with the opportunistic infection called Kaposi's sarcoma. The tumors were caused by human herpesvirus 8 and were one of the defining illnesses of AIDS. Plump purple and black nodules surrounded and crept into her nasal passages, distorting her facial features. The fungating and necrosing lesions infected her lips and gums, forcing the woman's mouth to hang open. It was evident that her soft palate and tongue were affected, not only because of the blood on her sari, but because of her skeletalized condition. She was dying. "Fucky sucky," she rasped.

"Acquired immune deficiency syndrome," Paul read. "Full-blown AIDS is diagnosed when a syndrome of opportunistic infections occur such as thrush, herpes simplex and Kaposi's sarcoma."

"This human being was sold into the Pawar's brothel at age nine," Agent Berkshire told Belhaj, who was sweating even more profusely and flushing deeply.

Paul turned to another marked page in the book as the third woman unveiled. She blinked with eyes like a treasured harem girl, lips that turned up at the corners in a perpetual, though enigmatic smile. Her nose, pierced with a tiny diamond, was short and upturned like an old fashioned pinup girl. She dropped her pallu and that is when we saw that her hands were a petrified mass flecked with bloody, white-crusted scabs, her fingers eaten away into mere nubs. "Sexy fun, Bel-ji. Fucky sucky."

"Leprosy," Paul read. "Caused by the organism *Mycobacterium leprae*. All forms of the disease result in peripheral neurological damage which causes sensory loss in the skin, nerves in the hands and feet, and lining of the nose."

"Seems the Pawars were not discriminating about their clientele," Berkshire said into Belhaj's ear.

Belhaj exploded from his chair, screaming like the proverbial stuck pig. "*Zhat bitch*!" Two Indian policemen blasted inside the room, tackled him, and held him down on the ground. The men were young and strong and overzealous and their profiles were firm, mouths set, eyes black with hatred for this man who represented more suffering in their country.

"I demand medical treatment!" Belhaj squealed.

Berkshire calmly chuckled. "Well, that's rich, old man. Seems the wheels of justice turn very slowly here in India. May have a little wait on your hands."

One of the Indian cops pressed his boot onto Belhaj's face, mashing his cheek into the gritty floor. The room seemed even stuffier with nine people jammed inside, body odors and secretions commingling with the moldy plaster, the slimy floor, the musty odor of the old medical book. My emotions were jumbled. Out of revenge, I had helped these women prostitute themselves. They had defiled themselves one last time. How could I have justified such a thing? I felt as if I were suffocating under my veil and that any minute I would lose control and rip the fabric away from my face so that I could breathe.

"If you tell us where we can find Dr. Fitzgerald," Berkshire said, "I'll see what I can do about getting you some medical attention."

"I don't know where she is," Belhaj blubbered. "I swear I don't know. I would tell you. I swear to God I would tell you."

Paul brandished an American passport in front of his face. "This is Doctor Fitzgerald's passport," he said, his voice cracking. He stood up and threw the passport against the wall. He turned away, hiding his eyes with a trembling hand.

I had seen enough. I couldn't see him feeling for me when I knew he would hate me if he knew what I had become. I stooped to pick up my passport. "Get me out of here now," I whispered to Ghanshyam.

Ghanshyam turned to McCarthy hurriedly saying, "She is the mother of one of the girls. She must be taking her leave of this distressing examination."

"Ve don't need her," the Indian inspector said. "But *you* stay around Mumbai."

I walked softly out of the room. A young policeman pressed past me, looking as if he were on a mission, stopping to talk to Ghansyham in hushed tones. Then I nearly ran into the shackled Mr. Chandraram who was tethered to a steel chair. "Keep these fucking Dalits away from me," he bellowed at the brush of my sari.

I pulled my pallu from my face, and flashed him a glimpse. "I'm no untouchable."

"Doctor Deva." He snorted a little blast of indignant air out of his nostrils.

"Your sister is dead."

"It was *you* who did this."

"I didn't kill her. You did. She's been dead for a long time. Now it's your turn."

I expected him to weep repentantly, but that is what one would do whose body housed a soul. Instead he laughed again. "Oh no, I think you are mistaken. The Lord of Death vill pass me by."

"Really. How so?"

He lifted his shackled arm showing me his golden threaded bracelet. "The Lord of Death, Lord Yama had a sister Yamuna who tied a rakhi to his wrist to bestow immortality. Yama was so moved that he promised life immortal to whoever received a rakhi from his sister. You see, every year growing up ve vould celebrate the festival of Raksha Bandhan. My sister vould tie the rakhi onto my vrist asking me for my protection and love. I voud accept the rakhi as confirmation of the gift of immortality. It vas a family event vith all members bedecked in finery gathering to celebrate."

Everything clicked. "You raped her when she was a girl."

He sneered. "Ve vere in love. But you vould not understand."

"When you couldn't afford to pay for your celebrations you sent your beautiful sister to Paris. But you were jealous. When she got away from you, you used brutality to bring her back. But she didn't love you like you loved her, so you turned your twisted attentions on destroying as many women and girls as you could get your hands on."

"Vhat kind of doctor are you?" he asked in a bloodless tone, a quiver of one spongy cheek giving away his fury. "As I am quite certain that psychiatry vas not your specialty."

"You don't need to be psychiatrist to understand that you're a madman."

I wanted to say more, but on my heels was Ghansyham, followed by Inspector Singh. The young policeman with the lathi must have told the inspector that Chandraram was here, in shackles. I quickly swept the pallu over my face.

"Mr. Chandraram!" the inspector exclaimed breathlessly. Camille *had* been telling the truth about the depths of corruption in India. And this inspector with the pretty moustache and tidy turban was one of those who had taken baksheesh to turn a blind eye to girls being tortured, raped, and killed.

There was an exit door out of the station. I walked toward it.

Chadraram sputtered, "That is her! Doctor Deva!"

The inspector, his ears closed to anything but the rattle of his own fear, hissed, "Chandraram, I insist that you are keeping quiet until the arrival of your solicitor!"

I opened the door as Chandraram called out to me, "My goondas vill find you no matter vhere you run."

I ducked out of the station. Just another beggar woman, vanishing into the throngs.

NINETEEN

Sitar music and drums filled my head as I rode with Ghanshyam and his wife, her pallu hiding the multi-tiered emerald necklace, bold riches against her ghee-colored skin. In the back of the bullock cart, with me, was the frail, hare-lipped servant girl Ekanta cradling Ghanshyam's baby daughter.

After leaving the police station, Ghanshyam had shown me to a clinic near the zopadpatti where he went to collect his family and meager belongings so that they could escape to his ancestral village. A harried doctor filled a prescription for enteric-coated erythromycin tablets in lieu of fragile penicillin, which was the preferred antibiotic for rat-bite fever. "In the U.S., human rabies immunoglobulin is no longer administered through the abdominal wall with a large bore needle," I informed her. But she merely wove her head around as if to placate my ignorance. "One half of the dose should be injected near the bite, the remainder intramuscularly," I asserted, to more head weaving as the doctor plunged the syringe into my abdomen.

I lay clutching my guts during four days of travel. Four hundred kilometers northeast of Mumbai, I was to take a train from the Aurangabad Station in Ellora, to Varanasi. In Ellora we found a clinic for my second rabies shot. Then we said our good-byes on the platform, shell-shocked by the events that had radically altered all of our lives, making passionate declarations of eternal friendship and oaths to keep in touch. "Good-bye," I said to my friends, not wanting to show them any trepidation. "Thank you for your courage." I did namaste and Ghanshyam returned my prayer, his head weaving.

And then, so suddenly that I was stunned, I was alone; traveling the rest of the way by train, where I expected to lean out of the window and feel the hot wind on my face and enjoy intoxicating freedom as I listened to the shrieking of the wheels on the tracks and the cars thundering over the rails. But it was not that romantic. Instead the air seethed, stuffy and hot; the air conditioning was dysfunctional, and the windows were sealed shut. Inside my choli I carried Belhaj's cash, my passport, the antibiotics, the *Gita*, the stolen jewels, and my father's ashes. It was uncomfortable lugging all of the things in my sari top, but I had no bag and furthermore couldn't afford to lose any of the items. The minor discomfort was nothing compared to the tenacious anxiety that had begun in Belhaj's room, which had mushroomed in the police station, and now settled in my stomach like the mice that scurried under the tracks at the station. Was I being paranoid?

I looked at my passport, with my mug shot with the suppressed smile—as the clerk at Kinko's had warned that the passport agency didn't like people to look too happy. But I had been happy that day. I had been happy most days. And I hadn't even known it. That was the tragedy. It was a sad revelation.

I could not stop thinking about Camille and Zarina, wondering what had happened to them. There had been no mention of them at the police station. Were they safe? I brushed away a fat black fly that had found its way into our sealed compartment, and then slumped into my seat trying to keep calm.

A young boy hung over the seat, staring at me curiously as he sucked, slack jawed, on a stick of licorice. His face was smeared with the black candy and the smell of it wafted over to me. If I made it to Varanasi, would Mr. Chandraram's network of thugs find me? I'd wake up in the night with a goonda sitting on my chest, razor switchblade pressed to my throat. *The smell of Pernod.* My mouth filled with saliva and the needles of adrenaline prickled up my extremities.

As the distance and time grew between my captors and me I began to ponder whether I had fought hard enough? Had I simply given up and let them do terrible things to me? Was it my fault? I covered my ears but it was no use; the charges repeated, swirling around in my head: *My fault. My fault. My fault.* I understood what the Victorian novels meant by swooning and felt myself falling out of control into a merciful sleep. But there remained a wretched lack of serenity to my slumber. Hours and days passed, yet the pulsing of the train's mechanism along the tracks couldn't deafen my tormented dreams. By the time I eventually saw the signs nearing Varanasi, I was nearing a breakdown. *Manikpur, Allahabad, Vindhyachal, Mirzapur, Chunar*, and finally *Varanasi-Banares*. Dozens of men and children squatted, defecating as they watched the train go by.

Then the blast of the whistle, chaos, shouting, the grating of metal on metal, the train slowing to a stop, screeching. A belch of fetid steam laced with stagnant fumes of human waste greeted me as I stepped off the train onto the platform. A wet heat sucked at me, luring me out of the station. A swarm of urchins ran to meet me, barefoot, their tangled hair blotched with white dust—an uncanny, ageless look. Some had been intentionally maimed, their stumps swathed in bloody bandages. Careening into me, they called, in tiny voices, "One pen, one pen, madam."

I plowed through the riotous crowd, staggered by the sheer numbers: the ancient wobbly coolies, bodies stretched prostrate, holy men and pilgrims, cows and begging monkeys, and long narrow bundles of corpses being carried through the streets. A strong sense of foreboding settled uncomfortably in my chest as I boarded a rickshaw. "Take me to a hostel," I said, "something not too expensive."

The vehicle swerved through the decadent grandeur of the city while I held my hand over my nose against the ammonia fumes, curry, diesel, incense, hashish, dust, and sewage. Everyone seemed sinister. The rickshaw pulled through the labyrinth of alleyways papered with yoga advertisements and film posters; inching and weaving around people, cars and bicycles like a worm in soft earth. The rickshaw puller stopped in front of a narrow corridor, no more than four feet, between two rows of buildings. Retail shops flanked the opening of the lane. To the left, a tiny tailoring shop where a man sat on the floor laboring over a sewing machine. To the right, a betel nut concession.

"Madam, go there. To hostel," the rickshaw puller said, pointing into the darkness of the corridor between the betel nut stall and the tailoring shop. "Madam must valk."

After all the weeks in isolation, I couldn't face going through that dark passage. "Is there another way around?"

"Long way. Madam vant ride long way?"

"Yes," I said. "Long way."

I finally arrived at the hostel, surrounded by a white picket fence and resting under an arbor of kumquat trees and pink bougainvillea. Through the gate was a garden and through an open door, a reception office. Inside sat a man at a desk reading a newspaper from a stack of papers a foot thick. He was about fifty, bald, and bespectacled with Mahatma Gandhi eyeglasses. A pencil moustache defined his lips, full and lush as a woman's though with a dour, sullen look about his face. He rose when he saw a guest had arrived. He was thin but carried a little paunch. He paused to take a long, slurping draught of his Kingfisher lager—thus the insulin resistant belly—and then walked around a massive mahogany desk stacked two feet high with more newspapers and books.

"Do you have a room available?"

"Of course, a very, very, very nice room I am having for your accommodation."

"Oh, that's good. I'm Doctor Meredith Fitzgerald." I handed him my passport. My credentials felt made up and I felt my face go hot and the redness rise on my cheeks.

"Doctor Fitzgerald, did you say?" His face lit up when he smiled, changing his countenance completely from sullen to cheerfully impish. "A pleasure to be making your acquaintance. I am Shreeram Jhombarkar." He did *namaste*. "Velcome to Vananasi."

"Thank you."

With barely a flicker of his eyes this man took me in, the soiled sari emanating body odor and soot, my shaved head, and Paul's engagement ring on my finger. His face showed no opinion, no judgment. "I am thinking that you are being a much famous physician in America, Doctor Fitzgerald!" he crowed. For a moment I thought it was just Indian hyperbole, until he added, "You see, here at Shreeram Jhombarkar's hostel the one and the only Doctor Fitzgerald has had a gentleman caller."

"What did you say?"

"Yes, he is coming by two days ago inquiring about you. I am having the distinct impression that he is going around the city as vell. He is seeming most eager to be finding you. Yes, yes, yes. He said he vas looking for a Doctor Meredith Fitzgerald. That is being you, is it not?" Jhombarkar's eyes flared with the intrigue of it all. He giggled.

"What did you tell him?"

"Vell, I am not exactly conversing vith the gentleman myself, you see, as I vas not available at the time. You see, my mali—the gardener—is knowing that I am highly respecting the privacy of my guests, employing all manners of solicitousness necessary for such high standards that I am aspiring to. Therefore the mali is informing the gentleman that he is not in the possession of any such information regarding the party he is seeking. At the time it was being much true, you see, I only am just making your acquaintance this very morning!"

"Did he say he would come back?"

"I'm afraid I cannot be telling you much more. After I said I didn't know of you, he simply is disappeared."

"Did the mali tell you what he looked like?"

"I am not being sure of the certainty. He vas apparently in possession of very, very, very dark circles under the eyes, definitely spoiling the appearance of his facial features as one's eyes cannot help but to be traveling to such flaws and the mind asking itself why the gentleman is not spending more time in pranayama and shavasana? Ah, but I am noticing that you, the most venerable of Vestern doctors, perhaps are not familiar with Ayurvedic terms?"

"If he comes back, please let me know immediately."

"Of course, of course, I vill not be breathing a vord of your vhereabouts if that is your vishing," he said conspiratorially. "Now I have been giving you my vord of honor, you may be resting very, very, very easily. The privacy of my guests is my utmost concern." Jhombarkar smiled, transforming his face again. "For additional surveillance measures, I vill be informing the mali to be vatching out with all due vigilance and to be checking regularly for any out of the ordinary eventualities. He is arriving every day at dawn and staying until the last plant has been vatering. He vill be informing me if there is anyone here that is not a paying guest. Now then, vhat are you saying is the purpose of bringing such a charming lady doctor to our holy city?"

"I've brought my father's ashes to scatter in the Ganges River."

"Ah," Jhombarkar sighed contentedly in this knowledge. "You have not come to our grand city solely as a tourist. I applaud you, Doctor Fitzgerald. You are having a more important mission to be accomplishing."

I smiled even more thinly.

"Yes, I am seeing now that you are appearing very, very, very, very veary from your travels," Jhombarkar said, with his lilting accent, a look of deep concern falling over his face so that his features once again settled into the unattractive sullen pall. "Now then, ve must be getting the heralded doctor situated in her accommodations. My best room. The only room vith having a shower!" His head wove back and forth.

I followed Mr. Jhombarkar up a flight of wooden stairs to a second floor room, a plain stucco room painted bright saffron. The walls could have used a good washing and the bed was merely another Indian rope bed draped with a gauzy mosquito net. Above the bed was a revolving fan, which, Jhombarkar declared, ran constantly, day and night. "No mosquitoes are being here," he boasted. There was a simple stucco shower room attached to my room, with the end of a pipe sticking out of the wall in lieu of a showerhead, situated above a porcelain, Eastern-style toilet. In all, the room was not much different than the one I had shared with Camille and Zarina at the Pawar's.

"Now, if everything is being satisfactory I shall be leaving you. But I shall be returning presently, vith fruit and chai to be giving you sustenance after such a long and arduous journey," Mr. Jhombarkar proclaimed with enthusiasm that was appreciated after the hellish train trip.

I shut the door after him and leaned heavily against it, listening to my heartbeat throbbing in my head. I lay down on the bed, feeling the relief of my body flattening supine into the rope weave. The train journey, like a diseased vector, had infected me with fear, doubt, confusion, paranoia. I squeezed my eyes shut, but remained alert. No more than five minutes passed and there came a tentative rap on my door, and I started.

"Fruit and chai," Mr. Jhombarkar announced, barging in and placing a tray down on a small table, setting out several bananas and a pot of chai with a cup and saucer. "After imbibing of the chai and perhaps the ingestion of a banana or two, you shall be feeling quite refreshed, I am thinking."

"Mr. Jhombarkar," I said, deciding to keep things on a formal basis with him, "I have only this sari to wear. My luggage was stolen on the train." I smiled to season my lie with sincerity.

"You vill be leaving your sari out of the door and I vill be returning it presently, laundered and pressed." He turned bowing, doing namaste, and left. I undressed and handed my sari, pavada, and choli out of the door.

I had not showered since the bath Mrs. Pawar's servants gave me. I reeked. And so I stood under the hot shower for thirty minutes, soaping with a bar of LUX and rinsing and soaping again. Then I lay, wrapped in a wet towel, on the bed in a fetal position. In a perverse way I felt grateful for the heat. It was almost as if I craved physical suffering to keep me from spinning off into insanity now that I knew that Mr. Chandraram's goondas were in the city looking for me. "I'll never be safe," I whispered.

It wasn't just the reality of being stalked by Chandraram's goondas. It was the mental torment. My mind swirled with the vicious, taunting, accusatory voices. I thought about the night Mrs. Pawar had spilled her secrets to me. It was clear that she had melted down from acute post-traumatic stress. Was I suffering from post-traumatic stress, too? It was so hard to admit that something like that could happen to someone like me.

Where was my only friend when I needed her? If Camille were here, she would have the answers. Completely alone in the world, all I could do was repeat my mantra, "I will find a way out."

TWENTY

Inexplicably—and this was only one of the countless quandaries I would encounter in India—Mr. Jhombarkar didn't appear to find it odd that a bald American tourist with one common sari to her name would proffer a handful of rubies, diamonds, emeralds, and sapphires. He inspected the gemstones from his perch on a woven mat where he sat modestly diaperized in his white dhoti, his left foot in half lotus, his right leg wrapped around his neck, his palms pressed together in namaste.

"Is it possible to exchange these for cash, Mr. Jhombarkar?"

"I am very, very, very certain that such an eventuality can be arranged," he said, smoothly unwinding from his yoga asana, rising to standing, and scooping the jewels from my palm into the pocket of his kurta like a practiced casino dealer.

No more than an hour passed when Mr. Jhombarkar appeared at my door, knocking tentatively. "I am having for you rupees in exchange for the gemstones," he hissed as if he feared being overheard, though I had noticed that, unlike American tourists whose propensity was to unleash their most despicable manners when they checked into hotels, his other tenants were Indians who moved soundlessly around the hostel like ghosts, whispering genteelly in Hindi. They never seemed to understand a word I said when I passed by murmuring *good-morning*, or *good evening*, or inanely, *have a nice day*. I peeked inside the leather pouch he handed me, designed with a long leather strap, perfect for carrying around my few other possessions. There was a stack of rupees neatly arranged.

Was Mr. Jhombarkar honest? I was in no position to question his integrity. I smiled. He beamed. Yes, *he'd profited by this exchange.*

It seemed a good idea to exchange some cash into American Express Travelers Checks. After all the months of depravity and intrigue, the idea of having this small security was appealing, and so I found myself in a long line that wound slowly toward a counter where customer service representatives operated on Indian time. I waited with my head down. When I got up to the front of the line I suddenly felt the penetrating stares of a group of Americans dressed in bright, crisp, department store cruise wear. I heard one of them talking, something about a junkie, something about a hippie. "I've seen them at the river, buying drugs." The entire group turned to look at me. I pushed through the crowd, out of the glass door, to the street.

My rickshaw puller, a twenty-year old barefoot man, with a rumpled, grubby turban tumbling off his head stood chatting with a group of other rickshaw pullers and drivers who were in the midst of a paan break. I noticed myself reflected in a crazy garland of mirrors that one of the drivers had rigged around the bonnet of his tut-tut carriage. My black hair bristled out of my scalp. My tawny face had grown gaunt, exaggerating the patrician bones my father had teased me as being my regal flaw. My reflection reminded me of the empty, tortured stares of the patients I'd seen in my psyche rotation. No wonder the antiseptic Americans mistook me for a drug user.

Indians were betel aficionados even though the nasty habit stained the teeth, tongue and lips bright red, rotted gums, and cracked teeth. The paanwalla smeared betel leaves with white germy looking paste, concocting something like a triangle shaped hors d'oeuvre. The pots filled with flavorings were filthy and repugnant. But the betel nut contained arecoline, a narcotic stimulant that produces a euphoric high, so I understood the men greedily grabbing for their fixes. Clinical studies have demonstrated that the mere sight of heroin paraphernalia elicits acute cravings even years after a person kicks heroin. Thinking about the men getting high started my mind reeling and the urge for heroin pounding in my head.

Then I remembered that paan was also thought to be an aphrodisiac and I felt a well of anger bubbling like the chaiwalla's brew at the sight of the giggling men and their jeering expressions. I imagined vulgar comments blurting from their despicable red lips, and the anticipatory fantasies reeling in their depraved heads about the whores they would visit later.

"Madam go hotel?" the puller asked, his mouth agitating a jumble of the masticated green betel leaf and red areca nut.

"No, take me to the river." His eyes flickered at my harsh tone and then I felt sorry that I'd lashed out at the boy out of my own twisted paranoia. "I'm sorry," I said, and his head wove back and forth and he smiled tentatively.

Sixty bathing ghats, which are stepped embankments, line the Ganges River. When we arrived at the entrance to the nearest ghat, the puller helped me from his carriage. "Madam go river," he said. "I vait."

The morning beckoned worshipers to the river where every living organism prepared for the inevitability of the midday sun when heat would subdue ambition. I descended the motley concrete steps to the water. Behind me were towering, ancient buildings defaced by crumbling plaster and tilting alarmingly as if in danger of tumbling into the river. The water stirred slightly, a murky green, like slightly turned vegetable soup. A breeze blew across the water like a blast furnace, evaporating my perspiration. The ghat was a confusion of clanging temple gongs, bells, cymbals, shouting, chanting, praying, bathing, washing. The chaos and heat were stifling.

Standing at the edge of the Ganges, I watched a priest sing over a tiny alcove, which housed a smooth phallus-shaped stone, the mark of Shiva, creator and destroyer, the ruler of Varanasi who promised to breathe on those cremated in his city, guaranteeing safe passage to Nirvana. I felt so out of place, removed from life in general, vulnerable and lost. I felt lulled into a shallow trance. The activity around me blurred, the noise softening to a hum as I stared across the green water.

"Lady want buy drugs?" A boy's voice barged into my thoughts. I turned slowly to look at this eighteen year old dressed in a wife beater tee-shirt and a dhoti. "Not much money. Very cheap." He smiled, his head weaving. He opened his palm. He held a packet made of folded paper. "Good drugs. Cheap." His eyes were deep brown and friendly. "Pure heroin."

I swallowed. "How much?" My voice sounded small, far away.

"Only four thousand, two hundred rupees."

I turned away.

"Lady for you, three thousand rupees."

"I don't have a needle," I said in a dry whisper.

"I have for lady. Together same price, three thousand rupees."

I turned and walked up the steps.

"I give lady best price. Two thousand, three hundred."

I stopped walking away and, without further thought, opened up the leather purse that hung from a cord around my neck and sorted through the bulging stack of rupees. But before I could offer the man the money, a Caucasian man stepped between us, grasped the young dope dealer by the throat. He throttled him as if to emphasize what he said in Hindi. "*Haramzade.*" The young man's bare feet left the ground momentarily, the friendly eyes registering fear. "I don't want to see you here again," the man said in an American accent. "If I see you bothering this woman again, you're in deep shit, understand?"

"No bother lady," the boy said, choking and coughing. "Lady ask me."

"Shut your fucking mouth," he said, prying open the drug dealer's hand and snatching the paper packet from his grasp. "Tell your friends. *Nikal jao yahan se*. Get out of here." He let go of the dope dealer, who bled quickly into the crowd. The man called out, "*Haramzade,*" and then muttered, "Fucking thief." He studied me for a moment. "People come to Varanasi to die. If you're not already dying it can be arranged." He crumpled up the packet and threw it into the river.

I stared at him, immobilized with mortification, anger . . . relief. My throat felt as if it were closed completely.

"Where're you staying?"

"At a hostel."

"I'll walk you there."

"No." I left him at the ghat and skipped hurriedly up the steps. When I turned to look, he was gone.

I found the rickshaw puller. When we got near the hostel, a wedding procession blocked the entrance to the street. "Rickshaw no go here. Madam valk."

I paid the man and slipped from the carriage. The wedding procession continued noisily, trampling the flowers strewn in the street, filling the air with a suffocating bouquet, the bells and drums reminding me that the dramas of other's lives continued to play on. Why had I gone to the river? It was as if I had known the young man with the white packet would be there. I walked faster, but the scent of the flowers grew stronger. At my feet dozens of marigolds appeared like glaring eyes. I stumbled and ran. The crowd closed in on me and I fell, looking up to see Belhaj's face looming over me. I fought to breathe.

"Madam!" The rickshaw puller dragged me away from the wheels of a bullock cart. He helped me to stand. I gasped like an asthmatic fighting for air. I met the man's gaze but he looked away, confusion and embarrassment in his eyes. "I take Madam hotel."

I brushed off my sari, which was streaked with gold and green stains from the marigolds. The puller walked with me back to the hostel. I opened my purse and handed him the wad of rupees I had almost given the drug dealer. A light in his eyes flared at the sight of so much money and he pressed his palms in namaste.

The full impact of the midday sun blasting like the heat from a foundry beat down upon the hostel garden. Mr. Jhombarkar stood in the tall Indian grass, which spiked like a white, silver and gold fringe between the fastidiously-raked paths, pouring water through his nostrils from the spout of a neti pot. "Good day, Doctor Fitzgerald." He stood tall, snorting, scrunching his nose, and adjusting his belly in his dohti.

"Hello."

"Please be forgiving my expectorate. I am feeling the discomfort of a small amount of sinus disturbance from the clogged atmospheric pressure of the too many diesel vehicles within our great city," he said, holding up a small pot. "The neti pot is an

Ayurvedic detoxification for the purpose of purifying the impurities. Perhaps Doctor Fitzgerald vould like to try?"

In my former life the word *detox* was barely tolerated and only in five star hotel spas. But now I just smiled.

"I am seeing that you are appearing very, very, very veary."

"Yes, you're right. I suppose I do need a rest." I sunk to a garden bench. Under the shade of the bench grew scaly corpse plants that lived off the remains of dead foliage, as Indians were, above all, avid recyclers.

"And how is your first day of being the tourist?"

"Fine. I went to the river, Mr. Jhombarkar, but you know, I find the derelict towers and palaces along the river disturbing."

He wove his head back and forth as if I should go on.

"Please don't take this the wrong way, but the fact that those incredible old buildings are sliding millimeter by millimeter into the Ganges . . . it's unsettling. Someday the Ganges is going to be clogged with the fallen relics of the days when Varansi had been great. Why aren't architects and archaeologists flocking to Varanasi to shore up the ancient structures like they are to the Acropolis in Athens, the pyramids in Cairo, like the old wall in Istanbul?"

"India is a mystery, Dr. Fitzgerald. And not everyone can decipher the many, many, many great treasures."

I thought of my father as our relationship had been a bit of a mystery too. I'd been ignoring the fact that his ashes were sitting up there in my room. I knew that I should just get on with the ritual of scattering his ashes and be done with it. But then if I did, I would have no reason to stay in India. I would have nothing left. I wouldn't know what to do. I couldn't simply get back on a plane and go back to the U.S. and resume my life. "Not all good things, all noble things, are considered worthy," I said sadly. "Some just come to an end."

"That is vhat you are missing Doctor Fitzgerald. You see, India is not simply the tangible aspect of being," Mr. Jhombarkar said consolingly.

Then I chastised myself for my inability to see that the breathtaking grandeur, the dignity, the spirituality of India was indeed more than the tangible. I had forgotten my father's training. I had forgotten how to accept. Moreover, I was angry with him, convinced that he never had to endure anything so terrible that he could not accept. Even my mother's death had been eased by decades of fucking other beautiful women. I refused to accept what had happened to me, and this new version of myself. I knew that it was counter productive to continue to wallow in negativity and self-hatred, but I could not stop the obsessive and tortured thinking.

"I suppose that I mirror my own soul when I see India," I confessed spontaneously to Jhombarkar in a rash moment of mindlessness. "That's probably why I only see the filth, the poverty, and hopelessness."

"If it is not too bold of me to say, I am thinking that perhaps your prana is being tangled up like one very, very, very big multi-vehicular traffic tie up?"

"I'm sorry?"

"Prana," he said, enunciating. "Prana is Sanskrit for breath. It is being one of the five organs of vitality: Prana, breath. Vac, speech. Caksus, sight. Shrota, hearing. Manas, thought. You are understanding? Nose, mouth, eyes, ears, and mind?"

"Uh-huh." Being a Western doctor this lecture would have been at one time a little too woo woo for me. Now I clung to the hope that he would tell me something that would ease my torment.

"Vedantic philosophy is coming from the Veda, that is being the ancient and very oldest sacred texts of Hinduism. Vedantic philosophy teaches of the vital, life-sustaining force of all living beings that are having the vital energy.

Prana is flowing through channels called nadis. Prana is suffusing all living creatures. Granthis are being the energetic knots that are blocking the flow of your prana through the charka channels, vhich are are being the energy centers, you are understanding?"

"I think so."

"Brahma granthi is being the physical knotting that is sitting in this region of the mooladhar and swadhisthana chakras." He put the flat of his hand on his sacrum. "Then you are suffering also from the Vishnu granthi, very, very, very emotional because you see it is covering the area between the manipura, anahata and vishuddhi chakras." He rotated his hand over his chest in the general vicinity of his heart. "Third is the problem of the Shiva granthi." He placed his forefinger delicately on his third eye. "It is the mental knotting of the ajna and sahasrar chakras."

"What can I do about these granthi knots?" I asked this man who had in the very recent past fenced stolen gemstones without blinking an eye. I suspected that Mr. Jhombarkar would proceed to tediously lecture me about oblique pranayama breathing exercises, equanimous yoga asanas, and impossible meditation in obtuse Vedantic terms. Instead, he shuffled into his office and returned immediately with a notebook made up of recycled paper, and several pencils sharpened into lethal graphite points.

"I am thinking that you are being a scholar and that the flowing of vords on the page is sometimes bringing the untangling of the granthi knots."

I looked at him and all I could do was smile. India was a nutty place.

I began in pencil in Mr. Jhombarkar's humble notebook: *Medicine is a system that processes human beings* . . . . The words poured out of me, the pain, the anguish, fear, guilt, remorse, self-hatred. And Mr. Jhombarkar was right. The knots didn't become untangled, but they seemed a little looser.

TWENTY-ONE

Three weeks passed. Mr. Jhombarkar delivered another notebook, then another. He brought trays of simple meals: Fish Amritsari—fried fish that had been dipped in batter flavored with carom seed. Green Chicken Pulao, Mughlai Biryani, and other chicken dishes that I suspected were expensive but that Mr. Jhombarkar was feeling a bit guilty for having skimmed a little too much off the top of the sale of the stolen jewels. In fact, when I complained about the complications of putting on the sari, he brought me two white salwar kameez outfits—apparently assuming I was in mourning—that had to have been costly with all the elaborate hand embroidery. He even went so far as to arrange for a doctor's house call to administer my third rabies injection.

Auspiciously, a light rain washed over the city, bringing a short respite from the heat—and fresh inspiration. I was determined to go to the river that night with my father's ashes. However, the upswing of my mood was only temporary. After a long rickshaw drive through the crowded streets, my mood soured. Still I was at the river, thinking *fuck it.* I gathered my courage and waved down the oarsman of a small boat. The craft was no bigger than a dingy, narrower, but not exactly a canoe. It was made of crudely-hewn lumber, slightly rotten, with an arched canopy of weather worn, but colorful canvas, just as I had seen in pictures. The man held out a hand, helping me onto the boat. Standing at the back end of the boat, he used a long pole to guide the craft from the ghat. The boatman continued along the river. The sun hung low in the sky and began to dip into the horizon. A dead monkey floated by, face down, like a discarded children's toy. The smell from the monkey corpse made me queasy. But it was not nearly as startling as the charred hand, and the chunk of flesh that looked as if there were a burnt femur bone sticking out of it. Not too far away from that, a half-naked man urinated into the water next to a group of women engaged in the curious process of bathing and washing their saris, while still partially dressed in them.

Purification is coming from bathing in the Ganga! Shabana had told me. Bathing in the Ganga was believed to wash away sins and liberate oneself from the eternal cycle of reincarnation. But I could not feel anything but disgust for this sewer. Just then, the oarsman leaned over the edge of the boat and, pressing an index finger against his nostril, blew a stream of snot into the water. I shut my eyes hard trying to forget the oarsman and his snot, the rotting primate, the burnt body parts, the urinating man. I revisited my image of the way the ceremony was supposed to be, of music and soft breezes, the ashes strewn on the holy river, mingled with fragrant white flowers. But it was no use. I instructed the boatman with sign language to return to the shore. He poled his craft back to the ghat.

I stepped off the boat, and as soon as the man had his rupees, he poled away. But I didn't recognize this ghat. "Wait!" I shouted. But the man was already approaching another customer farther on.

Night had fallen. It was Manikarnika, the crematorium ghat, the destination for the long, narrow bundles that were carried through the streets. A man worked a funeral pyre, flipping burning bones and flesh together as if stirring a pile of leaves, legs, ribs, head, arms, a jumbled mass. The stench of burning flesh mingled with the sickly fragrance of wilting flowers. I walked toward the road above. There, hundreds of people jammed the passageway with rickshaws, oxcarts, bicycles, motorbikes, and on foot. A few rickshaws and pedicabs passed through the narrow paths. But there were no cars, because even the miniature Indian Ambassadors and tut-tuts were too large to pass. In a city of three million people I didn't have a clue how to find my way back to the hostel—and I'd only brought along a few rupees, not enough for another hotel.

A chaiwalla served me chai from a tiny aluminum teapot holding the glass at arm's distance, pouring a long stream of tea precisely into the small glass. I paid for a tea and sipped it. Perspiration was the objective, for the moisture to evaporate on the skin and cool the body. The hot tea sloshed in my stomach, and then I began to sweat.

The evening brought even larger numbers of people to the water where meals were being prepared over small fires. Out of a long blue shadow a figure stirred, startling me. But it was only a man in filthy cotton pajamas trying to get comfortable on the stone. Someone clutched at me. "*Baksheesh*!" I stumbled away, slipping and falling, shredding my shin against the stone.

Sitar music and the clatter of horse's hooves echoed. I limped up the steps. There was nowhere to go but through a narrow alley. A vendor ran into the darkness carrying a torch, the fragrance of patchouli and musk trailed from his tray of goods. I followed the man but within a few yards was seized with horror. I was passing through a gauntlet of beggars with unthinkable deformities, some no more than heads lolling on stumps of torsos perched on small platforms with wheels. Some were riddled with dermal infections, mouths twisted with herpetic lesions, and milky eyes. Babies crawled about with withered limbs and other bizarre deformities, cleft palates, and the preventable neural tube defect, spina bifida. They called out, pleading. Those with arms reached out to touch my ankles. I doubled back and bolted to the river.

I could find a policeman, but then what if they were receiving bribes from Chandraram? I decided it was best to stay on the ghat. In the daylight I could find my way back. I shimmied under the shelter of a woven palm screen and slumped down the wall. I couldn't help but wonder what had I done that I deserved such a fate as this? What was karma, if not the evil karma interpreted from the Gita by Mr. Chandraram? I clutched the bag of ashes, looking over the dark river, frozen with the paralyzing hypervigilance that accompanies psychological trauma. What was my karma to be worked out? I stayed there all night listening to the rustling sounds of nocturnal creatures and other lost human beings like me.

TWENTY-TWO

A huge orange globe rose above the plain on the eastern shore of the Ganges. Behind me India's ancient holy city on the western shore was stirring awake. Nearby, a priest began to ring a gong loudly and the bedlam of the city burst into my senses. The commotion on the ghat undulated like an unstoppable centipede under the hot morning sun. My joints felt brittle, my muscles ached, and the smell of burning flesh saturated my clothing. The stench mingled nauseatingly with the fragrance of sandalwood and flowers. I was thrust back into the darkened room with the hot, dense scent of flowers and the smell of semen.

The air around me was still, except for the buzzing of flies. At eye level two chickens cannibalized a third, which looked at me with cold, watery eyes. The sanguineous pecking mimicked the beating of my heart and my breathing, in, out, in, out. The half dead hen had Belhaj's eyes and laughed his laugh and, when her beak opened to cry out in death, his white tongue flickered out.

"Meredith?"

In one instant reality took on a crystalline edge. My thinking became defined and crisp. I felt my body eject from my hiding place and bolt up the ghat. I tripped and sprawled on the ground. A heavy body fell on me, pinning me down. I fought him, wrestling. Against the sky, my attacker appeared as a black silhouette blurred around the edges into a white brilliance too startling to look at. Floating on the face of his black form were the eyes that invaded my dreams and relentlessly tracked me. The earth suddenly turned to quicksand.

"Meredith! Is that you? It is you. Meredith, it's me. Stop fighting! Meredith, I've been looking everywhere for you. Don't you recognize me? It's me, Paul."

I blinked against the brightness of the sun. Like waking from a dream I suddenly saw that it was Paul. He was laughing, his white teeth flashing in the sun. Tears streamed down his face. But then his face faded. It *wasn't* Paul. It was *Belhaj*. His nose was inflamed, his eyes brown, flecked with gold, like a reptile. "Deva, why did you run away from me?"

There was no oxygen in the earth's atmosphere. I twisted in the quicksand, thinking we would both be sucked under. "Leave me alone. Let me go."

"Calm down. You're safe."

"Safe?" The notion was so preposterous that I began to laugh. My laughter built until I was hysterical, laughing uncontrollably. My writhing stirred up a filmy cloud of dust, which hung low to the hot ground. I flung my head back, feeling the sun's heat stored in the earth, and screamed, and it was cleansing, like a good cry had once been. I screamed until my throat felt as if it were closing up. Then it was Paul who gathered me to him, holding me in his arms. "Meredith, Meredith, my God."

"Let me go," I repeated, but this time it came as a dull whisper.

Paul's eyes traveled from the stubby growth on my head to where my sleeve had fallen back on my arm. With his fingertips, he touched the flesh of my inner arm where needle scars flashed purple in the bright sunlight. He bent to kiss the scars, then turned my hands over and kissed my scraped palms. His eyes welled up at the sight of the engagement ring on my finger, his hand automatically clinching around mine. His eyes traveled to my face. A small laugh formed and then he wiped away a tear. "What happened to your leg?" he asked, sniffing, unashamed by his display of emotion. He inspected the long wet scrape on my leg, waving away the flies attracted to it. He pulled a bandana from his khakis and dabbed tentatively at the edge of dirt outlining the red wound. "Your arms, they're covered with mosquito bites. Don't worry baby, we'll get you medical attention." But when I didn't reply he said, "You're not well, Meredith. I'm going to take you home."

After leaving the police station, I assumed that Paul would go back to the States and wait for news from the Interpol agent. I didn't think he would stay in India tracking me. But now Paul's appearance on the ghat was like receiving an emissary from another planet, another time, light years away. He was solid proof that life as I used to know it still existed, but, simple as it seemed, the gulf was too large to cross. "I can't go home, Paul."

"What are you talking about? Of course you can go home." Paul picked up the plastic bag of my fathers ashes, which had fallen to the ground. "You still have your father's ashes?" The plastic was scored and pockmarked like hieroglyphics recording the history of my journey. I wiped my damp palms on the fragile silk of my salwar trousers and took the bag from him, clutching it possessively. "Why haven't you scattered them in the Ganges like you planned? Let's do it today, and then I'll take you home." He pulled me up, and didn't move away but stood there, strong arms encircling me.

He was an apparition, incongruous with the setting, like the actors he cast in his films, his blue eyes staring imperviously from the big screen. But he wasn't the same after all. There was a definite change. He had never looked that exhausted, even at the end of a problematic shoot. If I saw the changes of his face, how much more would he be able to see in mine? Then I couldn't look at him, with my ugly heroin tracks, rat bite scar, and my hideous shaved head growing in. I broke free of those muscled arms and walked along the ghat. He followed, his hand on my shoulder. We pushed past a group of tourists, but then fell back to let several women with huge baskets of laundry on their heads pass by. Ropes of bells at their ankles made a shimmering noise. Paul caught my elbow. "For God's sake, Meredith, stop walking away. Please talk to me."

"How did you find me?" I asked, not knowing what else to say.

"I was in Mumbai. There were four of us. A guy from the American consulate. Kind of a useless doofus. But there was an agent for Interpol who knew what he was doing. And an Indian detective."

Right. A man who allowed women to be bought and sold so that he could afford his Marlboros and his fake gold watch from China. I wanted to run then, but I stayed put, listening.

"We knew you had been there.

My fingerprints on the drug blister pack—and everywhere else.

"We thought you left the city and so I came to Varanasi, since I figured this is where you would come. I've been coming here to the river every day, looking for you." Paul's voice was strong against the clamor around us. A monkey swung down from the shoulder of a passing musician and began to bang a little drum in his face. Paul turned aside, his expression tight as he waited for my response. Maybe he wouldn't despise me if he knew everything I had done? But if he did hate me, it would be unbearable. I stood there calmly, like the yogi who maintains a pleasant expression, if not a faint smile, through a painful pose.

"I'm sorry, Meredith. You have to believe me. I was at your

back the entire time, but just one step away, I guess. We just missed you in Istanbul. When we got there, the house was cleaned out, but we found something that belonged to you." He handed me the photo of my parents.

I stared at the photo recalling the turning point, the frivolous decision that had rotated my life like a cumbersome craft in questionable waters, steering my future away from my hard earned hopes and dreams toward the dark unknown. I thought back to the day I stood in my father's rose garden overlooking the azure Pacific Ocean when I had held this picture in my hand and decided to bring my father's ashes to India. Now I held the impetus of my decision in my hand, for it was this very photograph that had sparked my stupid plan to bring my father's ashes here. *Why*? I asked. *Why? Why? Why*? Worse than any pain I felt for myself was the anguish I felt for Paul. His eyes swam with tears, his fear reflected in them, as black and bottomless as a well of India ink.

"How did they find the house?" I whispered.

Paul pulled out a folded piece of paper and unfolded it, handing it to me. It was a Xerox of the piece of tape that I had scratched with my fingernail, HELP KIDNAPPED MEREDITH FITZGERALD. Someone *had* found my SOS.

"You were seen at a market too. Apparently you made quite an impression. The report came in third hand, through one of the Consulate's operatives. They got wind somehow that the operation was leaving for Mumbai. The American Consulate scrambled an AWAC. But they lost the plane you were on after it left Turkish airspace. There are over 300 airports in India. They were all alerted. But the plane must have landed on a private strip. A G4 can land on a tarmac of hardened earth out in the desert."

Since nine-eleven ve are having all planes land at our secret land-

ing strip to avoid exposing ourselves to the possibility of the eventuality of dangerous security procedures.

"How did they know where we were going?"

"We got a tip from a driver at the airport."

I caught my breath, remembering the driver who had gotten the visas, who had said, *Allah go with you*. And then it was me tearing up, thinking, *there are good people on this earth*.

"After Interpol raided the place on Falkland Road, they sent an agent from the American International Police to look for you. One thought he saw you on a train from Aurangabad Station in Ellora. He followed you here and saw you again, here at the ghat."

I felt my face flame. It was the hippie guy who prevented me from buying heroin. Had he told Paul that I was a junkie? Then all I could think of was that that man didn't try to stop me, didn't cuff me, or force me to go to Paul. That had to have been Paul's instructions. He never would have tried to make me do anything I didn't want to do. All he wanted to know was that I was safe. Paul smiled at me and I remembered so well why I fell in love with him. He had a penetrating way of looking at whomever he was talking to, which had always made me feel that he was really listening to me, that he was not preoccupied, or formulating what he was going to say when I finished talking.

"I've been here looking for you ever since I left Mumbai. I've been to every hotel, every hostel, every flophouse in Varanasi. I would have kept looking for you, until I found you." Mr. Jhombarkar had said the man who came to the hostel looking for me had dark circles under his eyes. It was Paul who came to the hostel, not one of Chandraram's goondas!

"Meredith, listen to me. I know you've been through a lot." Paul said, shaking me gently. "But so have I." His face was close to mine, the tiny lines that defined his laugh appeared magnified. "It's been almost three months. I've been out of my mind." His uncut, tangled brown hair fell forward on his forehead.

"It's all my fault," I whispered.

"Is that what those monsters told you?"

A group of pallbearers arrived with a long emaciated corpse, shrouded in orange gauze. The crematorium burners were finishing up one cremation, scooping burning fragments together. Tiny molten ash swirled in the azure sky over the dusty rubble of the city. The burning particles flared and sparked out almost simultaneously in the hot air, just as souls do while the higher powers look on. Several fresh corpses lay waiting to be cremated and the men who burned bodies were busy with last minute adjustments of the funeral pyres lying on piles of dried reeds. One pyre was completely engulfed in flames. The smoke rose in a column and then wavered as a breeze stirred the particulate across the river.

"Say something," Paul said, worry saturating his voice.

I waved my hand through a thin veil of ash. "It brings good luck. The ash."

"Say something else," Paul said, his eyes frightened. "Say something that makes sense."

"Makes sense?" I squeezed my eyes shut trying to imagine my cool, hygienic life in Los Angeles. I pictured walking through the front door of my condo in Santa Monica. The rooms would need airing. Someone must have kept my cats all this time. They would be returned and they would need taking care of. The newspaper would be delivered. Groceries would be shopped for. My father's estate would have to be unraveled after my long absence. A million inconsequential details rolled into something called life that I could not deal with. Then there were the larger issues.

My wedding to Paul. My fellowship. Pursuing a medical career. Having children. But opening my eyes to see the dust and decay of Varanasi, I felt foolish. "There's nothing to say that makes any sense. There is nothing that can bridge the gap between my old life and me, and I already have all the pain I can tolerate. You have to forget me, Paul."

Paul squeezed my arm so it hurt. "What are you talking about, forget you? I am not sure about a lot of things in life, Meredith, but one thing I *am* sure of is that I could *never* forget you."

"Don't be a fool, Paul."

He folded my hands within his. "You think I'm a fool? When you lose everything, being a fool seems unimportant. I love you. All the months I prayed they would find you, I thought about how it would feel to kiss you. How it would feel to hold you, to touch you. Is that being a fool? Because if it is, it feels so good that I really don't care."

I bit my lip to keep from weeping. "You're right. I don't feel well."

"You're dehydrated. I'll get you some tea." When he dropped my hands I felt a stir of regret. His hiking boots climbed just two steps and he stood, almost at arm's length, ordering chai from a chaiwalla.

Over the water hundreds of golden and orange marigolds, their tips flicked with crimson, meandered on the gentle current caused by a group of sadhus bathing nearby. The slow swirl of the flowers mimicked the pace of the holy men, ponderous, rhythmic, yet determined. The sadhus waded by, their foreheads all bearing the same red mark, the tilak, their robes billowing like big orange bubbles in the water. Just then I felt awash in a fresh look at my life. The clarity of the moment allowed me to realize a different reality. It was purging and cathartic to accept how much Paul loved me and to grasp all the reasons why I could go on with my life. The exhilaration welled up inside me. I wanted to smile, to enjoy the hopefulness. Paul had not forgotten me! I wanted him at my side again, so I could tell him how much I loved him.

But then when I looked at the man at the chai stand I saw that it wasn't really Paul. *It was Belhaj.* I understood how deeply troubled I was, that my psyche was so fragile, so damaged. Yes, it was clogged with knots. That was the reason Belhaj was able to trick me. I could not go back to that life. I rose stealthily and turned, pushing through the crowd, and ran along the ghat, dodging through a herd of dusty water buffalos, away from Belhaj up the steps in the direction of the street.

"Deva!" Belhaj's repulsive voice rose above the clamor and if I would have been closer, if the noise on the ghat would have been less deafening, I would have heard the sound of two glasses shattering furiously on the concrete steps. I turned to see him searching for me. My name sounded like a long low howl. "Meredith." But it wasn't Paul. *It was Belhaj.* I could not allow myself to be fooled again. They would rape me, torture me with acid, kill me.

I ran blindly down the street until a side ache pierced my ribs. I paused at the mouth of a dark lane where tall buildings swallowed up the narrow alley. It was the passage that led to Mr. Jhombarkar's hostel! A man sat on the floor of his shop industriously fashioning a garment on his ancient Singer. Opposite that stall, people milled around, shoving wads of paan into their mouths. I'd passed by the night before and not recognized the neighborhood. I'd been so close all along. So close.

I caught my breath, and ran into the darkness of the passageway.

TWENTY-THREE

At the end of the passage where the hazy light streamed, I burst into a flat run, knowing the hostel was just on the other side. Under the arbor of kumquat trees laden with fat orange fruits, and the shocking pink bougainvillea that grew into the fencing stood the picket fence with its friendly white gate that swung on creaky hinges.

To my utter incredulity, in the courtyard sat Kilmar under a palm tree playing with Zarina. "Zarina! Kilmar!" I called out, breathlessly.

Kilmar smiled and waved, looking laidback and content as he peeled and ate a tangerine. But Zarina squealed when she saw me. She wore red trousers with a white flowered blouse, and her blonde hair was tied into pigtails. She darted across the path and threw herself into my arms. A smile stretched across her face, showing the open spaces, gradually filling in with serrated and oversized teeth. She slid from my embrace. I climbed the stairs. Zarina's laughter faded as she ran back to Kilmar. I slipped the photo of my parents inside my blouse and pushed at the decaying door.

Inside my room she appeared like a ghost, wearing a white sari. I set the plastic bag of ashes on my writing table. Her face was devoid of makeup, the bruises from Belhaj's beating had vanished, leaving only the tiniest bump on her nose that somehow looked okay. Even though I had always admired Camille's beauty, there was something else about her now. She slipped her arms around my waist. I breathed in her scent, pressing my cheek to hers, closing my eyes, letting the sensation register. "Camille, what are you doing here?"

She moved away from me and pressed her balled fists to her waist. "I got me a sixth sense when someone I care about's in trouble."

"I'm not in any trouble," I lied.

"Oh yeah? Hidin' out in some fleabag in Very-Nasty?"

"Well . . . . " I bristled at the characterization of Mr. Jhombarkar's hostel, as I had grown rather fond of him and his establishment.

"I thought you was goin' to the 'merican Consulate 'n I come to find out that you did no such thing."

"I thought *you* were going to the . . . . How did you know where to find me?"

"I called Ghanshyam on his mobile phone, well, on Mrs. Pawar's, that is." She giggled.

"What?" I stuttered. "He stole her mobile phone?"

"Dude, we been lookin' all over this town fer you!"

I didn't know what to say.

She giggled. "Hey look, yer roses. Mr. J got these fer you. Told him I was yer sister."

"So much for protecting my privacy," I muttered, but was immediately sidetracked from being irritated at Mr. Jhombarkar for his lack of vigilance by the flat, woven basket full of white rose petals that was being proffered to me by Camille. The fragrance made me feel faintly nauseous and I pushed the basket away.

"Me 'n Zarina pulled them petals off the blooms so you could toss 'em in the river with yer daddy's ashes."

"Camille, listen to me. We're in trouble," I said without conviction, as I was now beginning to feel a little squeamish about my mental state. "I saw Belhaj at the river. He *attacked* me."

"Yer a mess, girl. Sit down right here and I'm gonna call on Mr. J for some shit to calm you down."

"God, no." Clearly she was never going to get that drugs were not everyone's panacea. I wiped away a tear.

"Have yerself one big ole cry 'n be done with it. Belhaj was *not* at the river, girl. He's in the shit holes of shit holes in Mumbai, probably gittin' mud packed by some donkey-fucker as we speak."

"Is that true?"

"You think I ain't got a stake 'n keepin' up? Chandraram's not doin' so good neither, due to the fact that he horned in on territory that belonged to some bigger fish."

If it wasn't Belhaj at the river, then could it really have been Paul? I felt so confused. Camille walked over the W.C. "I'm gonna some run hot water fer you." The hostel had plenty of hot water, and the tiny room quickly filled with steam.

I couldn't tell Camille that I had an imaginary conversation with Paul who I thought was Belhaj who I thought was Paul. Was I having a psychotic break? "What about Zarina's mother?" I asked, stammering, wanting to get my mind off my mental state. "Shouldn't we take Zarina to the authorities and give her a chance of being reunited with her?"

"I thought about that," Camille said with a hint of the tightness people get in their voices when they discuss dividing property, children, love. "Thought about it a lot. What kind of a life would she have, bein' in a family what's gonna up 'n sell her the next time they needed cash. Zarina's stayin' with me. I love her, 'n I'm her mama now."

"You're right, Camille. But if we part now, will I see you and

Zarina again? Will you ever come back to the U.S.?"

Furrows appeared between her eyes and her pretty pouting mouth turned into a frown. "Told you about my Japanese friend. She was the best friend I ever had, till you. We didn't know what we was getting' into, thinkin' we was gonna be runway models on the Ginza. Belhaj come into the club where we was workin', 'n offered us modeling contracts 'n we jumped at the opportunity. We was as stupid as you was that day at the Egyptian bazaar when you done took the chai from the strange lady in black." The tower of strength was crumbling.

"Please, go on."

"Belhaj was up to his usual tricks, collectin' a stable of girls for Mrs. Pawar to ship off to destinations unknown. 'Course we figured it out purty quick when his goon Théodore raped 'n cornholed us. He locked us up with a bunch of other trashed tourist girls. We was in that particularly nasty pit fer three weeks. Finally, Belhaj done come fer me. I figured I'd play my cards right with him, then get my friend out too. But it didn't work out that way. Théodore was a sisterfucker that made that fucktard Vadim look like yer garden variety guardian angel. He made sure my friend got shipped off with the other girls." Camille stopped talking, chewing her lip. "Before we left for Mumbai I stabbed Théodore in the back, 'n left him to bleed like a stuck pig all over that hotel futon. Belhaj blew off Théodore's disappearance as part 'n parcel of the man's flakey nature. I was only sixteen 'n didn't have no sense, so's I left my prints on the knife. That's why I ain't felt exactly comfortable with the notion of crossin' borders."

Her fear of being extradited and prosecuted in Japan for murder explained why she hid her appearance when she was out in public. "Well, now that you've come back I realize that it was stupid to let you go," I said in a practical voice that I hoped was commanding. "I can't imagine life without you. We should stay together like a family."

"That's just freaky talk. You lived yer whole life without me. Yer goin' back to California with yer fiancé 'n I'm travelin' off with Kilmar. He's a good friend."

"Is that all he is? Because I worry about you. You've never done anything without a man telling you what to do."

"I never knowed how it could be with a man. I was always forced." Camille stood in a shaft of light like a goddess in cut glass, a small smile of anticipation on her face. Before I could reply she said with the dead-on elocution of an American movie star from the nineteen thirties, "Perhaps something will come of our friendship, perhaps we'll remain friends. Either way, it's a mutually beneficial relationship that I'll cherish for the rest of my life." Tears sprang to her eyes and she doubled over, cracking up. "You should see yer face. Oh my God."

I laughed too.

"Kilmar says if I don't stop talkin' like white trash that I'll never be able to leave Nasreen behind. He's been teachin' me how to talk like he learned in English classes back in Deutschland."

"It's good, Camille. You're an unbelievable mimic."

"So to answer yer question, a new way a talkin', quality passports 'n me 'n Zarina can go where we like. Who knows we may turn up in California someday. Anyway, if we stay together you'll use that for an excuse not to go home, and yer supposed to go back to your life, to your docterin' business, to yer fiancé."

"I can't face anyone . . . him now."

"Why not?"

"Everything I did."

"What'r you talkin' about, *you did*?"

"I don't know. Now that it's over it seems like I should have fought Belhaj harder. I should never have let him rape me," I said, my voice quavering.

"Girl, you was drugged, he's a big man, and he had that razor knife."

"Okay, but there's more. Remember that girl in Istanbul who died, then I harvested her organs? I was a coward, Camille. I did it to save myself."

"You done everthin' you could to save her life. Maybe somebody else, someone good's livin' now 'cause a her body parts."

She was right. But still. "But what about when I ran away, after Vadim burned Zarina? He could have *killed* her."

"Vadim was a turd but he didn't have the license to kill."

"That's a relief to know after all of this time, but there's so much more. Down in the dungeon at the Pawar's, I murdered a girl with heroin. Did you know that?"

"I suspected you'd do that when you saw her state. But that ain't murder. You just put her outta her misery like we done with animals on the farm back home. Nothin' wrong with sparin' a fellow creature from sufferin'. 'Sides, when my grannie laid in the hospital dyin' at age one oh two them doctors come in and cranked up the morphine. So don't be tellin' me doctors don't kill in hospitals."

She had a point, and it did make me feel better about Christyn. "Camille," I cried tearfully, "I let those young women be traded off. Right now, right now they are being raped. Some of them might even be dead."

"I know how you feel. I got my own guilty conscience to bear at what I helped them do fer six long years. But *you* . . . *you* ain't got no reason to feel responsible about that particular batch'a girls.

There was nothin' you could'a done. *Nothin'.*"

"Besides all of that, I prostituted myself to Mr. Chandraram," I whispered feeling the roiling gurgle of acid in the pit of my stomach.

"That man done wicked things to women who weren't as smart as you."

I was on a roll, hating myself. I stomped back and forth in front of Camille, thinking. I could have slit Belhaj's throat, but no, what I did was much worse. And the pleasant rush of feelings was what made me so uncomfortable. I was a doctor who swore to *do no harm*. "I used my medical knowledge to help three beggar women prostitute themselves for my own self serving needs for revenge." Camille laughed lightly.

I stared incredulously. "How can you laugh? How *dare* you laugh?"

"Accordin' to Ghanshyam them women 'r heroes in the zopadpatti. Everbody in that slum hated the Pawars 'n 'specially that slime bucket Belhaj. Them ladies gonna die happy. So now that's all settled." She smiled prettily.

It wasn't exactly settled. I had so much turmoil in my head that I could not sort it out with just one brief conversation, no matter how wise Camille was in the world. And something else was bothering me. I found myself blurting involuntarily, "What about Shabana?"

"*Shabana*? What, the two'a you best friends 'r somethin'? Well, her death was just a happy accident that you ain't got no call to be guilty about." She paused for a moment. "I didn't wanna tell you 'cause I knew it would bum you out, but that pimpin' fool husband'a hers called in one last favor 'n had her ashes brung here to the river."

I hadn't realized how amped up I was until Camille's words pierced my inflated bubble. A painful sob lurched in my throat as I deflated into a heap onto the concrete floor, crying so hard my words were unintelligible, "*Shiva will blow on her soul . . . she'll be spared reincarnation.*"

"What honey?" Camille asked tenderly as she pulled me to my feet. "I'm sorry I said anything. Them people don't deserve no favors 'r pity.

Camille would never understand. It was my secret. Mine and Shabana's. I picked up one of Mr. Jhombarkar's thick leaded pencils. "I'm sure my phone numbers are disconnected by now," I said, my voice husky with tears, my hands shaking so hard I could barely write. "But here's my father's attorney's number. You'll always be able to find me through his firm because they are managing my father's trust."

"Shh." Camille touched my lips. "I got me a Blackberry on the black market."

The door creaked open and Zarina walked through the steam. "Kilmar says we got to amscray cauth the carth leavin' thoon."

"Kilmar got us a ride in a Hummer down south. We're headed off to the West coast to some island. Supposed to be some paradise."

I nodded, picturing them all buck-naked on the beach. It was right. She needed that escape to heal her own psychic wounds and I could not deny her that. "Zarina." I held out my arms and the girl ran to me.

"Gueth what?"

"What?"

"I ain't gonna thuck my thumb no more. Mama thaid it give me cooties."

"Good for you." Zarina would be pretty. Not stunning, but pretty.

Camille took one of my hands and put it on top of the flower petal in the basket. "No," I said, pushing the basket away again. "I can't bear the smell of roses."

"Yes, you can." Camille took one petal and placed it in my palm and closed my fingers around it. "Remember in the garden? When you gave me that flower? It was the first time anyone ever said anything like that to me. You did mean it, didn't you?"

I remembered in the Pawar's jungle garden, handing Camille the broken rose. *This flower is like you.* Camille's allure was like an invisible net that she threw over everyone she came in contact with. Like a mythological maiden, favored with a power that came from deep inside her nature.

"There are hundreth of petalth." Zarina stood on tiptoes to reach and fluff the flowers, stirring up a waft of fragrance in the steamy air. "I know, cause Kilmar teached me how to count, all the way to one hundred."

The scent of the flowers didn't seem to bother me as I felt a surge of joy knowing that Zarina and Camille could quite possibly find happiness with Kilmar, that they could become a family. "That's quite an accomplishment."

"Touch them," Zarina ordered. "They're tho thoft."

I hesitated and then reached out and brushed the white petals with my fingertips. "Yes," I said. "They're as soft as your cheek."

Zarina cocked her head, smiling, waiting to hear more.

"And I love you very much."

"I'm in love with you too!" She hummed a tune, her little body undulating like a Bollywood dancer.

"When I see white roses I will think of you." I interrupted

her dance, pulling her close, feeling her miniature ribs and tiny shoulder blades. She was so small. So vulnerable. I thought of the first time I saw Zarina with her hysterical mother in the rain, Zarina's dirty bare feet slipping on the wet pavement. "Don't forget me, Zarina, my dearest."

"I ain't never gonna forgit you," she said solemnly. I felt a dèjá vu, hearing the words the hallucinatory Paul had spoken earlier. Zarina began to cry melodramatically. "I'm gonna mith you!" Zarina kissed my lips. "Good-bye," she said in a small teary voice.

"Camille," Kilmar said, walking into the room. He smiled, weaving his head back and forth like a native. He would be good for Camille and Zarina, and that made our parting bearable.

I unstrapped my Piaget watch and fastened it on Camille's wrist. I was babbling, stretching out the time. I knew we were falling, out of control, toward the awful moment when we would say our final good-byes. "The crystal got scratched, but you can take it to a jeweler to have it polished."

"Ain't necessary. A flaw just makes somethin' more interestin'."

"Keep your scar out of the sun, okay?" I touched Camille's collarbone where I had stitched her wound.

Camille took my hands in hers and turned them over. "Hey, you scraped yer hands." She kissed one palm and then the other. I looked at her, dumbfounded. My palms had been kissed twice that day by the two people I loved most in the world. Yes, it *was* Paul at the river. How foolish I had been. I closed my eyes and felt Camille's lips on mine. When the kiss ended, she picked up the white petal that had fallen from my hand and pressed it back into my palm. She whispered in my ear in her honey-glazed voice, "We ain't got to cry ourselves to sleep no more. It's over."

TWENTY-FOUR

Crushed in my palm was the one white rose petal. Nothing could have prepared me for the dull loneliness permeating every corner, every shadow. Alone in my room, I stared at a zany color portrait of Mr. Jhombarkar with his guru Sathya Sai Baba at his latest pilgrimage to guru-ji's ashram. The silence was interrupted only by the fan and by the water spraying from the shower. I hadn't had anything to eat or drink for over twenty-four hours, but realized that pain was its own kind of sustenance. Coolness enveloped the room as the hot water in the shower had run out. The mist felt incredibly good and I wondered how it was that pleasure seemed to go so well with pain. The ruined petal fell to the floor as I stood and crossed to the W.C., turning the shower faucet off. Without the sound of the spray the only noise was the fan rotating, an annoying rattle of its defective mechanism apparent to me for the first time.

Outside the window, cumulous clouds piled one on another in the bottom of the sky. I pushed aside the mosquito net and lay down on the bed under the fan, in hopes of avoiding the constant swarm of mosquitoes that would light on me the instant I left the netting and the zone of swirling air. On my writing table sat the basket of roses. Next to it, the bag containing my father's ashes. In California, when I had originally planned on taking his ashes to the Ganges, it was merely intended as a memorial. I hadn't pictured a spiritual experience. It was only a way of reuniting my father and mother in a symbolic way. In Istanbul at the Egyptian Bazaar

I had impetuously settled on the romantic plan to scatter white rose petals with his ashes. I thought that the white blossoms floating on the water would attest to the purity and perfection of the symbolism. As the trauma built over the months of my captivity, the idea of taking my father's ashes and the roses to the river had become something more significant. And even though Shabana Pawar was a sociopath, her muddled lectures about escaping the never-ending cycle of reincarnation still echoed in my mind.

A profound exhaustion fell over my being as I tried to sort everything out. I had not intended to, but I fell into a deep sleep. I may have kept on sleeping had it not been for Mr. Jhombarkar's insistent knocking. "Um, what?" I mumbled indecorously and woozy, when I opened the squeaky door, aware of my bristled head and the fact that I had slept in my clothes, the festively mournful, now torn and grimy salwar kameez.

"Dr. Fitzgerald I am seeing you are grieving for the departure of your dearest sister, whom I am noting has very different coloring than yourself," he said, his eyes flitting to those black bristles that were growing in. "And now that I am looking with greater attention to the details I am seeing that your eyes are blue, vhereas your *sister's* eyes are being green like the Ganga after the monsoon."

I smiled noncommittally.

"I am asking your forgiveness in advance for my lack of knowledge in the field of medicine," he said in the way he had that always seemed to harbor a happy chuckle at the back of his throat. "Vhen I am comparing my humble learning to your eminence, that is."

"Well, hardly," I replied, my voice froggy.

"I am bringing for you the Ayurvedic herb we are calling Indian ginseng. You see this is ashvagandha. Very, very, very good for the eventuality of fatigue." He wafted it under my nose and I recoiled at the odor. "Yes, yes, yes, it is the fouling smell of the sweat of the horse coming from the root ashvagandha, vhich is not coincidentally being Sanskrit for *horse's smell.*"

"Thank you, Mr. Jhombarkar."

"Perhaps you are joining me in the garden for a spot of tea, as ve used to say in the days of the Raj? Though I am being aware of your American heritage, and in fact, I vas not even being born into this incarnation until ten years after the revolution."

"Yes, thank you, that would be nice."

Presumptively, downstairs in the garden, Mr. Jhombarkar had set a wicker table with a tea tray, along with a plate of cookies. "Nan khatai," he said, offering me the plate. "Coconut cookie, very, very, very good for the immune system."

I chewed a cookie, wincing at the burst of saliva from my salivary glands. Mr. Jhombarkar poured tea as he spoke. "Dr. Fitzgerald as you are being a medical doctor of the Vestern persuasion, perhaps you are not finding the Ayurvedic medical system of India worthy of discussion?"

"On the contrary."

"That being the case, Ayurveda is dating back to the Vedas, more than six thousand years. It is very, very, very ancient form of medical treatments. Ayu, Sanskrit for the root, and ayus, meaning life, and Veda, that is being science, wisdom, and knowledge. This is vhy ve are believing that human life is being a combination of mind, body, senses, and the soul. Resuming our previously discussed conversation of energies, Ayurveda is teaching of the three fundamental energies that are dictating our health and happiness. These energies are being called doshas. First there is the Vata, and that is being air and vind. Vhen a person is having too much Vata, they are having hysterical needs for attention and much drama is ensuing. Then there is Pitta, and that is being fire and sun. Vhen a person is having too much Pitta, they are easily becoming angry and strident. They are running in circles and needing a cold shower. Lastly, there is being Kapha, and that is earth and water. Vhen a person is being too much Kapha, they are very, very, very lazy vhen unhappiness strikes, and at the same time eating vith very, very, very much passionate enthusiasm too much food. Every human living being is carrying the doshas in unique and variable proportions, vhich, given any thought, is making sense that these combinations of doshas are creating our human diverse natures—and that any changing of the composition of the doshas in any single individual is also changing that individual's nature."

"You are seeing through me, Mr. Jhombarkar."

"I am being pleased to be offering you another nan khatai," he said, brandishing the plate. And when I took a second cookie, he poured a fresh cup of chai as I had gulped the first cup in response to my dehydration.

"Naturally it stands to reason that certain balancing of the doshas is being optimal for health and happiness."

"I see, you mean like homeostasis?"

His head wove back and forth, "Thus my gift to you of the ashvagandha, as Ayurvedic herbs are very, very, very potent and the most powerful on the planet of Earth to restore dosha balancing of the resistance to stress, trauma, anxiety, and such exhaustion as you, Dr. Fitzgerald have been demonstrating."

"You're right that my spirit is suffering," I confessed glumly. "I must have done something to deserve this karma."

His head wove back and forth, and although I wasn't acculturated to Indian head rolling, something told me, from the sad look on his face, that it was not an affirmative head bob, but it was more like an empathetic gesture. "This is being the tragedy of Indian society, the misinterpretation of karmic law, that is. Not to being a Nosey Parker but I have been seeing that you are reading the *Bhagavad Gita*? The *Gita* is a summary of all the knowledge contained in the Hindu holy texts, the *Vedas* and the *Upanishads*. In a nutshell, as you Americans are saying, the *Gita* is a guide to life. Today many Indians who are not properly educated in the *Gita* are believing that vhen the bad eventualities are occurring that the beneficiary has brought such bad eventualities on themselves by having done something bad. But karma is not being isolated to each individual. Rather, the cosmic vorld is a very, very, very complicated stew, if you will, of karmic activities of all human peoples. Thus the vorld ve live in can be a cruel and harsh environment because ve can only be controlling our own actions and reactions, but ve cannot be controlling anyone else's."

"So you're saying that shit just happens because of this karmic stew and that people have the choice to react in either good or bad ways?"

"To my knowledge there is being no such vord as shit in the original Sanskrit iteration of the *Gita*, but I am understanding and agreeing vith your Vesternized interpretation."

"You're saying it wasn't my fault . . . what happened to me?"

Mr. Jhombarkar wove his head. "Not your fault, no. Not your karma. No, no, no." Unsmiling, my teacher's face was sullen and sad looking, but then he grinned. "Moving it right along, as one of my American boarders used to be saying, the ultimate karmic goal as espoused by the *Gita* is to achieve universal harmony by each individual abondoning attachment to the I. Vorldy desires are being the instigating factor for the most of our karmic downfalls instigated most definitely by this vell-established attachment to the I that humans are so characteristically demonstrating."

I couldn't help but think of Mr. Chandraram and the depravity he claimed to be endorsed by the *Gita*. Wasn't I just as immoral? "What if someone does something really terrible to you and you have no choice but to hurt that person to save yourself and save others around you?"

"The *Gita* is the story of a vor for righteousness, told in a dialogue between the lower self and the Higher Self. This conversation is occurring on a battlefield, just before the commencement of a vor. Ve are seeing a Arjuna, a brave and very, very, very great vorrior who is feeling very, very, very much as you are experiencing, Dr. Fitzgerald, vith the veighing of depression, fear, and grief upon his shoulders. So afraid is he because he must go to vor with an enemy who is also being his relative. And if you are to be giving this situation any thought, is making sense that all human beings are related and therefore any adversarial situation that one Dr. Fitzgerald has been finding herself in is also vith a relative. Relatively speaking," he added, being Indian to the core. "Coming to the aid of the vorrior Arjuna in his confusion and moral dilemma vas being a princely character who was in actuality the Lord Krishna—in other vords, the Supreme Being. Admonishing Arjuna in his vor for righteousness, Lord Krishna is instructing Arjuna not to be running away from his responsibilities and his righteous duties that vere necessary for the individual and also for the collective velfare. Lord Krishna's one caveat to Arjuna going to vor was that his actions be vorshipful and not for personal gaining of beneficial fruits."

"But that's just it. What I did, I did for revenge."

"Perhaps vhat you have been doing vas for the greater good of all, the only problem being that you did have this one teeny-tiny, ity-bitty, ensee-veensie bit of intention, vhich Lord Krishna refers to as to 'hanker after the fruit.' In more simplistical terms, you have perhaps lusted for the results of your actions. But let me say this, Dr. Fitzgerald and then ve vill speak of it no longer as I am seeing that you are needing the ashvagandha more prodigiously than you are needing further discourse in the areas of the *Vedas*: God realization does not come easily to human beings as infinitely flawed as we humans have proven to be. Sometimes vun must be satisfied vith accomplishing a smaller aspect of the goal, and the failings are for the learning to be utilized at a future date."

I nodded, thinking that Mr. Jhombarkar's explanation of the *Gita* was just another way of Camille telling me to get on with my life. "I have learned a lot."

His head wove back and forth. "All Lord Krishna is asking is to be desirous of the truth. That is sufficient. And no more vorrying about karma?"

"Okay."

"I am sensing that you vill be leaving my establishment in a short period of time?" he asked, which appeared to be his way of pushing me out of the nest.

I nodded again. "Regretfully. I've enjoyed our talks."

"As have I." The avuncular Mr. Jhombarkar collected the teacups and tidied up the tray, with minimal clinking of porcelain, and clanking of flatware. He rose. "I am bidding you a pleasant journey, Dr. Fitzgerald. Please be visiting to my humble hostel vhen you are returning to Varanasi at a future date?"

"It's a deal."

His face lit up with an engaging smile as he pressed his palms together in namaste, then picked up his tea tray. I watched him walk away, knowing what I had to do. I had to finish what I came to India to do.

When I left the hostel a few minutes later, I had my passport, the remaining rupees, dollars, euros, jewels, the ashwagandha, the *Gita*, the photograph of my parents, and my father's ashes in the leather purse Mr. Jhombarkar had given me. Tucked under my arm were my notebooks. Something caught my attention as I turned to leave the room. Barbie's head. I reached for it under my writing table, smoothed the doll's tangled yellow hair. Zarina's doll's head went into the bag. I juggled it all with the basket of rose petals and left the room, leaving the door open, the fan whirring. I descended the stairs and paused in the garden. The lights were on in Mr. Jhombarkar's office. I walked quietly by, hoping to leave unnoticed. We had said our good-byes.

When I reached the white gate, I stood searching the street. The flower petals from the wedding procession were long gone, trampled into the dust. Temple gongs rang out in the distance. The street was crammed with oxcarts carrying bags of rice and bright bolts of Varanasi silk. Women walked with baskets on their heads; bodies flowing gracefully under their heavy loads. Trinket salesmen with odd assortments of cheaply made gadgets roamed, scouting for foreigners. A boy hounded a group of tourists offering to show them burning bodies. I pulled my chunni over my head and walked through the dark passageway, which led from the hostel to the ghats.

The sun, at three quarters in the sky, cast long silver fingers in the ripples on the water. The phallic stone of Shiva, the symbol of the life force, the great yogi, oldest God, sat alone, splattered with that day's offerings of food. Temple gongs rang out in the distance. Endless conversations, prayers, chants, and inhuman sounds undulated across the water. There were boats on the river, with lanterns swinging at their bows that would be lit in another hour or two. There were boatmen who could take me out on the water, who would wait, making themselves inconspicuous while I attended to the ashes. Indeed, a man in a rowboat oared toward me. He beaconed me with his hand.

I flashed a wad of rupees. "I want to buy your boat."

"*Mai nahii samajhti hu*," the man said.

"He say he not understand." Behind me was a dirty little beggar boy with long stick-like limbs and a head that seemed to big for his body.

"Tell him I want to buy his boat. I'll give him this." I flashed the wad again.

The boy talked to the man in machinegun Hindi. The man limberly leapt off his boat, onto the ghat. He held out his hand. I peeled off a few notes and gave them to the boy, then handed the rest to the man. He counted it. His eyes lit as he examined me curiously, then he jerked his head and the little boy helped me onto the boat.

The constant noise on the ghat seemed to hush as I settled my worldly possessions in the bottom of the craft: the leather pouch of treasures, the plastic bag of ashes, the basket of rose petals, my notebooks. In the distance a stringed instrument began to play lamenting chords across the river. And then I rowed. It wasn't difficult as the current swept the little boat along. I rowed for an hour, listening to my breathing and the swooshing of oars into the water. My palms were blistered and the city was long gone.

The sun was beginning to set with apocalyptic pink strokes

against the sky. The fiery sphere was falling into the forested horizon on the western shore. The eastern shore—while littered with lean-tos within the city—was barren here. I let the boat drift while I turned the bag of ashes over in my hand, examining the gray matter. I remembered the funeral director's simpering expression as he handed the bag to me across the gleaming mortuary conference table. "It's what you asked for," he apologized.

I tore back the zipper strip, alarmed at how easily it opened, imagining all the ways the ashes could have spilled out during these past months. In the fading light the ashes appeared matte black, like a portal I could stick my hand in, then my arm, up to the elbow, and then to the shoulder, eventually diving in, vanishing. I touched the ashes that were once the living flesh and blood of my father. They were warm. Soft. I poured the contents of the bag into the basket. I let the dust settle back into the heap, then tossed the bag aside. Tomorrow someone would scavenge it in the boat for some other purpose.

The basket tipped in my hands as if guided by another being. My father's ashes encompassed the craft, the white rose petals lapping gently against the rotting wooden vessel. They were floating, and the ashes were melting into the holy water of Mother Ganga to rest on the velvet river bottom where my mother lay waiting to be joined, at long last, with my father.

I spoke the names of the girls who'd been sold into sexual slavery on my watch: "Lauren McCarthy . . . Olivia Coolidge . . . Tessa Rizzo . . . Imelda Conti . . . Karen Yamagata . . . Rita Kagoshima . . . Claudia Yager . . . Amelia Getman . . . Joanie Patterson . . . Danielle Fournier . . . Gabrielle Rosseau . . . Sharon Martins . . . Maria-Maarens Van Vleck." As the last girl's name left my lips, at a distance the last petal vanished. "Christyn Landseer," I whispered, honoring the acid burned girl who I had hastened to die.

Dusk was approaching. It occurred to me that I should be afraid, out on the vast river alone. But then I heard Mr. Jhombarkar's reassuring voice explaining about the ever-shifting energy doshas that make us what we are. No matter what had happened to me, and what I had been compelled to do, I was still my father's daughter. I was part Dr. Meredith Fitzgerald. I was part Paul's future wife. But now I was also Deva. There was much more to be learned on this karmic journey. Some of it would be painful, but there would be happiness too. A verse came to me from the Gita, and I repeated it in my mind, *Oh Lord, please guide me through this difficult uncertainty as I am your disciple and you are my Teacher.*

And then I called out, "Paul!" My voice rang clear and strong, and carried across the river.

A Note From The Author

In September 1968, after turning eighteen, I set out hitchhiking from Europe to India with my boyfriend. During those ten months I first heard about what was then called "white slavery," and that I should be careful. I didn't worry about it too much at the time, though I probably should have. Flash forward four decades to the global marketplace wherein trafficking in flesh has become more lucrative than trafficking drugs and international sex slavers have become emboldened and greedy. Today, all women and children, no matter how privileged, are potential victims.

People ask me, "What is the genre of your novel?" I characterize *Karma* as a psychological thriller, but really it's a horror story. The horror of sex trafficking is taking place right now all over the globe to 2.5 million women and children.

The three characters in *Karma*, Meredith, Camille, and Zarina represent the three major ways of recruitment by sex traffickers: kidnapping, coercion, and buying children from their parents. All of the descriptions in this fictional portrayal are based on documented reports of women and children held in sexual captivity.

This was a difficult novel to conceptualize because there is no way to fully capture the grotesque travesty of forced prostitution and drug addiction without writing an unreadable book. On the other hand, I didn't want to betray the people who are enslaved by making up a fantasy story. I know that some people have a hard time reading about what really goes on in the world of flesh trading. But my wish is, however difficult this subject is to face, that *Karma* will spark an awareness to help pass legislation that will thwart the traffickers and encourage the prosecution of both the traffickers and the rapists who buy women and children from these dealers, and that reading *Karma* will forewarn the unaware of the very real danger of the sex trade.

Although I used Turkey and India as venues for my story, these two countries are merely colorful backdrops and no more involved in sex trafficking than any other country on earth, including the U.S.

Regarding the title, *Karma*, I want to make it perfectly clear that blaming the victim is not the message of this story. Because Meredith is in India and learns about karma, she at first interprets it to mean that she is to blame—which is also a hallmark manifestation of post-traumatic stress disorder. But she learns from Mr. Jhombarkar that blaming the victim is the result of a misinterpretation of the *Bhagavad Gita*. The law of karma presents us with the opportunity to react to situations that would ultimately result in a better future, but it's not cause and effect. In this work of fiction, Meredith did not bring her fate on herself, and in real life, the victims of sex trafficking are not to blame.

Acknowledgements

My respect and acknowledgement goes out to all the victims past, present, and future of sex trafficking. My indebtedness for writing this novel reaches back forty years to Heini Baumgartner for introducing me to Istanbul, one of the most historically fascinating cities on earth, and to the wildly exotic, infinitely mysterious and confoundingly zany subcontinent of India.

The first person who helped me with my research on sex slavery was the librarian at the Santa Barbara library, Olivia Flisher, who probably doesn't remember, though I remember her. I have quite a few people to thank for reading drafts and offering opinions. I hope that they are all counted here. Agnes Perpere, Alexander E. Gowen, Amy Hazard, Anna and Dave Grotenhuis, Anne Lowenkopf, Barbara Deal, Betty Hatch, Camille Pasarow, Elizabeth March, Elizabeth Pomada, Karin Finell, Grace Gabe, Grace Rachow, Jitka Gunaratna, Kate Cashman, Keely Cormier, Ling Lucas, Louise Moore, Marie-Jose Ragab, Maureen Lehman, Sandra Alexander, and Sheridan Rosenberg.

For technical details, I thank Carol Crump and Dennis Freely for their graphic explanations of heroin addiction and withdrawals, Pravrajinka Vrajaprana for explaining bits and pieces of Hinduism, Glenn Miller, John Matrisciano, and Nadine Saubers for medical descriptions and terminology.

My gratitude to Rocky Lang who believed in this story through numerous iterations, who kept me believing in it, and gave me many suggestions and comments along the way. Thanks to Marjorie Gies who actually took the manuscript on vacation to vet the medical and psych, and if I didn't get her corrections right, I'm to blame. Thanks to Chris Germer for teaching me Metta meditation and for inadvertently putting some of the words in Shreeram Jhombarkar's mouth. Thanks to Gary Heidt for saying, "The best villains are like the ones Tolstoy created who you end up sympathizing with." It was because of Gary that Meredith comes to understand her persecutor, the heinous Shabana Pawar.

Thanks to Duane Unkefer and Jennifer Weiss Hander who edited earlier drafts. I am grateful to Ron Kenner for his thorough edit, so light-handed and thoughtful, yet with exactly the perfect word and phrase suggestions. He made *Karma* a much better book. And thanks, too, to his assistant and associate editor Tom Puckett at RKedit for some good catches and suggestions. Eternal thanks to my husband, John Davis for dropping his own work and giving my proof a final polish.

Thank you to Mike Vezo for taking over the publishing and distribution process, and Kimberly Pieper for doing all the yucky unmentionable stuff writers don't want to know about. I couldn't have done this without you.

Rocky Lang gave me the initial input on my trailer, Nadine Saubers pulled together many of the images, Julio Macat lent his weighty guidance and I can't thank him enough, but mostly it was Vidu Gunaratna who took the basic elements and brilliantly edited the final version. Still I wouldn't have been nearly as happy with the trailer if Ray Reich hadn't contributed his talent in composing the original music. It helped to have the input of someone as experienced in music production as Thaddeus Kryczko who generously reviewed iterations at the eleventh hour. What is a book without a website? Matt Haltom, thank you for creating a beautiful venue for *Karma*.

Mostly—and I've said this before in other books but can never say it enough—thank you to my husband John who for twenty years has put up with my writing obsessions and never once lost patience but has always believed in me. Love you, J.